BY ALEXANDRA OLIVA

The Last One

Forget Me Not

FORGET ME NOT

FORGET
ME NOT

a novel

Alexandra Oliva

BALLANTINE BOOKS | NEW YORK

Published in the United States by Ballantine Books, an imprint of Random House, a division of Penguin Random House LLC, New York.

BALLANTINE and the HOUSE colophon are registered trademarks of Penguin Random House LLC.

LIBRARY OF CONGRESS CATALOGING-IN-PUBLICATION DATA
Names: Oliva, Alexandra, author.
Title: Forget me not: a novel / Alexandra Oliva.
Description: First Edition. | New York: Ballantine Books, [2020] |
Identifiers: LCCN 2019059284 (print) | LCCN 2019059285 (ebook) |
ISBN 9781101966846 (hardcover) | ISBN 9781101966853 (ebook)
Classification: LCC PS3615.L49 R46 2020 (print) | LCC PS3615.L49 (ebook) |
DDC 813/.6—dc23
LC record available at https://lccn.loc.gov/2019059284
LC ebook record available at https://lccn.loc.gov/2019059285

Printed in Canada

randomhousebooks.com

2 4 6 8 9 7 5 3 1

First Edition

Book design by Jo Anne Metsch

FORGET ME NOT

1.

A woman whose name shouldn't be Linda stands inside the locked front door of her apartment, listening. Footsteps: a neighbor, walking. Linda knows her neighbors only from names on lobby mailboxes and glances through the peephole, doesn't care to meet them, can't chance being known. She gives the footsteps enough time to reach the elevator. To press the button, step in, and begin their descent. Then she unlocks the door, exhales the breath she was hiding from the passerby, and steps out onto the hallway's checkered carpet.

The carpet doesn't look any different from yesterday, and Linda wonders if it'd feel different beneath her toes if she was barefoot. She was trapped yesterday afternoon, waiting for a vacuum to be turned off and taken to another floor. By the time it was gone, her excursion window had passed: School was out, the evening rush about to begin. And though it's in some ways easier to slip away into a crowd, it makes her skin crawl: the talking, the laughter, the heavy-heeled steps. All these people who don't care who overhears the intimate details of their lives as they blather into their earcuffs. Even when they aren't talking, they're tapping and typing, creating hashtags for their confessions and trying to make them trend.

Linda doesn't understand how anyone can seek out the public eye. Yet every day her social feed bleeds the secrets of strangers, willingly shared.

She locks her door, then walks toward the stairwell. She wants to sprint, but that would send the message she's worth looking at. Pushing through the door, she feels a little better. This high up, the stairs are nearly always deserted. Sometimes children dash short distances to visit a friend above or below, but they're loud, echoing creatures—easily avoided—and those old enough to roam are now at school. The stairwell rings only with Linda's footsteps. Still, she pauses to listen at each landing. The casual hello to a stranger, eye contact—she can do it, but it drains her. She can never shake the fear that the person will recognize her, the fear of what they might say or do. She thinks of the woman last summer. The disgust in her eyes as she hissed, *What did you do with the bones, freak?* The glob of spit that hit Linda's window as a hired driver whisked her out of that neighborhood for the last time.

Linda exits the stairwell. The lobby attendant is sitting at his desk, a blue leopard-print earcuff screaming from his pale ear. Nick. Linda sometimes gets the two white attendants confused, but the earcuff is a dead giveaway. Nick doesn't look at her, and he isn't talking into his earcuff, isn't singing or bobbing his head along to some starlet's vocal fry. He's probably listening to one of the self-help podcasts that are popular. *Tips in Attention Splitting* is the one Linda keeps seeing mentioned on SocialHub: *TAS Tips for Maximum Efficiency,* or *TASTMEs.* Layers of acronyms; Linda likes to make up her own meanings. She hurries past the attendant, thinking: *Totally Anonymous Shitheads Tell Man Everything.*

She didn't want a doorman building. She didn't want to be in the city at all, had asked for a small house in the mountains, where it would be just her and the trees, maybe even the occasional fox. But Arthur insisted: *It's for the best.* That's what Dr. Tambor used to say and what Arthur still says. They'd been born to this world, so they should know.

Just as Linda is about to push her way through the lobby's revolving door, a woman buckling beneath the weight of a plastic crate backs into the door from outside. Linda steps aside. The woman with the box is shorter than she is, looks to also be in her mid-twenties, and her skin is dark enough that it's clear she's not Caucasian, though Linda can't identify her ethnicity. She often can't distinguish ethnicities. Dr. Tambor told her this made sense, given her isolated background; she compared it to Linda's inability to distinguish among commonwealth accents—a matter of exposure, no more. But interacting with darker-skinned strangers always sends a special nervousness spiking through her. She worries they can sense this wrongness of hers: an ignorance and curiosity she's learned to never admit to aloud.

And Linda *is* curious about the incoming woman. She's striking. Her black hair is short and spiky, save for a violet-dyed swath that falls across one temple, and even burdened with the box she moves with a grace and confidence Linda covets. When the woman emerges into the lobby, it's as a conqueror. Her eyes catch Linda's and she chirps, "Afternoon." Her irises are the color and pattern of crystallized honey. Linda shifts her gaze to the floor.

As the attendant scurries to help the newcomer, Linda pushes out into the wet, heavy breeze. Above, scattered clouds bask in winter daylight. A passing man pulls his coat tight as he hustles by a large shipping pod parked nearby.

Linda thinks of the elderly couple who moved out of the apartment down the hall from hers a few weeks ago—they were ideal neighbors: quiet, unprying—and hopes the eye-contact-seeking woman isn't moving onto her floor. In a building this size, there must be other open apartments.

She squeezes her eyes shut for a moment, allowing the damp air to calm her, and thinks of how she used to love waking in her tarp-lined nest, feeling the dew on her eyelashes, listening to the good-morning drip of gentle rain, and watching the mist retreat. It was her favorite time of day as a child. Waking with a brief spark of hope that maybe something new would happen.

She misses that: the naïveté of assuming *new* meant *better*.

Linda burrows her chin into the collar of her wool coat and walks forward in a quick hunch, blending as best she can. But everything feels wrong: the weight of her coat, the pressure of her Sheath against her left forearm, even her gait. She's wearing the thinnest-soled sneakers Arthur's assistant could find, but even after all these years she still misses the give of the fern-lined forest floor—running and playing Hide-and-Find. Sleeping in the trees; the white-faced fox who followed her around one summer. That Christmas, the only one she can remember celebrating, where the snow fell swift and heavy and there was a green disc sled waiting, slick and new, and she skid-ded down the hill, laughing, toward welcoming arms.

She was loved once.

She knows it, she feels it. Some days the loneliness tears at her so hard, it seems the only thing that keeps her breathing is the tiny, stu-pid hope that since it had happened once, it might happen again. Though maybe cause and effect runs in the opposite direction: Maybe her mind kindles this hope *because* her body refuses to stop breath-ing. She isn't sure it makes a difference.

A gas-powered car drives by, louder than the rest; Linda feels a pulse of adrenaline, and she pushes past the catch in her step, telling herself, *It's just a car.* She has a route in mind, one that will take her away from cars and buses to a nearby park. She needs somewhere quiet so she can make up for missing her excursion yesterday.

She pushed it once, to see what would happen if the tracking app on her Sheath recorded that she hadn't met her mandated hour a day of excursion time. She opened all her windows, burrowed into her chair, and waited, rising only for bodily needs. Friday evening a warning had blipped across her Sheath. The following Monday, Arthur's assistant called: *Are you okay, dear?* She even sounded sincere. Or so Linda thought; she often has trouble discerning sincerity. She mumbled an affirmative and what she knew was an unconvincing lie—*I've been out, but I forgot to wear my Sheath*—and ended the call. Then she hurried outside, walking forty minutes in one direction before turning back, accounting for the fact that she always moved faster when heading toward home. The pressure of strangers' gazes felt especially intense that day, and it was only after she returned and saw her sneakers sitting by the door that she realized she'd been walking barefoot.

Linda pauses at the corner and waits for the light to change. The word rolls around her mind: *home.* Home used to be twenty wooded acres. A pond choked by native cattails and invasive bamboo. An old fox hutch with fallen mesh pinned to the earth by moss and clover. A big-leaf maple where she built her nest: a single tree that, long before Linda's memory began, started as three trees. Saplings that sprouted too close together and merged without thought, without consciousness, cell by cell, to become one.

She shouldn't miss it. Growing up, she'd wanted nothing more than to see the world beyond the wall, the *people* beyond the wall. But she never thought it would happen the way it did. She thought—

Linda isn't sure what her child-self thought. Probably something stupid like that her sister would be standing outside waiting for her. That Emmer would grab her hand and ask, *What took you so long?* That they'd skip together into town, and town would be like in the picture books: a butcher, a baker, a candlestick maker. A trouble-free happily-ever-after for two brave little girls.

A bus passes, then the intersection is clear. Linda could cross safely, but it's said people don't jaywalk in this city. A lie. It happens, but it's a thing to be noticed. She keeps waiting. The white stick figure soon flashes on; she continues toward the park.

Ahead, two men round the corner, one Asian, one white and bearded. They're laughing and holding hands. The Asian man wears a yellow-and-purple scarf, the white man a hat and gloves to match. Linda glides to the inner edge of the sidewalk to give them space, and as they pass she feels it: a wave of happiness coming off the couple like a physical thing. She wants so badly to follow them, to experience a joy like theirs even from the outside. She crushes the urge. They might notice; they might recognize her; they might not be so happy after all.

When she turns in to the park, Linda's eyes go immediately to her preferred bench, which is tucked away near a cedar hedge. A woman with a toddler-stuffed stroller is sitting on it, bundled against the chill and drinking from a Starbucks cup. Anger bubbles through Linda. How is she supposed to fill two hours outside the apartment if someone else is sitting on her bench?

If she could make the woman disappear with a thought, she would. There are too many people in this world anyway.

She bites her lip. That wasn't a healthy thought. That wasn't a good thought, a constructive thought. It's the kind of thought that would have concerned Dr. Tambor. *Let's dig into this, shall we?* Linda shakes off the rancorous thought as she starts a slow lap around the park. The woman has a child, a fragile larva she'll need to get out of the cold soon. That she'll coddle and coo over, the kid having no idea how lucky it is.

Linda is nearing the water fountains—turned off for winter—when the toddler begins to wail and kick its sleeping-sack-encased legs. Did Linda ever make such noises as a child? It seems impossible. She watches, side eye, suspecting this means the woman will be on her way soon.

Indeed, the woman bursts up from the bench to rock the stroller back and forth. When that doesn't calm the child, she digs into a bag and gives it a packet of food. The crying and kicking cease.

Don't sit, don't sit, don't sit, Linda pleads silently. *Go.*

She feels a brief thrill of victory as the woman pushes the stroller toward an exit.

Linda hurries to the vacated bench. Taking a seat, she closes her eyes for a few seconds, focusing on the sound of the wind, the scent of wet cedar in the air. When she opens her eyes, she sees an older woman with formfitting athletic pants and a puffy vest turn off the street into the park. The woman's close-cropped hair is its earned gray, and she doesn't appear to be wearing an earcuff. Instead, she's looking around the park, bright and observant—unusually engaged with her surroundings. She seems like the kind of woman who might want to tell a harried-looking stranger that retirement is the best time of her life, so just hang in there.

And she's coming straight toward Linda.

Linda shoves up her left coat sleeve to access her Sheath, exposing its simple tether: two intersecting bands between her wrist and elbow. The Sheath's thin, flexible, waterproof screen is clicked into place at their nexus, which also hosts an extension to store her neoprene earcuff. The Sheath is constantly active, constantly connected, and though Linda has hers set to *Visual Only,* text bubbles pinged soundless announcements as she walked and continue to ping as she sits: The café one block west has the highest Yelp rating in a ten-block radius, and here's a coupon for 15 percent off any baked good with the purchase of a handcrafted beverage; there are seven new comments on a SocialHub post you clicked this morning—no, make that eight; and, look, a sale on pet-cloning services, today only (promoted content).

The gray-haired woman draws closer. Linda taps SocialHub's *Quick Reads* icon. Ducking her head, she scans the headlines: LARISSA CONWAY VOTED SEXIEST TEEN IDOL; FOUR DEAD AND DOZENS INJURED IN MIAMI PROTEST; SEVEN ONE-HIT WONDERS DEAD BY OVERDOSE—YOU WON'T BELIEVE NUMBER FIVE!

Linda stares and scrolls, her true attention on the approaching woman. *Don't stop, don't stop, don't stop.*

The woman doesn't even look at Linda as she power-walks by. Instead, she laughs, gazing off into the distance. She's wearing Augments, Linda realizes. She's used to seeing this kind of behavior from people with glasses, as the tech overlays their visual field with running commentary, but augmented-reality contact lenses are still prohibitively expensive for most. Of course, this is Seattle; there is no way of knowing how much a plainly dressed stranger might be worth.

Linda taps the home button on her Sheath and pulls her sleeve to her wrist, willing herself to calm down. She isn't sure how identification software works with Augments—the amount of information that can be legally gleaned with a glance seems to be in constant flux—and she's glad she hid her face.

She lifts her face now as a gust of wind rustles through the hedges. In the distance, a crow caws. Linda sucks in a deep, steadying breath.

There were crows on the Cedar Lake property too. Her real home from a lifetime ago. She'd watch them for hours when she was little. Once, she threw a trout into the grass to see what would get it first: the chickens or the crows. Neither touched it until it was dead; then the chickens pecked away its flesh, and at dusk the crows flew its bones over the wall.

Restless but unwilling to give up her bench, Linda decides to play a game: If Anything. She and Emmer used to play it, curled together on a couch cushion or in their tree or on the dock. One twin would ask the other: If you could do anything right now, what would you do?

Fly to Mars.

Find a Bigfoot.

Bake a cake.

Eat a cake.

Catch a fish in a jar and teach it to sing.

Limitless answers, limitless possibilities, seeded by the limited books and games available to them.

So, Linda asks herself: If you could do anything right now, what would you do?

Break my Sheath to pieces.

Climb that tree.

Run until my breath comes heavy and my legs are soggy, rotten stalks.

Find Emmer.

The last time Linda saw her twin sister, their mother was leading Emmer through the maw of the basement door. In this flash of memory, Lorelei is tall and slender like a ghoul and Emmer glances back, tossing Linda a superior smile as she takes a step down. Then the door closes, and Linda never sees her sister again.

At first, Linda didn't realize Emmer's leaving was permanent; she was only five or six when it happened, and it wasn't unusual for Emmer to disappear with their mother for hours at a time, occasionally for even a day or two. It wasn't until Lorelei reappeared and said, "She's gone," that Linda realized this time was not *another* but *the last*. And though Linda can barely remember the details of Lorelei's face after all these years, she remembers what she saw in her mother's eyes that day: They were dry and red and full of accusation. Under that rough gaze, Linda felt the weight of her sister's disappearance and understood that—somehow—it was her fault.

But she simultaneously also understood that Emmer was free. That her sister had been released beyond the wall into the larger world, and that this was Emmer's reward for being the better twin, just as being left behind was Linda's punishment.

Sometimes Linda dreams of Emmer finding her and making everything right. She knows better than to believe this will ever happen, but she allows herself the dream.

This is how Linda passes the rest of her excursion: dreaming of Emmer. In the dream, the only differences between them are the shade of their eyes and the shape of their noses: Emmer's a sweet button, while Linda's ends in a subtle, inferior hook. In the dream, these differences don't matter. They're both grinning—laughing—as they walk through the woods in step. Together.

2.

The moving pod is still parked outside Linda's building. Inside, the lobby attendant is on the desk phone, talking to a tenant. He waves at Linda, and she forces a nod on her way to the stairwell. As soon as she pushes through the door, she hears a commotion above. She peeks her head around the railing. A flash of an arm a few floors up. A woman's voice: "Turn it left!" Male grumbling. The woman again: "Dude, you're—" A tuft of brown pops over the railing, teeters, and then falls toward Linda. The woman shouts, "Heads!"

Linda jumps back, pressing herself against the wall, and the brown thing smacks the floor. Adrenaline pulses through Linda, and she feels the hard lump of a fire alarm against her back. Footsteps clomp toward her as she stares. The projectile is just a couch cushion, out of place on the tile and harmless now.

The brown-skinned woman from earlier pops into view from around the landing. "Whoa," she says. "You okay?"

Linda nods, and her eyes slip to the woman's T-shirt. It's purple, a few shades lighter than the swath of hair lying over her temple. Black cursive across the front reads *PhD Bitch*. The *i* in *Bitch* is dotted with a glittering skull and crossbones. The Sheath on the woman's left arm also sparkles, a dazzling, thick white band that covers most of her skin between her wrist and elbow.

"Sorry about the scare." The woman pats Linda's arm as she passes, the touch quick and casual and yet as sharp as fire—Linda can't remember the last time she was intentionally touched. Arthur's last visit, probably. Months ago: a stiff and awkward hug. "I told them we should take these off first," says the woman, picking up the cushion and examining it for damage. She props the cushion against the wall and juts her hand toward Linda. "Anyway, I'm Anvi."

Linda stares at Anvi's hand. Wide, twisting strands of gold decorate her middle finger above the knuckle; the strands have tiny leaves or thorns coming off them, like vines. Linda flicks her gaze upward; the woman's earcuff matches her Sheath's case.

Long seconds pass. Anvi withdraws her hand and peers at Linda. "Is it a germ thing or are you in shock?" she asks.

Linda's already done everything wrong. "Sorry," she whispers.

"Nothing to be sorry about." Anvi picks up the cushion again and hugs it to her chest. Her honey-colored eyes burn with curiosity. "What's your name?"

Her attention is so intense it's making Linda sweat. She hates sharing her chosen name. It doesn't feel like *her*. But she has no choice. "Linda," she says.

"Nice to meet you, Linda. We have the stairs blocked, so you probably want to take the elevator." Anvi lifts her hand in a little wave, then darts back up the stairs. "You two almost killed a girl," she shouts ahead of herself.

Linda retreats into the lobby and taps the elevator call button. She's so distracted she forgets to check if anyone else is in the lobby, and as the elevator dings its arrival, a middle-aged white man steps up next to her, startling her. She reddens at his glance. She's seen him in the lobby a few times before. He said good morning to her once as he collected his mail from near the top of the mailboxes.

The man gestures for Linda to enter the elevator first. She can feel his gaze. He's curious or possibly annoyed, she's not sure. Either way, if she gets into the elevator with him, he might want to talk. He might say, *You look familiar.*

"My mail," she blurts; she turns and strides back through the lobby toward the mailboxes, keeping her ears pricked in case the man follows. But he disappears into the elevator. Linda jams her key into the mailbox. As she pulls out a week's worth of coupons and fly-ers, she wishes a pestilence upon stairwell-blocking Anvi for throw-ing her so out of sorts. She closes the mailbox. The attendant is listening to his earcuff; the lobby is otherwise empty. Linda beelines for the elevators. This time no one joins her.

She rides upward with her jaw clenched, reminding herself with each slow, pinched inhale: *You're not trapped.* And with each exhale: *The doors will open.*

As long as her exhale statement is true, the inhale's is too.

Six floors, no stops. Today's trip lasts seven breaths, the first few quicker than the last as Linda calms herself. And then— This is the worst part, when the doors open and there's no knowing who might be on the other side, no window to peep through, to make sure the way is clear. But unless the doors open, she *will* be trapped, so it's a necessary terror. She braces herself as the elevator settles. Her neck and shoulders ache with tension. She needs to be home. She needs to take off her Sheath. She needs to close her eyes without fear or worry of who might be watching.

The doors slide open. The hallway is beautifully empty. She hears a dim ruckus from the stairwell; Anvi and her movers must be close. Linda steps out of the elevator and walks quickly toward her apart-ment: a one-bedroom corner unit. The recently vacated apartment that she hopes isn't Anvi's is across from the elevators. Linda can see the door from her peephole. She can see about half the doors from her peephole.

Inside, she locks her door and tosses her mail on the kitchen island. After hanging up her coat, she peels off her Sheath and drops it into a box she keeps by the door. Kicking off her sneakers, she falls into the wicker basket chair by the windows. It's the only piece of furniture in the room that she uses regularly. The sofa along the wall is for Arthur, for the pictures of the apartment he insisted she send and for his rare visit. Other than that, there is only a small coffee table and a wall-mounted television. Arthur's assistant sent Linda a potted plant when she first moved in—a succulent. Linda watched it die slowly, needing more sunlight maybe and certainly more water, since she gave it none. The plant's desiccated husk huddles in the corner. Linda pulls her knees to her chest and stares at it for a moment before closing her eyes. The plant's death was a choice: Succulents don't belong in this climate. If it'd been a fern, she would have watered it. Maybe even if it'd been bamboo, which had fought for and earned its place here.

It occurs to her that she hasn't eaten anything today. Resigned to the physical necessity of consuming calories, she gets up and grabs a can of ravioli from a kitchen cupboard. She heats the contents in the microwave until there's a loud *pop* and a new red splatter joins months' worth of stains inside the machine. She brings the steaming ravioli back over to her nest chair, then turns on the television, selects the PBS app, and puts on a quiet documentary about orangutans.

She eats quickly, then allows herself to drift toward rest as a wheelbarrow of big-eyed orange orphans coasts across the screen. She thinks of ferns and bamboo and the special softness of cattail blossoms—how she used to tie them into pillows and the one summer when she constructed an entire mattress. She thinks of Emmer waving at her from the far side of the pond, her earliest memory of her twin: three or four years old, with a mop of dark hair and freckles drawn out by the sun. They were the same age, so in the memory Emmer doesn't feel like a little girl, she feels like an equal—a peer, a sister. Maybe even like her better, since Lorelei loved her more.

Emmer wouldn't have. Emmer didn't. Lorelei's favorite phrases before she turned mute. Blame settling over Linda every time she did something wrong, an endless, nameless something wrong that she never understood. Or she was stuck holding a ratty teddy bear while Emmer cuddled a stuffed puppy with long ears. She can't remember the contests in which she always came in second place, but that sense of competition—and losing—is omnipresent. Whatever Linda wanted, Emmer got, leaving Linda with whatever remained.

But sometimes—*sometimes*—Linda came out ahead. These moments were magic, as rare and mysterious as a miracle. Lorelei might even touch her hand and smile. *Good girl.*

She remembers coloring a circle. She had a vague sense that the circle was meant to be a sun, but she used a thick green crayon anyway—she liked green, most of her world was green—and Lorelei's hand fell atop hers afterward. A gentle squeeze.

Warmed by this memory, Linda falls asleep to the sound of a motorboat chugging up a Sumatran river.

A piercing buzz wakes her. Linda jerks upright, heart pounding. It's dark—outside and in the apartment too. Not true dark but city dark. The sun has set.

She folds over, processing. The doorbell buzzes again. Linda lurches out of her chair, shooting a glance at the digital oven clock in the kitchen: 7:06. It's early yet, not even prime time—she shouldn't be sleeping. Never mind that it's been dark out for hours now; in this world people don't rise and fall with the sun.

Linda approaches the peephole. Looking out, she sees the new tenant. Anvi is wearing a zip-up sweater over her purple shirt but has the sleeve pushed up and is looking at her Sheath.

When Linda opens the door, she's startled to find a fluffy, knee-high black dog at Anvi's side.

"Oh hey," says Anvi. "Linda, right?"

Linda is transfixed by the dog, whose eyes are wet and dark. His black nose is twitching, processing the stale odors that must be drifting from Linda's apartment. She thinks of the golden retriever she had access to during her initial transition—as Dr. Tambor called those especially rough months immediately after she climbed the wall—an elderly dog who curled against her side and placed her head in her lap. Whose soft presence and silky fur calmed her, made her feel like, yes, her world had ended but maybe she could survive into the next. She thinks also of the fox she saw and who saw her—who she used to imagine following her everywhere, secretly, like a protector.

"I guess we're neighbors," says Anvi. Linda forces herself to look up from the dog. Anvi's smiling. Linda isn't sure what to do, why she even opened the door.

"Hello," she tries.

"Hi," says Anvi. "I'm sorry about before. The cushion."

"It's fine." She wants to close the door. She wants to pet the dog. To wrap her arms around his neck and hold him close.

"I'm just introducing myself around," says Anvi. "And I wanted to apologize for the ruckus." She waves at the dog. "This lump is Nibbler. He's probably going to bark a bit as we settle in. I hope it's not too annoying."

Linda has a habit of assuming animals are male and knows it was only luck that she was right. It's a holdover from childhood. She never heard a male voice, saw a man in the flesh, until the day she left, so as a girl she guessed most animals were male, to create balance. She isn't sure why she thought there had to be balance.

Nibbler's still sniffing the air. Linda wants him to bark—loud enough to remove the need for her to dig up some socially acceptable response to Anvi's introduction.

"Well, I'll let you get back to your evening," says Anvi. "Nice to meet you. Again."

"Goodbye." Linda closes the door and puts her eye to the peephole. She watches Anvi reach down to pet Nibbler then move out of sight to the next apartment.

Linda goes into her bedroom—dust atop the covers; she prefers sleeping in her wicker chair—and grabs her tablet from the desk. "Input," she says, "how is the feminine name *Anvi* spelled?" She dislikes using voice control, but it has its uses.

The tablet replies in the soft soprano Linda selected from dozens of options—the voice of a girl, not a woman. "The name *Anvi,* of Hindu origin, is most commonly spelled *A-N-V-I.*"

Hinduism is a religion from India. Linda remembers that from studying for her GED, but she also knows this doesn't mean Anvi is from India. *America is a salad bowl.*

She opens SocialHub and engages its proximity search, guessing that Anvi is the kind of person who keeps her profile open. Most people are.

Search name: Anvi

Search radius: .1 miles

There are two results: Anvi Mehra and Anvi Hendrickson.

Linda unpinches Mehra's profile picture to expand it. The photo is mostly of the woman's bust. The face above that bust is surrounded by long, lush hair and doused with makeup. Linda pinches the photo down and checks Hendrickson.

It's her, purple hair and all. She's giving a wistful look over her shoulder as she gazes toward a clock tower.

Linda taps to access her profile. Anvi's last two public posts are both pictures of Nibbler—one in a car; one beside a thick tree, his tongue lolling. Linda starts to scroll, then her breath catches: Anvi has over two thousand contacts. Two *thousand.* Linda has four: Arthur, Arthur's wife, Arthur's assistant, and Dr. Tambor's memorial page. Eventually she blinks away her shock. Maybe two thousand is a normal number. She knows four isn't.

She devours the rest of the information available on Anvi's page. Anvi is twenty-nine—older than Linda thought—and originally from New Jersey, has at least two brothers, is listed as being employed as a PhD student at Cornell, wore a huge bell-shaped dress and goggles made out of gears for Halloween, and posts a lot of links to articles about superintelligence and something called "the singularity." She also seems to have a thing for cheese plates, posting a picture of one almost every month. But above all else, Anvi's page makes one thing very clear: She *really* likes her dog. There's Nibbler running through tall grass. Jumping to catch a blue disc. Sleeping in a yellow bed. Wearing a Santa hat with a stuffed toy in his mouth.

Linda continues scrolling and tapping back through time, reading every comment, looking at every photo. Nibbler regresses into puppyhood, then disappears. Eventually she reaches Anvi's college graduation: a younger-looking Anvi grinning in her cap and gown with her arms around her brown mother and white father. Prisha and Clark. Linda taps both their faces, opening their SocialHub pages in different tabs. Dr. Prisha Hendrickson's is private and shows nothing except her picture. Clark's is a public memorial page established less than a year ago. He was a professor and, by all evidence, beloved.

Hours have passed. Linda's vision is fuzzy, and her eyes feel not just tired but sore. As she sets down her tablet and blinks her focal point to her dark kitchen, a sense of guilt rushes through her. But why should she feel guilty? Anvi shared all this information intentionally—publicly. This is why people open themselves to proximity searches, isn't it? So others can know them.

And she *does* feel like she knows Anvi now: a dog-loving, scientifically inclined extrovert with a dead father and a fondness for Brie cheese. Underlying Linda's guilt is another feeling, a rarer feeling: She feels powerful. She never knows more about someone than they know about her.

It feels good.

3.

Linda is curled in her chair, watching the sun rise, when furious barking erupts in the hallway.

"Nibbler! Quiet!"

She walks over and puts her eye to the peephole. Anvi is standing near the elevator, and Nibbler's pulling on his leash. The elevator doors are open, one of Anvi's legs between them. The doors slide shut, hit her leg, and bounce back open.

"Nibs, come on," says Anvi. Her voice is pinched but carries: a loud person's show of being quiet.

The dog dips his front legs and barks again—at the elevator. There's a white patch on the underside of his jaw Linda didn't notice yesterday.

"Oh my God, fine." Anvi extracts her leg. "We'll take the stairs. Brat." Nibbler follows her into the stairwell.

Linda watches the empty hallway.

Another day. Another useless morning. Another excursion she doesn't want to face. Another afternoon staring at televised wilderness, wondering why she isn't out among the trees.

She goes into the kitchen and drinks some water from the tap, then slumps into her chair with her tablet and checks SocialHub. Anvi has already posted today: a close-up of Nibbler's face; his eyes are closed, his nose elongated and richly textured. *Too tuckered out from moving for his morning walk.* The post is only minutes old and already has a dozen reactions, mostly thumbs-ups and hearts but also a few crying faces with comments like *Miss you! XOX.*

Linda taps out of Anvi's profile into her main social feed, where she finds a barrage of posts by people she's never met: the many contacts of her few. She's connected to most by way of Arthur's pro-social assistant. Her eyes slide over pictures of babies and deconstructed lunch pies, a political rant, and a meme equating "white male" to "privileged ignoramus." She can't help wondering if Arthur's seen the last and, if so, what he thinks of his assistant's laughter-emoji response.

She swipes over to trending topics. The Miami riot and a celebrity chef's just-announced pregnancy have top billing. A mix of laughter and rolling-eye reactions pelt a BUN IN THE OVEN headline. Linda rubs at her eyes, and her gaze drifts back to the window. The sky is a pretty blush, but Linda misses the stars—watching them fade into daylight. She wonders if the transition is still as beautiful as she remembers. If it ever was.

Soon, Linda hears Anvi and Nibbler in the hallway again. She slips over to the peephole just in time to see a black tail disappear. A door slams elsewhere. It's edging toward the morning rush. Linda eats dry cereal from the box and stares out the window some more. The urban view bores her—overwhelms her.

She checks SocialHub again. There's still the riot and the pregnant chef but also news of a winter storm swirling across the East Coast. There's a famous comedian who was accused of plagiarizing sections of his bestselling memoir; at first he denied the allegations but now he's asserting it was all part of a long-game gag. Earthquake-relief efforts in Bangladesh are being hampered by weather and—some insist—Western apathy. Under local topics, there's a report on home-lessness trends and a story about a programmer who claims to have created a computer simulation indistinguishable from life.

Linda rolls her head into the cushion and sighs. Her excursion window is still hours away. She thinks of Anvi and Nibbler and wonders what would happen if she walked over there and asked, *May I pet your dog?*

Instead, she reopens Anvi's SocialHub profile. There's another new post: the same local article about computer simulations Linda just skimmed past.

Anvi has scrawled across a screen grab: *I call shenanigans.*

Linda taps to continue reading, more curious about Anvi's reaction than anything else. The one-paragraph announcement—labeled *unverified* by SocialHub fact-checking algorithms—was posted this morning by someone using the initials G.H.:

> *The world needs to know what is happening within spitting distance of downtown Bellevue. I was part of a group of software engineers focused on creating ancestor simulations making use of immersive VR technology. After more than a decade of work, our efforts paid off in a way we never anticipated: We created a world indistinguishable from our own. The program isn't lifelike, it's life. Anyone familiar with Bostrom's simulation hypothesis knows what this means. The hypothesis is confirmed: The probability of our existence—our universe—being a computer simulation is near one. I don't expect people to believe me without evidence. I wouldn't believe it without evidence either. I spent months seeking cracks in the simulation before accepting the enormity of our creation. Unfortunately, my former colleagues have decided to keep our findings a secret. They believe this truth is too large to be shared. I believe it is too large not to be shared. When I spoke against them, they revoked my access to the project. I need your help: Only through pub-*

lic pressure will they change their minds. Help me change their minds so we can explore the truth behind all of us.

The top comment on the post is just one word: *Bullshit.* Linda stares for a moment, watching notes and highlights tick up. Bellevue is just across the lake, a short light-rail ride away. At this rate, the post will be trending nationally soon. She scrolls to read more comments. People want to know who G.H. is, why he—a sub-thread has already developed on this sexist assumption; Linda minimizes it—is bothering to post under SocialHub's anonymous feature, since his former colleagues must know who he is. There are posts Linda doesn't fully understand, including technological jargon about things like *computational limitations, error-correcting codes,* and *base reality.* Then, finally, a link to an article explaining the simulation hypothesis.

Half an hour later, she thinks she understands. The hypothesis comes down to this: If humanity can create a simulation indistinguishable from our reality, then that simulation would by definition also be able to create simulations indistinguishable from its—and by extension our—reality. Simulations could then stack like endless nesting dolls, each as "real" as the next. Therefore, the creation of one such simulation would in effect prove the existence of myriad others. From there it became a numbers game: It'd be vastly more probable that our reality—the universe as we know it—is just one among innumerable indistinguishable simulations rather than the single base reality that started it all.

Linda picks up her box of cereal from the floor, wondering what kind of simulation would allow for her existence. A faulty one, maybe.

There's only cereal dust left, and Linda suddenly feels hungrier than she has in days. She goes to the kitchen, smiling a sad little smile as she scours her cupboards, looking for something else to eat: *Maybe I'm the result of a coding error.*

It's an oddly comforting thought.

But most commenters claim it's impossible: that even if the world of the program looks perfectly lifelike, there's no way characters within that world can't be discerned from real people. AI simply isn't that advanced yet.

Linda doesn't have the firsthand experience necessary for an opinion. Arthur's wife has a gaming room in the Connecticut house, and Claire offered to show her how to use the VR set once, but Linda panicked and said no. She'd seen the woman play, and the goggles—you were blind with those on; anything could happen on the outside while you roamed a fictional world. She couldn't do it. Mixed reality seems more manageable—she tried Arthur's assistant's Augments once, at her insistence—but even then, how is one to know what is really there and what isn't? Why would anyone invite such uncertainty into her life?

Linda finds three more cans of last night's ravioli. Her cupboards are otherwise bare, except for what Arthur's assistant called "the staples": flours, sugars, spices, all unopened. The only thing Linda knows how to cook are eggs, and she hasn't been able to stomach eggs since leaving behind the feral hens of her childhood.

She doesn't want ravioli, doesn't feel up to exerting even the amount of effort it would take to open the can. It looks like today's excursion will be grocery shopping. Of all her guidelines, this is perhaps the most chafing: She isn't allowed to have her groceries delivered. She checks the time: 9:10. Another door slams, and she huddles in her chair, eyes closed, letting the time pass. At 10:27 she puts on her coat, grabs her Sheath and shopping totes, and makes her way down to the lobby.

She hears Anvi before she sees her: standing at the desk talking to the attendant—Eddie, recognizable by his dark skin and easy smile. Nibbler sniffs the floor at Anvi's feet. Linda keeps walking.

The dog is the first to look up. Anvi is next; her face brightens then falls, and Linda feels the responsibility of somehow having ruined her day.

"Hey, Linda," says Anvi. "You okay?"

The sour sting of her own musk hits Linda's nose, and she realizes she hasn't bathed or changed her clothes in several days. To her, a thick layer of dirt across her calves—splashed up from running—or the salty crispness of dried sweat upon her skin are signals to wash. She often forgets without these physical cues of exertion.

You don't owe strangers explanations, Dr. Tambor told her once. *Or apologies.* Linda tries to smile. "I'm well." After a second, she remembers to add, "How are you?"

"Fine, thanks." Nibbler tugs toward Linda, sniffing the air. "Can he say hi?"

Linda's heart leaps; she nods and sticks out her hand, palm up, but Nibbler's nose goes past her hand, jamming in between her legs. Anvi jerks on the leash.

"Nibbler! Rude. Sorry."

Linda blushes, but she kneels and offers her palm again. This time Nibbler smells it, and then he smells her face. His whiskers brush her nose, and Linda feels a real smile pulling at her cheeks.

"Where are you off to?" asks Anvi. Linda is so enamored with Nibbler, it takes her a moment to realize the question is directed at her. She tells herself it's okay. This is small talk, not an interrogation. She can suffer it to be close to the dog.

"To purchase food," she answers.

Nibbler sits and sniffs the base of his tail. "Mind if I tag along?" asks Anvi. "I'd love to see where the locals shop."

Linda lets her eyes dart to Anvi's Sheath—a far more useful guide than Linda could ever be.

Anvi interprets her silence as assent; or maybe she was never really asking. "Come on, Nibs," she says, and she heads for the door. "Bye, Eddie. Thanks."

Linda could retreat. She could run upstairs and hide. But she's drawn toward Anvi. Toward her purple hair and thousands of friends. Toward walking beside someone who knows nothing about her— and about whom she knows so much.

Plus, maybe she'll get to pet Nibbler.

A comforting drizzle chills her hot forehead as she steps outside. Beside her, Anvi pulls up her jacket's hood.

"You don't use an umbrella or anything?" asks Anvi.

Linda shakes her head. The rain is beading on her face; she feels a drop run down the side of her nose. As a child, she would shelter herself from the rain at night, but except for the occasional down-pour, she rarely bothered to try to keep dry during the day. Even on frosty days, she might put on a few extra layers from her clean cloth-ing pile, but mostly she kept warm by moving. She remembers the squash of her feet through long, sodden grass, how the clumps of blades clutched at her ankles as she chased after her sister. How much thicker and more cumbersome the grass felt after Emmer left.

Anvi allows them to walk in silence for a block, but Linda feels the weight of her new neighbor's contemplation. This was a mistake, she thinks. Anvi's a talker. She's going to ask questions. She's going to—

"Oh, neat!" says Anvi, and she raises her Sheath; Linda's heart thuds, but the picture Anvi's taking isn't of her. It's of an alleyway painting—graffiti or a commissioned mural, Linda's not sure—a brown woman with a rainbow for a smile and tears dripping down her cheeks. Anvi holds her arm where Linda can see as she swipes between the macroshot and a handful of microshots automatically framed by the Sheath's photo software. In one, the camera focused on the rain instead of the wall, and the rainbow smile bleeds behind crisp, glistening raindrops. "What do you think? That one's pretty cool, right?"

Linda manages a nod.

Nibbler whines and strains at his leash. "Okay, okay," Anvi says, pulling down her sleeve. "He gets antsy when I spend too much time on this thing," she tells Linda. "If I'm not careful, he'll go on one of his rants about how screen time erodes social bonds."

Linda stares.

"I tell him every generation since TV has said that, and he's just like, well, this time it's true."

Linda can sense Anvi's mind churning, trying to determine why Linda isn't laughing or making a joke of her own. "What does Nibbler think about the simulation hypothesis?" she blurts.

Anvi grins. "You saw that G.H. nonsense this morning? Nibs and I are of one mind there: That post is crap."

The supermarket is on the next block. Linda just has to make it that far, then the conversation should die naturally. "I hadn't heard of the hypothesis before today."

"Oh, Bostrom's reasoning is dead genius, and his writings on AI were a big part of why I started studying machine learning. The first time I read his stuff, my brain was like—" Anvi brings her fist to the side of her head and flicks the fingers outward, making a soft exploding sound. "But this post? It shows a puerile understanding of his work at best. The simulation argument hinges less on how realistic any one slice of a simulated world might be and more on whether or not that world can evolve. Not to mention the state of consciousness of its inhabitants."

Nibbler stops to squat in a patch of grass.

"You didn't believe it, did you?" asks Anvi.

"I . . . I don't know." She watches Nibbler. She thought male dogs always lifted their legs to pee. "It seemed far-fetched, but I've never used virtual reality, so—"

"You've never used VR?" exclaims Anvi. "Once mine is set up, you've got to come give it a try. It's amazing. It's not *reality*, but it's amazing. You'll love it."

A sour thread twists through Linda: This woman has no idea what she could or could not love.

"Here we are," she says, gesturing toward the supermarket's sliding doors.

Anvi ties Nibbler's leash to a bike rack, where a metal bowl is filling with rain. "Be good," she tells him with a pat on the head. Linda glances back as they pass through the doors; the dog is staring at them, his head cocked to reveal the patch of white under his chin.

Usually, Linda goes straight for the items she knows she wants—canned and boxed goods, a bag of apples—but Anvi snags a cart and starts pushing it aisle by aisle, and Linda feels compelled to stay with her. Anvi moves quickly at least, leaning over her cart and exclaiming over products she isn't even buying. "Who the frack is Best Foods?" she asks, holding up a jar of mayonnaise.

One of Linda's very first excursions was to a supermarket—more than a supermarket, a massive world of a store that contained everything from bicycles to laundry detergent, from cat food to fleece pajamas, from a selection of books to a teeming realm of electronics. Dr. Tambor chaperoned this early step toward "conquering the everyday," telling Linda it was okay to just look but that she could also touch anything she wanted. It took Linda a while to gain the courage to touch, but eventually she ran her hands across frilled pillows and tapped a button on a child's toy—it barked and lit up with bright colors, startling her into a small laugh that made Dr. Tambor laugh too. It went well until they wandered into the frozen-food section. Seeing the freezers there—Linda had seen them on television, but in person it was so different, the way they stretched down the aisle and the fog that appeared on the glass after you opened and closed the door.

She began to panic. Dr. Tambor noticed the signs and quietly ushered her outside. Linda chose a lonely tree trapped in the sea of parked cars and stared at its leaves. They were a beautiful autumn red—it was a maple, a smaller maple than her maple, a different species and all alone—and the wind shifted them before striking Linda's cheeks. She breathed deep, settling breaths and imagined she was smelling the woods of her home.

That night and many after, her nightmares shifted to include ones in which she sprinted through endless corridors of snow and ice and chunks of frozen meat containing copies of a face she was never quite sure was Emmer's, her own, or that of another girl. A girl decades dead, who Linda learned about only after leaving the property: Madeline Rose Niequist.

Over the years, Linda has thought so much about Madeline's death that the story sits in her mind almost like a memory. She can close her eyes and see the fourteen-year-old spinning on her heel and storming down a trail, ordering her parents not to follow. She can see her brash determination, the flare of confidence as Madeline decides to take a shortcut. Her wiry arm brushing tall ferns aside, her foot slipping off a hidden edge. Her yelp as she tumbles, a short free fall, then the *whomp* of air from her lungs as she lands. Linda imagines it happened so quickly it took Madeline a moment to feel the shattering pain. To realize her chest had crashed atop a broken branch at just the right angle for jagged wood to slide through flesh, between ribs, and strike something deeper. She can see Madeline gripping the broken branch and pulling it free. Most of the articles Linda's read suppose this was an act of panic, but in Linda's head Madeline's hands are steady; she's making a horrible mistake, but she's doing it mindfully.

She can see Madeline stumbling a quarter mile through the woods, lost and desperate, spiked with pain. She can hear her rasping breath as her chest refuses to fully rise. Then movement becomes impossible and she slips to the forest floor, her fingers dabbing blood on green leaves. There she sits, hoping for rescue—or perhaps in too much pain to hope for anything.

As shadows fall over the woods, Madeline rests her head against a tree, still clutching the stick that pierced her chest. Then a volunteer rushes into view. *Don't panic,* he says. *I'm here.* Madeline's eyes widen and she claws at the volunteer's shirt, desperate. Her skin is so pale, her lips edged with blue in the moonlight. The volunteer checks her pulse—weak, fast. Briefly, he's distracted by a bloody but superficial head wound, then he notices the dampness at her chest and lifts her shirt to reveal a sucking puncture wound just below her small right breast.

The volunteer shoves his hand against the wound. It doesn't help. Nothing he tries helps. He's radioed for help, and the ranger leading the search effort arrives. The ranger slaps an impermeable dressing over the wound, but it's too late: Madeline's chest cavity has filled with air. Her lungs struggle and fail to expand. Repeated checks of her vitals reveal only a worsening state; she begins to moan gibberish, and her dilated eyes grow wild and seeking. The ranger and the volunteer try to get her out, take turns carrying her, but she's too far gone. On a beautiful summer night, Madeline Rose Niequist suffocates to death in the arms of a stranger.

And if she hadn't, Linda never would have been born. Madeline was her older sister; she and Emmer were birthed to replace her: an impossible task, and one Linda didn't know she was supposed to complete until it was far too late.

Your mother wasn't well, Dr. Tambor told her. *She wanted the impossible. It's not your fault.*

But if it was impossible, why did it come so naturally to Emmer?

Perhaps it was only ever a matter of looks. The first time Linda saw a photograph of Madeline, all she could see was her twin. But while Emmer and Madeline were spitting images of each other, Linda's wrong nose and discolored eyes allowed for no illusion that they were the same girl.

Anvi has led her into a freezer aisle. Linda watches her toss a package of cold-brew-coffee ice pops into her shopping cart. There's a puff of cold air as the freezer door shuts; Linda envisions a small, lonely maple and pretends she remembers what Dr. Tambor's voice sounded like and that her voice is soft beside her, urging her to breathe.

Linda can feel her jaw trembling. Anvi is chattering about an ice-cream brand with familiar packaging but an unfamiliar name. A woman glances their way. She's in her forties, maybe, and Linda shrivels from her gaze, thinking that if Madeline hadn't died, that's about the age she would be today. And Linda would be a frozen nothing in a dish—that or medical waste, discarded long ago. Emmer would be too. Like Madeline, the two of them came from in vitro fertilization. Linda wonders for perhaps the millionth time where Emmer is now, if she has ever wandered down a freezer aisle and thought of her.

Finally, they're heading toward the checkout. Linda gets into line for a cashier. "You don't use the app?" asks Anvi, nodding toward the automatic checkout.

"No." She tried it once, but there'd been a weight discrepancy between her basket and scanned items, and the handful of minutes in which a worker scoured her purchases was far worse than the passing attention of a cashier.

She places her items on the conveyer, acknowledging the cashier's bright politeness with one-word mumbles and tapping her Sheath to the pad to pay. Anvi takes longer, engaging with the cashier's chipper small talk like it's an invitation to actual conversation. Regarding her sparkly Sheath case: "Oh, thank you, I got it for myself as a happy-moving-across-the-country present." Then the follow-ups: "Just a few days ago, from New York." "No, not the city. I was in school upstate." "Yes! It does get dark awfully early, but at least it's not snowing." "No, not Amazon—SocialHub."

Linda's head swings toward Anvi. She works for *SocialHub*?

Anvi is a spy, a plant. The elderly couple in 705 were forced out in order to allow a SocialHub insider an apartment on her floor. Linda's being tracked, monitored, analyzed. Does Arthur know? Was it his idea?

Calm down, she commands herself. Anvi doesn't know who she is. Today wouldn't have been possible if she did.

But still—SocialHub?

Anvi finishes paying, and Linda follows her outside. Nibbler hops to his feet, wagging his tail and whining. Anvi coos hello, then frowns at the four bags hanging from her hands. "I didn't think this through." She looks over at Linda, who's holding only one large tote. "Do you mind taking Nibbler?" she asks.

It feels like a setup. Like the request must be connected to the fact that Anvi works at the largest, most pervasive social-media network in the world.

Maybe she has Nibbler trained to jump or bite or piss on command. Anvi could be planning to record Linda, issue the command, then post the resulting footage. But if that was her plan, she wouldn't have mentioned SocialHub. Most likely, Anvi doesn't have a plan at all.

The disconnect between understanding this and the pit of dread in her stomach vexes Linda. Even though she knows she's being irrational, she can't banish her fear.

And if Anvi *does* have some indignity planned for her, at least Linda will get to hold the dog in exchange. "Okay," she whispers.

The nylon of the leash fits snugly into the crook of Linda's hand, and as Nibbler sniffs at her shin, she feels a thread of happiness crack through her. But also more anxiety: What if Nibbler pulls away, runs into traffic, and gets smeared across the asphalt?

She tightens her hold on the leash.

Nibbler trots between them as they walk; Linda focuses on keeping the leash just taut enough that it doesn't hit the ground or get tangled in the dog's legs—but also loose enough that she doesn't make him uncomfortable.

Something about having the dog in hand, she dares to ask, "You work for SocialHub?"

Anvi doesn't even break stride. "I start a week from Monday."

Her profile says she's a student, but Anvi doesn't know she's seen that. "Where did you work before?"

"I was in school. I finished my PhD in November, went home for the holidays, and now I'm here."

Anvi doesn't seem to mind answering questions, so Linda dares another: "What will be your role at SocialHub?"

"My specialty is natural language processing and machine learning. I'm joining SH's news division with the goal of improving real-time fact-checking and clamping down on the VP index of outright lies."

"VP index?"

"Viral potential."

"Interesting," says Linda.

They're passing the painting of the rainbow-mouthed woman; Anvi waves at it. "I think so," she says, a lilt of enthusiasm in her voice. "My thesis was an analysis of the proliferation of disinformation from the 2016 election through the pandemic." The former was Linda's last winter on the property, and like all of American history it feels distant and impersonal to her—facts to memorize, not events that affect her life in any meaningful way. The pandemic she remembers more clearly: months of isolation, shut into Arthur's Connecticut house, Linda barely leaving her room while Arthur fielded endless conference calls and Claire oscillated between panic and almost frightening peaks of optimism. As the rest of the world struggled to adjust, Linda's life hardly changed at all. If anything, that time was a reprieve.

"The election devastated me as a teen," says Anvi. "I was too young to vote but old enough to care. And then COVID-19—I had to move out of Cornell, and to come home and see all these people walking around as though nothing was wrong?" She shakes her head. "If I can contribute even a little to keeping that kind of massive proliferation and validation of lies from happening in the future, I'll consider mine a life well lived."

Linda feels a disorienting internal rocking. It never occurred to her that there might be a moral purpose beneath someone's involvement with SocialHub.

"So, how . . ." Linda wishes she was better at turning her thoughts into spoken words, that there was a way to ask what she really wants to ask without giving herself away. "How do you know what's true?"

"Most of the hogwash out there can easily be proven false," says Anvi. "But you have to catch it in time. It's a matter of constant vigilance and having the right databases. My thesis focused on prioritization by way of examining the frequency of emotive words as well as absolutes versus ambiguities. Turns out, the more *certain* a piece is, the more likely it is to correlate with falsehoods, especially if that certainty is paired with negativity." Linda has never been as excited about anything as Anvi is, talking about her work. "It's a lot more complicated than that, of course," continues Anvi. "For one thing, there are these self-propagating what-about bots, and they're a *huge* pain in the ass—it's difficult to get AI to recognize false equivalence." She pauses, then gives Linda an odd grimace-laugh. "Sorry, I get a little carried away, but it all boils down to language. That's the basics of the approach I'll be taking."

Linda watches Nibbler's swishing tail and wonders if Anvi ever wallows in a chair for hours, aching as time passes too slowly. It's hard to imagine.

They reach their building. "Thanks for taking Nibs," says Anvi. She stops in front of the elevator and presses the call button.

"He's okay with the elevator?" asks Linda.

"Did we bother you this morning? Sorry. He seems to be better at going up, for some reason. My little weirdo."

Nibbler follows Anvi into the elevator, and because she's holding his leash, Linda follows too. She feels her normal tension creeping through her. As the elevator doors close, she inhales shakily through her nose: *You're not trapped.*

"I'm serious about the VR," says Anvi.

The doors will open.

"I should have it up and running today or tomorrow. You're welcome to come give it a try."

"I, uh . . ." Linda's curious, so curious—and she knows this dynamic with Anvi can't last, so why not take advantage while she can? "Okay," she says. A mingling of terror and excitement runs through her.

"Great," says Anvi. "I'll let you know when it's ready to go."

The elevator doors open. For the first time, Linda isn't sure how many breaths the ride lasted.

4.

The next post from G.H. is short: *I'm not surprised you don't believe me. In a way, I'm glad: I've not yet offered proof. But I will.*

It's early Saturday afternoon and Linda is sitting with her tablet, staring at Anvi's comment: *Yeah, proof of your butt!*

A reply pops up from someone named Conner: a series of buttock emojis. *Which is the base posterior?*

Linda wants so badly to be the kind of person who could laugh at this. Who could add an irreverent comment of her own. It's like she's standing in the corner, watching a group of longtime friends sling inside jokes. But at least they don't know she's watching. She tells herself this is a good thing, but she's had an odd twist in her gut ever since her walk with Anvi yesterday. It's the pain of knowing she likes her neighbor. She hates feeling this way: this need for others, knowing they don't need her back, that she could only ever be a burden. But she also doesn't know how much longer she can bear feeling so alone. The weight of this truth sucks her deeper into her chair, but it isn't a surprise; she understands she is lonely. She understands humans are by their social nature intrinsically clingy creatures and it's natural for her to crave interaction and acceptance. But she also understands she is broken—incapable or perhaps simply unworthy of such connection.

The doorbell rings. Linda puts her tablet aside and checks the peephole. A swath of purple hair dominates the view.

As Linda opens the door, her heart thuds—she forgot to close SocialHub. If Anvi sees her tablet on the counter, she'll see herself.

She stops the door, leaving it open barely a foot. The tablet glows in Linda's peripheral vision; she wills the screen to dim.

"Hey," says Anvi. It's disconcerting seeing her in person when Linda was just staring at her SocialHub profile. "My VR system's set up. I was wondering if you wanted to come over and give it a try?"

"I, uh—now?"

"Sure, now works. Anytime, really."

The tablet's screen darkens. Relief flushes through Linda and she eases the door open another few inches.

"Warning," says Anvi, turning away, "my apartment's still a bit of a wreck."

What would happen if Linda were to close the door and pretend she didn't understand she was meant to follow?

Make friends, Arthur so often urges her.

This can't last, and Linda knows it's not a real friendship, but it's the closest thing she's known to one since Emmer. She grabs her keys but leaves her Sheath in the basket by the door. This way if Anvi asks to add her to her contacts, they won't be able to sync.

Nervous sweat seeps out along her forehead as she steps into her neighbor's apartment. Her eyes slip first to the brown couch, which faces an industrial-looking coffee table and a wall-mounted television so large Linda briefly thinks it's the wall itself. The living room is otherwise lined with bookcases, about half of which are filled with a mix of books and brightly colored boxes she thinks are board games. Stacks of plastic crates dot the room. As far as Linda can tell, the layout of the apartment is identical to her own. This calms her. She knows which door is the bathroom, which the closet. There are no surprises here.

Nibbler prances up to Linda with a fluffy red something in his mouth. He huffs, the sound striking Linda as somehow proud. Looking closer, she sees that the item is a stuffed crab toy with a white beard and red hat. She recognizes it from SocialHub.

"That's his Santy Claws—with a *w*," says Anvi. "He got it for Christmas and just loves it. This is the first time since he was a puppy that he hasn't immediately eviscerated a stuffy."

Linda smiles as she puts her hand out toward the dog. Nibbler brushes against her knees, still huffing, then drops the toy and runs to lap up some water from a bowl by the kitchen.

Anvi leads the way to the bedroom. Linda's perception wobbles: The hallway here feels longer than it should. It doesn't make sense; Linda's seeing things wrong, something's *wrong*.

Then she registers the second bedroom door.

It's just a larger apartment than hers. That's it.

Embarrassment creeps through Linda as she follows Anvi into a nearly empty room. Something so obvious, so silly—and still her first instinct is that something must be wrong with her.

A small desk with a computer and some other equipment, including a sleek headset, sits in the corner of the room. Anvi fiddles with the computer, then picks up the headset and hands it to Linda. "Nibbler, out," she says, pushing the dog into the hallway. The toy crab is back in his mouth, and his eyes are hopeful even as the door closes in his face.

"Have you gamed much at all?" asks Anvi.

Linda shakes her head. Holding the headset, she feels herself tensing.

"I'll ease you into it. You see the taped box on the floor? The system recognizes that as a boundary and won't let you walk beyond it. Like, you'll see a blue warning wall show up if you walk too close in-game, and that's a sign to turn or stop. So you don't have to worry about walking into the wall or my desk or anything. Also, I have this microphone keyed into the system"—she picks up a small headset from the desk—"so I'll be able to talk to you and I'll be seeing a flat version of what you're seeing on the monitor here. If you have any questions, just ask. Actually, here, give me that back." Anvi takes the headset and hands her a set of gloves instead. "These are your controllers, put them on first."

Linda shoves her hands into the gloves, which are tight and stiff and extend nearly to her elbows, and then Anvi positions her in the center of the taped square and helps her put on the headset. The goggles settle over her eyes, digging into the bridge of her nose.

Everything is black. Linda's throat cinches shut. She can't do this.

"How's that feel?" asks Anvi, muffled and faint.

Linda's voice is lost; she doesn't know what will come out if she tries to speak. "Looks a little loose," says Anvi. "Here." There's pressure around Linda's head as something is tightened. Anvi's hand brushes her ear and Linda nearly screams. The compression on her nose lets up; she feels tightness around her whole skull instead. "Shake your head a little," says Anvi. Linda manages to comply. "It's not too tight, is it?"

"No," she squeaks. She's standing in a void. She doesn't know where Anvi is, what is happening around her.

"Okay, cool," says Anvi. Her voice is clearer now, being fed directly into Linda's ear. "Are you ready?"

Linda nods; the motion is slow and heavy and a lie.

"I'm going to try you out on this RPG I like. It's a bit campy but fun. Bear with me one sec. . . . Okay, here we go."

Sharp, flame-colored letters flare to life directly in front of Linda. She takes a gasping step backward. The text shimmers: *Fury and Honor*. She lifts her hand, though she isn't sure if she wants to touch the letters, ward them off, or tear the headset from her skull.

"Go ahead," says Anvi. "Touch them."

Linda stares at her hand: gloved not in the VR controllers but in some sort of chain mail. The metal glitters in nonexistent sunlight. She turns her hand palm up, opens and closes her fingers. The hand in front of her moves exactly as she tells hers to. It feels like it belongs to her. She's still on edge, but her panic is fading. She reaches out and taps the *H* in *Honor*.

The text crackles, then cracks, falling in sharp pieces to Linda's feet. She watches them fall and sees that her feet are in armor similar to that on her hands. She looks back up. The game's title has been replaced by an options menu in three-dimensional black text atop a mountain backdrop. Linda turns in a slow circle. The background extends all around her, like she's standing in the valley of a great mountain range. The flush of color, the depth of the horizon, is astounding. It's the kind of color she remembers from childhood: vibrant, rich, and full of promise.

Linda completes her circle and returns to the menu. "Select *New Game*," says Anvi, and she guides Linda through a series of additional options—including *Noob* for difficulty, which from its placement Linda guesses means easy. Then Linda taps *Start* and is thrown into another world.

"Out of the way, peasant," sneers an old, vaguely cartoonish man wearing a purple cloak. He brushes past Linda so that she dodges right to avoid him. Anvi's light laugh in her ear reminds her the man can't touch her. None of the people around her are real, nor is the city that towers above her.

It's like nothing Linda has ever seen. She's surrounded by crooked wooden houses and shops with pictorial signs hanging out front— two crossed swords, a shirt. Framed on the horizon beneath a too-blue sky with perfect wisps of clouds is a castle with sharp-roofed turrets. She looks down. Dirty cobblestones. Even those are oversaturated, surreal. The whole world is. The crowd is parting around her. She can almost feel the breeze of their passing. And then there's a young squeak of a voice to her right.

"Pardon?"

Linda looks over. A waist-high humanoid creature with bulging black eyes like a spider's is staring at her. She has dark, greasy hair hanging to her shoulders and is wearing a ratty brown dress atop her yellow skin, which—Linda realizes as she looks closer—is covered in tiny scales.

"Please," says the girl-creature, "I need your help. Come with me." She darts toward an alleyway, stopping at the entrance to look back. Linda stares after her, and the creature waves for her to follow.

Linda takes a step, and the alleyway slides toward her, too fast. Disoriented, she nearly falls.

"I should have warned you," comes Anvi's voice. "When I had you select *Dynamic Movement* in the options? It's tile-based to make up for the limited space. Takes a little getting used to. If you don't like it, we can change it to *Stationary,* where you tap arrows to indicate movement, or to a game pad. There are also these platforms you can buy, kinda like treadmills, that integrate with the dynamic setting to smooth things out, but they're crazy expensive."

The alleyway is all around Linda now, dark and dank, and lined with trash—she can smell the dampness, the rot; how is that possible? An adult-sized creature of similar design to the girl sits against the wall between a dirty, knotted sack and a wooden crate.

"Hello?" says the adult. The voice is shaky, feminine. The girl-creature is kneeling with a concerned posture, her hands on the woman-creature. Her body language—clear to even Linda—reads: *This is my mother.*

"Hello," whispers Linda. The girl continues to comfort her mother.

"You might have to speak louder," says Anvi. "The voice recognition can be a little wonky."

"Hello," Linda tries again.

This time the mother looks up. Her spider eyes are cloudy. "Who are you?" she asks.

The world freezes and a new menu pops up. More flaming letters; this time: *Character Creation,* above what Linda thinks is supposed to be a mirror, except that the reflection is of a skinny white man in rags. To the side of the mirror are options like *Name, Gender, Race, Appearance.*

"What do I . . ."

"Touch what you want to change," says Anvi.

She looks at *Name.* Taps it with her dirty, skinny hand so that a text box opens. There is a button labeled *Random* beside it.

"You can spell it aloud or tap that little icon to bring up a keyboard," says Anvi. "Or just tap the random name generator until it comes up with something you don't hate."

"I don't have to be Linda?"

Anvi laughs. "God, no. That's the whole point of these games—you can be whoever you want."

She can rename herself. Her options are endless. It's too much; Linda can't decide. She can feel Anvi watching her. She wants to type *Emmer,* but what if Anvi asks where the name comes from? She taps *Random* instead. Ysafa. She taps it again. Gretta. Altara. It's exhilarating imagining these names as her own, but they don't fit. Chorka. Trinity. Briggs.

Briggs. It's simple, solid, and it makes her think of the woods. She taps *Accept* and the game moves on to *Gender.* There are three options: *Male, Female,* and *None.* Linda selects *Female,* and the image in the mirror morphs into an emaciated white woman wearing a different set of rags. Her pallor, her too-thin frame, her long, greasy hair. She reminds Linda of Lorelei.

She doesn't want to look like Lorelei. She taps the next option—*Race*—and immediately regrets it, thinking of Anvi watching her cycle through skin colors like costumes.

But the options aren't only skin colors. They also include entirely different beings: a dragon-like woman with wings and flaming eyes; a diminutive elf with huge ears; something like a fox standing on her hind legs—Linda pauses over this one, but she wants to see what else there is. A dozen strange and wondrous options, though none of the yellow spider-eyed beings; she wonders why. She goes back to the fox—a *Vulpinoid,* the game calls it—and hits *Accept.*

There's a mind-boggling array of options under *Appearance.* Eye color, fur color, jaw length, fur length, ear position, ear size, teeth size, height, shoulder width, thigh thickness, and so on. There is also another *Random* button.

"This is where you can get trapped forever," says Anvi. "I once spent like an hour on eye size and position and I could never get it to look right."

Linda taps *Random* with her now-furred hand, and her reflection becomes a little shorter, a little redder. This will do. She hits *Accept.*

She's back in the alleyway before the spider-eyed creatures.

"A vulpinoid," says the mother. "How wonderful. I thank you for heeding my daughter's call for help. I'm ill, you see, and the apothecary won't sell goods to our kind. We have the coin for the medicine I need, but we need a helpful soul to make the purchase. Will you help us?"

Linda waits while the mother-creature stares at her. The mother coughs into her hand and shifts slightly, then resumes her hopeful stare.

"Okay," says Linda. Nothing happens. "Okay," she says again, louder. "I'll help."

"Excellent," says the yellow creature, clapping her hands with delight. "Thank you, kind vulpinoid. My daughter has the coin. If you'll just take her hand . . ."

The little girl-creature stands and extends a scaled hand. Linda reaches for it, and suddenly the girl hisses, revealing sharp teeth and a forked tongue. She pulls a dagger from her pocket and jams it into Linda's stomach. Linda lurches backward with a gasp. Her vision is pulsing red; she looks down. The dagger's hilt is sticking out of her fur. Panic thrums within her as she tries to grab it, and she has to remind herself it's just a game, there's no blade in her belly. But she can almost feel it. The game wants her to feel it—the way the visuals are pulsing and growing dimmer into a point around the girl-creature's grinning face. There is a pounding in her ears—a simulated pulse—and, more faintly, the laughter of the two creatures.

Everything fades to black. Linda has lost already, died already, and all she tried to do was be kind. She goes to yank off her headset.

"Wait!" says Anvi. "That was supposed to happen. It happens no matter what."

Linda drops her hands. The visuals return. This time she isn't in a city or an alleyway but a cave lit by a single candle. She hears a drip of water, sees it splash near her feet. The visuals shift—her character moving from sitting to standing. And then nothing happens. The water continues to drip.

"What do I do?" asks Linda.

"Look around," says Anvi. "See what you can find."

The cave is a prison cell, complete with a thick wooden door that's locked from the outside. Linda walks cautiously around the space—there is no rushing motion this time; the cave is small enough for free movement. She finds a bucket of water by the door and another empty one in the corner. There's a tiny hole in the wall near the second bucket; a rat twitters in its mouth before disappearing. She steps onto a straw mat—this is where she started. Her foot is bare, covered in dirty, damp-looking fur. Her sharp nails glitter in the candle-light—a tiny flame is set atop a short stool.

"You can touch things," says Anvi.

Linda had been walking with her hands by her sides. She reaches out to touch the candle's flame and is surprised by a burst of warmth in her finger. She snaps her hand back. "How?" she asks.

"The gloves. They've got all sorts of sensory enhancements built in. The headset can do some odors too."

That's why she can smell the damp. Awed, Linda turns and lifts her hand to the cave's wall. She meets resistance: the glove stiffening, creating the illusion of a wall. She moves her hand a little farther forward, just to see what will happen. Her character's furred hand slips into the wall, and an electric-blue mesh overlay appears.

"That's how you know it's not part of the game," says Anvi. "Not like if you push through water or something."

Linda retracts her hand. She needs to figure out how to get out of this cave. She returns to the door, running her hand along the surface. Nothing. She picks up the water bucket—and gives a small laugh as she does so, because she can feel it: the press of the handle against her palm, the bucket's weight. The other bucket feels the same, only lighter. Linda places them both back in their original spots, then turns in a slow circle around the cave. Then—reminding herself it's just a game—she picks up the candle and drops it on the straw mat.

Flames leap up from the floor. Linda steps back. The fire looks so real. She can smell the thick smoke rising. She takes another step back, and another, until she is standing by the bucket of water. She thinks about grabbing it, flinging the water over the flaming mat, but already the fire is dying. The cave drips with moisture. The flames fade, leaving an ashy stench. The small cell is filled with smoke.

"What's goin' on in there?" comes a voice from the door. Then, more quietly, "I told 'er we shouldn't give 'em candles. We need 'em fresh. But, no, 'We have to let it heal,' she said. 'It needs warmth.' Bloody fool."

A screech and a clang and then the door opens outward. A burly male spider-eyed creature steps inside. "Burn yourself up, did you?" he says.

Linda thinks of the water bucket, of grabbing it and swinging it into the guard's face. Then he takes another step in, to peer through the smoke. She steps past him and slams the door shut, dropping the latch. It's an amazing sensation—the heft of the door, the lock.

"Ha! Go, Linda." Anvi laughs in her ear as the guard yells and bangs on the door. "You're a natural."

Linda is in the middle of a long corridor. To the left is a dead end.

Far to the right there's a huge metal door. One step rushes her to a door identical to her cell's, but she doesn't stop. Reaching the corridor's end, she yanks open the metal door, revealing a dazzling blue sky, the same surreal shade as before but cloudless. For a second that's all she can see, then she takes a step into the doorway and the horizon materializes. There are craggy mountains in the distance, and below her: an endless ravine.

She's standing in an alcove in a cliff face, the highest she's ever seen. She can hear the wind howling around her, can imagine how it might feel against her cheeks. The height brings a bubble of laughter to her throat. As a child she leapt and swung, moving through the woods in a way the city doesn't allow. It wasn't that she didn't fear falling, but the fear of falling made sense to her, and because she understood it, she could control it—judge the height, judge her abilities, and determine whether or not the risk was worth it.

Falling from here would kill her. If it were real.

She's standing on a slender path: a switchback leading both up and down. Looking down, she sees a bloodied bandage wrapped around her stomach. The stab wound. She forgot.

Her rag of a shirt flutters in a whistling gust of wind. Her vision rocks—a simulation of the gust's strength.

It's a glorious feeling: being here in this just-real-enough world, sensing the wind but not the pain. She looks down again. An endless drop; what would happen if she stepped off the edge? Would the game suddenly end, or would she experience the fall? She wants to know, but Anvi is watching, and even if she wasn't—a lingering sense of self-preservation keeps Linda from taking that step. She knows she wouldn't fall, but she feels like she might—a thrilling disconnect. She'll stick to the path. The only question is whether to go up or down.

She chooses up.

Three tiled steps bring her to the top of the cliff, where she sees an expansive, glittering forest—each leaf shining like a gemstone. The cheeps and chirps of little birds fill her ears as a pair flies a tight circle around her head before flitting into the sky. A rainbow blooms over the forest, celebrating her escape.

Linda finds joy burbling up within her, drawn out by the other-worldly display. She starts laughing, stifled at first, but it grows into a loose, unfettered laugh like she hasn't expressed since losing Emmer. The release she feels, laughing like this. She can hear Anvi laughing in her ear too—an equally happy laugh, a shared laugh. Linda feels dampness in her eyes. She lifts her headset to wipe them, laughing still, and finds that she's facing Anvi. The monitor next to her displays the same forest Linda left behind, flat and dulled but still beautiful.

"Pretty great, right?" asks Anvi.

Linda laughs again. She can't stop laughing.

5.

She chooses the most expensive option—diamond plus—because she assumes it's the best. It comes with a CircleTread and professional next-day installation, which won't actually be until Monday. Ten thousand plus tax. Linda rarely buys anything other than food; Arthur will notice this charge. She wonders if she'll be asked to justify it to him. The thought of having to do so is almost enough to keep her from tapping *Buy,* but that feeling of cresting the cliff, seeing that rainbow—she needs to see what else Fury and Honor has to offer.

It's Saturday night, and she's alone in her apartment. She wishes there was a same-night installation option. She wishes she had the courage to knock on Anvi's door and ask to play more. The afternoon ended with Anvi saying she was welcome to come over "anytime," but Linda knows she can't possibly mean that.

She looks at her digital receipt. Growing up, she sometimes found odd bits of currency around the property—coins between cushions, a stash of moldy bills in a plastic bag stuck under a rock once—but payment for goods and services wasn't part of her life. Even now, cost is an abstract concept that feels more like inscrutable ritual than honest exchange. She taps *Buy* on a screen or touches her Sheath to a sensor, and the item is hers. The effect on her account is usually negligible. Even this purchase won't have that much of an impact—the last time she checked, her accessible funds were in the six digits. A fraction of her "worth." The intangibility of her wealth, the monthly uptick of numbers on a screen as Arthur transfers her stipend without any effort on her part—when Linda buys something, it never actually feels as though she's giving up anything in exchange. Perhaps that's why she doesn't do it more often.

Just buy her a friend, Arthur's wife once said. Linda wasn't supposed to hear; she was lying in the crevice between the couch and the wall. It was one of the few spots in the huge house where she could find dust and cobwebs. If she closed her eyes and pretended her breath was a breeze, she could almost feel at home there.

Arthur laughed. *If only it were that easy,* he said.

It perplexed her at the time. Now it hurt. Linda doesn't entirely understand what Arthur did to earn his riches—something with hardware or software. Possibly both. She tried to look it up once years ago but was overwhelmed by the technical jargon—but he had near-limitless resources. And even that wasn't enough to make up for Linda's wrongness.

Her Sheath buzzes from the box by the door. Notifications don't buzz, only messages do. It's probably Arthur; he must have seen the charge. Linda doesn't want to type out an explanation right now. She grabs the TV remote and searches for a wilderness documentary she hasn't seen. Her Sheath buzzes again as she lets a preview about the Grand Canyon autoplay: sweeping views of craggy, striated rock. It reminds her of the view in Fury and Honor but less beautiful. She skips forward to a documentary about giraffes.

Another buzz. Unease prickles through Linda, and she puts down the remote. Arthur must be more upset than she anticipated to be sending this many messages.

When she's halfway to the door, knocking erupts ahead; Linda freezes like prey. The knocking is so frantic, some part of her expects the door to crack and shatter.

"Linda? Are you home?"

It's Anvi's voice.

Linda opens the door.

"Are you okay?" asks Anvi, her eyes wide and intense. Linda looks down to Anvi's T-shirt, which is hugely oversized and has a dragon on it. The dragon's ruby-colored tail curls around Anvi's hips.

"Linda?"

She blinks up from the shirt.

"You don't know, do you?" asks Anvi.

Linda's Sheath starts buzzing. A different buzz. Linda grabs it.

Incoming call: Arthur Niequist.

"I have to answer this," she says. She fumbles for her earcuff, slides it around her ear, and jams in the bud until it hurts.

"Is that your father?" asks Anvi as Arthur's gravelly voice sounds in her ear.

"Linda? I called as soon as I could."

Linda's eyes are stuck on Anvi, whose question reverberates through her: an echoing ache. "You know?" she whispers.

Anvi's nod is shallow, her eyes sad.

"Of course I know," says Arthur. It's too much input, and Linda can't process it all. The VR system, she remembers. That's what Arthur's talking about. But the purchase feels suddenly unimportant—when did she give herself away to Anvi?

Why is Anvi here now?

Arthur. His voice in her ear. "The important thing is you're safe," he says.

A dull, chilling fear seeps through Linda—this call has nothing to do with her bank account.

She turns her back on Anvi and asks, "What happened?"

A beat of silence precedes Arthur's answer. "You don't know?

Then why— Never mind." She hears him take a steadying breath. The same kind of breath he took before telling her Dr. Tambor died. Linda doesn't want to hear this. She needs to hear this.

"The Cedar Lake house is on fire," says Arthur.

His words suck the moisture from Linda's throat: a fear she didn't even know she had. Absurdly, she thinks of the cell from Fury and Honor, of dropping the candle herself. Straw bedding becomes cattails and bamboo, the dock and her nest tree. The couch and the creaking floorboards, the second floor where she rarely ventured, the basement in which she's never been. Her big-leaf maple. Her *home,* burning.

It can't be.

"I'm sorry, Linda." Nothing makes sense, not Arthur's words leaking into her ear, not the presence of Anvi beside her, infringing on this most private of moments. She squeezes her eyes shut and sees flames.

"I know this must be unsettling," says Arthur. "But don't worry, we'll get to the bottom of it. Everything will be okay, Linda." Even now it's impossible not to hear the repetition of her name as a reminder of who she isn't.

She flails at her Sheath, revealing the home screen. Texts are overwhelmed by notifications: so many, headlines cascading down the screen. She struggles to absorb context as fear tears through her. She settles on one headline and taps to enlarge it so the others don't infringe: FIRE AT CEDAR LAKE: CLONE GIRL HABITAT ENGULFED IN FLAMES.

A video autoplays below the headline: silent, towering flames, dark smoke racing toward the sky. Her home, burning. She hasn't been there in twelve years, but still it's *home* in a way no other place could ever be. The video entrances her, awful and sucking: Every day she suffers the discomfort of an exile, and now the only world into which she ever fit is burning to the ground.

She never should have left.

"Linda?" says Arthur. "Are you there?"

A hand on her arm; Linda spins away, flailing. Anvi. Staring at her, standing too close.

"What do you *want*?" cries Linda.

"For you to answer me," says Arthur.

"Nothing," says Anvi, stepping back.

She doesn't trust either. Linda storms away from Anvi, tosses her Sheath onto the couch, and picks up her tablet.

Arthur is still in her ear. "Maybe it was an accident," he says. "But it seems unlikely." Flames leaping and licking and consuming. Have they reached the hutch? The dock? Her tree? Will any of her home survive? "I want you to be prepared—this is going to bring attention back down on us, on you. You understand that, right?"

Extinguished. The word leaps from her tablet's screen. The fire has been extinguished. The video is from its peak, after a couple driving a fussy infant to sleep noticed smoke against the moonlight and called 911. It's an old house in a rural area: no fire hydrants. Water tenders were called in, their loads dropped at the mouth of the drive-way and connected to thick hoses from the two fire trucks that forced their way down the overgrown path. There were concerns about a wildfire, but the damp forest resisted flames in ways the rotten house could not.

"Linda?"

It's too soon to know the cause, authorities say, but there aren't any reports of lightning, and the electricity has been turned off for years. Arthur isn't the only one to assume intent. As the house smolders, corners of the Internet already whisper: *arson.* Also: *abomination, cleansing.*

Others treat the destruction of her home as a cause for levity:

I bet Clone Girl set it. Lashing out at mommy dearest.

Someone's annoyed she hasn't been in the news lately. #CloneGirl

*Maybe #FrankenMom came back to try again and left the
stove on.*

With every not-clever joke or jab, Linda wishes a wish, guiltless
and pure: that each of these trolls' homes too would burn to the
ground.

"*Linda.* Answer me."

She doesn't remember a question, and her fear and anger have
twisted together into a kind of courage. She voices a desire that has
been fermenting within her for years. "I need to go back," she says. "I
need to see."

Arthur is silent for a moment. Then, "It might be a crime scene,
Linda. Do you understand what that means?"

"I understand what *crime* means." She looked it up the first time
she heard herself referred to as a crime against nature, when she was
just weeks out of the property.

"They'll have to investigate is what I'm saying," says Arthur. "And
it might not be safe."

"It's my home."

"I understand, but it's for the best if we give things time to settle
before making any decisions."

Linda feels her courage retreating, and she doesn't reply. She sits
in her chair and swipes at her tablet. Curiosity and sick joy mock her
from her lap.

After a moment, Arthur asks, "Would you like me to fly out and
be with you while this gets figured out?"

She might not be adept at identifying sincerity, but Linda recognizes Arthur's tone. It's one she's known from the very first day, when
he showed up at the clinic in Cedar Lake and she was told, *Your father's here.* She thought, *I have a father,* and her heart swelled in a way
she didn't know it could; as the door opened she felt an urge to rush
forward, wrap her arms around this stranger who wasn't a stranger

because half of her was him and she was so alone and so scared and here was her *father,* come to save her. All her little-girl hope and courage had gone into taking a step toward the opening door, and then his face crested the frame and his eyes met her eyes—and he recoiled. She saw it, she felt it; it was small, but it was there: a twitch of distaste that opened a chasm between them. When he finally stepped forward and hugged her, she stood stiff and unresponsive, feeling the weight of her existence on him: She was a burden he accepted not out of love or even hope but because he had to.

"No," she says.

"Okay," he replies. Linda taps *Play* on the video and again watches her home burn. Seven seconds in, Arthur says, "I should go."

Four more seconds of silent flames.

"I'll be in touch soon." Another pause. "Linda?"

"Goodbye, Arthur," she says. She taps the disconnect button on her earcuff, then tears it off and drops it on the sofa.

"Are you all right?"

Her heart leaps; she pivots toward the door. Anvi. Linda forgot she was there.

"Just take your picture and go," she says, defeated. Her thoughts flick briefly back to last September, when a young man introduced himself to her on one of the semiannual organized outings she agreed to in exchange for living alone—in this case a guided tour of the Olympic Sculpture Park. *Make friends,* Arthur told her. She didn't understand how she could possibly make something Arthur's money couldn't buy, but still, she tried, wanting to please him. She even allowed this young man—Matt—to take her photo with a piece she liked. And then facial-recognition software kicked in and the Social-Hub app suggested he add #CloneGirl to his post. He laughed at first. "This thing thinks you're the girl from when that crazy bitch tried to rebirth her dead daughter over in Cedar Lake." But Linda's face—its expression this time, not its structure—gave her away. The *joy* in that man's eyes as he announced his discovery to the rest of the tour group. Then the questions came from everywhere, everyone, pummeling her. Madeline's grave had been desecrated only a couple of months earlier—the sun rising one day to reveal loose soil and grass hastily stomped back into place. An investigation revealed that someone had clipped off three of Madeline's fingers and then put the rest of her back in the ground. Most of the people were asking if Linda was the one who'd taken her sister's finger bones. But one elderly woman who didn't speak English engaged a translation app to ask, *At what location do you think your mother is?* And at Linda's blank stare, the follow-up: *Do you feel hatred toward her?*

"I don't want a picture," says Anvi. She sits on the couch, looking concerned but also very much at home. Her assumption of belonging, of being wanted, astounds Linda.

"Then what do you want?" she asks.

No, it wasn't me who dug up Madeline's grave.

She's not the sister I care about.

"Nothing. Really. I just saw the news about the fire and there were pictures of you everywhere. I wanted to make sure you were okay."

Linda resumes swiping at her tablet. Online chatter is regurgitating the same few facts as it spirals into circuitous speculation. She sees one of the pictures Anvi is talking about: Matt's from the sculpture garden. *Smile,* he said. It looks like she's baring her teeth.

She'd known it couldn't last—Anvi's ignorance—but she never imagined she'd be forced to suffer the woman's presence while watching her home burn.

"You're upset," says Anvi. "I get it, and I'm sorry I didn't tell you I knew who you were, but it wasn't malicious, I swear."

Linda looks up, thoughts reshuffling. "How long have you known?"

"Since my first night here."

This further rocks Linda. Two days. It's nothing, and yet it's everything. "How did I give myself away this time?"

Anvi laughs. A small laugh and not unfriendly, but it makes Linda feel stupid. "A Linda R. who's friends with Arthur Niequist found my SocialHub profile via proximity search."

"You can see that?"

"Yeah, it's a notification option when you make your profile public. When I realized I'd gotten a click from Clone Girl, I—"

"I'm not a clone," snaps Linda. That old stinging wound, like a sore never allowed to heal.

"Right," says Anvi. "Sorry. Catchy hashtag, though." She smiles, like catchiness makes using the ridiculous misnomer okay. Deeply rooted anger burbles within Linda, and part of her wants to claw the smile off Anvi's face.

#CloneGirl. #FrankenMom. She'll never understand why those were the hashtags that stuck and not #GhostGirl, #MaddyRedux, #CedarLakeMistake, or any of the others. They don't even make sense; Linda's neither a copy nor cobbled together from parts. It *is* true that she wasn't naturally conceived, but neither was Madeline. There were extra embryos; Arthur and Lorelei kept them in storage for years. After the divorce, disposal was mandated and recorded— but it was a lie. Once Linda climbed the wall and fell into the public eye, a former lab technician came forward, eager for limelight and protected by the statute of limitations. He spoke of a bribe. He spoke of placing the long-frozen embryos in a cooler with dry ice and se- creting them away to a late-night transfer; the envelope of cash that filled his pocket afterward. There's no record of how Lorelei impreg- nated herself, but one of the charred scraps of paper the police found on the basement floor after Linda left was from a chart: a daily record of body temperature and cervical mucus. It's supposed that with careful timing, Lorelei used a syringe and catheter to impregnate herself.

Another scrap of paper was filled with frantic cursive: *Be her.* Over and over: *Be her be her be her.* Then: *Why isn't it her?*

From that scrap, the public narrative sprang: Lorelei Niequist,

mad with grief, birthed a child but in doing so thought only of re-
placing the one she had lost. When her broken mind finally grasped
that Linda wasn't Madeline, she abandoned the girl to raise herself. It
was an unfathomable level of neglect, said the authorities; the child
was lucky to even be alive.

Is she? asked some, and their voices were louder and more persis-
tent.

Lorelei used to breed foxes. It's a fact articles like to mention—
sometimes to demonstrate what a fascinating and intelligent woman
she was before her fall, sometimes to frame her as always having been
a little mad. Both interpretations use the same photo: Lorelei holding
up a droopy-eared red fox with a white muzzle, smiling so hugely
Linda didn't initially believe the photograph was really of her mother.

Something about this photo merged with knowledge of Lorelei's
inherited wealth and her lay interest in genetics, and someone created a link between Madeline and then-nameless Linda that didn't
exist. The word seeped into discourse: *clone*. It might even have been
a joke, but it stuck, senselessly and painfully—virally.

And like a virus, the hashtag—the attention—sweeps through the
populace in seasonal waves. The last outbreak started when Madeline's grave was dug up last summer, and it was a bad one. Linda's gut
is telling her this will be bad too.

She's still swiping through stories about the fire, waiting for up-
dates. More and more pieces about her are popping up, including a
timeline connecting Madeline and Linda—not as a tragedy but as a
conspiracy. Standard practice. The date Linda climbed the wall is
circled in bright red with a comment: *WHY THIS DAY?*

Because of a voice, thinks Linda. Because of a man she spied
through a window. A man standing in the kitchen, the first man she'd
ever heard or seen.

Let me help, the man said to Lorelei, and that's when a sunbaked
jawbone tumbled out of Linda's pocket onto the deck—the jawbone

had belonged to a predator, and Linda liked to run her fingers along its teeth as a good-luck charm. The man looked up at the clatter. His eyes locked onto hers.

She ran, not to her tree—where she was supposed to be being scarce—but to a damp bramble, where she burrowed deep. There she waited, the cold seeping through her, until the frogs began to sing. When she finally crept back to the house, Lorelei was gone, the man too. And the door to the basement was ajar, which was beyond un-precedented—it felt impossible.

That's why she climbed the wall: An open door turned her home into an alien place, and she had to get as far away as possible.

Back then, she didn't know Madeline existed—much less that that night was the fifteenth anniversary of her death.

Anvi clears her throat from her seat on the couch. Linda refuses to look; she doesn't care that Anvi's not used to being ignored. She can feel pity radiating toward her.

She sometimes wonders if this is why Emmer hasn't found her: She doesn't want to be pitied. She doesn't want to be a hashtag too.

"Linda?" says Anvi. "Do you want me to leave?"

"Yes." She scrolls through more live reactions to the fire. Nothing new, nothing surprising.

But Anvi doesn't leave. She sits there like the couch is hers. After a moment, she says, "I'm not sure you should be alone right now."

Linda looks up, uncomprehending. Alone is her sanctuary.

"That was your father on the phone, right? Is he coming over?"

Father, thinks Linda with a sad, internal laugh. The day Dr. Tambor told her she needed to decide on a name, she'd been in Arthur's custody for a few weeks. She had a room in his Connecticut home, though most of her time was spent in outside facilities, receiving what he called "specialized care"—which seemed to mostly involve being forced to wear shoes and being told to walk, not run, and please, dear, don't climb that. Plus seemingly endless hours of speech therapy. But Dr. Tambor never told her to stop fidgeting or to keep her feet off the couch. She was a fat, soft-spoken, yet steely woman with dark eyes and a tuft of orange hair that people—even Dr. Tambor herself—for some reason referred to as being red. When she first met Dr. Tambor, Linda's first thought was, *Wow, people really do come in all sorts of shapes, colors, and sizes.* She didn't know back then that being fat was considered a sign of weakness. She didn't know that weight was a thing to be judged at all.

Dr. Tambor suggested she choose a name distinct from Madeline Rose. *No one is denying your connection,* as Dr. Tambor liked to say. But this time also: *We believe it'll be best for you in the long run if that connection isn't immediately obvious.* When Linda didn't offer any ideas, Dr. Tambor provided a list of options and Linda chose at random, closing her eyes and running her index fingers individually up and down the two printed columns. She counted silently to six and stopped. "Those," she said.

Dr. Tambor frowned at her method and encouraged more-measured consideration—even suggesting she discuss it with Arthur. But Linda shook her head, and in the end Dr. Tambor respected the outcome. Bureaucracy churned into motion, and it was only when her government identification arrived weeks later that Linda comprehended that she hadn't been picking a first and middle name but a first and last. She was not to be Linda Russell Niequist but simply— achingly—Linda Russell. The knowledge blindsided her; she felt it physically, a light-headedness as she shot from understanding to disbelief to a new understanding: She would not be permitted her living father's surname.

"Leave me alone," Linda whispers to Anvi. "Please."

Finally, Anvi stands and goes to the door. "I'm sorry," she says, pausing with her hand on the knob. "If you ever want to join us for a walk or, you know, spend some time with a fluffball who can't take your picture, you know where we are." She lets herself out.

Linda leaps up to lock the door, then returns to her chair and watches the video of the fire again. And again. She studies the flames against the night sky, the familiar outline of the house's roof flickering among them. She wonders briefly who's holding the camera—why they're not helping if they're close enough to record the scene.

On her next play through, Linda notices that the garage door is closed. She can see only a sliver of it past the nose of a fire truck, but the fire doesn't appear to have spread there. She's never seen the garage door closed before. Its natural state was wide and welcoming, the cement floor littered with dust, leaves, and pine needles, a thick layer of moss encroaching each winter and drying to a crisp each summer. Spiderwebs pinned hand tools and a tennis racket to a pegged wall, and an old white Civic squatted in the center of it all like a permanent object.

Linda blew into the valve on one of the car's cracked flat tires once. She wanted to see if she could get reality to match a picture she'd seen in a book: *C is for car*. She wonders if the Civic is still there. She's the legal owner of the property, but Arthur manages it on her behalf. She's so uninvolved, she didn't even know someone had closed the garage door.

One of her hidey-holes was beneath the car's front passenger seat. She stored the alphabet picture book there, a sticky gray gaming controller too. She liked to lie atop musty blankets in the back seat and scurry the controller around like a long-tailed mouse while languishing in a favorite memory, one of her earliest and the only one she then had of going beyond the wall: the day Lorelei took her to the lake. Back when the Civic's tires were still round, she'd bounced along in that back seat. The car moving—it had thrilled her to imagine such a thing. After they'd parked, she hopped out and ran in her blue-frilled bathing suit. Grass gave way to rocks, then to drying mud starkly cracked like kitchen tile. All leading to a lake that surprised her by being so small. So shallow. And there were tree stumps—*giant* tree stumps, wide and tall—poking from the mud, from the shallow water. The lake had been choked by dead trees the way her pond was choked by living cattails. She remembers the squish of the earth between her toes as she stared. Then the gentle pressure of Lorelei's hand against her back, urging her forward.

There's not enough water to swim.

Then climb.

She'd clambered up one of the giant trunks; she'd laughed and declared herself Queen of the Lake. She'd had the time of her life.

Linda taps *Play* again. She understands so much more now than she did back then. She understands Emmer wasn't her only sister. She understands they had an older sister they never knew about. She understands she and Emmer wouldn't exist if not for this other sister's death. She understands that her childhood was a test and that she had failed by being herself instead of being Madeline—and that Emmer faced these same tests and somehow passed, possessing an instinct that was the *right* instinct.

The worst part is, if Linda had understood what Lorelei wanted, she would have done it. She would have done anything, been anyone, for her.

From: Lorelei Niequist   Draft Saved 3:06 A.M. 1/20/2004

To: Arthur Niequist

RE:

I can't sleep. It's so quiet without her. Without you. I want to call you. I almost did. Are you awake right now? You always got up so early.

Captain died today. Clipper's grandson. I buried him and released the others. Far side of the wall. (That's right, I had the property fenced in. You'd hate it.) But I wonder if it would have been better to keep them inside the wall, docile as they are. At the time it seemed better to return them to the wild. Sounds cheesy when I type it. They don't have a chance. I made sure of that, didn't I? Breeding the soft. The weak. The ones who made me feel needed. Bought some roosters too. The chickens probably have even less of a chance, but I figure I'll at least open the door for natural selection. Because I just can't do it anymore. It feels so pointless maintaining them without her. Everything feels pointless without her.

How do you do it? Work. Sleep. Live. I don't understand how you do any of it anymore.

6.

nvi closes the door and sinks down to receive Nibbler's squirmy, hot-breathed welcome. Closing her eyes against his snuffling, she tries to imagine a scenario in which she handled that worse. If she'd taken a picture, maybe.

Nibbler runs off for some water. Anvi leans back against the door and taps the voice-control button on her Sheath. "Call Mom," she says. It's instinct—she needs her best friend—but at the first ring, her stomach drops.

She slaps at her Sheath. "Cancel call!"

The icon switches to red, then dissipates. Anvi rubs at her face. That was stupid. She can't talk to her mom about Linda without telling her who Linda is, and if she did that, it'd be all over SocialHub in minutes.

I thought your brothers should know.

Sure, Mom, but you realize you're not telling just them, right?

It was one thing with her breakup last fall. As sucky as that was, Anvi could at least understand her mother's thinking—that she was saving Anvi the pain of telling the rest of the family herself. Her mom promised it wouldn't happen again. Anvi doesn't doubt her intentions, but she's also shown her mother at least a dozen times how to restrict posts to specific social nodes—family, bridge buddies, med school friends. It never seems to take. She still just unthinkingly clicks *Post to all*. Every time.

And even if she didn't post about it, she's getting old: She'd slip in person and tell someone who'd tell someone else, who'd tell someone else. Next thing you know, the tale of Anvi moving in across the hall from Clone Girl is a twisted bit of family lore, and cousin Greta is texting her for details to post on that trashy gossip site she keeps insisting is meaningful work.

Yes, hanging up was the right thing to do.

Anvi watches Nibbler nose his food dish as though it might have refilled itself since dinner. She smiles—she can't talk to her mother, but at least she has him.

Her Sheath buzzes. As she glances down, Anvi gets a whiff of the sweat trapped beneath its case. She felt so cool the first time she strapped on a Sheath, but the novelty has faded. The device strikes her now as little more than a puffed-up smart watch: a trend posing as necessity. She's heard rumors the major players are going to move away from wearables back toward devices that fit in your pocket. She can't wait.

Anvi answers the call. "Hi, Mom."

"What's wrong?" Her mother's voice is edged with worry and sleep, and Anvi remembers it's almost midnight back home.

"Nothing's wrong. I was just calling to say hi, but I forgot the time difference."

"You don't sound like nothing's wrong."

She shouldn't have said *nothing*. Her mother knows how scared Anvi was to make this move, how hard it's been. "I mean, nothing major," she says. "Just feeling a little lonely."

"Hang in there, *meri rani*. It'll get better once you start work."

My princess. Anvi's mother has only a handful of Hindi phrases, but it's what her own mother called her. It's what Anvi hopes to call her own daughter someday.

"Thanks, Mom. I'll let you get back to bed."

"Give my grand-dog a kiss for me."

"Will do. Good night."

Anvi heaves herself to her feet and goes to the kitchen for a beer, randomly selecting a local brew from a sample pack. Then she sinks onto the couch and pats for Nibbler to join her. Instead of turning on the TV or checking her Sheath, she stares at the door. Every instinct she has is telling her Linda shouldn't be alone tonight. And though it's not her place, she aches with the need to help. She's used to playing the cheery, chirpy friend when hard times strike others—she mastered that role in undergrad. She *likes* playing that role; she wishes the anxious itch of inadequacy inside her would let her play that role always.

She digs at the tiny space between Nibbler's eyes with her index finger as his tail sweeps across the couch cushion that nearly hit Linda. Tiny hairs shed onto the pad of Anvi's finger.

She meant to tell Linda she knew about her when they went to the grocery store. That was why she tagged along despite Linda's obviously not wanting her there. But she saw the full-bodied flush of terror that ran through Linda when Anvi lifted her Sheath to photograph the mural. For someone who walks around like she's wearing a full set of battle armor, Linda's eyes are astonishingly unshielded. After that—especially once they started talking about SocialHub—Anvi couldn't think of a way to tell her that didn't sound like *gotcha*.

She tried again when Linda came over for Fury and Honor, and again the words failed to find her lips.

She's not surprised she failed and that it ultimately came out in totally the wrong way. The last decade of her life has been about feigning bravery; she's gotten good enough at it that most of the time it feels easy and natural, but she's always been inept at things like this.

When she was fifteen, she researched her favorite teacher online, scouring his social-media accounts—it was less centralized back then, a smattering of platforms all competing to dominate the attention economy. She'd done it out of childish love and hero worship, but the web of his online presence eventually led her to an Instagram account overflowing with risqué photography. Woman after woman just shy of nude, one of whom looked an awful lot like Anvi's third-grade teacher.

Anvi burned with the shame of this knowledge for weeks, until Mr. Quinn asked her to stay after class one afternoon. "What's wrong?" he asked.

Anvi cracked and told him everything.

His face flashed with horror. She still remembers the panic of his stuttered *How?* And then he'd offered extra credit for her silence, an uptick to her already stellar grades, a bye on any homework assignment of her choice. Whatever she wanted, just please don't tell anyone. He wasn't doing anything wrong, it wasn't meant to be part of his school life, it was art, a private hobby. *Private*—the word suctioned into Anvi's mind. If it was so private, then why was the account public? If it was art, why was he so ashamed?

She hated herself for knowing, hated him for being just another horny man, hated realizing that a flesh-and-blood person could never be the kind of hero she wanted. She ran from the room in a panic. She and Mr. Quinn didn't make eye contact for the rest of the year, and she made straight A's. She'd been making straight A's before, but the possibility of accidental blackmail has haunted her ever since.

Her mother doesn't know about that.

Anvi can count on one hand the meaningful secrets she hasn't told her mother. And now here's another. She wishes she could tell her about Linda and ask for advice. Dear Mom, how do I convince a traumatized meme I mean her no harm? Also, her house just burned down and she thinks I'm a liar.

She should let it go. Wave in the hall, hold the elevator, be a decent neighbor and nothing more.

But Linda is the first interesting person she's met since moving, one of the most interesting people she's met in years. Not just because she's famous—it's how the entirety of her demeanor begs the world not to notice her, and yet you can see her noticing everything. And she set fire to the prison cell in Fury and Honor—that never occurred to Anvi, who dismantled a bucket and used the handle to pick the lock. She likes the idea of a person who is so outwardly meek but who can also be like: Fuck it, I'm going to set this room on fire.

Anvi finishes her beer and watches Nibbler's paw twitch in his sleep. She needs to do something. She can feel the desire to learn more about the fire, about Linda, about anything, building inside her. She's already compiled gigs of data—articles, PDFs, podcasts, video files—about Linda and her family. Once she figured out who she was, she couldn't help it. That tireless compulsion to know more. But it feels disrespectful—almost dirty—when she knows Linda is across the hall, mourning the loss of a place she loves.

She taps her Sheath. "Find cake," she says. "Sort by currently open." She scrolls through the options. "Exclude keyword marijuana." She compares critic reviews, lay reviews, and photographs, then selects a snack shop a few blocks away. She kisses Nibbler on the top of his head. "That one's from your grandmother." Then she slips her coat on over her pajamas and follows the glowing blue arrow on her arm out into the night.

Linda wakes before sunrise, feeling as dreary as the early-morning sky. A sense of horrible wrongness grabs her and for a moment she can't place it, can't recall the reason for her panic. And then she remembers the fire and it's as though the room around her collapses, grinding her into the worn cushion of her nest chair.

Hours pass and she doesn't rise, doesn't even reach for her Sheath or tablet, can't find the energy to. Midmorning, the doorbell rings. Linda can't find a reason to stand and answer. It's probably Anvi, and any further interaction will just give Anvi more fuel for the Social-Hub posts she's undoubtedly authoring by the dozen:

I just moved in across the hall from #CloneGirl! She's SO weird OMG!

#CloneGirl's *still* just sitting in her apt. Maladjusted much?

#CloneGirlWatch continues! No new sightings. I'll get a clump of her hair next time as proof.

Eventually, the pressure of Linda's bladder forces her to rise. After she pees, she grabs a glass of water. Turning back to her chair, she notices a white rectangle on the floor by the door: a piece of paper with a bold arrow drawn on it. The arrow points toward the hallway. Linda's tempted to push it back under the door with her foot. Instead, she checks the peephole. All clear. She cracks open the door to find a small cardboard box sitting on the carpet. Inside the box are two paper bags and an envelope with *Linda* written across it. Linda snatches the envelope and retreats inside. It's a card: a cartoon skunk surrounded by squiggly stench lines and the words: *This Stinks.* She unfolds the card to find a phone number and a note:

> *Dear Linda,*
>   *I'm sorry your house burned down. Perhaps cookies and a distraction will help?*
>   *(Or at least not hurt.)*
>   *Let me know if you need anything.*
>
>

Yours in Neighborliness,
Anvi
>

Linda stares at Anvi's slanted, slender handwriting. She can't remember the last time she read hand-inked words, and there's an intimacy to the irregular print that makes her want to trust it. After a moment, she checks the peephole again, then opens the door and slides the cardboard box inside. One of the paper bags contains assorted cookies; Linda sets these aside—she never developed a taste for sweets. The other bag contains a small rectangular package wrapped in bright polka-dot-print paper. She slides her thumbnail through the tape and unwraps the box. Inside is a set of brainteasers, one metal, one wood. Little interlocking parts meant to be broken down and reassembled. Linda takes the card and the puzzles back to her nest chair.

She holds the card for a long time, examining the rotund, brightly colored skunk—his wide eyes and human frown—and the message within. She memorizes the number but doesn't add it to her Sheath.

Eventually she sets aside the card, takes out her tablet, and opens SocialHub. Anvi hasn't posted anything today—not publicly, but who knows what her two thousand friends are seeing. Linda taps the magnification-glass icon in the corner of the screen, then selects *#CloneGirl* from her recent searches. The most recent hit is from three minutes ago, an I-wonder-if-she-did-it post featuring video of the fire alongside an old, iconic photo from the night Linda climbed the wall: a grubby child standing in the middle of the street, recoiling from an EMT who has her hand outstretched. The girl's ragged T-shirt is too short, revealing a concave midriff, and the frayed elastic waist of her shorts droops to display sharp hipbones. Her dark hair is a nest of snarls, sap, and thorns, and the nails of her raised hands are long and jagged, except for the left thumbnail, which is freshly torn at the base and bleeding. There's a light shining on the girl's freckled face. Her eyes are pure terror.

You're right to be afraid, thinks Linda.

She recognizes now how monstrous her child-self was, with its long, craggy nails like something out of a real child's nightmare. But she also remembers how she felt before that photo was taken. How the smudges of earth had felt as much a part of her as her freckles and she hadn't known to be ashamed of being dirty. How she'd loved to run and leap and climb, all these motions she'd since learned aren't part of moving from here to there in civilized life.

She scrolls past the photo, aching. If a girl like that were to emerge from the woods today, Linda too would pity her—not for her past but for her future.

Hundreds of posts speculate over the cause and meaning of the fire. An investigation is pending or has already begun. Linda sorts the posts chronologically and reads them all, even the cruel ones. Even the ones that call her a monster and openly express hope that she was caught in the flames and burned to death. Few use her legal name—it's known, but not widely, and using it might force people to think of her as an actual person. But a man whose avatar is the sun being skewered by a rapier posts:

The creature that uses the name Linda Russell shouldn't exist. This fire is the universe righting itself. She will be the next to burn.

Gregory T. Every time #CloneGirl trends, he's there. He was especially vehement last year, positing that it must have been Linda who dug up Madeline's grave. He said she was probably driven mad by her own inhumanity and seeking to usurp whatever remained of her dead sister. He even suggested she ate the fingers as part of some arcane ritual.

To which someone else replied with Linda's address and a dare for others to go look for the bones there. That's how Linda ended up in this apartment. She preferred the last—at least it had a dog park nearby.

Eventually Linda reaches posts she recognizes from last night. She rubs at her eyes and glances out the window at the stocky horizon and stone-colored sky. Then she navigates back to Anvi's profile and swipes through pictures of Nibbler.

Anvi knows who she is.

Anvi knows she's checking her public profile.

Anvi says she doesn't want anything from her.

Add contact. The button stares at her. Linda looks toward the skunk card. Her own SocialHub profile is essentially blank. If she adds Anvi, she'll get access to Anvi's private posts; Anvi will gain nothing.

Fuck it, she thinks—words she's never said aloud, but she likes the weight of the curse sitting in her throat—and she adds Anvi to her network.

It takes less than a minute for the notification to pop up: Anvi accepting her request and adding her in return. Linda's contacts list ticks up from four to five. She reloads Anvi's page.

It doesn't change. She reloads again, assuming the data was cached. Nothing. She puts down her tablet and checks on her Sheath, but Anvi's private page is still exactly the same as her public page. There isn't a single post claiming to have run into Clone Girl in a stairwell. Nothing about leaving cookies outside her door. Nothing about what the inside of her apartment looks like or the fact that she calls her famous father by his first name.

Anvi hasn't shared anything about their encounters.

Linda spends the rest of the day and night struggling to understand this impossibility, not quite willing to accept the most obvious explanation: that Anvi's being sincere.

She's still pondering possible ulterior motives the next morning, when Arthur's assistant calls to tell her that the officer investigating the house fire is coming to speak with her. "I'll organize a call," chirps Victoria. "Your father wants to be there."

The lobby attendant buzzes her a few minutes before noon to announce a visitor, and when Linda opens the door she finds a short, bulky white man in a gray suit. He flashes his badge, introducing himself as Officer Baldwin, and confirms Linda's identity before stepping inside. In the heavy authority of his presence, Linda feels callbacks to the discomfort of her first days outside the wall—all those stern-faced men and women telling her they were there to help but not giving her access to the one thing she wanted: her home. Linda swallows this feeling and, as instructed, texts Arthur's assistant that the officer has arrived.

"Nice place," says Officer Baldwin, standing in the center of her sparse apartment. "I don't usually do this in person, you know, but given who—" He stops and clears his throat. "How do you like the neighborhood? I haven't been here much since the upzoning."

Linda was instructed not to answer any questions until Arthur connects. She stares at her Sheath, silent. Officer Baldwin shuffles toward the couch. Victoria's reply comes through: *Turn on your TV. You should still be synced from last time.* Linda presses the power button. Arthur's assistant's face pops up on the screen—pale skin, bright-red lips, the stark gold frames of her Augments—and the camera at the top of the TV blinks on, a little green eye telling Linda she's being watched.

"Linda, hello!" says Victoria. "Connecting you now."

The picture blinks to black, then to a view of a conference room. One of Arthur's lawyers, a middle-aged Asian woman, sits next to him. Arthur looks as worn-out and stately as always. Linda even recognizes the blue paisley tie he's wearing. *It's okay,* he told her once, as they stood together before a closet he'd paid his assistant to fill. *I get overwhelmed by having too many options too. That's why I cycle through the same seven ties.* And though it wasn't so much the number of options as the presentation of those options—so clean and organized, folded and hung with purpose, whereas she was used to yanking items from a heap on the floor—that overwhelmed her, she'd loved him in that moment. A painful pull. This was before she'd been denied his surname, back when she still held out hope that the crevasse between them might be bridged.

Officer Baldwin steps up next to her. "Good afternoon, Mr. Niequist," he says.

"Hello. Thanks for your patience. I believe you have some questions for my daughter?"

Linda prickles. He only ever calls her his daughter to other people.

Officer Baldwin turns to Linda. "Yes, but first off, I wanted to offer my condolences. Property loss is never easy, though I'm sure we're all glad no one was hurt." He pauses, perhaps waiting for Linda to reply. After a few seconds, he continues. "Anyway, we've examined the property, and it looks like it was a chimney fire that spread to the attic. There's some trash spread around the building, which suggests people might've been using it for shelter, and we suspect squatters. Our best guess is it was an accident: They were trying to keep warm, but the chimney hasn't been maintained or cleaned in years. We found a number of substantial cracks and evidence of animal infestation."

Linda tries to envision it: Strangers crouched in the couch room, tossing logs into the fireplace, setting them aflame, then . . . Would it happen all at once, the chimney igniting like an explosion? Or was it slow and they didn't notice until they felt the heat from above?

"That being said, Ms. Nie"—the correction comes smoothly— "Russell, do you have any knowledge of anyone who might have been staying at the property?"

"No." A short, true answer, just as she'd learned to give as a girl newly thrust into this prying world. Never offer anything they don't ask for. Regret. Emmer.

"Have you had any recent contact with your mother?"

"Lorelei? No. She—"

"Officer," interjects Arthur. "We agreed—"

"You think it was her?" asks Linda. As the weeks turned into months and years without any sign of Lorelei, her mother had become to her like the wind: an everywhere-and-nowhere presence she would forever feel but could never touch. Most people assume she's dead, but an irrational part of Linda can't shake the belief that the woman might actually be immortal. It suddenly seems ridiculous she didn't think of it herself. Lorelei's being involved makes more sense than random transients. Cedar Lake is a small town, and its Wikipedia page doesn't mention anything about a homeless population.

A new itch of a thought: Emmer. Maybe she's finally reaching out after all these years. Linda feels a horrible blossom of hope that maybe she'll get to see her sister again after all.

"We don't have any evidence she was involved," says Officer Baldwin.

The words wash over her thoughts of Emmer. Sometimes Linda resents that such a big part of her life is omitted from the public narrative of her childhood, but a larger part of her is glad to have kept such a substantial secret. Her true sister: the answer to the question no one has ever known to ask.

"Is there anything else?" asks Arthur. He sounds irritated. He rarely talks about Lorelei in Linda's presence; she can recall only a handful of times in the last few years, each having to do with handling the money she inherited from that branch of her biological family.

"No, that's all." Officer Baldwin turns back to Linda. "I discussed this with Mr. Niequest already, but you'll want to contact your insurance regarding cleanup."

"I'm taking care of all that, Linda," says Arthur.

Officer Baldwin pulls out his wallet, extracts a card, and hands it to Linda. "In case you think of anything we should know or have any questions," he says.

That's it? thinks Linda, relieved but also somehow disappointed.

Officer Baldwin opens the door to let himself out.

"I can go?" she blurts. He turns around, a quizzical look on his face. Linda clarifies, "To the property?"

"It's your house, Ms. Russell. We did contact a board-up service, per protocol, and I'd advise you to be careful, but yes, you can go. Is there anything else?"

Linda shakes her head.

"Have a good day, then."

Linda locks the door behind him.

"Linda." Arthur is still on the TV with his silent lawyer. Linda doesn't know if the camera's eye can reach her at the door; she steps back to the center of the room.

"When can I go?" she asks.

"It's still unsafe," says Arthur. "I think it's for the best if . . ." Linda stops listening. After she ends the call, all the things she didn't say roil within her. It's *her* property, *her* home; she should be allowed to go anytime she wants. Even the investigating officer said so.

She wonders suddenly what Arthur told Officer Baldwin while arranging the visit. She can practically hear him begging the officer not to "unsettle" her. One violent fit a decade ago, and she is forever a volatile compound to be tightly contained and tiptoed around.

Linda, I have bad news. Arthur's tone had been so dire, it sent a full-bodied flush of alarm through Linda. After two years in the real world, she no longer held any illusions of it being a magical place, and she braced herself. But her thoughts assumed blood: Emmer had come forward and—as much as Linda wanted to see her again—Emmer was all Arthur ever wanted in a daughter, so would Linda please vacate the house? Or Lorelei had been found and—what would be worse, if Lorelei wanted her back or if she didn't?

She was entirely unprepared for the words *It's Dr. Tambor . . .*

She remembers shrinking into herself, pinned down by a sense of loss so deep it precluded sorrow. It was at Arthur's *It'll be okay* that she exploded. Everything from there is a blur in her memory: Her voice, loud, Arthur's voice, rising. Wanting to hit him, kick him, harm him, and throwing herself against the wall instead. The crash of the mirror, a spray of her blood marking the birth of a scar that still hugs her elbow today.

It wasn't the first mass shooting Linda had heard about, but it was the first she paid attention to, the first that felt real to her: A man with a rifle tucked in his coat walked into a store and started firing. It was the same store where Dr. Tambor had taken Linda on her very first excursion. The man's ex-girlfriend worked there, but she was stocking the cereal aisles and the killer was incapacitated by a security guard before he made it that far.

But his bullets found others. Linda pictures it often: Dr. Tambor's soft body being punctured over and over, sparks of blood puffing from her chest, bullets passing through her to shatter packs of gum and pocket-sized toys. She was lionized briefly in the media afterward—the photo from her practice's website posted everywhere—because she used her bulk to shield a stranger and that stranger's stroller. The young father and his infant both survived. The man and his wife shared their grateful tears with the world, called Dr. Tambor a "remarkable woman" and a "hero."

Linda still doesn't really understand it, any of it: the why of the shooting or Dr. Tambor's actions. She wishes Dr. Tambor had shielded herself instead.

Her death was a lesson: Trusting isn't worth the risk. Caring isn't worth the risk.

The intercom buzzes; Linda jumps up and answers, wondering if Officer Baldwin forgot something.

"Ms. Russell?" says the lobby attendant. "You've got a work crew here, say they're supposed to install an entertainment system."

The diamond-plus package. It feels like a lifetime has passed since Linda ordered it. She thinks of looking down and seeing a dagger in her stomach. Of dropping a candle. Of standing on the edge of a cliff and wondering what it would feel like to step off. Of a world in which nothing could truly hurt her.

"Send them up," she says.

From: Lorelei Niequist   Draft Saved 6:50 P.M. 2/1/2004
To: Arthur Niequist
RE:

Sometimes I wonder what my mother was thinking before she took those pills. Poured the whole bottle down her throat. She was tucked under the covers when I found her. I wanted to talk to her about this boy in my biology class, so I laid down next to her. I was halfway through the story before I realized she was cold.

She had to know I would be the one to find her. I was always home before Dad, and Will wouldn't walk into their room like that.

I hope I'm a better mother than that, at least.

I have an idea. I want to tell you, but you'd think it's crazy. Maybe once you can see her. Hold her. I think

7.

Linda-as-Briggs claps her orange-furred hands, then spreads her palms, shooting a ball of electricity into the crowd of goblins before her. Their tiny green bodies shudder and flash, then all seven drop to the ground, dead. It's her most powerful spell, and it saps the last of her mana pool. She's out of rejuvenation potions; she'll have to rely on non-magical skills from here. She hopes this is the last group of foes in this dungeon. It has to be; she's already defeated the old king's ghost and collected his helm as proof for the villagers. The exit is just around the next bend in the corridor. She feels her character's fatigue as her own—heavy legs, aching neck. The exertion, the momentum, is exhilarating.

She moves a tile forward, loots the bodies, then peeks around the rocky corner. Deciduous trees shine in the sunlight beyond the dungeon's exit. All clear. She moves another tile, emerging into sunlight she can't feel, then she taps her right pinky and thumb together to bring up the game's menu. The current time flashes in the corner: 8:23 P.M.

Linda blinks. She's been playing for nearly five hours.

She should stop, but there's a path through the trees, beckoning. And if she gets lost, she can toggle on a map awash with stenciled towns, stars, and pulsing orbs. It's so easy to set a goal here—and to accomplish it. Ease leads to compulsion, and with every quest completed, Linda finds herself drawn into the next.

But now that she's aware of the time, she also becomes aware of how her whole body is aching. She hasn't eaten since morning. If she's going to stop, it should be now—before a distressed NPC entices her into something new.

She taps *Save,* then pulls off her headset, emerging into darkness. The sun was still in the sky when she started playing. While she waits for her eyes to adjust, she tugs off her gloves. Normally she'd be fine walking in the dark, but her apartment's layout is newly unfamiliar. She thinks she can see the lump of the CircleTread in the corner. The installation team centered it in the room, but walking in it made her feel unstable and slightly nauseated, so she pushed it out of the play area.

After the installation team left, Linda downloaded Fury and Honor, remade Briggs, and spent hours roaming the simplistic, cartoonish land of Rothram, distracting herself from the pain of knowing her home was ash. She hasn't left her apartment in the two days since. She's barely taken off her headset.

She rolls her neck, then shuffles to the kitchen and flips on the light. While she's heating canned pasta, her Sheath buzzes. It's Arthur. *I see you haven't been out in a few days. Are you okay?*

Linda's tempted to ignore him, but that will just incite more messages, maybe even a call. *Yes,* she replies.

The pasta has another minute. She checks SocialHub. There's a direct message from Anvi. Linda's never received a direct message before, not from someone she actually knows. She taps to read it.

Hey! I don't like to send personal messages on here. (SH might not sell your data, but they certainly collect it.) Text me directly so we can talk? Please?

The pasta pops; Linda startles, though she was waiting for the sound. There's another pop before the timer ends. She's staring at the message. The food will be hissing hot now. The number in Anvi's message is the same one from the skunk card. After a moment, Linda copies it into her contacts, but that's it.

She swipes back to her news feed. The Cedar Lake fire is already old news, and of the few people still paying attention, most don't believe the official explanation that it was an accident. They're seeking connection when the simplest answer is coincidence. Linda's been doing the same, thinking Emmer might be involved. Because why would Emmer return? And if she were to, why would she start a fire? She loved their home too.

Frustrated, Linda scans today's trending stories: catastrophic flooding on the other side of the globe, a celebrity divorce. Then: *Why has G.H. gone silent?* The question catches her eye, but it takes her a second to remember the engineer who claimed to have created a simulation indistinguishable from reality. That's why she wanted to try VR in the first place. Fury and Honor isn't like reality, it's brighter— better. But she wonders; she's seen trailers for darker, more-realistic games—ones where the only races you'll find are the ones here on earth.

It seems there hasn't been any activity from G.H.'s account since his post on Saturday. Has he retreated from a lie? Been murdered for exposing a truth? Theories abound, stoked by his silence. Linda feels a kinship with G.H., whoever he is. She knows the pain of staying silent in the face of hounding speculation.

She puts down her Sheath and looks at her VR headset.

The pasta needs more time to cool.

She'll just return the old king's helm. Then she'll stop.

Her apartment is replaced by green leaves with pale undersides that flash like sequins, simulating a breeze. Sometimes it seems like this game was designed specifically for people who hunger for the natural world. There's all of the beauty and none of the inconvenience. As much as she loves it, Linda wouldn't mind a little more inconvenience—as long as it came in the form of mud and gnats, and not intrusive neighbors. Or homes going up in flames.

The village is only a handful of tiles away, and the village mayor—a pale human—is exactly where Linda left her: milling around the town center, visibly fretting. "Oh dear, oh dear," whispers the mayor as Linda approaches.

"I have the helm," says Linda, clearly and loudly.

"Oh dear," says the mayor again, turning to face her. Her eyes are a shocking purple, an unexplained characteristic of the characters who populate this region of Rothram. "You found the helm?"

"Yes."

"Wonderful!" the mayor exclaims. "May I have it?"

Linda selects the item from her inventory. "Yes."

"Thank you! With this returned, the countryside will be at peace once more." The helm disappears into the mayor's slim-fitting tunic. "You are a true friend to this village." She holds out a skeleton key. "As a reward, here is a key to our Temple of Shya. I believe you will find sanctuary there." When Linda takes the key, the mayor dips her head and walks away.

Her pasta is probably cool enough to eat. This is where she told herself she would stop, but having a key in her hand has dulled Linda's hunger. She knows where the temple is, and she makes her way there, taking a shortcut across the back sides of several cottages. As she passes through a garden, cabbages crumple beneath her, and a peasant-farmer calls out thanks for saving the village from the old king's curse. Word for word, he echoes a woman two cottages back.

Anvi was right about that much: There is no consciousness here, no evolution.

Linda likes it, the ease of these empty interactions.

The temple towers above her, all sharp turrets and vaguely Celtic carvings. It's hugely out of place in this poor village, but all of Rothram's temples look like this. She's arrived at the back side and follows the fence to the front. The fence is wrought iron, tall and spiked, and the gate when she reaches it is massive—for wagon access, maybe, or just effect. Linda slips the key into the lock. There's resistance as she turns the key, then metal screeches as Linda pushes the gate open. The sound sends a shudder through her.

Before she climbed the wall to leave her home all those years ago, she stood at the gate across the driveway. It was open, evidence of Lorelei's departure, and as wrong in its way as the basement door left ajar. Linda stood there, knowing she could run down the overgrown driveway to the road. But even in her panic, leaving that way felt wrong. There was a particular spot on the wall, a span where an alder grew close and a branch brushed the rusty barbed wire, a spot where—after Emmer's disappearance, when she had first considered the possibility of leaving—she would sometimes run her hand along the lichen-crusted sheet metal and think, *Here.* Everything else that day was going so wrong, was so far out of her control, but she could still leave the way she imagined she would. She could pretend her leaving was a choice.

She closed the gate—the basement was wrong, she didn't want the gate to be wrong too—and its rusty squeal rolled over her like a storm, making her tremble. It was a sound she'd never heard, a sound that signaled change and invited fear. She ran to her chosen spot, seeking the familiar, even if it was only to say goodbye. There, she stemmed between the slick wall and the tree trunk, creeping her way up with tiny shuffling steps and careful pressure. Her leg and arm spans were just long enough to reach, which allowed her to tell herself, *This is what I'm meant to do.*

And then the spiky wire at the top, so much sharper than it looked. She'd grabbed a thin shirt to toss over it, but the wire had a greater bite than the nettles she'd learned to avoid, and it tore a rift in the shirt. She kept going, having already come so far. She felt rusty teeth bite into her thumb, deep into the soft skin beneath the nail, then nip at her abdomen, thighs, and calves as she crested. Then a leap and a roll, and she spun across a span of the earth new to her. It hurt: branches and rocks demanding to be known. But she was limber and determined and not once in her life had someone ever asked her, *Are you okay?* She knew no other way but to keep going.

She knew where and what the road was, had heard engines and air-filled tires, had even occasionally glimpsed a mystical flash of headlights on the nights when she'd sat at the gate and strained to see to the end of the driveway. Climbing back to her feet, she trudged toward the memory of those lights. She avoided the driveway—this felt important—and wound through the trees, her body throbbing from the fall, her chest tight with the thrill of pushing through terror.

Things get blurry after she left the forest. Following the road one way and not the other, hiding from a handful of hugely loud vehicles, and then emerging into an alien landscape that upon noticing her devolved into chaos. Everything was taken from her, even the shirt she wore, her favorite, a green one she'd loved for the mystery it presented: an acronym of unknown origin. Every time she wore it, she'd cycle through possible meanings. *To Me Never Talk. Think Mother Noted That? Tame Me? Not Today!*

She used to be untamable, before the fear took over.

Linda blinks at the virtual gate now open before her. Ivy creeps up the temple walls and over a dry fountain. There was a birdbath in front of the Cedar Lake house, similar in shape to this fountain but smaller and overrun by massive, leggy rhododendrons that would burst with pink blossoms each spring. She'd sit there and watch the bees. Dozens of bees, maybe hundreds. They swarmed the flowers as though of one mind. Such a source of wonder, and she hasn't thought of them in years.

She didn't notice the birdbath in the video of the fire. She wonders if it was destroyed or just hidden from view.

A golden bird flies past the temple fountain, and a single luminescent feather drifts down in its wake. Linda moves to pick it up, but after one step a blue barrier flares before her. She's reached the edge of the play area. It's a simple thing to tap her middle fingers to her thumbs to freeze her view, then turn her body until the barrier is behind her, but the necessity of the action irritates her in a way it never has before.

There shouldn't be barriers here.

No, that's not why she's upset. Not truly. She feels the desire thick and undeniable: She wants to be back at the birdbath, the house, her tree and dock. She wants the barriers between her and going home to be as easy to circumvent as Fury and Honor's flaring blue wall.

She closes her eyes, then taps her fingers to pause the game.

For years, all she's done is pine for her home. She told Arthur she wanted to go back. It felt bold at the time, but, really, she was just asking for permission. Permission he denied. As Briggs, she's never asked permission. She tramples gardens, rushes into dungeons, saves the empty townsfolk, and collects whatever loot catches her eye.

She removes her headset and gloves and finds her Sheath. She takes a deep breath. She thinks of the T-shirt she loved, which she now understands references a cartoon Madeline must have liked when she was young. *Text Man*, she thinks. *Not Timidly.*

I'm going back. A statement, bolder than she could voice, but she can type it. Barely. Anxiety flares through her as she taps *Send,* but she does it.

About a minute later, Arthur replies. *I don't want you to go alone. I'm coming out this weekend.*

Linda knows he thinks of the property as his too, but in her mind he doesn't belong there. She can't stomach the thought of going with him, and she can't get there without a licensed driver, even if she were to rent an autonomous vehicle—some legal stipulation guarding against software failure.

Her eyes slip to the puzzles Anvi left her.

Time trickles by while she stares. This isn't like texting Arthur. This isn't even like storming a virtual dungeon. This is like opening her arms and saying, *Go ahead, stab me in the chest.*

Anvi hasn't posted anything about her. Not a word.

Trusting is too risky.

But she wouldn't be trusting Anvi; she'd be using her.

Is that better or worse?

She can't take it: this constant tearing of her desires and fears, the bite-back of wanting something and then immediately feeling, *How dare you?* She hates this meek version of herself, feels trapped in it. With a burst of frustrated rage, she throws her Sheath across the room. The smack of it hitting the wall thrills her. She feels the urge to tear the apartment to pieces and to bloody herself in the process. To use her muscles, to accomplish *something,* even if it's destruction. To for a moment be anything other than her mother's victim, her father's hapless charge.

There is a bowl on the counter. Bigger than her head. She picks it up and brushes her thumb along its raised pattern of swimming fish. Another useless nothing chosen by Arthur's assistant to decorate a space for which Linda feels nothing.

When you break pottery in Fury and Honor, there's often gold inside.

In this world, gold is the last thing she needs.

Linda flings the bowl against the wall and watches it shatter.

You're acting like an animal. Arthur's wife's voice, when all Linda was doing was searching for a snack, her bare feet on the kitchen counter as she pawed through a cupboard, the granite cool against the softening skin of her once-callused feet. The disgust in the woman's eyes. *If you need something, just ask for help.*

How does one do that—ask for help?

She slides to the floor and rests her head against the side of the kitchen counter. There's an overhang. Linda looks up. Her shelter is a synthetic material she can't name.

The last time Linda remembers crying was when Dr. Tambor died, and she feels a decade's worth of tears swelling inside her. But she fears that if she starts crying now, liquid will flow from her until she's as dried out as the dead succulent in the corner. Why did humans evolve to feel? Physical pain she understands—warnings against *hot* and *sharp*—but what is the purpose of this kind of hurt?

Flames. Devouring her childhood home, her only home.

She tucks her face into her hands, pressing hard. She doesn't want to be this version of herself.

There's only one solution she can see, as clear as any quest.

She rises and in her bare feet steps carefully through shattered clay to retrieve her Sheath. She opens her contacts and taps Anvi's number. It's just words, she tells herself. Just a question. *It's okay to ask for what you want,* Dr. Tambor used to tell her.

She holds her breath and, trembling slightly, types in a rush: *This is Linda. Do you have a driving license?* She hits *Send* without rereading the message, checking it for errors, or searching for better wording. If she doesn't send it immediately, she knows she never will.

Anvi replies within seconds: *Yes.*

Linda types her next question even faster. *If I pay to rent a car, will you take me to*—how to phrase it? Her real home? The place where she was born? No, no meaning. Just a name Anvi will know—*Cedar Lake?*

This reply takes longer to appear, a handful of weighty seconds. But then there it is:

Hells yeah.

The mansion stood exactly ninety-eight meters ahead, according to the subtle green text that floated in Graham's vision. The building was mostly glass. Interior lights flared through ground-level windows, and moonlight glinted off the opaque second floor. A garden patch meandered between here and there. A timer ticked in the corner of Graham's eye; he had only ten minutes before the security lapse would be detected. Time to get moving.

As Graham rounded a hedge, a pond appeared to his right. There was an eruption of chirping and croaking from an army of frogs. The mansion loomed closer. Twenty-five meters. Fifteen. Eight. The interior shone with stiff white furniture, massive abstract paintings, and wire sculptures of animals and music notes. Clearly, this was a home meant more for display than for living.

Graham circled the immaculate patio until he reached a door. All of their previous missions had involved obvious monsters—child molesters, murderers, one particularly corrupt politician—but these next two missions were different. Each involved a girl. In this case, a girl whose name didn't deserve to be known. She had catapulted to fame after starring in a soft-drink ad, and her second role was the lead in a romantic comedy that was neither funny nor charming yet still earned nearly two billion worldwide.

Graham tried the door. It was unlocked, and there was no backup to the hacked security system. Adoration had made this girl complacent.

Now that she'd conquered film, the girl was pivoting her career toward the music industry. The mission brief had included a quote from an early review of her upcoming album: She's completely tone-deaf, but I can't stop listening.

There was only one explanation for such baseless success: code error.

Inside, Graham followed a set of crosshairs to the spiral staircase at the home's center. As he climbed, he heard the girl's recently released single blaring from upstairs. It was a preview of her album and already a chart-topper, boppy and electronic.

He crested the stairwell, emerging into a hallway. Here, the walls and ceiling were cloud white and the floor was carpeted in lush grassy green.

The crosshairs centered on a door at end of the hall. Five meters. Suddenly Sergei's voice sounded in Graham's ear: "We have a problem. Security is self-repairing." With its next tick, the timer in Graham's vision lost a minute instead of a second.

He pushed through the door.

The girl was sitting in an armchair, wearing jeans and a white tank top. She was pretty in the generic way of skinny blondes, but without makeup she wouldn't have earned a second glance on the street. No talent, no real looks. She shouldn't have this life.

She leapt to her feet. "Who are you?"

The crosshairs tightened over her face.

IDENTITY CONFIRMED

As Graham stepped forward, the girl backed away. Her leg caught on her chair. She stumbled, and fear blossomed in her eyes.

Only fifty-five seconds left.

The girl scrambled backward, cornering herself.

Graham pulled a Taser-like device from his belt. In the last mission, a madman had charged him while wielding a meat cleaver. Somehow, walking toward this terrified girl was even more unsettling.

"Stop," said the girl. "Please."

They couldn't all be monsters, Graham reminded himself.

He jammed the device into the girl's shoulder.

CODE ERROR DETECTED

Graham pressed a button, and the girl screamed, a wrenching cry like she was tumbling off a cliff. A progress bar appeared below her crying face, ticking toward 100 percent.

REPROGRAMMING COMPLETE

The girl collapsed to the floor.

"Security is coming online in ten seconds," said Sergei. "Get out of there."

Graham looked at the motionless girl. He could still fail this mission if he got caught.

He ran.

8.

inda walks stiffly through the gray morning, hyperaware of Anvi and Nibbler's presence beside her as they traverse the few blocks to where the rental car is parked. She still isn't sure why the car couldn't come to them, but she follows the directions on her Sheath. They duck into a garage and find it: a sleek black luxury crossover that gleams in the overhead lighting.

"Fancy," says Anvi.

Some people will want your money. Arthur, four years ago, explaining her ten-thousand-dollar-a-month stipend.

"It says the keys are inside." Linda taps at a lock symbol that's pulsing on her Sheath. The car's lights flash and it emits a soft *click*.

Anvi tries the driver's door, which slides open. "We're in business." She opens a back door and pats the seat; Nibbler leaps inside.

They input their destination, then the vehicle weaves them out of the garage and onto the freeway.

Anvi turns to Linda as they inch through traffic. "Thanks for asking me to come with you. I know that couldn't have been easy."

Linda keeps her eyes on a red car to their right. There's a small child in the back, rear-facing in a throne-like seat. His tiny hands hold a tablet, and his eyes are rapt, staring.

After a moment, Anvi asks, "Do you prefer a podcast or music?"

Linda doesn't care as long as the podcast isn't *TASTMEs*—but she can't imagine voicing a stipulation. "Music," she says. Anvi syncs her Sheath to the car and plays something with a heavy beat and warbling vocals.

After a few songs, traffic loosens. As they gain speed, Anvi declares, "Vehicle, warp speed ahead!"

The vehicle replies in a cool, subtly feminine voice, "I don't understand." Anvi laughs, then she turns to Linda. "You know, I'm honored to be your fifth Hub contact." Shame prickles through Linda. "Seriously," says Anvi. "I am."

Anvi shouldn't feel honored. Linda only did it to make sure she wasn't posting about her. But even as Linda tells herself this, part of her calls out the *only* for the lie that it is.

"Are you worried because I'm going to be working there?" Anvi must see her answer in her posture or averted eyes, because she continues, "Just because I'm going to be working at SocialHub doesn't mean I'm some crazed proponent of the platform. Necessary evil if you ask me. I'm glad they make some basic nods to privacy and truth, but only a fool would think that's anything other than a business decision. They had to know it was the only way to unseat Facebook. Not to toot my own horn"—she mock-honks the steering wheel—"but I feel very strongly that they need people like me to keep them honest."

Linda steels herself and says, "I was surprised to see that your public and private profiles are the same."

"Just because they don't sell your data doesn't mean they don't track it," says Anvi. "Nothing you do on there is truly private, no matter your settings. Besides, participation in social media is an inherently performative act—why pretend otherwise?"

Anvi keeps surprising Linda. She wants to ask about the recurring posts about cheese, but she also doesn't want to admit that she's examined Anvi's profile that closely.

For the next hour, Linda lets the music seep through her as she wonders about what's waiting ahead. Anvi spends the time cooing over the car and making more jokes that neither its voice-recognition system nor Linda understands. Nibbler remains curled in the back, blending into the black leather as he naps. The city recedes and they leave the freeway behind. White-clad Mount Rainier towers in the distance.

They pass a small sign that reads WELCOME TO CEDAR LAKE, then turn away from the mountain view onto a road that Linda, as a child, didn't know had a name. *Mill Lane*. It looks as unexceptional as it sounds, just like any other rural road in the Pacific Northwest, flanked by trees with sweeping limbs and the occasional mailbox.

Anvi's mooning over the rental car some more, her hands hovering above the wheel as she pretends to drive. Her chatter has become white noise. Linda wonders if that is what it's intended to be.

Another mile, then Anvi rests her hands on her lap. "We're almost there."

Such a short drive. Linda hates herself in this moment, for taking so many years to act. She should have come before the fire. A lost opportunity to see her old home as it will never exist again: whole.

The car slows and announces, "Now arriving at your destination."

Linda doesn't recognize any of it, not the crooked, dented mailbox at the driveway's end or the mouth of the driveway itself. The car pulls in, rocks slightly as its tires slip into deep ruts, then stops.

"Impassable terrain," states the car. Linda wishes she felt half as calm as its voice sounds.

Anvi takes the wheel. "Vehicle, engage manual control." Then, to Linda, "It looks like the fire trucks really tore up the driveway."

"I can walk from here," says Linda.

"Parking, roger," says Anvi; she taps *Park* and powers down the car. Nibbler is on his feet, his head poking up between their seats.

Linda opens her door and steps out. The driveway was laid with gravel decades ago but is now mostly crushed weeds and muddy divots crusted with paper-thin ice. Brush and saplings encroach from either side, and every so often there is a freshly fallen branch—knocked free by the fire trucks, she guesses. There is a soft scuttling behind her, then Nibbler darts past, romping leash-less up the driveway. He stops to lift his leg over a branch, then sniffs in circles.

Anvi steps up next to Linda. Linda wants to tell her to stay here, but Nibbler is already moving ahead, and Linda wouldn't be here if not for her neighbor. She starts walking.

On either side of the driveway, moisture has frozen in the dirt, leaving a series of crystalline structures like a scaled-down cityscape. As a child, Linda loved watching the soggy earth freeze and grow, then crushing it beneath the pad of her foot. Playing Hide-and-Find, she and Emmer used to avoid the crunchy, expanded turf—or sometimes skip backward across it or dart one way before circling around to a less telling path. *Crunch crunch crunch:* little lies intended to help them win.

Linda takes a subtle step to the side and presses her foot into a tire track. She feels the give of the dirt, hears the ice crumble. This is how winter earth is meant to feel.

The driveway curves slightly, bringing the gate into view. The sheet-metal wall extends from either side of the gate's vertical bars. The wall is less impressive than Linda remembers, but seeing it still makes her pulse spike. For twelve years, this rust- and lichen-clad plane of metal defined her world. She's never seen the gate from this side, this angle, and some small part of her has trouble accepting that this is the place she remembers.

She keeps walking toward the gate, watching as the driveway beyond curls into a circle around an unruly mass of beaten-down weeds and rhododendrons. There's no sign of the birdbath. Linda imagines it felled by time and ground into the earth by the fire trucks.

And then she sees the house. Her head and heart lurch toward buoyancy: Forget the birdbath, her home is still standing, still *here*. The flames had blazed with such abandon in the video, she expected to find little more than a pile of ash.

But the roof is charred and gaping in sections, and blackened eaves glisten with an odd, icy shimmer. It takes Linda a moment to puzzle out that it *is* ice: a frozen and jagged overbite. She remembers whispers of snow on the drive here, puddles crusted with ice. Overnight lows, she reasons. The firefighters saturated the house with water, and now that water freezes at night. Still, it's a jarring sight. She'd imagined the ruins might still be smoking.

At the gate, there's no sign of the padlock Linda remembers. The hollowed-out house looms about a hundred feet ahead. Anvi is a step behind Linda. Nibbler is tracking nearby scents. The wall seems taller now that Linda is beside it. Above, the barbed wire has snared so many leaves and twigs, it looks like a nest. She remembers that now: Part of the reason she was so surprised by the wire's bite as a child was that it had looked to her like a place a bird might live.

She pushes the gate open, the screech milder than she expected. Then, with another step, Linda crosses the line of the gate. She clamps her gaze down to her sneakers and the frosty mud hugging their sides.

She's never worn shoes within these walls before. She feels the urge to kick them off. The urge to run. The urge to find her tree and climb.

Growing up, she rarely noted time, instead following cycles of sun and hunger and her body's need for sleep. But she remembers a brief obsession in which she timed everything with an old stopwatch she'd found: How long it took to run from the west wall to the east, and from the north to the south. Corner to corner. Around the perimeter. From the pond to the big-leaf maple and back again. All quicker than she expected. She'd read stories in which people ran for hours, hiked for days, and here was the map of her world defined by seconds and single-digit minutes. The property felt so big; it was strange to have data in hand telling her it was actually quite small.

She feels similarly now. It had taken barely an hour to drive here. It's extraordinary, thinks Linda, how dissonant time and distance can feel.

She forces her gaze upward. In Madeline's lifetime, the house was painted a happy yellow. Linda has seen pictures in which she barely recognizes her home—so sunny and full of promise. In her memory, there's still yellow, but it's faded and flaking, speckled with colorless pockets where the paint bubbled and burst like sores. Now the exterior is a grayed-out nightmare.

"How are you doing?" asks Anvi. Linda can feel her standing close. A few more inches and they'd be touching.

"I'm fine." Linda's voice sounds strained even to her.

"You've got this."

She takes a deep breath and resumes walking. This time, she tells herself, she won't stop until she reaches the house. But she doesn't know where to go first: The closed garage? The nailed-in sheet of plywood where the front door should be? Should she circle around to the back deck or perhaps skip the house entirely and explore the rest of the property instead?

Indecision leads her down the cracked, uneven driveway to the front door. The stairs to the small landing are winter-slick, and the railing—rickety but intact in Linda's memory—lays on the ground, encased in moss and ice. Climbing up feels like cresting a mountain. She faces the plywood slab; toothy, cold stalactites hang from above, and the house smells of wet ruin. Linda feels herself beginning to shake.

Pressure on her lower arm, light but sudden. Linda jerks her head to look at Anvi, who's standing at the base of the stairs in her cream-colored coat, reaching up.

"This doesn't seem safe," says Anvi.

Linda twitches her arm away. She spent most of her childhood outdoors, but this house holds memories too. Clicking through channels on the television, trying to find meaning in endless static. Walking the top of the couch like it was a log across a river. Sitting with Emmer beneath a fort of musty pillows and whispering guesses about what their mother might be keeping in the basement. Emmer's refusal to answer.

The basement is almost directly below her.

As a child, Linda imagined her sister slipping away through a secret passage into the real world. This narrative followed Linda through adolescence and into adulthood, a belief so fundamental to her sense of self as to be unchallengeable truth. When she wondered where her sister might be, she imagined faraway cities and exotic landscapes. She imagined her around the next corner or two blocks back, watching.

But her understanding of Emmer's disappearance suddenly strikes her as absurd. A five- or six-year-old child being released into the world like a farm-raised fish into a river? Lorelei was mad, but her madness was defined by grief—if Madeline was what she wanted and Emmer was like Madeline, why would she have let her go?

For the first time, Linda thinks Emmer might not have ever left the basement.

Lorelei's cruelty was mostly in her eyes and voice, the way she held herself apart, but Linda remembers the occasional flare of anger. Intense and frightening, usually targeting inanimate objects—she threw a lamp through a window once. Maybe despite all her promise Emmer did something unforgivably un-Madeline-like, and Lorelei snapped. Maybe Emmer's breath was snatched from her in a violent burst. Maybe she was left in the corner to rot. Maybe she died of thirst and sour disdain, like the succulent in Linda's apartment.

And maybe that was why Lorelei looked at Linda with such hate that day, why she locked her from her affection ever after—because if perfect-seeming Emmer had failed to be Madeline, then Madeline was truly gone.

Linda suddenly feels immensely stupid for believing it could have happened any other way. For believing Emmer might be out there somewhere, living the well-adjusted life Linda herself can't manage.

Her sister's bones are in the basement. It's a devastating thought, but it also feels true.

A drop of water splashes onto Linda's cheek. She looks up and sees glistening icicles. Another drip on her shoulder. The droplet coalesces atop the fabric of her jacket, bits of gray trapped in the water. Linda feels the liquid on her face and imagines it looks like an ashen tear—that since she can't cry, her home is doing it for her.

She digs her fingers around the edge of the plywood.

"Linda—"

She won't let Anvi stop her. She always thought Emmer was the one who left her behind, but it was the other way around. Linda crams her fingers in behind the wood as far as they'll go and spreads her feet for balance.

You must have been so scared, the well-meaning often said. But she wasn't scared. Lonely, sometimes. Sad. But not truly fearful—not until the day she left.

She pulls at the board, straining her fingers.

She used to fling herself through trees as a girl. One time a branch snapped and sent her tumbling. She had bruises and scrapes, a throbbing numbness in her wrist for days afterward—but she survived. She healed and climbed again.

The plywood board creaks but doesn't move.

Linda misses the girl she used to be. Even if she wasn't the child Lorelei wanted, there was something in her that was better than the woman she is today.

She extracts her fingers from the board. She needs leverage. Linda turns around and looks past Anvi, scanning the ground, hoping the firefighters left something of use. There's nothing.

The shed. There are tools there.

Anvi looks like she has about a dozen questions on her lips. Linda steps past her.

As she rounds the corner of the house, Linda's expectations shift like time-lapse; she sees saplings mature, seedlings sprout, thorned brush invade and expand, a handful of old trees snap and fall. Twelve years of change in an instant. She blinks, searching, and then there it is: the shed. Its roof is sagging and it's closer to the house than she remembers, but it's there, tucked in an embrace of sweeping branches.

One summer an animal took up residence in the shed; every time Linda or Emmer opened the door, the lumber and buckets and garden tools that were stored inside rattled. The ruckus thrilled them, the mystery and danger. Then one day Linda caught sight of the beast: a midsized rabbit with ratty ears and a twitchy puff of a tail. He squeezed out through a hole in the wall when she tried to catch him. The next morning she found tufts of brown-gray hair outside the shed and knew that a fox had eaten him.

She forgot about that—the guilt she felt over causing the rabbit's death and how that had thrilled her too.

The power of this place, it pulls at her, runs through her. This is who she is.

She pushes through brambles and a slough of collapsed, sodden grass to reach the shed. It looks as though it might come crashing down if she opens the door, but Linda doesn't hesitate.

The door squeals. The walls hold.

There's a window in the back. Linda remembers it being fogged; now it's broken. She teeters across rotting boards, ducking beneath the sagging roof, to where a handful of gardening tools hang from pegs. She digs her hand through a spiderweb thick with insect carcasses to grab a trowel—and then she remembers the shovel. There should be a shovel in the corner. She turns but doesn't see it. She feels her way through the dim until her foot taps against a metal spade.

Exiting the dusty shed with the shovel in hand, Linda sneezes. As her eyes refocus, her gaze slips past Anvi and falls on the house. The destruction is worse from this angle. Most of the roof and the uppermost walls are gone, revealing jutting blackened innards and the broken frames of two bedrooms. It's as though the front of the house was hiding its damage behind a brave face.

"It's a lot worse from this side, huh?" says Anvi, and Linda hates her briefly, hates that anyone who doesn't love this house would see it like this.

She hurries back to the front door and slips on the steps; her shin cracks against an edge and the shovel clatters to the ice.

"Are you okay?" asks Anvi, grabbing her elbow and helping her up. It happens quick, and Linda wonders if Anvi's chatter and touching is as much animal instinct as Nibbler's urinating and scent-tracking. If so, it's an instinct Linda lacks. She wonders what it's like to be able to touch another person without thinking about it first.

"I'm fine," she whispers, and because Anvi didn't laugh when she fell and hasn't taken any pictures, she adds, "Thank you."

Linda picks up the shovel and jams its blade behind the plywood. Her feet slide as she tries to crank the handle back. She braces one foot against the house. Then she pulls, huffing out a breath that wants to be a cry.

The plywood groans and pops free. Linda stumbles but manages to keep her feet.

The front door is open, its lock hanging from the jamb. Beyond is a maw of blackness, a warning and invitation both. Fury and Honor leaks into Linda's mind. But this isn't the game, it's home, and when an icicle drips, Linda feels its splash.

"Linda," says Anvi. "I don't think this is safe."

Linda steps inside.

The windows are boarded over, but weak light creeps in from the door and the stairwell. Her eyes go first to an overturned couch, which is sprouting sad springs from its underside. Officer Baldwin said the fire started in the fireplace, and in that direction there's rubble everywhere: bits of ceiling and wall that fell or were torn down. The stench of mold and char clogs Linda's nostrils.

She catches a glimpse of what look like magazines under some of the torn-down drywall. There is a crushed water bottle too. She wonders if these are from the firefighters or from the squatters Officer Baldwin thinks were responsible for the fire.

She makes her way toward the cooking room. *Kitchen,* her mind corrects. But in the context of this house, the word feels odd. Though she knew the term *kitchen* as a child—she'd read it and maybe Lorelei had said it, early on—she still thinks of each room by its main function or a defining feature. Cooking room. Couch room. Toilet room. Only bed room sounds the same, though she always imagined the syllables separated by a space.

A sharp clatter at her feet startles Linda. Looking down, she sees a rocking shadow. She crouches and picks up a large glass bottle. She can't make out the cursive print on its gold-and-black label, but the stark square text below that is legible: CHAMPAGNE BRUT. She puts it down and continues toward the cooking room.

She pauses in the archway. Remarkably, there are few signs of the fire here. The windows are fogged and dirty but intact. One of the kitchen table's legs has buckled. Linda runs her hand along its top, leaving a trail of char. She remembers sitting here one winter evening with her sister, eating soup that must have come from one of Lorelei's scheduled deliveries. They were sounding out the words on the packaging: *Chicken Noodle.* She remembers being puzzled about how the soup connected to the birds roaming the property; it tasted only of salt.

She could probably taste it again, Linda realizes. Buy it at a store.

She catches a glimpse of a pattern on the inside of a table leg: a dark swirl that isn't mold or fire damage. She kneels, curious. Then, with a rush of revelation, she remembers huddling beneath the kitchen table with Emmer. They'd taken some pens from a drawer, or maybe just a pen. Plural, singular, on this point the memory wavers, but however many, they cracked them open—the snap of the plastic in her hands, this feeling she *knows*—and then there were pieces, two at least, sitting in the black ink as it pooled beneath her and Emmer's knees. They'd dabbed their fingers in it, padded their hands across the tile and up the table legs, leaving trails of tempestuous whorls and crashing waves. Black ink everywhere, running. They'd laughed themselves silly, the two of them, *tap-tapping* their separate paths across the grain, twining them together. Afterward, giddy and exhausted, they'd laid side by side beneath the table, admiring their handiwork: their fingerprints patterned across the underside of the table, resting above them like stars.

Then: Lorelei's rubber clogs and pale, hairy ankles as she crouched, bringing the hem of her long white sweater to the ink-wet floor. She looked at the girls, her angular face in exhausted neutral, then her jaw tightened. That was all, but it was enough; Linda knew who was getting blamed. She remembers turning her head and seeing black ink on Emmer's chin, like the darkest of bruises on her skin, and she remembers wishing that it *was* a bruise. That it hurt.

Linda touches the table leg with her soot-marked hand, gently, as though she could reach back through time and soothe her younger self. She feels a ringing certainty that if she could replay that day from morning to night, the next thing to happen would be Lorelei taking Emmer by the hand and leading her into the basement. Closing the door. Linda's cries—*I'm sorry, please come back*—but, no, that part was from another day.

She lifts her hand to rub her temples. There was at least one day before she left when she was truly scared—she just doesn't like to admit it, even to herself, because one outlying example can easily be blown up until it's larger than the truth.

When she opens her eyes, she sees fresh ash fingerprints alongside the ink. One of the inked sets is a scaled-down replica of the whorls she just made. Here is proof beyond memory that she's been here before. That as a girl she laid here with her sister and laughed. A silent part of her feared none of it had happened. Her current existence and her childhood are so dissonant, it sometimes seems impossible that the same person could experience both.

But she did. She exists now and she existed then: a different, budding her in a world that shouldn't have been possible but was all she knew. The truth of her physicality overwhelms her. The way her nostrils pinch against the stench of ash, the tightness in her legs from sitting so tensely in the car, the brush of her hair against her neck, the way her toes are compressed in her shoes, the pressure of the soles against her arches.

She *exists*.

She sticks her head under the slanted table and looks up. There they are: the constellations she and her sister made together, obscured by a fog of mold but there. They're stunning. Proof of Emmer. Proof that she hasn't always been alone.

She wishes Dr. Tambor were alive and standing here now, beside her, so Linda could point at this table and tell her everything she held back before.

She can't leave the table here. The door to the back porch is boarded, but Linda turns the knob and slams her body into the wood. On her third try, the door pops open a few inches as the plywood splits from the house. Her shoulder throbs and wood cracks as she forces the door open the rest of the way.

"Linda?" Anvi calls from out front. "Are you okay? What was that?"

Linda drags the broken table to the back door, heaves it onto its side, and shoves it onto the deck. Before leaving, she looks back at a short hall leading to a space she never named as a child. It hadn't seemed to need one, but she knows now that most people would call it a laundry room. But before that room, partway down the hall, is the door to the basement. It's exactly as Linda remembers: thick, solid, closed.

She has to go down. She has to look for Emmer. But she's not ready. She needs to get this table out of here first.

Outside, Linda glances to the right. Across an expanse of feral yard slump the remains of the fox hutch where she and Emmer used to play. She can barely see the structure beneath the creeping greenery reclaiming it. There's so much memory here, sucking at her. One thing at a time. Right now: the table. She drags it down the stairs with a clatter, then starts around the side of the house. It feels as though the hutch and shed are watching her; the basement door too. Everything is watching her, judging her return. Nibbler meets her halfway to the front, panting, and Anvi appears a moment later.

"What are you doing?" asks Anvi.

Linda doesn't want to answer, but Anvi is blocking her. "I need to take this back with me," she says. She's sliding the table upside down from the broken end so that the fingerprints face the sky. She takes another step, and Anvi moves out of her way.

And then Anvi is on the opposite side of the table, lifting. "Anything else?" she asks.

A pulse of warm confusion runs through Linda. "I don't know yet."

They leave the table in the driveway. Linda doesn't feel ready to face the basement yet. She goes through the front door and turns right. She opens another door, then scuffs her feet down a single concrete step. The garage looms over her, dark and unwelcoming. At its center is the shadowy hump of the white Civic. How many times did she sit in its back seat and imagine she was on her way to the lake? How many times did she bounce in place to simulate being driven, telling herself the story of that wonderful day over and over? Remembering Lorelei's soft hand on her back. *Then climb.*

She opens the rear passenger door with a great creak and sticks her hand under the remains of the front seat, patting. Her hand falls on plastic and, below it, damp paper. She pulls the items free. The picture book is sodden, the pages merged into a single thick clump, the art of the cover made abstract by water damage—but the plastic controller is whole. She can still read SUPER NINTENDO ENTER-

TAINMENT SYSTEM across the top center. She has to stop herself from skittering the controller across the back seat. Instead, she presses the blue-purple B button; it indents and sticks. She understands how this might work now; how one could press such buttons to navigate a fictional land.

She places the controller in her jacket pocket and rolls the book into a tube, which she places in her waistband. It's cold and damp against her skin. Bits of paper fleck off on her fingers.

There is nothing else in here she wants. She retreats from the garage, wiping her hands on her pants to leave thick black-brown smudges. Anvi is in the living room, brushing her foot through a pile of rubble while Nibbler sniffs around. Linda watches as Anvi absentmindedly pats his head.

Upstairs next.

The stairs creak as she climbs. Cobwebs hang in the corners and between railings, black with ash. Halfway up, it's as though the walls have been painted dark gray; the line is so stark it takes Linda a moment to realize it must be from smoke damage. She crests the stairs into ruin. The ceiling is gone, the roof intact above her but burned away over much of the rest of the house, and she can see straight through the burned-out walls into what remains of the bedrooms. The chimney stands stark and exposed—its brick blackened and cracked.

There were boxes in the attic; that was where she'd found many of the books and much of the clothing that sustained her through her childhood. Items that seemed so mysterious but she now understands were relics of Madeline. All that is gone now, turned into ash. The floor is thick with cold, slushy char that squishes around her sneakers like mud.

There is nothing to salvage here. Nothing to see but destruction. A cold breeze rustles through the ruin. Linda takes a last look around and retreats downstairs.

No more delaying. She needs to go into the basement. Her insides rebel against the notion, and she has to remind herself that the basement does not belong to Lorelei anymore. It belongs to her. All of this rubble and char and dust belongs to her. And she owes it to Emmer to see what she can find.

If she hesitates, she'll lose her courage. She goes to the basement door and puts her hand to the knob.

It turns a fraction of an inch, then stops.

She nearly sags to the floor to bury her head in her hands. How can she be locked out again? Still?

Come back. Her fist on the door, banging.

But she isn't that little girl crying at the door, she tells herself. Not anymore. She wishes she were; that little girl had been mostly brave, had drifted into sorrow and despair only on occasion. It all seems so wrong; she was trapped here as a child, and yet she didn't feel trapped until she was "free." Everything is backward.

She grabs the doorknob—visions of the door swinging toward her to reveal Lorelei, swinging away to hide her—and yanks it inward.

It pops open with a groan. All she needed to do was pull harder, and now here is the one threshold in the house she's never crossed. Linda gathers her breath and steps through the doorway.

She feels a cold flush of déjà vu. But, no, this is something she has never experienced, has only imagined. The first stair creaks; Linda's faint shadow disappears into the darkness below. She steadies herself with a hand against the wall.

She hears a wooden groan from behind her and turns to see Anvi's profile in the doorway, surrounded by floating dust particles.

"What's down there?" asks Anvi.

"I don't know." It can't be as simple as Emmer's skeleton sitting in a corner. The police would have found that. It has to be something only she will recognize.

"Wait," says Anvi as Linda takes another step. "Linda, stop!"

"What?"

"The stairs are broken. Look."

Linda gazes hard into the darkness, willing her eyes to adjust. And then she sees it: a four- or five-foot gap in the stairs, just ahead of her. Now that she sees it, she wonders how she missed it before.

Looking down, she sees a shimmer that might be the basement floor. She would survive the fall, but she might break something. Maybe she can jump across the gap, but there's no guarantee the stairs on the far side are stable.

One risk or the other. Her choice.

She tests the next stair with her foot. If it's strong enough to hold her, she can dangle and drop. As long as she lands loosely—and not on anything sharp—she should be fine.

"Linda." Anvi again. Hovering.

You can't stop me, thinks Linda.

"Why don't you use a ladder?"

It takes her a moment to process the suggestion. Then she rejects it. She wants to laugh at Anvi. She wants to ask her, *Did you bring one?*

"I saw one by the shed. Come on."

Anvi sounds so certain, Linda wants to see her be wrong. She follows her through the kitchen, out the back door, and toward the old shed. Anvi's coat is dusted with gray and black, as though the air itself is leaving a mark. Linda feels an uncommon smugness as she follows; she memorized every inch of this property as a child. There is no ladder here.

Except—there is. Propped horizontally against the side of the shed, moss and lichen growing over its rusty metal rungs, it looks as though it's been here forever. Linda has no memory of its existence, but it doesn't seem out of place to her either. It *was* always here, she realizes. She just didn't know it was a ladder. She never tried to shift

it, stand it up, climb it. She'd simply accepted it as part of the landscape. She didn't even notice it when she got the shovel. Her stomach
twists; she thought she understood the world of her childhood.

Anvi heaves the ladder upright, leaving deep imprints in the
earth. Exposed beetles skitter away, and hard, curled larvae shine in
the cold light, unmoving. Anvi bangs her hand against the ladder's
side. "Seems solid." She doesn't seem to think it's strange that Linda
didn't think of the ladder herself, and Linda is grateful for this. Together they carry the ladder back to the house.

Inside, Linda sits on the second stair. Anvi slides the ladder to her
and Linda guides it into the gap, easing it down until the bottom
finds the floor. The top extends only about six inches above the last
stair. If the bottom slips, the ladder will plummet.

"I'll hold it," says Anvi, crawling up next to Linda. Her coat is
filthy now. Nibbler whines from the kitchen. Linda removes her
hands from the top of the ladder, and Anvi's take their place.

"You sure you want to do this?" asks Anvi.

Linda nods and sneaks a foot onto a rung. As she descends, the
ladder rattles. Its rungs are slick beneath her sneakers and palms.
Then her foot finds the floor. All around her is musty darkness, with
only a few rays of dull light creeping in from above.

"What do you see?" calls Anvi.

"I can't see much of anything." She looks away from Anvi's spiky-
haired silhouette to let her eyes adjust.

"Use your Sheath."

Linda rolls up her sleeve and turns on the Sheath's flashlight function. She shines her arm around her in an arc, then at the rubble on
the floor. She chooses a direction and follows the light of her Sheath.

"Linda," calls Anvi. "If you hold the bottom, I can come down and
help."

Linda doesn't answer. She wants to be alone for this. The first obstruction she finds is a metal desk. She runs her hand over the sur-

face, which is thick with dust. There is a keyboard, a mouse, and a computer monitor—all connected to nothing. Lorelei sat here. Typed at this keyboard, clicked this mouse, stared at this monitor.

Did Emmer sit at this desk too? Snug in Lorelei's lap, reveling in her latest reward?

Linda realizes she doesn't know what happened to any of the technology the police took from the basement. Was the rest of the computer here when they came all those years ago? Did they find anything on its hard drive? No one told Linda, and she didn't know to ask.

She pulls open the desk's top drawer; the metal screeches. There are only a few pens and paper clips inside. She checks the rest of the drawers. They are equally noisy and equally empty. She takes the pens and sticks them in her pocket with the gaming controller.

A few feet away, she finds a whiteboard that bears faint marks of use. She takes a photograph spread with her Sheath. Beyond that, there is an overturned rolling chair and a couple of empty storage units—including what must be the freezer Linda and Emmer were stored in before being implanted. It's empty now, the same temperature as the rest of the basement.

Reaching a wall, Linda traces the perimeter of the basement and finds a back room containing a furnace and water heater. Beside them, encased in dust, is a piece of equipment she doesn't understand, and it's attached to a wooden hatch in the floor. Linda heaves the hatch open, revealing a deep, dark hole. The underside of the hatch drips. Some sort of water access. Around her, the stench of ash mingles with that of organic decay. As she steps away from the equipment, her foot squishes into something. She shines her Sheath to find a pile of rot and bones. Her heart wrenches—*Emmer*—even as her eyes note a third component: fur. Damp gray fur and the glistening of sharp teeth. The remains are that of a raccoon, perhaps an opossum—not a sister. Still, her heart races.

When she returns to the stairs, she notes a small bathroom tucked beneath—a sink and a toilet, a single disintegrating towel on a hook.

And that's it, the full extent of the basement. She's not sure what she expected to find, but she feels like a failure. She checked everywhere except that hole in the floor, which isn't wide enough to climb into. Though perhaps a child could fit. She thinks of Emmer tripping and falling into the slender pit. She thinks of Lorelei tossing her down. She can't quite believe either.

"Coming up?" calls Anvi.

Her tree, thinks Linda. That's where she's going next. She had another hidey-hole in the tree; perhaps she can find it. She doesn't remember what she stored there, only that it existed.

The ladder creaks as she ascends. Anvi scoots out of the way, offering Linda a hand she doesn't take. Linda climbs to her feet past her. Nibbler brushes up close, panting and eyeing his human.

"Find anything?" asks Anvi.

"Not really," replies Linda, fingering the pens in her jacket pocket. Her other hand is pressed against Nibbler's soft fur. This close, he smells slightly fishy.

"Should we put the ladder back?" Anvi steps down onto the first stair as she asks, and the wood beneath her creaks sharply. She turns toward Linda, eyes wide—and then she plummets as the top of the stairwell collapses.

From: Lorelei Niequist   Draft Saved 9:41 P.M. 2/11/2004
To: Arthur Niequist
RE:

You said you watned another child but I only want her. The nightmares theyr endless i see her, she's alone crying and im not there and how am I suposed to live without her? Our last words wwere a fight and we weren't there.

9.

Between two thuds of her heart, Anvi feels herself fall. Her hands react before she can decide what to grab, her nails digging into the doorframe like a fail-safe device. She's dangling at an angle, her chest pressed to the edge of a stair as her feet scramble for purchase. Her toe finds something jutting from the wall; it takes her weight—some of it—and she stops sliding.

Nibbler rushes forward and nuzzles her face, and all Anvi can think is, *No, you'll fall too.*

And then Linda is there, throwing herself onto her knees to take Anvi's wrists in an iron grip. She pulls, dragging Anvi's chest against the edge. Anvi kicks off the wall and swings her leg up and over. Together, she and Linda scramble away from the broken stairs.

Anvi's heart thuds again, and now all she can feel is its panicked racing and the tile floor cold and solid beneath her. Then the pain hits: her hands, her shin. Survivable pain, but loud.

"Thanks," she says to Linda. Nibbler crams his face into hers, licking. Anvi pats his warm side. "Yes, you helped too." She sits up, hanging her head over her knees to catch her breath. Linda is stone-still beside her, watching. After a bit more huffing and nuzzling, Nibbler settles his flank against Anvi's shoulder. His tail wags nervously in her face.

Anvi pulls up her left pant leg to reveal an ugly dripping wound along her shin. It hurts worse now that she sees it, and she sucks in a breath to keep her stomach steady.

Nibbler twists around to sniff the wound, and Anvi pushes his head away.

"Any chance there's a first-aid kit lying around here?" she asks Linda. It's a joke—mostly—but Linda answers with a serious shake of her head, then starts fiddling with the sleeve of her oversized jacket. Anvi looks back at the cut, half-wishing she were the kind of woman who carried around a handbag stuffed with handkerchiefs and breath mints. She could clean herself up *and* get the taste of her fear out of her mouth.

Linda shoots forward and presses a sleeve-covered palm against Anvi's shin. Hard.

Anvi yelps, less from the pain than in surprise—Linda moving so quickly is like a statue coming to life—and then she steadies, watching. Linda's brown hair is hanging forward, hiding most of her face, but Anvi can see one eye. It's flashing with concentration—and so much confidence, it makes her look like a different person.

Anvi watches that steady eye, fascinated. Finally, Linda peels her hand away. The bleeding has stopped. "We should wash and bind the wound," says Linda.

Anvi limps upright and turns toward the kitchen sink. Her shin is shrieking. "Want to place any bets on whether or not there's running water?" she asks.

"The indoor water stopped working years before I left," says Linda.

Anvi doesn't even try to hide her shock. Freshman year of undergrad, some friends in the agriculture program convinced her to go deep-woods camping with them. There were a handful of sublime moments—the image of a spotted fawn rising out of invisibility is stamped in her memory as one of the most beautiful things she's ever seen—but the lack of plumbing ensured it would be a once-in-a-lifetime experience. Enough years have passed that she has trouble believing she really did it—that she went days without washing her hair, that she dropped trou behind a tree stump and buried her excrement in the earth just as her nomadic ancestors might have done generations ago. Though they were probably a lot less worried about getting shit on their jeans.

"How did you drink?" she asks Linda. "Or bathe? Or anything?"

"There's a pond and a creek," says Linda. "This way." She heads out onto the rotting back deck.

Anvi hobbles after her. With every step, her shin hurts more. She tucks her hand under her sweater and touches the lesser pains there. She doesn't feel any blood, but she suspects there will be bruises. At least this will make a fabulous story, she thinks. It would be good for Linda's image too: her doing something proactive, helpful—saving Anvi from a broken leg or neck. All the Clone Girl stories Anvi has found are of Linda shying from the camera or doing something socially awkward. There's one particularly cringeworthy video of her as a teenager. She's at a charity function with her father, and Arthur is speaking with big sweeping gestures to a journalist. Linda's standing beside him, blank-faced, and then her eyes flick up and she startles, her face falling into toddler-like fascination. It's obvious she's staring at a novel stimulus. Then there's a twitch to her eye and mouth that could be read in so many ways, but one interpretation—the worst possible interpretation—is as finding the stimulus repellent. The camera pans to reveal that she's staring at a black man in a wheelchair. Both of his legs are amputated at the knees, and his face is heavily scarred.

The man was an employee of the nonprofit at the center of that night's event; he'd been injured years prior in a terrorist bombing abroad. Anvi couldn't find any record of his response to the video, but this occurred at the height of call-out culture, where a portion of the population reveled in identifying social missteps and labeling even the smallest infraction as bigotry. In their eyes, there could be no ignorance, only hate—and despite her father's wealth and privilege, Linda was still exceedingly ignorant. They pounced on the video, proclaiming Clone Girl's unguarded gaze a window to her ableist—and probably racist—soul.

Anvi gets it: She remembers the tension of those years. How she felt compelled not only to action but to continually signal her involvement. Online, she maintained a data-centric persona, sharing infographics, nonprofits she believed in, and well-reasoned arguments more than passion. Passion she saved for her father's side of the family, where she had a chance of achieving conversation instead of just an exchange of rhetoric.

What a terrible time to emerge ignorant into the world, she thinks. Not only did Linda have to contend with religious fanatics and everyday trolls, but the opposite extreme also exulted in finding fault. Between the two, Linda's every stumble was a fall into an abyss.

Anvi limps down the porch steps. Linda keeps moving, apparently confident in Anvi's ability to keep up. She can so far—barely.

If people knew about Linda throwing herself across the floor and heaving Anvi to safety—it would be an entirely new Clone Girl narrative. A positive one about something Linda did instead of what she doesn't know or who her parents are.

Not that Anvi can tell this story publicly. She can't even tell her mother.

As she follows Linda across the overgrown yard, she tries to imagine her doting, health-obsessed physician mother living here. Doing any of the things Lorelei Niequist is said to have done and not done.

It's remarkable Linda survived, she thinks. It's remarkable she can speak in full sentences and live on her own.

Linda stops, her feet straddling a slump of dead grass. Anvi stands beside her. Her leg is killing her and it's getting harder to walk. It makes the most sense to go back to the car. The navigation system showed a downtown area nearby, and she wouldn't mind some gauze and an antibiotic cleanser.

But confidence is still flashing in Linda's eyes, and she's standing straighter than Anvi's ever seen. Even more than Anvi wants to clean her leg, she wants to see what Linda's going to do next.

She sucks back her pain and waits.

The tree line is denser than Linda remembers. Whatever path once existed is now as wild as the rest. So she estimates, striking out where she thinks the path to the pond used to be.

As Linda pushes past a sapling, Anvi calls, "Linda." Her voice is soft, and Linda turns around to find her hunched over, breathing heavily. Linda can't see her face. She backtracks to Anvi's side.

"Any chance you can give me a hand?" asks Anvi. "I hate to be a wimp, but my leg fucking hurts." She laughs. It isn't her usual laugh.

"Okay," says Linda, and Anvi slings her arm over Linda's shoulder, so that her weight sags onto her. The scent of char wafts up from Anvi's hand, and Linda notices that her fingernails are painted a glittering opal. You would never know she was just clawing at floorboards to catch herself, except that the ring finger's nail is torn. Linda feels Anvi's coat brushing her back, the heat of her body.

Underneath these physical sensations is something else: a warm feeling that makes Linda want to be worthy of the trust Anvi is giving her.

The trees thin and the pond comes into view. The years have transformed what Linda remembers as a clear and cool body of water into a murky bamboo-choked swamp. The cattails are gone. As they limp closer, Linda sees the dock poking from the edge of the grass like a bucktooth jutting toward the water.

They reach a large rock Linda recognizes. "Wait here," she says, easing Anvi down. Nibbler dashes ahead. His nails clack atop the dock. Anvi's pant leg is bunched around her knee, and the cut is bleeding again. Her leg is a swath of crimson, her sock soaked where it peeks above her boot.

"You should sit on the ground and rest your leg on the rock while applying pressure to the wound," says Linda. She helps Anvi shift her position. She isn't sure what to use to apply pressure.

Anvi squirms. For a second Linda thinks it's from pain, but she's taking off her coat. Anvi rolls the jacket into a ball and jams it against the wound. "Ow," she says. When she sees Linda's surprised look, she adds, "It's ruined anyway. At least now it'll go out like a champ."

Linda nods. "I'll be right back."

As she moves to investigate the pond more closely, she realizes the feeling she wasn't able to identify while helping Anvi was that of being needed. For the first time in as long as she can remember, she feels useful. It's a good feeling, and she wants to get this right. Which means she needs clean water to flush out the wound, and then she has to bind it.

When Anvi fell, it was as though time stopped. Then Linda saw Nibbler clatter forward, heard his whine of concern, and she caught a flash of panic in Anvi's golden eyes. Suddenly she was running forward and throwing herself to her knees. She doesn't remember deciding to help; it just happened.

She reaches the dock and finds it half-sunken. Nibbler is back with Anvi, sitting with his head pressed to her side. The water is atrociously murky. Linda doubts even fish live here anymore. Maybe some frogs do. This water won't work. She circles the pond, pushing through thick clumps of brown grass, searching for the inlet. A third of the way around she finds it: a trickle. But the water is clean.

She needs a vessel. She has to go back to the house. She looks at Anvi, who is still applying pressure to her raised leg.

When Linda first saw the blood, it all came back to her, how she used to treat her injuries as a child—those she'd actually incurred as well as those she only pretended to. She would follow instructions from a book she'd loved and had completely forgotten about until this moment. That's what's rotting in her tree hidey-hole: her old first-aid book.

A remembered phrase: *Almost all external bleeding stops with firm, direct pressure.*

Linda pushes through the foliage, away from the water, beelining for the house. The brush is so thick, her pace is barely more than a walk; then she reaches the woods and quickens to a jog. She dodges trees, moving faster than she has in years. When she reaches the overgrown field, she lets loose, pumping her arms and legs, zipping through wild grass that tries to snag her sneakers. Her calves cry out, aching and free. She gasps and huffs and runs, the house looming larger, closer. She takes the porch steps two at a time. Pounding through the door into the kitchen, she slides to her knees at the cupboard by the sink. The huge pot she remembers is there, gloriously there, just as it should be. She yanks out the pot and is about to run back to the pond when she pauses. *Think,* she tells herself. What can she use to bind Anvi's leg? The towel in the basement pops to mind, but even if she could reach it, it's likely covered in mold.

She walks toward the laundry room. She used the machines sporadically as a child—the dryer until it started to smoke and smell, and the washer until the water stopped running. Then she kept her clothing in two piles on the couch room floor: clean enough and not. When the not pile got too big, she'd take an armful down to the pond and scrub, leaving them splayed on the dock to dry. She sometimes dropped bits here and there, leaving a trail of T-shirts and socks between the house and the pond. Anything out there is part of the earth now. And if any of the clothing is still in the living room, it's burned up or buried in torn-down drywall. But she may have left something in the laundry room.

The walls are lined with blooms of mold and netted with cobwebs. But Linda finds a single gray sock crumpled inside the dryer. There's a hole at the toe and another at the heel, but it's probably the cleanest item in the house. She crams the sock into her coat pocket and collects the pot from the kitchen, then runs back to the pond's tiny inlet. Anvi hasn't moved. Nibbler is nestled to her side.

Long minutes pass as Linda holds the pot to the trickle of clean water, trying not to upset the silt at the waterway's bottom. She can't get the pot submerged enough to fill it. She decides to follow the inlet upstream and look for a deeper pool. After only a minute or two of hiking through ferns and deadwood, she reaches a spot where the inlet opens up. Not much, but enough that she can get the pot a solid inch under the surface of the water. She fills it as much as she can, then hefts the pot up into her arms and hurries back to Anvi.

"Is it still bleeding?" she asks.

"I'm not sure," says Anvi. Her voice quakes slightly.

"Can I see?"

Anvi peels off the blood-soaked coat, breathing tightly as the cloth pulls away from the wound. There is a fresh dribble of blood, but it looks like it's just because the cloth adhered.

"I'm going to clean it," says Linda. "Let's have you sit on the rock again." She helps Anvi up. Anvi extends her leg and looks away. Linda picks up the pot of water and dumps it over the heart of the wound in one quick gush.

Nibbler scrambles to his feet as Anvi yelps and kicks her opposite heel sharply into the ground. "For fuck's sake," she hisses. "Ow."

Maybe she was supposed to have given more warning, but it's too late. Linda sets the pot aside and peers at Anvi's leg. She can see the gash more clearly now that some of the blood has been washed away, and she realizes it isn't just a gash; there is a thick black splinter jammed in on one side.

"We need to get this out," she says.

"Get what out?" asks Anvi. Then she sees it. "Yikes. I think I can grab it." She leans forward and pinches the end of the splinter between her fingers. Her hand is trembling. She hisses as she pulls, and the splinter slides out cleanly, a solid inch and a half long. "Gross," breathes Anvi. She flings the splinter aside and takes a handful of deep breaths.

Linda's trying to decide if she should flush the wound again, since Anvi touched it with her dirty fingers. Probably. She tells Anvi what she's thinking, then rushes off to refill the pot. When she returns, Anvi is hunched over with her head hanging toward her knees, shivering. Linda suddenly realizes that the quaking, the trembling, the tremor in Anvi's voice—it isn't from fear or pain; she's cold.

Of course she's cold: It's in the mid-forties, her coat is a sodden rag pressed to her shin, and she just had a pot of icy water poured over her leg. Linda puts down the water and takes off her jacket. "Here," she says, helping Anvi into the sleeves. She feels stupid for not offering it sooner. She rinses Anvi's leg again, then asks Anvi to hand her the sock in the coat's left pocket.

"Where did you get this?"

"I found it in the warm machine." Linda pauses, cursing herself silently. "The dryer, I mean. Inside." She folds the old sock, then reconsiders the wound. The skin is split pretty far; she doesn't know if it will knit together on its own or if Anvi needs stitches. But she can't do anything about the latter possibility; she presses the folded sock to the wound, then uses handfuls of long, twisted-together grass to tie it in place.

"That looks pretty badass," says Anvi. She's still shivering.

"We should get you warm," says Linda. "Let's go back to the car." She helps Anvi up and they walk slowly together back to the driveway. Linda's eyes are drawn to her sister's fingerprints as they pass the overturned kitchen table.

"How do you know so much about first aid?" asks Anvi.

"One of the books I had here was a first-aid guide," says Linda. "I must have read it a thousand times growing up." But she also has a vague memory of doing something like this before. Anvi's cut didn't surprise her or scare her. The gushing blood felt almost familiar. Perhaps from the fit in which she cut her elbow at Arthur's, but that doesn't feel quite right. She didn't treat that wound herself. She was too upset to care about a little blood, a little physical pain. After she calmed down, Arthur took her to a doctor. Five stitches. Anvi might need more. She might not need any.

Lorelei. It comes at her like a slap: At some point Lorelei came to her with a wound. It was well after Emmer was gone, well after Lorelei had stopped talking to her other than to tell her to be scarce. She emerged from the basement, silent and red, dripping blood from her throat—no, from her forehead, but it was running down her face and throat, dyeing the collar of her shirt and pooling in the divots of her collarbones. Young Linda had for a moment thought the blood was exploding from her mother's throat, traveling both up and down.

She doesn't remember being scared, though. Linda stanched the wound—she pulled sections of Lorelei's hair, yanking her scalp closed like a butterfly bandage, could that be right?—then cleaned and dressed it. Afterward, her mother retreated without explanation or thanks.

The memory feels like winter, and it chills her: How could she have forgotten something as momentous as Lorelei needing her help and allowing her to touch her?

Walking with Anvi, she feels weak. Her flush of competency is gone, replaced by a sickly fear: What else doesn't she remember?

They pass through the gate and reach the car. Anvi pats her pants pocket, then stiffens. "Crap," she says. "The fob's in my coat. I left it by the lake."

Pond, Linda corrects internally. Lakes are bigger, are magical. Are places where children go to swim and climb and play and not be alone anymore. She shakes away the thought and says, "I'll get it."

She leaves Anvi at the car and jogs down the driveway, relishing the quick *crunch crunch crunch* beneath her. Nibbler follows as far as the gate, excited by her running, then Anvi calls him and he darts back. Linda runs past the table to the side of the house, then down the path they made like a game trail through the dead grass. The pond pops into view and she stumbles to a stop.

Halfway around the west side of the pond, there's a man.

M ud squelched beneath Graham's feet as he passed through the rusty gate and spied the old yellow house at the driveway's end. Above, the sky trembled with ominous clouds.

He toggled off the distance indicator, wanting to see the house unobscured. Already, this mission felt different from the others. He could remember the first day he heard about this girl, his age or thereabouts, drifting from the woods as though freshly arrived from an alien planet. The sense of wrongness about her emergence, her life, like a klaxon. For years, a curiosity about her—if he's honest, a sense of awe—had floated in and out of his awareness as they aged together—and apart.

She didn't know he existed.

People said she shouldn't exist.

The mission timer ticked down. Graham stepped past a tangle of greenery. The house was everywhere, was all he could see. He lifted his hand to touch the front door.

And then his vision flickered—a brief, static flash. Graham stepped back, and his arm jerked upward and detached from his shoulder.

"Fuck," he whispered.

10.

Linda's first thought is that she must be hallucinating. She watches as the man across the pond lifts his head. His face is shielded by a baseball cap, but she can feel his eyes on her. Two breaths pass, then he turns and runs into the woods.

Instinct shouts for Linda to chase him, and for once she listens, sprinting along the side of the pond. But even as she tears through the foliage beside the pond, she knows she'll never catch the man. He has too far of a head start. Then her foot slips and she dips sideways, her right shoe sliding into icy water. She climbs out and continues the chase, her ankle aching but functional. She reaches the spot where the man was standing and sees his trail: bent foliage, prints through mud, and the bits of frost lingering in the shadows. Reading the land like this, she feels as though she's remembering how to see. She lost so much of herself when she left the property as a girl, and this is part of it: Having a knowledge base. Being in position to recognize when something is out of place. She follows his trail through the trees to the perimeter wall, where it ends.

A section of the wall is crooked. As Linda approaches the rusted surface, she sees that the piece is disconnected, propped up in place. She presses against it with both hands; the metal warps slightly but doesn't fall. It must be secured on the other side.

This man, whoever he is, has done this before.

She thinks about finding a place where she can climb a tree or about going back to the basement to retrieve the ladder. Then she thinks about Anvi shivering and bloodied by the car. She wants so badly to stay, to follow the stranger's path through the forest on the far side of the wall. But the longer she stands here, the heavier Anvi's presence back at the car weighs on her.

He's probably just some voyeur coming to see the charred remains of the Clone Girl habitat. Or he's one of the squatters Officer Baldwin mentioned, checking whether or not it's safe to return. He might even be the one who set the fire—accidentally or otherwise. That last thought makes her want to scale the wall and give chase after all, but she knows it's too late. And what would she do even if she found the man? The idea of her confronting him is laughable. Linda slinks back to the pond, where the flare of cream and red that is Anvi's blood-soaked coat reminds her why she came. She grabs the coat, then goes back to the house. Partway there, a clump of wet paper catches her eye. It's her picture book; it must have fallen out of her waistband. She picks it up, and when she reaches the driveway, she places it and Anvi's coat on the table. She's careful to put them in a corner where there aren't any fingerprints. Then she drags the table down the driveway, walking backward. The table clunks and groans as it slides, leaving a wide groove.

"Find it?" calls Anvi.

"Yes." Her throat closes around the words *I also saw a man*. Spending time with Anvi, liking Anvi, doesn't mean she has to tell her everything. And her inability to catch the man makes her feel weak. She drags the table the rest of the way, then hands Anvi her coat. Anvi digs the fob out of a sodden pocket and taps it to unlock and start the car.

"Will you open the back, please?" asks Linda, and Anvi taps another button before moving to help Linda lift the table into the rear hatch. They cram it inside the car, askew with its legs up. A moment later, they're belting themselves into their seats and Nibbler's digging in the back, making himself comfortable.

"Vehicle, set destination: nearest pharmacy," says Anvi.

"Nearest pharmacy is 2.6 miles away," the car replies. "Confirm destination."

"Confirm."

Linda stares out the windshield as her home retreats. Frame of reference: She's the one retreating. Maybe she's making a mistake. Maybe she should stay. Anvi could return the car herself. Linda could find her own way back. Or maybe she'd stay here for good. Bundle up in her nest and wait out the winter. In the spring she could rebuild. She has resources now. With a few taps to her Sheath, she could order whatever she needed to shore up the missing roof and broken stairs. She could paint it all yellow. Pull the weeds from the pond, expand the inlet, make sure the water drains and flows. Buy trout to restock it. She could have a home again.

As she fantasizes, the car backs out of the driveway onto the road and begins returning them to the city.

Except. It takes Linda a moment, but she realizes: They aren't backtracking. They're advancing toward the town of Cedar Lake, following the same stretch of road she walked down barefoot as a child. There's the ditch she ducked into to hide from a car—or was it that one? They're going too fast for her to be sure, and of course it's been years and it was dark then, and summer. She doesn't actually recognize any of it, but it's the same road, bringing her back. Anxiety thrums through her. *Vehicle,* she wants to say, *stop.*

A pickup passes them going in the opposite direction. Catching sight of the driver's bearded, sunglass-sheltered face, Linda's first thought is that he's the man from the pond. But that man wasn't bearded, was he? She doesn't think so, can't remember. Her thoughts spiral: Could the man in the truck have been there years ago when she stumbled into town? Was he the one who took that awful, iconic photo of her cowering in the dark? Did he recognize her as they crossed paths seconds ago, her pale face staring at him from the passenger seat? Anything seems possible, and her chest tightens as they snake down the road. Why are they going this way? Her mind rewinds: Anvi asked for the nearest pharmacy.

"Why?" she croaks.

"Why what?" asks Anvi.

"Why a pharmacy?"

"Oh, I want to get some Bactine or something. And a proper bandage. I appreciate what you did back there, but I can't imagine this sock is all that sanitary." She taps the temperature up a few more degrees. "Man, this heat feels good."

No, the sock bandage probably isn't that clean. Long before the water stopped running, they ran out of detergent. For a while it had appeared in Lorelei's deliveries. One jug per month, so that even when that particular delivery stopped, there had been a surplus. The dish soap had stopped then too, and the hand sanitizer. Pretty much everything but the food. But isn't there somewhere else they can stop? Somewhere Linda has never been? She wants to ask, but then she'd have to tell Anvi how scared she is, and Anvi just saw a side of her that Linda feared was dead. A side that can *act*. She doesn't want to destroy that impression.

She tells herself that no one will recognize her. But someone might. The fire has thrown her photo back into the public's eye.

Plus, they recognized her the first time.

That's not entirely true; she was likely less recognizable than she was a spectacle. If she'd walked through town clean and in the middle of the day, maybe no one would have realized who she was. And if her biological parents weren't Arthur and Lorelei Niequist, they might not have cared.

Ahead, a stop sign looms. The car slows, stops, turns right. And there it is: town. Sickly and gray in the winter light, slushy puddles along the sidewalk, a glaring neon bar sign that she actually remembers. She was mesmerized by the color, the light, and headed for it, moth-like, before being intercepted by a woman who asked, "Where did you come from?" The car slides past the bar, the post office. There aren't any people around. They take a left. She doesn't recognize this street. She can't remember where the police station or the clinic is.

She remembers a swarm of people pressing forward, trapping her in the street, more people than she'd imagined existed in the entire world. Why were there so many? It's a tiny town, she realizes now. Dead quiet on a Thursday afternoon. She doesn't know what day of the week she escaped, but it was at night. Why were there so many people out then when there are so few out now? It strikes her that maybe there weren't many people at all. Perhaps it was just a handful, but it seemed like a crowd because she'd never been around people before.

The car turns in to a parking lot. Linda sees the Walgreens that must be their destination. There's a bank beside it, followed by a pet-food store and a storefront featuring a FOR LEASE sign. The car takes a spot near the Walgreens, announces their arrival, and powers down. None of the other cars are as new as theirs. As clean. Most appear to be gas-powered.

"It's like going back in time," says Anvi, articulating a sliver of Linda's unease. She reaches down to arrange her pant leg over her cut. Her sock is noticeably bloodied, but once that is covered, the stains on her dark pants and ankle boots might be mud or moisture. She gets out of the car. "Are you coming in?" she asks Linda.

"I . . ."

"Please. In case I faint from blood loss or something."

Linda follows Anvi, matching her pace to Anvi's slight limp.

There are only a handful of people inside: a cashier, another worker walking the floor, three customers that Linda can see. All of them are white, and the customers are dressed plainly and clustered together—they might be a family. Linda sees flat winter boots, thick coats, flannels beneath. With her baggy pants and wet sneakers, she doesn't stand out here, but Anvi does: her swath of purple hair; the cowl neck of her sweater and its stark asymmetrical hem. Her comparatively dark skin. Linda was scared all eyes would fall on her, but she instead feels them turn toward Anvi.

"Good afternoon," says the cashier, and though the words are friendly, his voice lacks the I'm-here-to-please chirpiness Linda has become accustomed to.

"Afternoon," Anvi replies, picking up a handbasket. She cranes her neck to read the signs above the aisles, then takes off toward the far end of the store. Linda follows. She must be imagining it, she tells herself. The tension. Anvi is acting normally. She isn't even limping anymore. They reach the first-aid supplies and Anvi tosses a few items in her basket. On her way toward the checkout, she pauses to add a pair of cotton socks and then veers off to the refrigeration units and selects an iced tea.

They are both wet and soot-stained, and Linda's sneakers squeak with every step. Maybe that's why it feels like people are staring at them. Though anytime Linda flashes her eyes toward anyone else, they aren't actively looking their way. It just feels like it.

"You want anything to drink?" asks Anvi. Linda shakes her head. "What do you think, pick up some snacks here or get lunch on our way back?"

"I . . ." Linda frowns, more uncomfortable with every passing second. "On the way back."

"Sounds good." Anvi walks to the register and pays. The cashier doesn't offer any small talk, doesn't meet Anvi's eyes. Linda doesn't understand it, why this store feels so strange. Soon they are back outside.

"Sure is a different vibe than in the city," says Anvi as they get back in the car.

"You felt it?" asks Linda.

"I hate to jump to the it's-because-I'm-brown conclusion, but . . ."

"It's the first time in my life I've felt like someone else was the outsider."

Anvi looks over at her sharply.

Embarrassment flushes through Linda. People with skin as light as hers aren't supposed to acknowledge other people's skin color unless it's to document diversity, like how Arthur's company releases a report every year announcing their increasing percentage of African American employees.

"After all these years, you still don't feel like you belong, do you?" asks Anvi.

Linda sets her eyes on the dashboard. "No," she admits.

Anvi shifts her seat back and begins rolling up her pant leg. "How old are you again?"

"Twenty-four." Give or take. When the authorities first asked Linda her birthday, she blurted, "September third," having an association between the word *birthday* and the only date she knew. So that's what went on her paperwork. She later learned September 3 was Madeline's birthday and therefore almost certainly not her own. But by then it was in the system—wrong but official. Since moving, she's started calculating her age from the start of the calendar year, mostly to distance herself from the remembered strain on Arthur's face each year when he pretended to celebrate. He still sends a card each September. Linda wishes she had the courage to ask him to stop.

"You're still a puppy," says Anvi. "Plenty of time to adapt." She hisses as she tears the grass binding and sock from her wound. Then she sprays her leg and wraps it in gauze. She puts away the supplies and rolls her pant leg back down.

Linda notices how scraped Anvi's hands are from grasping at the doorframe. "Maybe you should clean those cuts too," she says.

As Anvi does so, she asks, "What do you say, should we head home? Or do you need to go back to the house?"

She didn't get to walk the property. She didn't get to visit her tree.

But she's cold and wet and aching—and Anvi clearly is too. "Let's go home," says Linda.

After all, she knows how easy it is to get here now. She can come back.

She will come back.

Graham should have aborted the mission, but instead he circled the house. An old garden shed materialized to his left. The woods behind it were a vast and repetitive morass. In the corner of his vision, minutes and seconds ticked toward zero. He turned toward the pond. His right arm lagged and wobbled as he walked, making his head ache. Long grass rustled about his legs. He thought of the frogs vocalizing outside the starlet's mansion. There should be insects here.

He crossed the tree line. A few seconds later, the pond slid into sight. Her pond. He imagined her sitting on the dock, dipping her toes into the water.

Then: A cracking sound so deep and loud it shook him. And a blur to Graham's left—a massive Douglas fir falling.

He took an instinctive jogging step forward, but the tree was too big and falling too fast.

Time's up, *he thought.*

11.

"What were you thinking?" Arthur's voice pounds in Linda's ear.

"I needed to see," she says.

A pause. Then, "I understand that, Linda. I really do. But I wish you would have waited for me."

She burrows farther into her nest chair, silent. She knew Arthur would find out, but she hoped it wouldn't happen this quickly. It was her Sheath that gave her away—the distance and duration of yesterday's excursion so far beyond anything she's done before.

"Who is Anvi Hendrickson?" asks Arthur.

The question blindsides her, and she stutters an inelegant "How did you—"

"You rented a car and listed Anvi Hendrickson as the driver. Did you hire someone?"

"She's my neighbor." She aches to say *friend* but is scared it isn't true. Anvi's voice filled the space between them on the drive back. She told stories about her time at Cornell and how she and her father used to play pranks on each other, how their pranks escalated to an all-out war during the pandemic: an effort to distract themselves from the peril her mother faced treating patients. Anvi looked so wistful as she shared, it was clear how much she loved him. There was a warmth in the air that begged Linda to confide—about the man she saw, about Emmer, about *something*—but she couldn't quite do it. Instead, she asked Anvi questions and smiled at her stories. It felt almost easy.

"Okay," says Arthur. "What's done is done. What was it like?"

"Most of the second floor was gone," she says. "But the kitchen is still there." She untucks her chin to look across the room, where the broken table squats beside the CircleTread. The table looks even more decrepit next to the shining chrome-accented equipment. The Super Nintendo controller and moldy picture book are on the kitchen counter.

"You went inside?" says Arthur. "Christ, Linda. You're lucky you didn't get hurt. But I guess I'm glad you're spending time with your neighbor. Have you been friends for long?" He so easily makes the jump she avoided.

"She moved into an apartment on my floor last week."

"So it's new." Linda can hear it in his voice: *Be careful*. For all the times he tells her to meet people and make friends, there is always this undercurrent of concern: People will want to use her.

There was a boy a few years ago, when she was still residing in Arthur's Connecticut house. She met him at a drawing class Arthur's wife, Claire, had signed her up for. Linda showed up exactly on time, sweating with nerves, her drawing supplies dangling from her fingers in a plastic bag. The only empty seat was between this boy and the wall. The way he smiled at her, so open and kind. "Hi, I'm Jason." She felt a flush come over her and was embarrassed by the strength of her reaction. She still remembers his gray-green eyes, the way gold spiked through the irises like sunbursts. His brown hair was shaggy, un-kempt, and each week he wore stained, ill-fitting clothing that re-minded Linda of how she used to dress. His ragged appearance felt familiar to her—safe. Slowly, over the course of the ten-week class, they began to interact. By week seven they were standing together outside during a break; Jason vaped and talked, while Linda listened, feeling special.

Week eight, Arthur rather than Claire picked her up from class, and Jason recognized him. "Holy shit," he said. "That's Arthur Niequist. I knew he had a house around here, but—" And then Arthur walked up to Linda and asked, "Ready to go?"

The next week, Jason was full of questions, his voice oscillating between declarative heights and soft, secretive whispers. But he was still friendly and he didn't take any photos of her, so Linda convinced herself everything was okay.

Week ten, their last class, he gave her his number. He watched as she entered it into her phone—she had an older model then; Arthur didn't get her a Sheath until she moved west—and had her text him so he could immediately add her too. That was when things started to get deeply uncomfortable. He texted her daily, questions and compliments. He started calling her *beautiful* and saying he missed her, was thinking of her. Linda felt like she should be flattered, but she was mostly scared. She replied rarely, usually only to say *thank you,* because she didn't want to be rude and didn't know what else to say. Then he started asking if he could see her again. If he could come over to her house. The intensity and frequency of contact overwhelmed Linda, felt wrong to her—but everything that was "normal" felt wrong to her, so perhaps this was right.

One day she asked Arthur if it would be okay for a friend from drawing class to come over. He said yes, telling her he was proud of her—and she believed him, felt his pride, allowed herself to believe that she was taking a step toward becoming a daughter Arthur could like instead of simply tolerate.

Jason came dressed as Linda had never seen him—in a suit. His hair was freshly cut and he was carrying a résumé, which he promptly handed to Arthur, talking about his degree, his love of technology, his hardworking spirit. He launched into a speech about how kind and admirable Arthur was for taking in Linda, for giving "the poor girl" a home and a good life. For buying her drawing classes—and hadn't she gotten so much better over the weeks? Arthur must be proud, so proud.

He barely looked at Linda. Barely said anything to her beyond "hello." And after he left, the conversation she had with Arthur was one of their worst ever, as he lectured her on all the things she'd already figured out for herself.

She stopped replying to Jason's flooding texts, which turned mean before finally stopping. One of his last was: *You're a lying bitch who shouldn't exist.*

She hadn't lied to him, but she couldn't argue the last part.

"Linda?" says Arthur. "I have to go, I have a meeting. Victoria made us dinner reservations for tomorrow. She'll send you the details."

"Okay."

"Bye."

She peels off her earcuff. She expected worse—some new guideline or restriction to counteract the fact that she left the city without Arthur's permission. But she'd barely been reprimanded at all, really.

He didn't even tell her not to go back.

Linda gets up. Her body aches from yesterday and is begging to move and stretch. She can't run outside, where people would see, but she knows the building has a gym in the basement. It was listed in her welcome packet.

It's ten-thirty in the morning, one of the building's quieter hours. She decides to risk it. She puts on her mud-caked sneakers, grabs her keys, and takes the stairs down to the basement. Once there, she doesn't know which way to go. The first door on the left reads MAINTENANCE and the second RESTRICTED ACCESS. She goes the other way and finds it: FITNESS CENTER. She peeks through the small window and doesn't see anyone inside.

The room is smaller than her apartment, with two treadmills, two ellipticals—she recognizes these from Arthur's house—a rack of dumbbells, a huge yoga ball, and a few other pieces of equipment she doesn't know. There's a television mounted on the wall, a remote dangling from it by a tether.

While Linda's examining the treadmill instructions, a woman walks in. She's young and white, with her light hair held back in a high ponytail. Her bright clothing clings like a second skin and exposes her midriff, which is heavily tattooed: Roses grow from the woman's navel. She stops just inside the door and stares at Linda.

Linda is suddenly aware of how out of place she must look in her street clothes and dirty sneakers. Shame shoots through her. The woman waves, expressionless, then climbs onto an elliptical. Instead of an earcuff or Augments, she wears a set of earbuds—meant not to integrate but to isolate. Linda hears the faint whisper of a beat. And then the woman starts the elliptical and the music is overwhelmed.

Linda retreats, frustrated by her own cowardice. It's as though she left her courage in Cedar Lake. Stepping into the stairwell, she sees a trail of dried mud, flaked off from her sneakers' treads—yet another reminder of how unfit she is for the civilized world. She makes herself take the stairs at a jog. Not being able to hear anything over her own heavy breaths feels like punishment—more so than the physical exertion, which she was seeking anyway. She lengthens her stride to take the stairs two at a time; if she's going to collide with a stranger, she wants to get it over with. Her thighs are weak and throbbing before she's even reached the second floor. *Keep going.* Sweat wells in her armpits, along her temples, under her breasts. Her pace slows, but she refuses to walk. By the time she pushes into her hallway, her legs have turned gelatinous. The hall is littered with dried mud. She kicks a clod aside and lurches into her apartment, where she collapses into her chair.

After she catches her breath, she looks at her VR headset. She'd have to stand up to reach it, so she grabs her tablet instead. Most of the day's chatter is about a bomb that went off in a Pennsylvania mosque that morning and a hairless cat who was crowned the winner of an ugliest-pet contest. Linda prefers the pictures of the goblin-like cat to those of the smoking, blood-splashed rubble. After the cat photos, she finds a *Deep Reads* article about the continuing epidemic of frog extinction. She makes it almost two paragraphs in before her thoughts wander to Cedar Lake. She wonders if her pond still fills with frogs each spring. She used to like to run her fingers through the jellied pods of their eggs and watch the tiny black tails swish within.

She puts aside her tablet. Arthur will be here tomorrow. She tenses just thinking about it. She needs to think about something else.

She heaves herself to her feet, grabs her headset, and slips into the world of Fury and Honor. She left the region of purple-eyed people last night, and Briggs awakens in a small inn run by dwarves. She ignores the barkeep's stare, which she knows means he has a quest to offer, and exits to the mountain woods. She's in the mood for wandering. She reaches out to touch a mossed trunk. It looks wet and cool, but her gloves don't pass along those sensations; they just stiffen to simulate resistance. It's still better than walking city streets in the real world. A rabbit darts across her path. She could skewer it with a thrown dagger, fry it with a bolt of lightning. The game would reward either action with a pelt, and she wouldn't even have to do the skinning.

But right now she's not interested in the creatures of this world; she craves the easy beauty of the world itself. She lets the rabbit go. After a time she emerges into a valley. She sees water in the distance and is drawn to it. It's a small lake, not much bigger than her pond. She stands there for a while, just watching the wind ripple across the water. Then she wonders: *Will it let me build a dock?*

She takes her dagger to the nearest tree. After only three light hacks, it snaps and falls. A handful of small birds flee, twittering in alarm. Cutting the trunk into logs is just as easy. After felling another tree, she has enough wood. She takes a coil of rope from her inventory—it's a common dropped item, she has sixteen—and begins lashing the logs together. This takes longer, and the game lags on some of the fine-motor movement, so that wood jitters briefly through her orange-furred hands.

The bindings and the rolling texture make it look more like a raft than a dock, but she pushes it halfway into the water and secures it to a nearby tree. She steps on. Her field of vision bobs slightly. She looks up at the sky; it's a sunny day in Rothram, as usual.

When she was young, Linda liked to sit on the dock and scrape the soles of her feet with her fingernails. Callus came away as a gray mash she flicked into the water. The skin cells would strike as a clod, then disperse, and she was always fascinated by how this dead part of her looked more liquid than solid as it swirled down to the bottom of the pond. She wishes Fury and Honor could replicate that experience.

A fish rises, rippling the water's surface, and the ripples distort a cloud's reflection. Linda eases herself into a cross-legged position. She could sit like this for hours, she thinks. After a few minutes, a buck emerges from the trees. He's close enough to attack. The game is goading her, but Linda lets him be. Watching the deer dip his antlered head to drink, she wonders what else she could build here.

From: Lorelei Niequist   Draft Saved 10:06 A.M. 4/15/2004
To: Arthur Niequist
RE:

I miss the foxes more than I expected. Haven't seen hide nor hair since I released them, and it's not like they couldn't just squeeze under the gate if they wanted. So much for domestication, I suppose. But the chickens are thriving. Who would have guessed? I like to watch them in the morning as they peck their way across the yard. They're leaner than they used to be but look happy. If a chicken can be happy.

It makes me think anything is possible.

12.

Linda spends the next twenty-four hours almost entirely in-game, emerging only when her body demands it. She's aching and proud and has barely slept. Putting aside her headset to eat that afternoon, she glances at her Sheath and sees a handful of messages. The most recent is from Arthur, reminding her about tonight's dinner. The other three are from Anvi, a short series spread over the last two days:

Hey! How are you feeling after our little adventure? Want to join Nibs and me for a walk?

Any interest in some Fury and Honor? I got a second headset—we can do co-op!

Everything okay?

The sense of peace Linda cultivated in Fury and Honor slips away. She was so drawn into her project, she never checked her Sheath for messages. All her worry and hope about whether or not Anvi could be an actual friend—she should have checked.

She taps to reply, but she doesn't know what to say. It's only been a day, but it might as well have been weeks. After about a dozen false starts, she writes: *Hi. I've been away from my Sheath. How is your leg?* She's proud of herself for the last part. She taps *Send,* and then she waits. She wants to go back into the game and continue her project, but there's a sour lump in her throat that won't let her do anything but stare at her Sheath. Hours pass. Anvi always has her Sheath; if she's not replying, it's for a reason. Linda checks SocialHub; Anvi's most recent post is from this morning: a photo spread from Pike Place Market. Produce and fish, trinkets and crowds. Before that is commentary on G.H.'s continued silence: *Liar liar, pants on fire.*

It's a phrase even Linda knows, but her gut still lurches at the word *fire.* She wonders if it's a sly reference to her.

Eventually it's time for Linda to get ready for dinner. She sets her Sheath on the sink as she showers, so she'll be able to see if a text wakes the screen.

She misses Fury and Honor. She understands the people there. If she helps them, they give her a free potion or a discount on enchanted boots; if she hurts them—as she accidentally has a few times while sheathing a weapon in a crowd—they run away or try to hurt her back.

Has she hurt Anvi with her silence?

Is Anvi trying to hurt her back?

She dries herself off and fishes her most expensive clothing out of the closet: a knee-length black skirt and a blue silk top that's snug to her torso with voluminous sleeves. Arthur's wife picked out the outfit for her. Linda hates how it looks and feels, like some weird cloth parasite has attached itself to her body, but it's the kind of outfit women are supposed to wear to nice dinners. Pulling her damp hair from the collar, she looks in the mirror. Her nipples poke starkly against the blouse. She forgot: This top requires a real bra, not just a camisole.

She unzips the top, takes it off, and changes into the one bra she owns. It's incredibly awkward feeling—the wires digging into her chest, the straps itchy and loose even when she tightens them as far as she can, the padding pressed against her flesh. She doesn't understand how people can wear these things every day. She puts the blouse back on; now her breasts are half-again their actual size, but they are smoothed to social acceptability. She just has to remember not to tug at the wires or straps during dinner. Arthur gets annoyed when she fidgets.

She wonders briefly if she can wear her sneakers with the skirt but remembers how Claire shook her head at that idea back when they purchased the outfit. She got her a pair of calf-high black boots instead. Linda digs these out of a box and shoves them on over a pair of long, thin socks. Her toes pinch and her calves ache against the compression.

Leaving, she pauses outside Anvi's apartment.

She desperately wants to kick off these too-tight boots and return to her game. There, if she wants someone to like her, all she has to do is complete the right quest. There, she doesn't have to worry about losing someone's friendship, because the someone in question is never real—and if she makes a mistake, she can always load her game and try again.

She misses Nibbler with an absurd intensity. On their drive back from Cedar Lake, he stuck his nose between the front seats and whined until Linda scratched his head. But Fury and Honor has a shop called Minions that sells all sorts of pets. She has enough gold to buy a companion. She could go do that now. She wants to. Even more than she wants to do that, she wants to sit and wait outside Anvi's apartment.

It frightens her how badly she wants to do just that.

That's part of the reason she didn't check her Sheath earlier. She wasn't just distracted; she was terrified there wouldn't be any messages.

It felt safer to be the one who retreated.

Her Sheath buzzes, and Linda nearly cries out with relief—but it's just a note that the car Arthur ordered for her has arrived. She slinks to the elevator like a kicked dog. The last time she took the stairs in these boots, her heels were rubbed to bloody messes.

As soon as she steps into the lobby, she sees the car outside: a sleek black sedan with a human driver leaning against its side. His posture reminds her of the stagecoach drivers you can hire when you want to fast-travel in Fury and Honor.

She blinks and tells herself to stop thinking about the game. But she's spent so many recent hours there, it's impossible not to see connections. Walking through the lobby, she automatically envisions how quickly a lightning spell would leap among the handful of people milling around. And when she exits to the street, it almost feels like she's brought the warmth of Rothram's perpetual summer with her; it's a January evening, but her jacket feels superfluous.

The driver is looking at her through a pair of Augments. His skin is darker than Linda's, lighter than Anvi's. His Augments must confirm she's who he's waiting for, because he opens the car's back door.

"Hello, Ms. Russell," he says. "I'm Javier."

Linda nods and gets in, struggling a little in the skirt, which restricts her movement just enough to be annoying. Javier closes the door and walks around to the driver's side. As they pull away from the curb, Linda sees Anvi and Nibbler round the corner at the end of the block.

Her heart leaps; she nearly calls for Javier to stop the car.

But then she sees how Anvi's laughing into her earcuff. How she gestures with her leash-less hand as though speaking to someone in the flesh—to her mother or a brother or perhaps a best friend back on the East Coast. Someone she loves who loves her back.

Linda made the mistake of reading Anvi's last text in a worried tone, maybe even a hurt tone. Now she imagines a far more likely tone: idle curiosity. Because what is one potential friend to someone as beloved as Anvi?

She ducks her head as the car passes Anvi, and she tries to banish her neighbor from her thoughts by focusing on the trial to come. The restaurant is about ten minutes away, an upscale place by the water that specializes in seafood. She and Arthur always meet there when he's in town. Every time he says it's his favorite. Every time he talks about how he can't come to the Pacific Northwest and not have fresh salmon and Dungeness crab. It's like a script.

They arrive. Linda gets out and marches toward the entrance. Arthur should be inside; his hotel is less than a block away and he always arrives early. Is always waiting for her at a table with a gin and tonic in his hand.

A hostess in a cleavage-baring top greets her and asks to help. Linda scans the dining room. She doesn't see Arthur.

"Miss?" the hostess tries again. "Do you have a reservation?"

"I'm meeting someone," says Linda.

"What's the name? I can see if they've arrived."

Linda scans the room again before relenting. "Niequist." Quietly, so no one at the bar can hear.

The hostess blinks, maintaining her wide smile, then glances down and taps the screen on her little pedestal. "Yes, he's here. Right this way."

Linda follows the woman to the back of the restaurant and through an archway she doesn't recognize—which seems impossible, given how many times she's been here. The archway leads to a dining room Linda didn't know existed, and there he is, his silver hair in its familiar sideswept style, a lime-garnished drink in his hand, facing her from a plush booth on the left.

The hostess melts away as Arthur stands to greet Linda. She recognizes his red paisley tie, still in rotation.

"Linda," says Arthur with a smile. "It's so great to see you." He puts his arms out and Linda steps into a brief, uncomfortable hug before slipping into the booth.

"How was your flight?" she asks. There is a glass of water waiting for her. She takes a sip.

"Fine," replies Arthur. "I was next to a young woman who'd clearly never flown first class before. She was too nervous to ask for anything, and I had to assure her it was all included, so she might as well take advantage. She took a picture of the chicken marsala and her champagne. It was adorable. I, of course, skipped the meal. I was saving myself for this." He pats the menu. "My favorite."

"Crab cakes, crab dip, and roasted salmon," says Linda.

"You know it. Though they seem to have expanded the menu to go with the expanded dining room." Expanded. She was right to not have recognized the space. "I'm tempted to try the prawn poppers. How do those sound to you?"

"Fine," says Linda. Even under normal circumstances, menus overwhelm her with their abundance of options. Tonight she's just going to order the same thing as Arthur.

A server appears and asks Linda if she would like a drink. "Orange juice, please," she says. Arthur ordered juice for her their first time dining out. The police in Cedar Lake had kept trying to give her sickeningly sweet soda and hot chocolate, so she was wary, but the interplay of citrus tang and natural sweetness delighted her. She remembers the taste as her first pleasurable experience on the outside. She's ordered juice at every meal with Arthur since. It's the only time she drinks it, so it gives her something to look forward to.

"You know," says Arthur, "you don't need to be shy about having a drink around me. You're old enough."

It takes Linda a moment to realize he's talking about alcohol. "No, thank you," she says. She had a sip of wine once and didn't care for it. Plus, anytime she considers trying alcohol, she imagines a video of a drunk Clone Girl stumbling down the street going viral.

Arthur leans back, takes a sip of his drink, then tips the lime wedge from the glass's edge to its interior. "You're just like her," he says with a small shake of his head.

Linda blinks, confused. "Like . . . Madeline?" she asks.

"Mads?" He laughs softly. "No, you're like Lorelei." He looks away to stare at the table. Linda feels nervous sweat dampening her armpits. Arthur rarely speaks of Madeline and never of Lorelei. Even more than she doesn't want to be likened to Lorelei, Linda wants him to keep talking.

Arthur puts his drink down. "Sorry," he says. "I . . . Claire and I are getting a divorce. She wants kids." Linda's throat feels like it's been soldered shut. Her silence doesn't seem to matter; Arthur continues. "I told her from the start that I couldn't. And that I didn't want to adopt. I'd rather . . . I give *tens* of thousands to those orphan charities each year, and we've got our youth initiative. Last year we raised nearly five million and put every *cent* toward getting STEM education into disadvantaged neighborhoods. And then there's . . ." He pauses and looks at Linda, then flicks his eyes quickly away. "But it's not enough for her. After almost twenty years, she suddenly needs kids? It's bullshit."

A heavy silence descends over their table. Happy chatter echoes through the rest of the restaurant, and Linda hears the distinct chime of two glasses meeting in a toast. Arthur sucks up the last of his drink, then raises his hand to order another. Linda's never seen him order a second drink before their appetizers arrive. She notices the pink tinge to his eyes and wonders if it's only his second.

"I'm sorry to hear that," says Linda.

Arthur shrugs and rubs at his face. "I knew it was coming. Or I should have. The baby thing is an excuse. She's too old for that anyway, just like me. Though," he laughs again, lightly, painfully, "apparently she froze her eggs years ago, right after you came to live with us. Didn't even tell me." He grips his chin; when he releases it, his face blooms into a forced smile. "At least they're not fertilized, right? Imagine all this"—he waves his hand, indicating Linda or perhaps the entire world—"happening again."

Linda has no reply. Replying to this is impossible. The ice in her water shifts, releasing a tiny clatter as it settles farther down into the glass.

"Anyway," says Arthur. "How are you? Go on any fun excursions lately?"

This is her first time leaving her apartment building since she went to Cedar Lake, but if he hasn't been checking the excursion logs, she's not going to tell him. "I walked with my neighbor's dog," she says. It's only been a week since she held Nibbler's leash, so it's not a lie.

The server arrives with their drinks and leaves with Arthur's empty glass and their order. More silence. They each take a sip. The orange juice must have been poured at room temperature; it's watery from melting ice.

"Maddy always wanted a dog," says Arthur suddenly. He's staring past Linda. "I guess all kids do. But Lorelei had her foxes and the chickens, and that was already a volatile combination. Plus, the kid we paid to take care of the animals when we were in the city was nice enough, and I liked helping him out, but it was all a hassle. It didn't make sense to get a dog too. We let Mads have anything she wanted in a tank or a cage, though. For her eighth birthday, all she wanted was hermit crabs. That was her list: a piece of printer paper with *hermit crabs* written in huge letters across it." He smiles, and this time it seems genuine, if sad. "We got her a tank half the size of this table, a dozen crabs, all sorts of extra shells and little castles for them to crawl around in. It was cute, but it *stank*."

Arthur's never talked about Madeline this much. If this is because he's having extra drinks, Linda wants him to have even more.

He takes another sip and continues. "She gave each crab a name, and every time one died—and those suckers didn't last long—we had a little funeral for it. *Every* time. We buried them all back by the garden and put little stones on top to mark the graves—"

"The shell garden," Linda whispers. She knows where he's talking about: a small extra-rocky patch of land. One day she decided to dig there to see if the rocks were a surface phenomenon or if they continued below. She found the shells—a confusing and wondrous discovery. Some were crushed and broken, others whole. A mix of colors, natural and painted. When she scrubbed the dirt from one, she found a chipped and faded blue flower. She spent days digging, looking for more, then spread the shells between her various hidey-holes, entranced by the color and mystery of them.

"The shell garden?" asks Arthur.

"I found them," she says, because in her surprise she already gave that much away. "I . . . the shells, I thought they might be from ancient snails." There were books on mythology in the house, and she imagined a primitive people living on the property, painting the shells to honor their gods. She remembers cupping the flower-painted one in her palms and whispering, "Bring Emmer back." Just to see if it might work.

Arthur drains his gin and tonic, shaking his head with a half smile Linda can't interpret. "It's so strange to think of you growing up there. I was so worried about Lor at first. She never replied to any of my emails, and I . . . I drove out there once, you know. On a work trip. I climbed over the gate and I found her inside, down in the basement. When she saw me, she said, 'You're back.' Like I was there to stay. But I just . . . I wanted to know she was *alive*." He flags down their server and orders drink three. "You're sure you don't want a real drink?" he asks Linda. She shakes her head. Arthur rolls his eyes and waves the server away.

"She thought I was there to stay," he says to Linda. "Can you imagine?"

Can she imagine Arthur being there when she was a child? Him and Lorelei happy together? Every Christmas like the one she remembers, except with two pairs of welcoming arms at the bottom of the hill instead of one?

Yes, she can.

"I should have realized she'd lost her mind," says Arthur. "I mean, look at her mother. From the timing, she . . . she must have at least had the embryos in her possession by then. She might even have already done it." In a low voice he adds, "She asked me to stay, told me everything could be like it used to be. I thought it was just normal bullshit, but, no—she was already working on creating you."

Linda twirls the skinny black straw in her juice. Tears push at her eyes with the pressure of what might have been.

"I thought the notes on the whiteboard were about her foxes," says Arthur. "I barely even looked at them."

By the time Linda was old enough to remember anything, the foxes were long gone, their hutch—she'd always known that the old hutch used to hold foxes, though she has no memory of being told that—falling into disrepair. It never occurred to her to wonder what happened to them; they were simply something that had once existed and now no longer did.

But a few summers before she left—when she was probably nine or ten years old—she saw a red fox with a streak of white like an hourglass down his face standing beside the dock just before dusk. It wasn't her first time seeing a fox on the property, but it was the first time the animal didn't dart away as soon as it noticed her. The fox was small, young, and he cocked his head at her, unafraid. Linda sat in the grass and cocked her head back at him. Eventually he scampered away into the woods, but he was there again the next day. And the next. He was a skinny thing, his fur ragged. Linda decided to feed him. She wasn't sure what he would like, so she made him a platter on a log: a whole chicken egg, a cracked chicken egg in a bowl, a trout from the pond. She thought about adding a frog too, but she felt a special fondness for the frogs and didn't want to kill one if the other options would do.

She set out the food in the late afternoon, earlier than she normally saw him, then retreated to a nonthreatening distance. When the fox appeared, he trotted soundlessly to the log and slurped up the cracked egg before yanking the trout into the grass. She couldn't see him as he ate, but she heard snuffling and faint tearing and cracking sounds. Afterward, the fox hopped atop the log and stared at her. She looked again at the hourglass pattern of white across his face and named him Chrono.

She'd forgotten that part. Chrono.

"Why are you smiling?" asks Arthur.

Linda startles. "I was . . ." Arthur is telling her so much, perhaps it's only fair for her to reciprocate in this small way. "I was remembering a fox. I think he must have been descended from the ones Lorelei bred." Chrono let her touch him once, weeks after he first appeared. She held a chunk of fish in one hand and extended the other. When he dipped his head forward to take the flesh, she ran her fingers gently along the fur of his flank. Chrono looked at her—a warning, she thought—and she stopped. But after that she started seeing him on different parts of the property at different times of the day, eyeing her from a distance.

"She wasn't still breeding them?" asks Arthur.

"No," says Linda. "Not that I remember." She and Emmer used to play in the hutch. They liked to pretend they were foxes, or sometimes human ghosts. Then a tree branch fell a winter or two after Emmer disappeared, crushing the roof. Linda tugged the branch off, but there was no salvaging the structure.

"She loved those damned foxes," says Arthur. "I remember when she bred her first silver. She was so excited. Always said that as much as she loved her work with the foundation, that was more her parents' thing. The foxes were all hers." He laughs slightly. "Did you know she wanted to give Maddy the middle name Mendel?" Linda doesn't know why that's funny, and Arthur doesn't explain. "I talked her into using Rosalind Franklin as inspiration instead. She liked that. Franklin wasn't much acknowledged back then."

His third drink arrives and, not long afterward, their array of appetizers. They eat in silence for a while, then Arthur asks, "Did anything *good* ever happen to you there?"

"On the property?" Arthur nods. What to give him? It has to be a story without Emmer. She stares at the shrimp poppers. "We celebrated Christmas once," she says. Dr. Tambor is the only person she's ever told this story, and voicing it is difficult. "It didn't snow often, not more than a dusting, but the night before there'd been a real storm. Several inches of snow, maybe half a foot. And—it's the only year I remember Lorelei giving me a gift—I walked into the living room and there it was: a bright green sled. Not one of the cart-shaped ones, a round one. A disc. It had a red bow on it, and it was there, perfect, this beautiful *new* thing. So I tore off the bow and ran outside to the back hill." Remembered joy bubbles up within her; it feels good to be telling Arthur this, better than she would have guessed. "I trudged up the hill and cascaded down, sliding atop the snow. I remember laughing, and spilling at the bottom, toppling off the sled as it slid to a stop. Lorelei was down there, her arms held wide, waiting for me. I remember her taking a scarf and wrapping it around me, then holding my hand and helping me back up the hill so I could go again."

When she finishes, she can't look at Arthur. She feels too raw.

Dr. Tambor told her the memory was probably so strong because it was such a powerful exception to her everyday. Those are the things that stand out the most in memory, she said: the exceptions. Linda's glad there was an exception.

Arthur is silent. Linda glances up, expecting to see that heavy pity she's so used to receiving from him.

But Arthur's face is set in hard disgust—his lip curled, his brow furrowed. Linda's heart beats toward panic. She doesn't know what she did wrong.

"That was *our* Christmas," he says. "We always went to Hawaii to visit my parents, but the year after we built the Cedar Lake house we went there instead, and that—that couldn't have happened to you."

Linda can't look at his face, but she sees that his hand is shaking. She's shaking too. She wants to curl into a ball, hide her eyes, her face, her everything. Anything to make this moment stop. "I don't understand," she whispers. "I remember it."

Arthur takes another drink. "No," he says. "*I* remember it. On the drive over, we heard a radio report about expected snowfall. Four to six inches overnight. We hadn't been home for Christmas since Maddy was born. I remember her squirming in her car seat, she was so excited. When we stopped at a gas station, I ran over to a hardware store next door, bought a sled, and hid it in the trunk while the girls were in the bathroom. It was a cheap green disc sled, and Lor tied a red scarf my mother had knitted around it to look like a bow."

She hears the ownership in his voice—the simmering anger—and a sense of guilt swarms her: How dare she take this memory from him?

But she didn't take anything. She was given this: one of her only two unequivocally good memories of Lorelei. She begins to feel angry too. She has so little. She can't afford for Arthur to take this from her.

"You really think that happened to you?" asks Arthur. His voice is softer now, his drink finished.

"It *did* happen to me." She's furious but feels as though she's going to cry. Anger shouldn't feel this way; she should feel strong—righteous. She can't even do anger right.

"Maybe . . ." Arthur's fingers drum the table. His voice takes on a tone of desperate reasoning. "God, maybe she reenacted it? The sled could still have been there; we kept it in the garage."

Linda doesn't want to believe that either—that it happened but it was staged.

A sick taste invades her mouth: That actually makes more sense than the experience being authentically her own. Somehow, her understanding that so much of her childhood was a test hadn't infiltrated this memory. She always thought of the sled as being a reward, but it could have been a test. Lorelei wanted her and Emmer to be Madeline, and if she seemed to love Linda in that moment it was only because she acted as Madeline had. As any child would on a snowy Christmas morning. Fresh snow, a sled. The easiest test she ever faced.

Linda squeezes her eyes shut. The pain is unbearable. She can't feel this way in public, where strangers can see. Where Arthur can see.

"I have to go," she says, and she can hear it in her voice: all her pain, bubbling to the surface.

"Linda," says Arthur. But that's all he says. Linda sits in his silence for three beats of her heart, and then she walks out.

From: Arthur Niequist   Sent 11:03 A.M. 6/1/2004
To: Lorelei Niequist
RE: Checking in

Hey Lor,

Sorry I overreacted about the fence. The house just felt so different walled in like that. But of course the fence isn't really what made it feel different.

I don't want to send mixed messages and I know this isn't my role anymore, but if you ever need anything, please let me know. I know things got heated, but I still care about you. I always will.

If I don't hear back, I'll assume you don't want contact. If so, I understand.

Art

From: Lorelei Niequist   Draft Saved 11:55 A.M. 6/1/2004
To: Arthur Niequist
RE: RE: Checking in

It started the same. The soreness in my left breast.

I kept waiting for you to notice. I know it's too soon, but part of me still expected you to notice. I even thought you might have somehow sensed it from afar. Nonsense, I know, but why else would you have come if not for her?

If I'd told you, would you have stayed?

13.

nvi flicks at her Sheath, trying to decide what to order for dinner. Thai maybe. She doesn't really care. Her heart aches from talking to her mother and pretending everything is fine. She's also annoyed at herself for not responding to Linda yet, but she's drained from the call and needs some time.

She drops her arm and turns on the television. Some animated inanity would be perfect right now. She navigates to her favorite show, then scrolls through seasons and episodes. Nibbler's Santy Claws is at her feet, its coat matted by saliva, and she lingers on a holiday special before scrolling by.

In her text, Linda said she'd been away from her Sheath. The only way anyone is ever away from their Sheath is if they use Augments. Which Linda doesn't. Anvi envisions Linda lying comatose in bed. So much has happened to Linda—in her life, in the last week—it would be surprising if she *wasn't* depressed. Anvi should really text her back, invite her over to play with Nibbler.

Her Sheath pings with an alert: *Butterflies*. Her code—chosen by a random word generator—for anything to do with Linda.

It's a news article translated from Portuguese. She skims to the highlight; it's just a typo or a poor translation and doesn't have anything to do with Linda: *Dr. Cardoso stated, "If I had funding to clone girl child I would be willing to try."*

Her keyword alerts catch the occasional article involving reproductive cloning—either because someone made a passing reference to how Linda isn't a clone and please stop calling her that, or because of slips like this. Anvi skims most of them, at first to be sure they weren't relevant and now because she finds them interesting. Turns out, human reproductive cloning is entirely possible but such an ethical morass that no reputable institution will fund it. Most nations even have outright bans in place. Anvi has considered the moral implications of duplicating a person before—some of her favorite books and shows as a kid were based on that premise—but what she didn't realize was that the process scientists use to replicate sheep and dogs—even a woolly mammoth—is so complex, no single instance can be guaranteed to work. For each successful clone, dozens if not hundreds of unviable embryos are also created. One article she found showed images of jar after jar of malformed mammoth fetuses that failed to reach maturity. The technology is getting better, but the more complicated the organism, the more things can go wrong. Any attempt to clone a human is all but guaranteed to produce failures: twisted creatures who never had a real chance at life. Probably a lot of them. It's a completely different deal from therapeutic cloning—stem cells—and as unethical as fuck. Anvi's seen references to this Dr. Cardoso before; he is one of the very few scientists who seem to think the failures might be worth the success, but even his interest strikes her as more intellectual than practical. If Anvi had to put money on it, she'd guess he's just playing devil's advocate. Still makes him a creep, though.

She files the article without finishing it. Nibbler pads into the room, stretching first into what Anvi likes to call his downward-facing me, then its inverse. Back in Ithaca, she would joke with her friends about how they should pool their money and make a bunch of Nibbler clones, so they could each have the perfect dog. She's also considered it more seriously as an option for many, many years from now, when he dies from natural causes at a record-breaking age. But thinking of the possibility of failed copies—she'll never do it now.

Nibbler nuzzles her calf, and Anvi slips to the floor to give him a hug. "What do you think?" she asks. "Thai? Mexican? Teriyaki?" He licks her. "Roasted squirrel, got it. I'll see what I can do."

She looks out the window at the night sky. It feels so strange that it's January and there's no snow, that she can walk outside and her nose hairs won't prickle and freeze with her first breath. She always complained about Ithaca's frigid winters, but now she wonders if she'll get used to their absence.

Worse is the lack of friends. She misses walking out her door and running into faces she's known for years. She misses throwing inside jokes over her shoulder as she exits a coffee shop. She wonders if she'll ever have that again. If getting as far away from Tasha as possible was worth giving up all the rest.

Nibbler pads toward the front door, ears pricked. Someone must be walking by. It could be Linda. She should check, but Anvi can't quite summon the energy. Tomorrow, she thinks. She'll check in with Linda tomorrow.

Linda doesn't know where the driver is, doesn't care. She walks home in the dark. Her heels and toes start screaming after a block. She refuses to limp, refuses to slow down. Soon, she can feel wetness collecting in her socks. A man sticks his hand out, asking for money, and she pushes past him—though part of her wants to give him everything she has, if only he'll take the burden of her identity along with her unearned wealth.

By the time she reaches her building, her feet are swimming in blood. But she's still angry, still hurt, and she takes the stairs. As she closes her apartment door behind herself, her legs begin to wobble. She kicks off her boots, peels away her blood-soaked socks, and changes into a T-shirt before grabbing her tablet and throwing herself into her nest chair.

The video she wants is easy to find. A quick search and there they are: Arthur and Lorelei Niequist, standing at a podium outside the Cedar Lake Police Department. It's been years since she last watched this recording, and she feels a jolt at seeing Lorelei's drawn face. She never sees her own face in any of the old photos of Lorelei smiling and laughing, but here, with sorrow weighing down her mother's features, she does. Their starkly different noses notwithstanding, it's like looking at her future self—one that never finds happiness.

"We want to thank the Cedar Lake police, rangers, and all the volunteers for their help during this hard time," Arthur's voice croaks from her tablet. "Our sorrow is immense, but so is our gratitude, and we know that our Mads—" His voice cracks here. Lorelei's jaw clenches, and she slides her hand into her husband's. Arthur closes his eyes for a second, then powers on. "Mads would also be grateful for all this community has done for our family. She loved this town. Thank you again, all of you, for your support and friendship." He lifts his free hand to pinch the bridge of his nose. "Thank you," he says again. Then he and Lorelei step away from the podium and retreat into the police station.

His darling *Mads*, thinks Linda. *Mads* is the one who was gifted a sled. *Mads* is the one who was loved. The nickname is symptomatic of a bond she can never penetrate or share. She's known that since before she even knew of the nickname, since the first moment she met Arthur—and yet she feels it as painfully as ever now, curled in her chair watching younger versions of her biological parents mourn the daughter they loved together.

Somehow, some indeterminate time later, she falls asleep. Her conversation with Arthur runs through fitful dreams: images of foxes and hermit-crab shells and a towering, frowning Lorelei.

In the morning, as she uncurls and sets her scabbed and painful feet on the floor, Linda gets a mental flash from a fading dream: Lorelei tying a red scarf into a noose around Linda's neck.

She can't take it; this hurts too much. She rises, kicks aside her bloody socks and boots, and, without putting on pants, brushing her teeth, or even taking a drink of water, retreats into the world of Fury and Honor. She imagines that the pain in her feet is part of the world—that her mana-boosting boots come with a blood price.

Her game resumes with Briggs standing on her dock. It's level now; Linda figured out how to shape the logs into boards using an ax. The pond—that's how she thinks of it, even if it's big enough to be a lake—extends before her, rippling in the sunlight. A dragonfly buzzes by her face.

Linda turns. Her house stands before her, not as she last saw it, not even as she remembers it, but as she imagines it could have been: the perfect yellow of a cartoon sun. It took her hours to build the house but only seconds to paint it. In this world, it stands close to the pond, only two tiles away. She's condensed the essentials of her childhood. All that's missing is her tree. She doesn't know how to shape a living tree.

She steps off the dock and walks the two steps to her perfect yellow house. She doesn't go inside. The inside is still barren; she wishes she could drag the fingerprint-clad table through the interface into this world.

The same stag she saw when she first discovered the pond crosses her line of sight. They've been sharing this land, but today possessiveness flares through Linda. This is *her* home. She claps and fans her hands, shooting a lightning bolt at the deer. He rears and sizzles, smoke rising from his antlers, then collapses as a black, charred mass.

She chokes back a surge of guilt, then goes to loot the corpse. Otherwise it won't disappear.

Then—her inventory one deerskin and a set of antlers richer—she wanders back to her dock. She wants to build her wall next, but she's not sure what material to use. Sheet metal doesn't exist in Rothram. Maybe there's a way to make it, but she doesn't know if that would require carpentry or blacksmithery. She's massively leveled up the former skill stat in the last few days but is still a beginner at the latter.

Her feet are screaming; it feels like she's standing in a pit of glass. It's better if she keeps moving.

She opens the fast-travel menu and taps *Rothram City,* this land's capital.

The pond fades to black. Helpful tips scroll across Linda's vision while she waits for the city to load. *Combine items to improve your crafting skill. You never know what you might discover!*

The town square generates before her. Linda ignores the elven woman crying on the temple's stoop and instead heads straight for Minions.

Baby dragons caw at her entrance, their price tags more than she's yet to collect in all her adventuring combined. Kittens peer at her from their cages, and one old yellow-white cat with a missing ear paces along the store's topmost shelves. Linda-as-Briggs walks past them and the two-headed-amphibian display to the back kennel, where three young pups topple over one another. She taps the purchase icon and enters the bartering screen, where the shopkeeper appears: a craggy, dark-skinned old man in a dirty apron.

Linda doesn't barter. She selects a fluffy white-and-brown male and pays full price: about half of her accumulated gold.

The puppy follows her out of the store, yapping. Linda watches him closely as he prances around her feet, worried he might run off into the streets.

"What an adorable beast," says a voice behind her. Linda turns to find a scaly-skinned Lacertilian smiling at her with pointed teeth.

The same species as the individuals who tricked her at the beginning of the game. They aren't all bad—an early mission involved working with one to take down the ring of thieves and murderers who kidnapped her to start—but she doesn't trust him. "What's its name?" asks the Lacertilian.

The naming screen pops up. Her only thought is Nibbler, but that feels somehow sacrilegious. She taps the *Random* button until *Pickles* flickers into place.

Pickles. It almost makes her smile. She taps *Accept*.

"That's a stupid name," says the Lacertilian. Pickles sits at Linda's feet and growls at him; Linda feels a flicker of affection for the virtual dog. The Lacertilian laughs and walks away.

She reaches down and picks up Pickles. She can feel the puppy's weight in her hands. He squirms, his brown eyes bright, his tongue lapping toward her face. Linda wishes she could feel his fur. Wishes she could sink her face into the animal's neck. But even at this physical remove, Linda warms to him. This dog might not be real, but he's hers.

While Linda stocks up on potions and carpentry supplies, Pickles yaps along beside her. In his company she feels the pain in her feet less. Her gold supply is getting low. If she wants to finish building her home, she needs more gold. She heads back to the adventure board at the center of town. Pickles prances along too; it seems he's programmed to stick to her side. The listings on the board range from collecting bear pelts to defending a family farm from a suspected werewolf. Linda chooses an easy-rated job clearing goblins out of an old watchtower. She doesn't want a challenge right now.

She fast-travels to the waypoint nearest the watchtower, then heads down a path toward the river. Tiny purple flowers sway in the breeze on either side. Pickles frolics among them, at one point chomping on a blossom, then sneezing as its fluff invades his nose. Linda finds herself laughing—and feeling something shockingly close to love.

The watchtower slides into view beside the curve of the river. She sees movement in one of its windows. She double-checks that her lightning spell is equipped and selects a poisoned dagger from her inventory for her belt slot.

Pickles at her side, she strides toward the tower.

A war cry sounds from above. Linda glances up and sees a round green face grimacing at her. The goblins are on their way. They pour out of the watchtower's entrance—a dozen, at least. She has to wait for them to get closer before casting her spell. The goblins spread out as they advance; it'll take at least two castings to get them all. She summons her lightning to its maximum power, then fans her palms. Electricity shudders and spikes through the rightmost group of goblins, killing about half of them. The rest keep coming. An arrow whizzes by her ear, shot from the tower above. She didn't anticipate that, but she should have.

Linda starts walking backward, drawing the goblins toward her, hoping to elude the arrows, and letting her lightning spell recharge.

She releases her next barrage of lightning just as the goblins come within arm's reach. She watches their faces spasm as they sizzle and fall. She equips her dagger—now to get the stragglers.

A yelp to her left. Linda pivots to see Pickles struggling against the grasp of a particularly fat goblin. Horror spikes through her. It didn't occur to her that they might be able to attack the dog.

The goblin sinks his teeth into the dog's neck; Pickles cries sharply as blood bursts across his soft coat.

Frantic, Linda tells herself the dog is not a *him* but an *it,* and barely even that—an unfeeling, unthinking program. That isn't blood soaking through its fur; it's just a graphic effect. This is just a game. And yet as Pickles goes limp, the loss hits her so viscerally she thinks she might collapse.

The goblin tosses the dog's body to the ground and advances toward Linda.

Linda's vision flashes red; she's being attacked from the right. Her health meter drops by a notch. The froggish croaks of enraged goblins sound in her ears. But all she can do is stare at Pickles, dead upon the grass.

She tears off her headset and throws it to the floor. Pickles's yelp echoes in her ears. She wipes at her eyes, but she can't stop the tears coursing down her cheeks.

Furious and ashamed that she allowed herself to be tricked into caring, she kicks her headset across the room. She tosses her gloves after it, then retreats to her nest chair and scrubs her eyes with her blanket.

It's just a game. But pulsing blood plays again in her memory. That yelp. Her throat feels clogged and her nose is thick with snot.

She hears her Sheath buzzing from the kitchen counter. Messages from Arthur, probably. Linda doesn't care. She curls deeper into her chair. She isn't crying anymore, but her sorrow hovers beneath her skin.

Time passes. Her Sheath buzzes insistently. If it didn't require her to stand, she'd throw it out the window.

Urgent knocking erupts at the door.

Linda startles, then settles back and pulls her blanket over herself. It's probably Arthur, coming to scold her about all the ways in which her existence encroaches on his memories of his real daughter. He has a key. She waits for him to either use it or leave.

Thud thud thud. Then the doorbell. Then more knocking.

Go away, she thinks.

"Linda?" Muffled through the door.

It isn't Arthur's voice. It's Anvi's.

Linda springs to her feet and looks out the peephole. Anvi's wearing a long, fuzzy robe and her hair is in disarray, half of her purple swath sticking straight up.

Linda wipes her eyes a final time, then opens the door.

Anvi grabs her by the arm. "We have to go."

"What? Why?"

"Didn't you get my texts? It's your address. Someone posted it online." Linda can't quite parse what Anvi's saying. Anvi elaborates slowly, peering directly into Linda's eyes: "Linda, those people who say you shouldn't exist—they know where you live."

14.

"Grab your things and come on," says Anvi. "We can at least get you as far as my apartment." Linda watches Anvi's eyes slide over her. "And you should probably put on some pants."

The urgency in her voice dazes Linda into compliance. She walks into her bedroom to change into fresh clothing. Anvi waits by the CircleTread.

"When did you get all this?" calls Anvi.

Linda pulls on a pair of pants. "Monday."

"Is *that* what you've been doing since we got back?"

Linda hesitates, sensing an opportunity. She slips on a fresh camisole and long-sleeved T-shirt, then steps back into the room. "Yes." Her cheeks redden with the half-truth. "I'm sorry I didn't text you back sooner," she adds. They're difficult words to say, even though she means them.

"Did you think I was angry?" Anvi touches Linda's arm. "Just because instantaneous communication is possible doesn't make it mandatory. Always feel free to take your sweet time." She smiles. "I'm just sad I missed baby's first VR bender." The smile fades as she looks down. "What happened to your feet?"

Linda follows her eyes to the split blisters and crusted blood. Red smears cover the floor, as well as the seat of her nest chair's cushion. "I walked too far in those," she says, gesturing toward the boots.

"Yikes. You can clean up at my place. Do you have a bag? What else do you need?"

Linda picks up her Sheath and straps it on. The screen is flush with texts, and it looks like most are from Anvi. She grabs her jacket and sneakers. "I don't need anything else." Linda locks the door and follows Anvi over to her apartment. Anvi waves her inside, looking warily toward the elevator. Linda is touched by her concern, but she doesn't share it. Over the years she's noticed that true vitriol and threats of violence tended to stay online. Even the woman who spat at her last summer hadn't tracked her down from her publicized address but was a familiar face from across the street. In fact, no one did anything in response to Linda's address being made public last year—no one except Arthur, who made her move. Truly, that's what concerns her the most right now: that Arthur will shuffle her to yet another apartment that could never feel like home. This nascent friendship with Anvi—if that's indeed what this is—is bound to be snuffed out as soon as they're no longer neighbors.

There are fewer plastic crates in Anvi's apartment than last time, and scattered clutter—dishes, books, electronic knickknacks—makes the space look more lived in. Nibbler is curled in a dog bed in the corner. He lifts his head just enough to look at Linda before groaning and settling back in. She thinks of fictional Pickles, dead—and then she thinks of Chrono the fox. She thinks of Arthur telling her one of her favorite memories isn't real.

It strikes her suddenly that Emmer isn't in her Christmas memory. She was young, young enough that Emmer should be there. This realization rocks Linda. It means Emmer must have been being punished at the time—which in turn means she wasn't as perfect as Linda remembers. Linda doesn't want to believe it. She wants to remember Emmer as flawless. That's the history she knows.

It's strange—since leaving Cedar Lake, she's felt the urge to go back to thinking Emmer's alive. Her instinct is to envision her out there somewhere, an adventurous maverick, like a heroine out of some modern fairy tale. Every cell of Linda's being wants to believe this.

But she won't let herself. Not anymore.

Her new theory: On some unremembered day, Lorelei told Linda to be scarce, and then while Linda sat in her tree sounding out the words in a book, Lorelei dug Emmer's grave. Probably outside the wall so Linda wouldn't find it.

It's such a simple and terrible answer. The only other one she can think of is that Lorelei crammed Emmer's body into that dark, dank hole in the basement—the well. After some research, she thinks that's what the hole must have been. Either option explains why the police didn't find Emmer's remains, but the latter is the one that's been giving Linda nightmares.

"Sorry about the text deluge," says Anvi. "I saw your address online, and this asshole was saying that the conclusions about the fire are a lie, that you set it for attention. *Let's give her the attention she clearly wants,* he said. It pissed me off and honestly made me panic a little." She sits on the floor next to Nibbler and scratches between his shoulder blades. "It was an unmoderated forum outside of Social-Hub. I tagged it as a privacy violation to prevent links, but there's really no going back from something like this."

"I know," says Linda.

"I was going to call the police, but I thought I should get you first."

"We don't need to call the police," says Linda. Officer Baldwin wasn't bad, but in general, being around law enforcement turns her into the scared little girl she was the night she left the property. She'll tell Arthur about her address being posted and let him handle it as he handles everything. But not yet. She isn't ready to talk to him again.

"Are you sure?"

"Arthur will take care of it," says Linda.

"Right," says Anvi, as though remembering who her father is. Then she asks, "Do you want something for your feet?"

There are tacky red smears across Anvi's floor. "Do you have any plastic bags?" asks Linda. "I can cover them, and I'll clean that."

"I don't care about the floor," says Anvi. "That's not why I asked."

"Oh." She can feel Anvi staring at her, and she refuses to look up. "It's just blisters."

"At least sit down and I'll bring you a towel."

Linda does as she's told; Anvi disappears down the hall, then reappears with a dry towel, a wet washcloth, and the antibacterial spray she bought at the Cedar Lake Walgreens. Linda thanks her and wipes as much blood from her feet as she can. A thumbnail-sized flap of skin dangles from her left heel. She carefully lays it back in place over a raw patch, then sets both her feet down on the clean towel. She doesn't use the spray.

Meanwhile, Anvi gets dressed and makes breakfast—eggs. Linda takes a few bites to be polite. It makes her think of the yellow scrambles she used to make as a child. The occasional crunch of shell between her teeth, and the time a half-formed chick fell into the pan—its eyes huge and senseless.

She didn't see any chickens when she went back. She doesn't know what happened to them. Maybe they were dispersed to local farms by an animal-rescue organization. Maybe they strutted out the open gate and were immediately eaten by coyotes.

They hear footsteps in the hallway. Anvi hurries to the peephole, then glances back at Linda. "It's just Mr. Lewis from 703. Hard to imagine he's in league with back-forum assholes."

A. Lewis is a chubby, middle-aged black man with a goatee. It took Linda weeks of watching through the peephole to match his face to the correct name on the mailboxes below.

Anvi just knocked on his door and asked.

As Anvi stacks their plates into the dishwasher, Nibbler unfurls from his bed and goes and sits by the door. He looks over his shoulder at Anvi and whines.

"I have to walk him," says Anvi. "You'll be okay here?"

Linda nods. She's sitting on the couch, her feet firmly on the towel. She thinks of asking to go with Anvi but doesn't know if she can stomach putting on shoes.

As Anvi locks the door from the hallway, Linda feels panic creeping in. But she catches herself—she can unlock the door from inside. She can leave if she wants.

It's strange being alone in someone else's home. In Connecticut, whenever she was alone at Arthur's house, she usually just stayed in the room assigned to her and read, watched nature documentaries, or stared out the window, feeling out of place. Which is exactly how she feels now. She sits stiffly on the couch, not wanting to get her bloody feet anywhere. Not wanting to move something Anvi doesn't want moved. Not wanting to have any sort of impact at all.

Her thoughts spiral toward Emmer. Maybe Linda was older than she thinks that Christmas. But it seems impossible that Lorelei would have acted so kindly toward Linda after Emmer was gone, because after Emmer left—after Emmer *died*—the contests stopped. Didn't they?

She's not sure. Her memories feel out of sequence now— suspicious. The narrative thread of her childhood is fraying, and the only resources she has are her own mind and memory. She can't confirm anything.

A key slides into the lock, and Linda wishes it could be Emmer opening the door. She imagines an adult Emmer being adjusted to this world, comfortable in it. Fashionable boots wouldn't make her feet bleed.

"I didn't see anything suspicious," reports Anvi as she lets Nibbler off his leash. His nails clack as he prances over to Linda, but she can barely pet him before he scrambles to the kitchen to lap up water from his dish.

"No frenzied townspeople with torches and pitchforks?" asks Linda.

Anvi cocks her head at her and smiles. "Was that a joke?"

Linda shrugs. Anvi hangs up her coat and comes to sit beside her, at the opposite end of the couch.

"Maybe I overreacted," says Anvi. "But when I saw it, I . . . You see what some of those people say and it's not hard to imagine someone doing something crazy. It just takes one."

"I know," says Linda.

"Have you told your father?"

"Not yet."

Anvi curls her feet under herself. She looks like she's formulating another question, but Linda needs a break from conversation. She turns to her Sheath. The top message is from Arthur: *I'm sorry. Last night got out of hand. Can we try again tonight?*

She swipes to minimize it. As soon as he knows what's happened, he'll take action, and Linda wants to pretend to be normal for as long as she can. Sitting beside someone who might actually care, a dog at their feet. Once she replies, she may never have another moment like this.

Anvi's living room is peaceful, but the day's headlines are not. There's a terrorist attack in London, a school shooting in Arizona, the tanking of a starlet's debut music album, and a death in China—the world's first successful human-head transplant patient, who just passed away after spending the last four months on a respirator. Wonder and horror build up in Linda as she stares at the last. The article preview says the transplant happened last October, and she's surprised she doesn't remember reading about it.

She keeps scrolling. There's nothing about Clone Girl's current address being released to the world. Last time, it was all over the news. Perhaps this kind of thing isn't as big a deal the second time around, or maybe Anvi reported it quickly enough to mitigate the damage. Hope darts through her: Maybe she won't have to move after all. She doesn't want to live in the city, but if she has to, she wants to be near Anvi and Nibbler.

Headlines update. The one about the shooting becomes more detailed: SEVEN DEAD IN SECOND SCHOOL SHOOTING THIS MONTH.

Linda didn't realize it was a second shooting. She thought she'd already read about this one. She taps to read more. It happened yesterday, after regular school hours. The middle school was equipped with a security system that upon detecting gunfire automatically locked down every classroom, magnetically securing bulletproof doors. But the shooter was already in a classroom when the system was triggered. So instead of keeping the other kids safe, it locked the boy's victims in with him. Linda skips over a link to a piece about the inevitable lawsuit against the security company.

SocialHub moderators blocked the shooter's livestream before any shots were fired—a feat possible because of their ten-second broadcast delay and a maze of algorithms designed to tag possible content code violations for real-time review. But from security footage, they know the robotics club's supervisor tried to talk the boy down, softly reciting empathetic talking points he learned during active shooter training, before taking a cluster of bullets in the chest. Next, the boy took down his terrified classmates. One girl rushed the shooter, holding her backpack before her like a shield, but it was useless. The boy didn't flinch as he pulled the trigger again. The article emphasizes that detail: He didn't flinch. Linda wonders why anyone would expect him to flinch then if he didn't before.

Finally, the boy let the semiautomatic rifle—his father's legal property—fall to his side and walked to the classroom's smartboard, where he wrote a short note, the lettering darting through the splatter of his teacher's blood, before pulling out a handgun and shooting himself in the head. His note quoted the theme song of a popular children's cartoon—a message of sharing and caring.

A pop-up announces that the producers of the cartoon have issued a statement condemning violence and offering condolences to the families. There's a video of the show's main character—a big-eyed sloth—urging children who feel isolated to seek help. Linda stares at the character for a moment, her stomach thick with a sense of wrongness she can't articulate, then she swipes the pop-up closed, returning to the main article.

One girl survived. An older boy pinned her beneath him under a desk. The boy died quickly from a shot to the back of the head, his last words reportedly a whispered *play dead*. Soaked in her savior's blood, the girl followed his directive until the security system was overridden and help arrived. Her only physical injury was a bruise on her chin from hitting the floor. The hero boy had three younger sisters at home.

The shooter was twelve years old.

That fact pounds into Linda. It's the same age she was when she left the property. She imagines an automatic weapon in her childhood hands as she stepped out into that Cedar Lake street. She imagines pulling the trigger, holding it down. Spurts of blood and brain as each onlooker falls to the pavement. She imagines one of those onlookers as Dr. Tambor, who did die by bullet. Who played the same hero role as the boy with three sisters.

Linda drops her Sheath arm. Children shooting children—there's no logic to it. Or to her own existence, or to Anvi's kindness, or to a man's agreeing to have his head cut from his body and swapped onto another.

Maybe it's all a mistake, she thinks, remembering a different headline from weeks ago. Maybe this reality is actually a failed simulation, a typo in the code spiraling society toward violence and

madness. News sources seem to agree it's getting worse: errors com-
pounding.

"The simulation hypothesis," she says to Anvi. "Whatever happened to the man claiming to have proven it?"

"As far as I can tell, he just disappeared," says Anvi, tapping at her
own Sheath. "Made a crazy claim and then ran off into the sunset."

"You think it's crazy?"

"Not the theory as a whole—that's sound—but the timing. We're
just . . . we're not there yet. He was rabble-rousing or it was some sort
of ploy."

Anvi seems certain, but Linda thinks of how easy it is to lose herself in Fury and Honor. Yes, the colors of the world are a little too
bright, the characters a little cartoonish—but those are choices the
game designers made. She's watched ads for other games, ones that
look like the world in which she now exists. A world in which a door
can lock behind a child with a semiautomatic rifle, and some people
respond, This wouldn't have happened if the teacher had a gun too.

Linda thinks of herself on the other side of the equation: As one
of the soon-to-be dead huddling behind a desk as her fellows fall
beside her. Knowing her turn is coming, that she can't stop it. She
glances at Anvi and imagines her head snapping back as a bullet
punctures her brain, imagines Anvi joining Dr. Tambor and Emmer
first as decay and then as dust.

Sadness swells within her. People bemoan the inhumanity of her
childhood, but the outside world is so much worse.

Anvi's busy on her Sheath. "I can't find anything about G.H.," she
says. "Just speculative nonsense." She looks up. "Maybe when I start
work they'll give me secret access to the anonymous accounts, and
I'll be able to track him down." She laughs. She's probably joking.
Linda's not sure. Anvi scoots off the couch onto the floor to give Nibbler some vigorous pets. "You know," she says, "the really interesting
thing about the simulation hypothesis is the way it's become interwo-

ven with the idea of the singularity—this presumption that technology can create consciousness. That self-awareness can arise from programming."

"Can it?" asks Linda.

"I've yet to hear a substantive argument as to why not. I read this fascinating article the other day about brain mapping and how neurological circuits are essentially mathematical patterns. We don't understand it all yet, but it's becoming increasingly obvious that our sense of self, our identities, can be expressed mathematically. I mean, *everything* can, from the atomic structure of sand to how our eyes perceive and communicate light. And it's like, if we can *express* it mathematically, it stands to reason that we should eventually be able to *create* it mathematically, you know? Even fingerprints can be explained through formulae. Curvature and force, that's all individuality is."

Linda thinks of the table she salvaged from the property. She remembers pressing her small, ink-soaked thumb to its surface, Emmer beside her.

"What about memories?" she asks. "Are they just math too?"

Anvi looks up thoughtfully. "I guess? I mean, it's all brain circuitry. But I don't know. The brain's a tricky little bugger." She reaches across the floor to grab Nibbler's Santy Claws toy, then tosses it toward the door. Nibbler scrambles and leaps, catching it in his mouth. Anvi claps. "Good catch, Nibs!" After a second, Linda adds her own applause. Warmth spreads through her as she realizes that she actually feels comfortable here.

Over the next few hours, two new messages from Arthur pop up on Linda's screen. She'll need his help soon, but for now she ignores them.

Anvi orders delivery for lunch; it's Linda's first time eating from any of the ubiquitous teriyaki restaurants around the city, and she's surprised by how much she enjoys it. Anvi even lets her give Nibbler a piece, ordering the dog to spin in a circle first to earn it.

Anvi crams the takeout containers into her compost bin, then pops up with a little "Oh! I forgot. I downloaded a demo I think you'd like. It's a first-aid thing. Want to give it a try?"

It takes Linda a moment to realize she's talking about VR. She thinks of her system still running. She didn't pause the game, just tore off her gear; Briggs is undoubtedly dead at the hands of those easy-rated goblins. Which means the game is waiting for her to okay a reload to the most recent waypoint—when she exited the fast-travel stagecoach. Pickles will still be alive, will be alive again. She expected spending time with Nibbler would make her feel less attached to the virtual dog, but it's had the opposite effect. Somehow, their similarities trump the fact that one doesn't actually exist.

She wonders if she can protect Pickles. Maybe there's a command database she hasn't yet accessed where she can instruct the dog to wait by the road during quests. If not, maybe she can return him to Minions—or contain him to the land where she's reconstructing her home. That would be the best solution. She can't watch him die again.

"Okay," she says to Anvi. She doesn't want to try a new game, but she's also curious to see what Anvi thinks she might like.

"To the holodeck we go!" Anvi starts down the hall, then stops. "Do you want some socks, or are you more comfortable with bare feet?"

Linda inspects her feet, which she's kept firmly on the towel this whole time. They don't appear to be bleeding anymore. "Bare. If you don't mind."

"Your call," says Anvi. Linda follows her into the VR room; Nibbler stands at the doorway, wagging his tail. Unlike last time, he seems to understand he isn't allowed inside.

Linda places her Sheath on Anvi's desk and slips on the headset and gloves. Though she doesn't feel the trepidation she felt last time, it's still slightly jarring to hear Anvi's voice in her ear as she says, "Here we go."

The game world flares to life. Linda is standing in a forest. Around her are deciduous trees with smooth white bark speckled with dark knots. At first she thinks they are the birches she remembers from the East Coast, but something about them looks different. The bark is too bright, and unlined. It's a new-to-her tree, or perhaps a fictional one. Sunlight dapples the forest floor as simulated clouds drift overhead. Linda's aching feet are overlaid with red-laced hiking boots.

About a yard ahead of her, a small red box with a white cross on its lid sits on the ground. Linda walks over and picks it up. A large latch on the front of the box glows briefly, and she opens it. Inside there's a small booklet; when Linda touches it, the booklet disappears and lines of text appear:

Warning: This Program Is Not a Substitute for Medical Training.
Completing This Program Does Not Make You a Doctor.
It Doesn't Even Make You a Dentist.

. . .

But It Could Save Your Life.

Linda taps the text to continue.

Lesson One: Lacerations.

"Help!" The voice—young, male—comes from her right. Linda swivels to find a white teenager stumbling through the trees toward her. He's wearing jeans, a T-shirt, and a backpack; his left arm is covered in blood. She looks at his face. Gone is the cartoonish veneer of Fury and Honor; he registers not as CGI but as human. There is even a speckling of acne across his cheeks, and sunlight reflects from his scared-looking eyes.

The boy comes to a stop before her, breathing heavily. He holds out his arm. A three-inch gash runs down his forearm. Blood pumps out of the wound.

Step One: Control the Bleeding Using Direct Pressure and Elevation.
Linda already knows this. The boy is wearing a bandana around

his neck. She reaches for it. The boy recoils. "What are you doing?" he asks.

"I want to use your bandana to stop the bleeding," she says, articulating carefully for the program.

"Oh." The boy sniffles. "Okay." He reaches up with his uninjured arm and pulls the bandana from his neck. Linda takes it and folds it into a square just large enough to cover the full width of the cut. She places it on the wound.

"Hold this here," she tells the boy. "And lift your arm."

He does. Linda can see blood continuing to drip.

"Press harder," she says. "As tight as you can."

Ding. A chime of success from the game.

"Hey," says the boy. "It stopped. Thank you. What now?"

Step Two: Prevent Infection and Support Healing.

The bleeding would take longer than that to stop, but Linda flows with the game. She needs to flush the wound with clean water. She looks at the first-aid kit, which is back on the ground. Though she thoughtlessly dropped it earlier, it landed upright and open—the game designers clearly didn't put as much effort into physics emulation as they did into character rendering. She kneels to search through the kit.

"Linda," comes Anvi's voice. "Can you pause for a second?"

Linda taps her fingers to bring up the menu.

"I hear something in the hall," says Anvi. "Someone's saying your name."

Linda feels instantly sick. She peels off the headset and gloves and follows Anvi to the living room. She can hear it now too—a loud knocking down the hall and occasionally her name in an irritated tone.

Linda recognizes the voice, but she checks the peephole anyway.

Arthur is pounding on her door. After a moment, he pauses and takes his key from his pocket. He calls out a warning and then lets himself in.

Linda opens the door to follow.

"Linda, wait!" says Anvi.

"It's just Arthur."

"Your father?"

Linda nods, then squeezes past Nibbler into the hall. She half-expects Anvi to follow, but Anvi only stands there, watching.

"Arthur?" says Linda, walking into her apartment.

He's standing in the doorway to her bedroom. He turns and something flashes across his face. Linda's not sure if it's relief or annoyance. "Where were you?" he asks.

"At my neighbor's."

Arthur looks exhausted, and his tie—the same tie from yesterday—is askew. On him, that's like being covered head to toe in creases and coffee stains. "I couldn't stop thinking about that Christmas," he says. "She really reenacted it for you?"

Linda dips her head, not wanting to meet his intense gaze. Perhaps it was wrong of her to ignore his texts. "All I know is I remember it."

Arthur walks over and sits heavily on the sofa. "What's with that?" he asks, waving toward the CircleTread and the dirty, flipped table.

It's like she's a girl again, standing in a dress everyone tells her fits though she can't stand the fabric's glossy texture, the pinch of its waist and shoulders. Trying to find the right answer, trying to tell Arthur what he wants to hear so he might love her. "I bought a virtual-reality system."

"I know that. I meant the table."

She doesn't want to answer—she's scared Arthur might somehow try to claim that memory too—but she can't think of a lie that works. "It's from the Cedar Lake house," she admits.

"From the kitchen?" At Linda's nod, he gives a little "Huh" but doesn't seem interested beyond that. "Look," he says, "I understand my reaction last night must have been upsetting, but I—"

Something within Linda cracks. *"Upsetting?"* she interrupts.

"I know," he says. "I keep trying to think of it from your perspective. You couldn't have known."

There's no apology in his voice. Just pity.

"That day is one of the only good memories I have of my entire life," she says.

Arthur stares at the floor. Linda's anger wanes, and a sense of guilt creeps forward in its place. Where would she be now if not for Arthur? She doesn't know what this world does with parentless little girls found living in the woods, but it probably isn't anything good.

"You didn't do anything wrong," says Arthur. "You're just a victim of Lor's mental illness."

Defined by another's poor treatment of her. Forever and always.

"Why are you here?" asks Linda.

Arthur's chin shoots up and he meets her eyes. "This is difficult for me too, you know. My daughter died, and it destroyed my marriage. It took me years to piece together a life after that, and then you show up looking *so much* like Mads. Tweak the nose, throw on some extra freckles and a couple pounds, and you could have been twins. My own private uncanny valley staring me in the face. It was . . . I did my best, Linda. I'm *doing* my best."

So am I, Linda almost says. But there's a tiny flame deep inside her, flaring with challenge: Does she even know what her best is?

She can't take the way Arthur is looking at her. Like he doesn't want this chasm between them, like he's trying to cross it. Terror shoots through Linda, a fear of change and chance and connection. An instinct to run away as far and fast as she can vies against her deep-rooted desire for something different, something better.

But when she looks at Arthur, all she can think is, *It's too late.*

So she gives in to instinct and runs, hating herself even as she bolts for the door and down the hallway to the stairwell.

"Linda!" Two voices behind her. Anvi's door was closed as Linda passed, but she must have been watching through the peephole. Linda doesn't slow. She pushes into the stairwell and darts downward, her bare feet slapping the cold steps. She doesn't know where she's going, she just needs to be somewhere else. Chest heaving, she reaches the lobby and runs straight across, ignoring the attendant, pushing out into the wet air.

Outside, she does pause. Beneath her feet, the sidewalk is cold and damp, covered with tiny bumps. The rolling gray clouds above look as though they might have the same texture if she could reach up and touch them.

She turns toward the park that is the usual focus of her excursions and starts walking. But she doesn't stop at the park. She keeps going, making arbitrary turns every few blocks until she doesn't recognize her surroundings. She's walking uphill and her calves ache. Pings of sharp pain shoot through the soles of her feet. Her eyes are misty with confused and exhausted tears that she blinks back. She feels as though she's on the verge of choking. People are looking at her. One even asks, "Are you okay?" but Linda keeps walking.

Finally, she reaches a block where she can't see any other pedestrians. The road here is slender and rough, much of it cordoned off for construction and abandoned on a weekend. Linda ducks into an alleyway. It smells of urine and fish, and she sees a needle on the ground. She leans against a wall.

Let this world not be real, she thinks, closing her eyes. It's a ridiculous plea—she knows that even as she makes it. But her swirling thoughts center on the possibility that G.H. was right. And even if he and his colleagues didn't prove the hypothesis, the hypothesis still makes sense—Anvi said so. It's only a matter of time until someone else proves it and Linda—and everyone—is revealed to be nothing more than code.

The only thing she doesn't understand is why someone would run a simulation as awful as this. Have they no compassion for a world filled with murder and pain? How can they feel nothing for the beings suffering here when Linda feels so strongly for a dog in a game? *Put us out of our misery,* she thinks. *Please.*

She thinks of Briggs in limbo back in her apartment. When the game resumes, its timeline will simply return to a version of that world where Pickles is still alive. None of the NPCs will know a stutter step through time occurred or that it wasn't the first time. Only she will, the outside player. The one in control.

What if this world isn't just a simulation but a game: Who controls it? Has she been paused? Reloaded? Are there even worse fates for her out there; did she experience them before being reset to the lifetime she now knows?

Could her whole existence simply be someone else's side quest?

She can feel the urgency with which she wants some version of this to be true. To wipe herself of responsibility—to claim it wasn't fear but an algorithm that made her run from Arthur.

Yet even as she releases these thoughts, she feels her heart rate slowing. She doesn't *feel* like a program. Her decisions don't feel easy, or inevitable, or like the outcome of some equation. They feel like choices, and often irrational ones at that. If she were simply part of a program, why would she—why would anyone—be irrational? Every action the characters in Fury and Honor take makes sense, or if it doesn't, it's portrayed clearly as madness. Mental illness. Like Lorelei—a rational woman by all accounts, committing the least rational of acts and following through with it for years before disappearing.

Lorelei's mother killed herself when Lorelei was a teenager. No one told Linda this; she read it on Lorelei's Wikipedia entry. Painkiller overdose. Lorelei was the one who found her. Her father died of a heart attack a few years later, when Lorelei was eighteen. There was an older brother—he would have been Linda's biological uncle—but he died young too: a car accident just weeks after their father's death. He was drunk behind the wheel.

What is Linda's pain in comparison to all that?

Quick, heavy footsteps interrupt her thoughts.

She opens her eyes to see a man barreling toward her. She tries to step back, but the wall is there, and in her second of indecision he's on her, grabbing her by the shoulders and shoving her to the wall. Her head knocks against brick, and it flashes through her mind that she should yell for help, but the cry dies in her throat. It's as though her body doesn't know how to produce a sound demanding attention from strangers.

"I'm not going to hurt you," says the man. But her head is already throbbing as he shuffles her toward a car parked at the mouth of the alley. The back door is open.

She pulls away, but the man is stronger.

She looks at the car. She thinks of the insults and threats aimed her way online all these years and the fact that someone told the makers of those insults and threats where she lived just this morning.

She slams her elbow into the man's stomach. He lurches back with a groan but doesn't let go of her other arm. She twists; his grip tightens. She claws at his face.

Suddenly she's facedown on the ground, the man's knee on her back, one of his palms on the back of her head. Her forehead screams from the impact, and her sense of balance wobbles as though the earth itself is convulsing. She struggles as the man's knee digs deeper into her spine. Her lips and nose are pressed to the cold, hard ground. The man lets go of her head to take her left wrist, and Linda twists her face to the right, gasping. As she blinks dirt from her eyes, she sees the discarded needle only inches from her nose. She lunges for the needle, intending to jam it into the man's throat, but her other arm is quickly twisted back. Linda yelps, and her vision flashes. Something hard presses into her side.

"Don't make me pull the trigger," says the man.

Linda freezes. The man pushes up her sleeves and binds her wrists, and then he too stops moving—the sudden stillness of something gone wrong. Hope shoots through Linda. Maybe he's realized he has the wrong person. Maybe someone's stepped into the alley and seen them.

"Fuck," says the man, a short, angry exhalation. He yanks her to her feet—Linda's hope bursts; there's no savior in the alley, it's just them—and shoves her into the car. Muttering a soft series of profanities, he slaps duct tape over her mouth. Leaving her on her side along the back seat, he closes the car door and walks around to the driver's seat. As she wheezes against the tape, Linda's head spins. Her mouth is sour and part of her fears she might choke on her own bile.

Another part of her fears that whatever this man has planned for her is worse than choking.

She focuses on slowing her breathing and stares at the back of the man's head as he begins to drive. The abduction happened so quickly, she barely remembers anything about his face other than that he's white.

If she can just free her arms enough to text 911—

Linda's pulse thuds in her throat, quick.

She isn't wearing her Sheath. She left it at Anvi's.

She can't call for help, and there's no way to track her.

15.

nvi watches the stairwell door swing shut. Nibbler presses his head to the back of her knee, wanting to investigate. She nudges him back.

"For Christ's sake," says a gruff voice.

Anvi turns and locks eyes with Arthur Niequist. She tries to keep herself from evaluating him against her expectations, but it's impossible: He looks heavier in person—and older. His obvious exhaustion probably doesn't help.

"You must be Hendrickson," he says.

Her throat is suddenly dry with nerves. "Yes, sir," she replies. The formality wasn't planned, it just came out—but standing before her is Arthur *freaking* Niequist. His are among the shoulders on which every tech company today stands.

Arthur rubs at his temple and asks, "Is she this moody when I'm not around?"

"She's not the most easygoing person I've ever met," says Anvi, keeping her voice as light and level as she can. She refuses to be the kind of person who goes to pieces before her heroes.

"Think she'll come back?"

"I hope so." Anvi feels her nerves loosening. Arthur's not acting like a titan of technology, and it's already getting easier to think of him as a man—a father. "She's not wearing shoes. Or her Sheath."

"She doesn't have her Sheath?"

"No, she left it on my desk."

"Shit," says Arthur. He rushes to the elevator and jabs the call button.

His sense of urgency shoots through Anvi. She locks Nibbler inside and follows Arthur. "You know someone posted her address on a public forum today, right?" she asks.

"Again?"

"Again." Linda never mentioned it, but Anvi read all about the first incident. After Madeline Niequist's grave was ransacked, someone posted Linda's address on SocialHub along with a challenge: *The bones are in #CloneGirl's apartment—go find them*. It was just some hacker kid having a laugh, but the bot network latched onto the hashtag before it was removed, causing a viral spike, and plenty of idiots took the post seriously.

The elevator arrives. Anvi follows Arthur inside. The look he gives her tells her she's not entirely welcome. "Did anyone show up at her place last time?" she asks.

"No, but some asshole sent a box of decapitated dolls."

"Creepy. How did she handle that?"

"She never saw it. I had her out by then."

They arrive at the lobby. "Did Linda pass through here?" Arthur asks the attendant. Anvi has only seen this attendant, a gender-ambiguous Latinx wearing a pair of black Augments, once before. She thinks he—she, they?—might be a temp. Anvi sees understanding click into the attendant's eyes as the glasses identify Arthur—and she wonders if he was allowed to walk into the elevators unchallenged earlier. Nonresidents are supposed to sign in.

"From 702?" pushes Arthur. "Thin white woman with dark hair and no shoes."

"Oh," says the attendant. "Yeah, she just left."

"Which way did she go?"

The attendant stutters an unhelpful response. Anvi taps Arthur's shoulder and nods toward the door. He follows her outside.

A look left, a look right. No sign of Linda.

"Do you want to search or wait here?" asks Anvi.

The dim afternoon sunlight draws out the exhaustion in Arthur's creased face. Even the most accomplished human is still just a human, thinks Anvi. And in this case, an old one.

"Don't worry," she says. She can feel herself growing steadier, her mindset shifting to fill the gap left by Arthur's obvious worry. "She'll come back. She has to." She continues to scan the street. She didn't notice any suspicious lurkers when she walked Nibbler this morning—two loops around the block—and she doesn't see any now. Not that she's foolish enough to think that means much. "People are lazy," she says. "She might get another creepy package, but the chances of someone actually doing something . . ."

Her empty assurances wither beneath Arthur's disdainful look. She swallows the urge to tell him she's not naïve, she's just trying to be positive. She's the one who got Linda out of her apartment, after all—even if she didn't get her very far. If this were Ithaca, she'd have a dozen retreats, but here she didn't know where else to go.

Arthur pushes up his sleeve, whips his earcuff into place, and says, "Call Victoria." After a brief pause he begins barking instructions. "I need you to enable notifications on all of Linda's accounts and let me know the second any are accessed. . . . Yes, social, financial, everything. . . . No, everything's fine, she's just having a tantrum. But someone put out her address today, so I want to be careful. . . . Good idea, yes, please do. I don't know, maybe somewhere a little quieter would be better—include some options on the Eastside. We'll give her three to five choices, let her pick. . . . No, send them to me first. And throw in something near the Westport house, just in case. . . . Okay, yes. . . .

Thank you." He taps his Sheath to end the call. Looking up, he asks Anvi, "So, what's your deal?"

Anvi stares, startled by his bluntness.

"What are you looking to get from my daughter?" He says it slowly, as though he thinks she didn't understand the question. "Connections? Money?"

"Nothing," she says.

"What, then? You find her charming?"

Anvi hopes the lilt of sarcasm in his voice is a test. "I like her," she says. "She's interesting." She remembers the first time she saw Linda in the lobby. Her baggy clothing and slightly starved look had Anvi wondering if she might be a social-media influencer shying from attention—which wasn't that far off, except Linda never chose the limelight.

"How long have you known her?" asks Arthur.

It feels like months since she left Ithaca. "Bit over a week."

Arthur lifts his eyebrows.

"I know," says Anvi. "It's not long, but maybe not knowing her when she was younger helps." She understands how the way others first see you can easily become a trap—can become how they always see you. Confirmation bias disregarding any sign of growth and change, forever pegging you as a meek little girl. She can't imagine what a shock it must have been for Linda, emerging from that dank, secluded property into a world dominated by hookup apps and a purposefully inflammatory twenty-four-hour news cycle. She can't imagine being thrust from silence *into* that news cycle, not just as a consumer but as a target. Anvi's native to it all, and she still gets overwhelmed; that's why she avoids all Augment and most voice-control technology. She may be addicted to her Sheath, but at least when she looks up from it, her vision is clear.

"Maybe," says Arthur, his voice flat. He looks away from the streets and meets her eyes briefly. "She does seem to trust you."

"I understand why you're wary," says Anvi. "But I don't plan on hurting her. Or using her."

Arthur sighs softly, and Anvi thinks they've perhaps reached an understanding.

"Why don't you wait here," says Arthur. "I'll take a quick lap around the block."

Anvi agrees, and as she watches Arthur stride away, she wonders if she should have told him the whole truth.

When Linda tries to sit up, the man barks, "Stay down, or I'll put you in the trunk and shoot anyone who sees us." His voice is cold, and she believes him. No matter the danger to herself, she can't let him hurt someone else. Linda lays her head back on the seat. The fabric smells of marijuana. Her stomach roils, and that afternoon's teriyaki creeps back up her throat.

The man switches on the stereo and a woman's voice pounds out of the speakers, "Multitasking is a necessary skill for survival in modern society. Maximum efficiency demands—"

The voice switches over to music, a classical piece heavy on the piano. Under the sound, vibrating through the seat against Linda's cheek, is the thrum of the car's gas engine. Every once in a while, she hears another soft "fuck" from the man. From the way he pushed up her sleeves, she thinks he probably wanted her Sheath.

She doesn't know how much time passes as she lies there holding in her vomit and breathing shallowly through her nose. After what feels like hours, the car slows and makes a sharp turn onto a gravel road or driveway—Linda can hear crunching beneath the tires. The slice of the windshield in her view displays only trees.

They roll to a stop and the man gets out of the car. The door by Linda's head opens and she's extracted from the back—the man gentle but insistent, somewhere between helping and pulling her out.

Linda's muscles scream as she unfurls to a standing position, and she snaps her eyes to the man's face.

He's around forty years old, she guesses, with blue eyes and shaggy light-brown hair. Uneven stubble shrouds his chin and cheeks, disappearing down his neck into the collar of his coat.

"Come on," he says, leading her by the arm toward a small, rundown house. Everything else around them is dense trees and overgrown shrubbery. There are no neighbors to be seen, nothing but wild. Sharp rocks prick the bare soles of Linda's feet.

The tape across Linda's mouth stings her stretching cheeks as she tries to ask, "Who are you?"

The man yanks her up the three steps to the house's front door. He takes out a key, unlocks the door, and leads her inside.

The room she enters is dark and musty, with the smell of grease creeping in from a small kitchen to the right; Linda can see pans and plates piled high beside the sink. To her left is a sitting area: a sunken couch and armchair, an old-fashioned box TV like the one she had on the property—though she assumes this one works. She sees a hallway with at least one closed door on the far side of the room. Directly ahead of her, a staircase leads to a second floor.

The man drags her toward the hallway, opens the first door, and shoves her inside.

"Sit," he says. The room is dim, its only window boarded from the outside so that just a sliver of light sneaks in. Linda sees a twin bed in the corner. It has a single pillow and a thin blanket that in this light could be either blue or gray.

The man gives her another small push. "I said sit."

Linda stumbles forward; her hands are still bound, and she twists so her hip hits the mattress first. The bed squeaks as she squirms to face the man. She can't breathe deeply enough through her nose to keep her head from swimming. She braces herself to fight—but the man just gives her a look somewhere between condescension and disgust and walks out. The door closes, and Linda hears the click of a lock.

She looks around, searching for a sharp edge to cut her bonds, a way to pry the board from the window. There's a small bedside table, but nothing else. The cave-cell from the opening of Fury and Honor pops into her churning mind. She wishes desperately for the game's candle. Here, the walls are made of wood. Here, a fire would be more than a distraction.

She heaves herself to her feet and circles the room with her back to the wall, feeling for a sharp crack of wood on the windowsill, a nail jutting from the wall, anything. But there is no secret to be found, no tool that will grant her a way out. Eventually, Linda returns to the bed, where she sits and tries to contain her panic.

The only thing she can think of is to rush the man when he opens the door. He has to open the door eventually. Every once in a while, she hears a muffled clank or bang outside the room, and she wishes she knew what was happening—what this man wants.

Unknowable time passes. Linda calms enough to feel the endless ache of her strained shoulders. Still, every small sound sends a jolt through her, and when she shifts she's startled by her own faint shadow.

A floorboard creaks outside the door, and she hears a key slide into the lock. She's still struggling to her feet when the door opens, and whatever chance Linda had to surprise the man passes—so she stands there, trying to project defiance despite her terror.

The man is unimpressed. He pulls something out of his pocket. "Turn around," he says.

Linda doesn't move.

The man fingers the object, and a short blade flips out, glimmering in the dim light.

Linda's eyes lock onto the pocketknife, and she remembers a lizard girl jamming a blade into her gut. She throws herself toward the open door. It's unplanned, reckless, but if she can get by—the man grabs her and shoves her back into the room.

"I'm just going to free your hands." He says it like Linda's inconveniencing him, and the absurdity of that roils through her. Then the man twists her around, pushing her chest to the wall. "Be still, unless you want to get cut."

He grips her left arm, hard, and she presses forward into the wall to get away from the feel of his breath on her neck. This is the most a man has ever touched her, and she'd give anything to make it stop. There's pressure, then a little pop, but the man doesn't let go. Linda can feel snot dripping down her face, slick around the duct tape covering her mouth. But her hands are free; if he doesn't let go, maybe she can—

He releases her and steps back. "Where's your Sheath?"

Linda flips around, bracing her back to the wall; the man reaches out and she recoils, lifting her arms to fend him off.

"For fuck's *sake*." He steps back. "Fine, take the tape off yourself."

Linda paws at her mouth, finds a corner, and tears off the duct tape. Her raw, released skin stings. She wipes away her snot and feels adhesive residue.

"So?" he asks. Linda blinks at him. "Your Sheath. Where is it? You never leave without it."

"I forgot it," she says. Fear and thirst have added a rasp to her voice.

The man rubs at his face. "Of course you did," he sighs. Then he walks out. The door locks again, leaving Linda alone and confused with a piece of duct tape dangling from her hand.

16.

nvi grabs Linda's Sheath from her desk, then walks to the living room and hands it to Arthur, who's shifting to avoid Nibbler's crotch-curious nose. After a moment, Arthur turns his back to the dog and thumbs the Sheath, unlocking it, then begins tapping through Linda's digital self. His own Sheath buzzes. He taps his ear-cuff. "Yes? . . . No, that was me. You can disregard anything from the Sheath." He ends the call.

"She's twenty-four," says Anvi, aghast.

Arthur looks up. "What?"

"You're using parental controls."

"Sure am."

Anvi bites back a reply. She met Linda barely a week ago and Arthur less than an hour ago. She doesn't know him at all beyond his public image; it's not her place to judge their dynamic. She tells herself this, and yet the judgment is there—and sharp.

Nibbler sits at Arthur's feet and cocks his head.

Anvi tries to imagine Arthur's perspective, how he must be feeling. "You're worried," she says.

"I'm always worried." He says it coolly. *Calm as a cauliflower,* as Anvi's mother likes to say.

Anvi isn't sure what to make of him. Arthur Niequist the Father is very different from Arthur Niequist: Computer Scientist, Philanthropist, and Public Figure. Though perhaps she shouldn't be so surprised he's monitoring Linda—he built his fortune on data collection and analysis.

She wonders if Linda knows how closely she's being watched.

"Are you calling-the-police-level worried?" she asks.

Arthur sighs and looks up. "Honestly, I'm not sure. I'd rather the public not get wind of this if she's just burning off some steam with a stroll. She must know the area by now, right? Or do you think she's going to get lost without her Sheath?"

Anvi flattens her voice, so he knows just how ridiculous his question is. "She knows her way around."

"Well, that's something." Arthur steps past Nibbler toward the door. "I'm going to wait in her apartment. Thanks for your help." He pauses. "Will you let me know if you hear anything?"

"If you'll do the same."

Arthur gives her a little nod, and then he's gone. Anvi flops onto the couch and lets Nibbler lick her face for a few seconds. Then she rolls onto her back, lifts her Sheath arm, and accesses her *Clone Girl* file, which is tucked away untagged several tiers beneath *Side Projects.* There are dozens of subfolders, including *AN Confirmed and AN Rumors:* everything she's been able to find about Linda's father. She did the easy people first, starting with the dead girl, Madeline Rose Niequist. There wasn't much to find: A-student, so-so athlete, tragic accident. Anvi can't help but wonder what else there would be if social media had been around back then; yearbook photos and obituaries don't seem like the best way to get to know a teenage girl.

She scrolls through the data for a few minutes, then double-checks her alerts to make sure nothing new has surfaced. The Internet—SocialHub and otherwise—is momentarily silent on the subject of

Clone Girl. She hopes it'll stay that way. She hopes Linda will knock on her door any second and no one else will ever know about today. She considers sending Linda a direct message via SocialHub, in case she accesses the network from somewhere else, but with the level of monitoring Arthur has enabled, he probably has access to that too. Soon she's staring at the ceiling, wallowing in a sense of worry and responsibility. Maybe she shouldn't have told Linda about the man knocking on her door; probably she should have run after her instead of shying in the presence of Arthur Niequist. Certainly she could have made sure Linda took her Sheath with her. And wore shoes.

She thinks of Linda asking for plastic bags to cover her bleeding feet and the assumption there: that the floors of a rental apartment merited more concern than Linda's own flesh.

She wonders how much of it is innate, if Linda would still be so deferential if her childhood was a few standard deviations closer to the mean. But Anvi's never been able to resist outliers: people who break the mold of normality not because they choose to but because they have to. Her thoughts flash to Tasha, who—if they were still speaking—would berate her for picking up another stray. She remembers the look on her then-girlfriend's face when Anvi stepped into their Ithaca apartment with a tiny puppy cradled to her chest. How Tasha had looked up from her dissertation notes and cocked one of her bleached eyebrows to ask, "What's that?"

He'd come from a cardboard box in the corner of the Wegmans parking lot; some instinct had told her the way the box shook wasn't just the wind. She remembers opening the top flaps and seeing the minuscule animal inside, how he could barely waddle around on his stubby legs. How his eyes sought her face and shone with a secret message: *I'm yours.*

"I'm allergic," said Tasha.

"To *cats*," Anvi replied.

"Close enough."

That night in bed, Tasha curled up tight against her and whispered, "I want to be your only stray." But Nibbler was named by then—and he'd lapped wet food from the palm of her hand after being startled by the noise of a bowl clattering across kitchen tile. Anvi knew she would never be able to let him go. Even if he'd already peed on the carpet twice.

A few months later, a friend texted Anvi, urging her to tune in to a livestream of an arts department Halloween party. Eager for a break and expecting some hilarious spectacle—Dr. Li was known to commandeer lab equipment in the name of a good prank—Anvi instead spied her girlfriend in the corner, her hand tucked beneath the elastic of an undergrad's skull-and-crossbones leggings, stroking.

Nibbler licked furious tears from her face that night and many after.

After Anvi moved out, it took her weeks to fully scrub Tasha's presence from her digital life. Untagging, unfriending, hiding all mentions—it was grueling work. That's what inspired her to write Scrub: a program that identified all of one's digital connections to a specified individual and made it easier to block and delete them. It was Scrub that caught SocialHub's eye. She might not be here if not for that program. She might not be here if not for Tasha. Those skull-and-crossbones leggings.

There are days Anvi considers this new job, this new life, and is almost grateful to Tasha for her role in getting her here. There are other days this same gratitude makes her hate Tasha. She doesn't want to feel indebted—even indirectly—to someone who hurt her so. And then there are the days when she resents that *she* was the one who had to get a new life, when Tasha's the one who fucked a twenty-year-old.

Sitting on the floor to scratch Nibbler's ears, she wonders if how Arthur feels toward Linda might be similar: simultaneously grateful to and made furious by Linda's serving as a constant reminder of loss. Yet he's also responsible for—and to—Linda in a way that Anvi could never be responsible for Tasha. She tries to imagine what she would have done in his place, if it'd been her half-wild, previously unknown

offspring found wandering down a rural street. She doesn't know—
can't know—but as she scratches Nibbler's ear, she can't help but
think she would have tried her hardest to help.

I'm always worried, he said. He's a data-driven man who's experienced inconceivable loss. Maybe surveillance is how he tries to help.
She can relate to that.

Afternoon transitions to evening, and Anvi's stomach begins to
growl. She walks over to Linda's apartment and knocks on the door.
When Arthur answers, she catches a spark of hope in his eyes that
dissipates when he realizes it's just her.

"Can I bring you some dinner?" she asks.

"No thanks, I'm good." He lifts his hand to the doorframe and
Anvi catches sight of his Sheath's screen, which displays a quiet night-
vision view of a graveyard.

Glimpsing the eerie scene, she expects some sort of otherworldly
creature to erupt from the soil. She wouldn't have pegged this as Arthur's brand of entertainment. "What are you watching?" she asks.

Arthur snaps his hand back, and Anvi's first thought is that it must
be porn. Judging from the discomfort that flashes across Arthur's face,
he can sense what she's thinking. "It's a security feed," he says.

"Of a—" Before the question's out, she understands, and her voice
drops into a soft "Oh."

The Halloween after Madeline Niequist's grave was disturbed, one
of Anvi's friends eschewed more-recent clickbait news to dress as the
unearthed corpse. She looked more like a zombie than anything else,
and it was only when she stood with a friend who was dressed as a
grave-robbing Clone Girl that her costume was discernible. Anvi had
done a tequila shot with them, the odd one out in her steampunk
garb.

Shame rolls through her—and then a jolt of something sharper.
She must have posted pictures from that night on SocialHub; it was
her last Halloween at Cornell.

Were Louisa and Viv in any of the pictures? It's all she can do to not whip out her Sheath and check. What if Linda saw them? How could she explain? *Sorry, Linda, it was funny at the time.*

Arthur's looking at her, his emotions zipped away.

"Sorry," says Anvi. "I shouldn't have—"

"It's okay."

An uncomfortable pause follows, then Anvi asks, "Are you sure I can't get you anything?"

"Thank you, but no."

In the elevator, she scrolls feverishly through SocialHub. Louisa is in the background of one of her pictures, but Viv isn't, and without her it's impossible to tell Louisa's dirty, torn costume isn't just a zombie. Anvi deletes the photo anyway. Wandering through the lobby and outside toward the nearest neon OPEN sign, she thinks of Arthur sitting alone upstairs, watching a live feed of his daughter's grave.

The least she can do is get him a couple of tacos.

Hands freed, Linda tries the light switch. There's no bulb in the overhead socket. The light from the window is fading. She searches the room again, racing against the dark. There is the plastic tie that was cut off her wrists, and pawing under the bed, she finds a small glass marble hidden in the dust. She places the marble, the plastic tie, and the strip of duct tape on the bedside table and wonders how she's supposed to manufacture an escape out of items such as these.

And why does the man want her Sheath? How long has he been watching her? He made it sound like he knew where she lived before today. Could he be the one who posted her address—but if he was planning on kidnapping her, why?

She sits on the bed, rubs her wrists, and takes a deep breath through her mouth, truly filling her lungs for the first time since she was abducted. The room grows steadily darker. When Linda can barely make out her hands on her lap, a light switches on in the hallway, illuminating the door in a thin outline.

Eventually, the man comes back. Light blares through the door-way at his entrance.

"Log in," he says, holding out something toward Linda. Blinking against the sudden light, she sees that the object is a tablet, an old one about twice as thick as hers. Its browser is open to her bank's website. "I need you to transfer half a million dollars into an account. If you do that, you're free to go."

A bubble of relief and disbelief travels through Linda. Money—could it really be so simple? She takes the tablet. He can have as much money as he wants.

The browser's design is slightly different than she's used to, and it takes her a few seconds to find the log-in. It needs her username and password. Of course it does. Linda's relief dissipates. She hasn't typed either in over a year: Her Sheath just recognizes her thumbprint and authorizes a banking app from there. She knows the username is her first and last with some punctuation between—but the password is a random combination of numbers and letters that Arthur picked. She has it written down at her apartment but hasn't looked at the thumbprint-locked digital-password book since he helped her set up the app.

"This can all be over tonight," says the man. Linda wants nothing more than to give him the money and go home. There's a seven in the password, maybe two sevens.

"Go on," says the man.

Shaking, she types *Linda_Russell*.

"Good girl," says the man. "Now the password."

There's virtually no chance of her guessing it correctly, but she has to try. She taps out an eight-digit code—including two sevens—and hits *Submit*. Please, she thinks; let the luck she's been missing all her life come together in this moment.

This username and password combination doesn't match our rec-ords.

Even though she expected it, her heart sinks. She looks at the tiny text below: *Forgotten password?* But Arthur's the primary on the ac-count, and she can't reset the password without his consent—and even if she could, the confirmation would go to her email, and she doesn't know how to log in to that without her Sheath either. She stares at the tablet, feeling helpless and stupid, and her trembling grows worse.

"Calm down and try again," says the man.

On her second attempt, she can barely tap the characters she means to. Not that it matters.

This username and password combination doesn't match our rec-ords.

The man is silent. Linda feels his weight beside her, indenting the bed so that she has to lean away to keep from touching him.

"If you're delaying, it's pointless," he says. "I've got the IP address masked and rerouted in so many layers, anyone tracking these at-tempts will need to next Christmas just to determine which hemi-sphere you're in."

This should be easy. This should be over. "I don't remember the password," she whispers.

"Then reset it."

"I can't without Arthur."

She can't bring herself to say *my father,* but he doesn't ask who Arthur is. Whoever this man is, he knows where her money comes from. "Are you shitting me?" he says.

"I'm sorry."

"For fuck's sake, Maddy, I—"

Any scrap of warmth and hope that was lingering in Linda flushes away, replaced by unadulterated horror.

Maddy.

This isn't about money. Not if he's calling her by that name.

"I'm sorry," she whispers again, wanting more than ever to avoid angering the man.

After a few beats of tense silence, she dares to glance at him. For the first time since he abducted her, their eyes meet; the intensity she sees there is terrifying.

The man snatches the tablet and storms out of the room, slamming the door behind him. The hallway light flicks off, leaving Linda in pure darkness.

Minutes pass, then hours. There are intermittent footsteps in the hallway. Linda curls up under the covers and stares at the pitch-black door. Her throat aches with thirst and she has to pee. When the urge to urinate grows painful, she goes to the door, feeling her way in the dark.

She knocks—an act of desperation, not courage. There's no response. She knocks a little harder as a cramp runs through her midsection.

"I need to use the bathroom," she says. Her voice is a dry whisper. She clears her throat and tries again, louder. "I need to use the bathroom, please."

She doesn't hear a single footstep, any sound or motion at all. Linda leans her forehead against the door.

"I tried to do what you wanted," she whispers. A rush of anger overcomes her, and she bangs her fist against the door, loud. She doesn't deserve to be left in here like this, nothing to drink, nothing to eat, nowhere to relieve herself. She *tried*.

It's taking all her control not to wet herself. She bangs on the door again. And again. She bashes her fists against the wood until the flats of her hands feel swollen and raw. She's never made so much noise in her life.

But no one comes, and as her anger fades back to fear, she knows that no one will.

She staggers over to the corner of the room farthest from the bed, then pulls down her pants and squats against the wall, low. As she lets her bladder release, a sob catches in her throat. This isn't like peeing in the woods as a girl. This is unlike anything she's ever experienced. Urine splashes her bare feet, warm and shaming. Her only other choice was to piss herself at the door—knowing this should help, but it doesn't.

When she's done, she dries her feet on her pant legs and goes back to the bed. The acrid scent of her urine follows her, and she buries her head under the pillow to escape it. There, burrowed like an animal, she somehow, eventually, falls asleep.

Deep in the night, she wakes, groggy and cold—and registers a clammy pressure against her right calf. A brief instant of confusion, then flooding terror: The man, he's here, holding her leg. She kicks wildly, throwing off the blanket and flailing at the dark. He lets go, but she doesn't strike him, doesn't see or hear him—there's nothing, no one, in the room. She doesn't understand: Where did he go? Then the agonizing pinpricking of rushing blood wakes her left foot. As she shifts against the pain, her waking foot flops against her right leg, and Linda realizes that was all she felt—not the man but her own limb, asleep, lying against her like a foreign body. The tingling spikes in intensity, and Linda bites her lip against the pain. But it soon fades, and her foot is again just that—part of her. The room, the house, everything but her own shaking breath is silence. She can still smell her urine.

She moves to her opposite side, to face the room rather than the wall, and curls up even tighter. The skittering of a rodent in the ceiling crosses above her, then all is again silent. After a moment, she reaches out to pat along the bedside table. She finds the marble and clutches it to her chest, just to have something to hold.

She lies there, curled in the bed, shivering and sleepless, until she hears a wooden groan and the clunk of footsteps passing her door. It's still dark out, and she can hear the man moving around the main room. A metallic screech, another *thunk*. More footsteps and the occasional gap of silence. Linda sits up. She's so thirsty she can barely feel her fear. She's still clutching the marble. Eventually, the footsteps come closer, then the key is in the lock and the door swings open.

"Christ, it's cold in here," says the man.

There's a lidless mason jar in his hand. It's filled with water.

The man sniffs. "Did you piss on the floor?"

Linda feels his disgust, but she doesn't care. All she cares about is the water. She can't take her eyes off the jar. She lets the marble fall to the mattress.

And then, magically, he's holding out the jar to her. She grabs it, so eager the jar tilts and spills—just a splash, but Linda nearly cries out, seeing the water run over the side. Then she's drinking. The water is so cold it makes her teeth ache. She drinks it all.

"Do you remember the password?" asks the man.

Linda clutches the jar. She can feel the tightness in her head loosening. She needs to think. Now that she's had water, she can think.

"I don't know it," she says. "But if you let me go, I'll transfer the money as soon as I have my Sheath."

She means it, but the man laughs. "Come on." He takes her by the arm and leads her out of the room, directing her through a door across the hall into a small, dirty bathroom. "You have three minutes," he says. Then he takes the mason jar from her and closes the door.

Three minutes. Linda moves to lock the door, but the knob doesn't have a lock. The tile floor is frigid against her bare feet. There's a window, but it's boarded shut just like the bedroom's. There's a wet toothbrush and a goopy uncapped tube of toothpaste on the sink. She thinks of the tube being pressed to the brush, the brush traversing the interior of her abductor's mouth. It's all she can do to not swipe the items to the floor. She pushes aside a moldy green curtain to find an old tub and shower with cracked tiles. A bar of soap, a crusty bottle of shampoo.

She has to pee again; it's like the water flooded straight through her. She relieves herself quickly, watching the door. Her exhausted mind is running in circles, looking for something in the room she can use. She's heard of prisoners making knives out of toothbrushes, but she doesn't know how it's done. She could break the mirror and slash at the man with a shard, but he would hear her. He would be prepared. And then he *really* wouldn't believe she's being honest about wanting to cooperate.

She flushes, then rinses her hands and face and drinks more water from the sink. Rubbing her wet face, she looks into the mirror. The surface is fogged with age and chalky flecks of toothpaste, and her reflection is more shadow than woman. This room, this house—it feels like some nameless nowhere separate from the rest of the world. It feels like she should be able to pull a headset from her eyes and be back home.

The door opens. The longest and shortest three minutes of her life. The man nods for her to follow him to the house's main room, then directs her to sit on the couch. Linda sinks into its worn cushions, and the man falls into a plush chair. He places his hands on the chair's stained arms and stares at her. A woodstove crackles behind him; Linda didn't notice it before. Much of the noise she heard earlier must have been him adding fuel.

"We need that money," says the man.

Linda swallows a new bubble of unease. First he called her *Maddy* and now he's saying *we*. His words seethe with complications.

"You can have the money," she says. "All I want is to go home."

The man nods. Yesterday he could barely look at her and today he won't stop staring.

"You look so much more like her in person than in the photos," he says.

Linda pulls away. Her skin prickles with danger. This man wants more from her than money; she can feel it. He must be a Madeline junkie. They pop up in discussion circles, and she received letters from a few while living at Arthur's—men who form attachments to dead girls on the Internet, who masturbate to old photos and croon about innocence.

The front door is maybe fifteen feet away.

He's faster than her. Less beat-up.

Thinking about running, Linda realizes something. "You're the man I saw at the pond," she says.

He blinks at her. His silence might as well be a nod.

Everything clicks into place: He *is* a Madeline junkie, but his obsession couldn't be contained online, even before now. He visited the Cedar Lake house, who knows how many times—Officer Baldwin's squatters. It wasn't coincidence that *he* was there when Linda saw him; Linda was the unusual factor.

He must have followed her home from Cedar Lake.

Maybe he even started the fire. To draw her to him. A gamble, but it worked.

Dread and certainty: The money's a ruse. It doesn't matter if she gives him every cent in her account—he will never let her go.

She bursts up and sprints for the door.

Her hand is on the latch when he grabs her by the waist. She fumbles with the lock and flails backward with her elbow. She feels it connect with his chin, hard, and he stumbles, swearing. The lock clicks, and Linda yanks the door open.

The man tackles her to the floor and kicks the door closed.

Linda rolls over, punching and clawing. The man pins her wrists. She thrusts her knee toward his crotch. He sits on her legs, trapping her. She snaps at his forearm and catches heavy flannel between her teeth.

"Stop it," he says.

She struggles to heave his weight off her.

"Stop it *now*." His voice is different, higher.

The man's weight shifts and stills, then lessens: an opportunity. Linda squirms out from under him. As she scrambles to her knees, she sees that the man is looking at the stairs. Her eyes snap to follow.

There's a woman a few steps from the top, watching the two of them.

Confusion coalesces as Linda realizes the voice calling for her—for them—to stop wasn't the man's. *We,* he said.

Linda's on her hands and knees in a hunched, feral position, processing the newcomer. White-gray hair falls nearly to the woman's waist, and static electricity suspends a handful of strands about her frail frame like a shroud. The woman is older, smaller, and she's wearing a long gray robe instead of a white sweater, but everything else about her screams of the familiar. Linda even recognizes the way her fingers curl around the bannister.

Impossibility crashes around Linda, sucking away her air, her pain, leaving her stunned and stupid and so overwhelmed she forgets every fear and thought that was coursing through her just seconds ago.

She understands nothing, feels nothing.

All she can do is stare as Lorelei takes another step down the stairs.

From: Lorelei Niequist   Draft Saved 10:17 P.M. 8/9/2004
To: Arthur Niequist
RE:

Do you remember Boise? I kept sneaking you my drinks because we were too scared to tell anyone. It didn't feel real yet. Then on the drive home the morning sickness hit, and we had to stop at that hick town Walmart so I could throw up? And you bought me every variety of peppermint and lemon candy in the store? Do you remember how we called her the Parasite? How it finally began to feel like it was really happening?

I'm fifteen weeks and I haven't felt sick at all. I'm worried that

17.

"That's better," says Lorelei. She descends the stairs, her movement stiff yet somehow ethereal. The man scurries to help, leading her to the couch.

Linda rises awkwardly, unable to take her eyes off Lorelei. The door is directly behind her. She should run; this is her chance.

Lorelei sits, waving away the man's concern. And he's very concerned, apologizing for the ruckus and doting over her like a servant or a son. Linda *should* run, but she can't. Not with Lorelei right here, just a few feet away. After all these years, she's *here*.

"This isn't going how I intended," says Lorelei.

That voice. Linda ached to hear it so badly as a child, almost as badly as she ached for touch. But now—she blinks, squeezing her eyes shut for a tight, impossible moment. When Linda's eyes open, Lorelei is looking straight at her, her gaze framed by crow's-feet as deep as crevasses. There's something in them that from anyone else Linda might have thought was kindness.

"Please, sit," says Lorelei. "Let's talk."

Linda can't move. She can only stare.

"This must be strange for you," says Lorelei. Her voice seethes with understanding, and Linda chokes on a childish urge to scream at her to shut up. She feels so lost, it's maddening that someone else could understand anything.

"Please," says Lorelei again. She pats the cushion next to her.

Dr. Tambor used to do that—pat a cushion, inviting Linda to discussion. She did it with a smile, like she was excited to see Linda. The only person who ever was.

"Where have you been?" blurts Linda. Of all the questions roiling within her, she doesn't know why this is the one that boils over first, and she's not quite sure how she manages to speak it.

"Here," says Lorelei—simply, as though Linda should know where *here* is. She leans forward and adds, "Percy told me you struggled. You weren't supposed to struggle. It wasn't supposed to happen like this."

Percy. The man has a name, and that name means nothing to Linda. She darts her eyes to where he's hovering by the couch. "Who is he?"

"Percy's family," says Lorelei. She turns to give him a small smile. There's a connection between them, a sense of exclusivity. The family Lorelei's referring to—Linda's not part of it.

Linda combs her memory for any mention of a Percy in the myriad blogs, comments, or articles she's read concerning Madeline. If he was mentioned anywhere, it was in too insignificant a manner for her to recall.

"I understand why you might be scared," says Lorelei. "But we don't want to hurt you. We need your help."

Linda thinks of herself as a child, tending her mother's spurting head wound. Looking at Lorelei now, it feels less like a memory and more like a wish, and she wonders if it ever happened. Her legs are beginning to feel weak; she allows the uncanny magnetism of the moment to ease her into the armchair.

A new level of focus clicks into Lorelei's eyes, and Linda can feel herself being studied. "I shouldn't have done it," says Lorelei. She shakes her head and looks away. "I wasn't well, and I thought I could do the impossible. I thought I *had* to. And for a time—I remember it so clearly, holding my baby again. I really thought it was her."

Linda's mind is churning; she thought Lorelei was talking about the kidnapping, but no—she's talking about *her*. This soft, regretful woman is not the Lorelei she knows—and what she regrets is *her*. Her and Emmer.

Linda doesn't know how to ask—*what* to ask. Where is Emmer's body? How did you kill her? Did you mean to kill her? *Did* you kill her? "My sister—" she starts.

"Don't," says Lorelei.

Be scarce. The same sharp, familiar tone. It's almost a relief to hear—at the same time, it freezes Linda's throat. It's a tone she can't disobey.

"It was never her," says Lorelei. "It could never be her. I understand that now—what I wanted was impossible." She lifts her hand, hovers it toward Linda, but then places it back on her own knee. "But what was impossible then is possible now," she says. "With your help, Madeline Rose can be reborn."

From: Lorelei Niequist   Draft Saved 2:03 A.M. 8/24/2004
To: Arthur Niequist
RE:

I can finally feel her. Not just my body changing, but *her*. Little shivers of movement. Only a few are big enough to be called kicks, but I can feel her. I keep whispering to her, telling her who she is. Who she will be.

18.

"All you have to do is give us the money," says Lorelei. "*My* money." She's looking right at Linda, but now it doesn't feel like she's seeing a person, a woman—her daughter. It feels like she's considering an annoyance.

"I don't understand," says Linda. She doesn't understand anything other than the way Lorelei is looking at her.

"The embryos weren't exact genetic replicas," says Lorelei. "It never could have been her, no matter what I did. But when Percy told me what they call you"—she gives a derisive sniff—"it gave me an idea."

Genetic replicas. What they call Linda. It's obvious what she means, but Linda doesn't believe it. "You're going to *clone* Madeline?"

She's almost expecting Lorelei to laugh. She's *hoping* Lorelei will laugh, call her guess ridiculous. But Lorelei smiles, bright and genuine. "It's taken years, but I have everything I need," she says. "All we have to do is pay him."

"But that's—" The word *impossible* curdles in Linda's throat. When she was still living at Arthur's, she went through a phase of researching human cloning, wanting to believe someone would do it soon and that the duplicated person could be her friend or—better yet—would inherit the mantle of Clone Girl, allowing Linda the anonymity she craved. She had trouble sorting truth from fiction, though, and came away from her research more confused than ever.

But now she thinks of the ads she's seen for pet-cloning services. She thinks of Anastasia the woolly mammoth and an article she saw months ago about attempts to create a saber-toothed tiger in South Korea. If these long-dead animals can be cloned, why not a human child? She believes Lorelei when she says she's at least found someone willing to try. And if all she needs is money—

Her skin prickles. It takes more than money to clone an organism. "You're the ones who dug up her grave," she says.

Lorelei's smile fades.

Linda expected to feel disgust at the confirmation, but instead a crushing sense of sadness flows through her. She thinks of a child genetically identical to Madeline being born. A *real* Clone Girl. She studies Lorelei's face for a moment, the heavy frown lines around her mouth, the frizz of her gray hair.

"It won't be her," says Linda. Her voice cracks. It's so hard to contradict this woman.

The frown lines twitch. "It's my money."

There's a tick inside Linda that pushes her toward acquiescence, not only because it's Lorelei, but because she's right: Linda didn't earn any of that money. It fell to her just as ownership of the Cedar Lake property did—some legal transference based on Lorelei's disappearance. But thoughts of Madeline help restrain her: a girl who existed once and can never exist again. Even identical twins can range from eerily similar to wildly divergent—there's no guarantee Madeline's clone would be like her. Even if her genetic makeup primed her to be, there's the role of a child's environment. Linda thinks of running through the trees, leaping from the dock, crawling through the fox hutch with Emmer. She thinks of the marriage Madeline Niequist's death destroyed, of pictures of a young, smiling Lorelei, a bright-yellow house. She looks at the dust- and dirt-crusted hovel around her. The old woman sitting on the couch. The strange man standing silent beside her, bleeding from a fat lip.

"No," says Linda. She tries to be strong, to put that strength into her voice and posture, but sourness rises in her throat—if she remembered her password, Lorelei would already have the money. Linda was so eager to do as Percy asked. She would have given him every cent.

But now she knows what it's for. Now she's saying *no*.

Linda expects Lorelei to harden—to demand—but she surprises her by doing the opposite. "This is your chance to do the right thing," says Lorelei. "It'll be easy. Percy will take you to the bank and—"

"No," interrupts Linda. She's staring at Lorelei's chin; it's as close to her eyes as she can make herself look. No, it's not the right thing. No, she won't do it. No, this woman can't control her.

Lorelei's lip curls to reveal deeply yellowed teeth, and she turns to Percy. "Put her away until she changes her mind."

Percy swoops over and takes Linda by the arm. He leads her back to the bedroom; Linda's too stunned and exhausted to fight, and it's a relief to take her eyes off Lorelei. Then Percy stands in the doorway, staring at her.

Something in his look makes Linda feel antagonistic, and knowing how easily she gave in earlier fills her with the need for defiance. "You can't bring Madeline back," she says.

Percy flinches, then glances over his shoulder toward the couch, where Lorelei must still be sitting. "I'll be back in a few hours to bring you lunch," he says. "Try to hold in your piss until then." He closes the door.

Linda sits on the bed, burying her feet beneath the blanket. It's a little warmer in the room than before, but now there's a closed door between her and the woodstove. She looks at the boarded window and imagines she can see the heat leaking out.

The marble she held last night is sitting on the bed; Linda rolls it around her palm as she sits, aching. It's swirled blue and reminds her of the first time she saw a photograph of earth taken from outer space. It was in one of her GED textbooks, and looking at it she experienced a brief flash of understanding: how tiny she was, how large the universe around her. Feeling the enormity of existence eased something in her chest and made her almost light-headed—then the moment passed, and her anxiety came crashing back down around her.

She read half a dozen books about the universe after that, hoping to re-create the experience, but she was never able to find that emotional equanimity again.

But she feels something similar now—a less pleasant cousin to that striking experience. Lorelei is alive. Lorelei wants to *clone* Madeline. Linda understands her place in the world less than ever. Refusing to give Lorelei money—is that all she can do, the best she can do?

Hours trickle by. The room grows steadily colder. Linda wonders if she'd be able to see her breath in the air if there was a light. She wonders what Lorelei is doing, what Percy's connection to all this is. She wonders what Anvi's doing and how many texts Arthur has sent her wayward Sheath. It's Monday; she's probably far from his mind. Anvi's too. Today is Anvi's first day at SocialHub; she's probably forgotten all about Linda. That or stepping foot on their campus cracked her Clone Girl silence and she's sharing details, creating narratives. Telling all. Trending.

Linda isn't sure which would be worse. If it even matters. She's been off SocialHub for about twenty-four hours and she's already having trouble remembering why she ever checked it at all. The rants and rambles of strangers seem so unimportant now that her mother is on the other side of that door planning a second attempt at the impossible.

Eventually, Percy returns. He's clutching a red notebook—an actual paper notebook, tattered around the edges. When he sees Linda's eyes on it, he tucks it closer to his body—making her curious about what might be inside. He gestures to the bathroom and says, "Go."

When Linda's three minutes are up, Percy takes her back to the bedroom. He lurks by the bedside table, where he's set a sandwich, a sleeve of crackers, and a jug of water. His body language is different from before—less menacing. It's because they need her to cooperate, Linda realizes. If she's to go to the bank in person, it has to look like she's there by her own choice.

Which means she has power. Maybe not a lot, but some.

"Why are you helping her?" asks Linda.

He counters with, "You don't remember me?"

"I do." At his silence, Linda adds, "You were at the pond."

"No, not that." He picks up the plastic ties from the bedside table and twists them between his fingers as he walks toward the door. Linda moves to give him wide berth. "I was there the night you left."

Linda's eyes snap to his face.

"I saw you through the window, then you ran into the woods," he says.

It's impossible. The man in her memory is huge and strong, a destroyer of worlds—nothing like this wiry, aging sycophant.

He must be lying.

But—she was just a girl, and he was the first man she'd ever seen, and so many years have passed since then. She knows her memory may have exaggerated him. She knows he might be telling the truth.

"Why?" she asks. Why him, why then, why now, why everything.

"Penance," he says with a sad little smile. His voice is odd—confessional—and Linda gets the sense he's been wanting to tell her this. "Maddy was my one true love," he says. "And she died because of me."

He shuts the door, leaving Linda stunned and alone.

Days pass. Percy brings her food and water and monitors her trips to the bathroom, but he rarely talks to her other than to issue simple directives. *Go,* he says. *Sit.* He also starts leaving the house during the day for hours at a time—she can hear the front door slam, the car come and go. She sits in the cold dark, listening to the creaking of the house and the intermittent patter of rain. She hears Lorelei occasionally, but when Linda asks to see her, Percy responds, "Are you ready to transfer the money?" then closes the door on her silence.

She can't make any sense of his confession. Madeline's death was a well-documented accident, and Lorelei wouldn't have anything to do with Percy if he were somehow responsible. His claim doesn't make sense. Nothing about Percy makes sense. Multiple times she reaches for her Sheath to search his name and is briefly startled when her fingers meet bare skin. She resented the device so much, but without it, all she can do is wonder.

Occasionally, Linda presses her eye to the crack in the window, seeking a reminder of the world beyond this room. The slender view afforded her is of a slice of forest: damp, swaying cedar branches. One morning she sees a squirrel pop from one limb to another. There is no sign of human life.

They must be close to the Cedar Lake property, she thinks. If Percy was there the same day she and Anvi were—and the day she left as a child—if he's someone who knew Madeline, then he must live near Cedar Lake. She might be in the town limits right now.

She remembers overhearing a conversation between Arthur and his wife: Arthur telling Claire he expected Lorelei's body to be unearthed in the woods by hikers or a dog. *She ran,* he said. *She panicked and ran and died in the woods.* This is the first time she's ever known Arthur to be wrong, and as she sits alone in this cold, dark room, there's a strange comfort in that. At the same time, bitterness simmers in her chest: She imagined Lorelei running endlessly, regret trailing after her like a dog. To think she was tucked away in this house formulating a new plan this whole time is more painful than Linda could ever admit aloud. And Lorelei won't talk to Linda. No matter how many times Linda asks, no matter what she says, Percy only asks her about the bank and then shuts the door in her face.

With each rejection, the truth settles deeper: She's not a person to Lorelei. She's a mistake and a means to correction. Even when Lorelei talked about Linda's creation, about her and Emmer's childhood— she only ever used the word *it*.

Lorelei probably wouldn't have even revealed her presence if Linda had been able to transfer the money with Percy's tablet. Linda might have never known she was here.

This is Linda's first time being denied fresh air. Sunlight. A breeze. She was wrong all these years, thinking she knew what it was to be trapped. Her muscles ache with disuse, and the scabs on her heels and toes grow thick. She shivers constantly.

Rescue scenarios play in her head: Anvi kicking down the door, Nibbler leaping forward to sink his teeth into Percy's calf. In these visions, it's never Arthur who helps her. She imagines him scolding her for walking the streets without her Sheath. She imagines his secret relief at having her gone—and the look in his eyes as the burden of her falls again across his shoulders.

Sometimes her daydreams turn toward violence. The bruises on her legs have faded to yellow, and she thinks of earning more. Of pounding her fists against the window until the boards pop. Of swinging one of the boards to the back of Percy's head. Lorelei's head. Tackling Lorelei to the ground and pressing her old-woman face into the floorboards until she agrees to give up her preposterous plan.

She thinks too of somehow slipping out into the night, silent and unnoticed. But she doesn't know where she is or where she would go, and this scenario feels the least likely of all.

There's no use dreaming. She knows the truth: She's stuck here until she gives Lorelei exactly what she wants.

This time, the door swung open at Graham's touch, revealing a dim living room with a sad couch and dirty fireplace. A stairwell stretched into the darkness above. There was a short hall to the right and an archway to the left. Graham explored the contours of the house, running his fingers through cobwebs, and then he stepped through the archway into the kitchen.

This mission was unique—more about the place than the person. But the person was why people would care. The person was why Graham cared, why he'd argued to save the mission for last. This was his reward for completing all the others.

Graham's exploration was interrupted by a hissing sound. He turned to find a white-chested fox crouched by the door to the back deck. The curl of its spine was catlike, as was the hiss it made.

Graham scanned the kitchen, keeping the fox in sight. Crosshairs blossomed and tightened. Text erupted just above the sink:

CODE ERROR DETECTED

As Graham reached for his reprogramming device, the fox sprang toward him. The device slipped from Graham's grasp and clattered to the floor.

The fox paced in a circle, then stopped to hiss again.

Graham frowned. This didn't feel right at all.

19.

The doorbell rings, sending Nibbler's tail thwapping. Anvi heaves herself off the couch. It's been a near-sleepless week with no word of or from Linda. She's delayed starting work, feigning illness. Lying to her HR contact and group leader probably isn't the best way to start her career at SocialHub, but Anvi didn't know what else to do. Starting a new job with her friend missing felt every shade of wrong.

"Morning," says Arthur, standing in the hall. He hands her a cup of coffee she didn't ask for but very much needs.

"Thanks," says Anvi. She moves aside so he can enter the apartment. Arthur's eyes are bloodshot, but his tie is straight and his collar crisp. She hasn't seen him without a tie. No one she met at SocialHub during the interview process wore a tie.

"Any news?" she asks.

"Nothing." Frowning, Arthur sits on her couch and reaches out to scratch Nibbler's ears.

Guilt weighs heavily on Anvi. She takes a sip of her coffee and is surprised by the earthy hit of the pea milk and the pop of the double shot. Her drink. She ordered one in front of Arthur the other day in a crowded shop while talking of other things. She doesn't remember what he ordered; drip maybe.

Nibbler leans into Arthur's hand. The white hair on Arthur's knuckles pops against the dog's dark fur. "Oh," says Arthur. "I got a little something for him, but I left it down the hall." He gets up. "Want to come with?"

"Sure," says Anvi. Her apartment has become their base of operations, and she hasn't been to Linda's since she accidentally caught Arthur watching Madeline's gravesite. On each of her previous visits, she was careful not to appear too curious, but this time when she steps inside, she openly scans the apartment.

Linda's CircleTread dominates the room. It's a top-end model, and sections of its sleek surface are still encased in protective cling plastic. It had to have cost thousands of dollars, and there it is, discarded in the corner. Anvi grew up more comfortably than most, but this is a whole new tier of wealth. She forces her eyes away from the CircleTread and sees the dead plant, still dead. She sees the blanket crushed into the wicker nest chair. She sees the puzzles she bought Linda. Both are out of the box, and one is solved. She imagines Linda curled in the chair, twisting the puzzle's metal pieces, maybe even smiling a little when she finished it. Like a needle to the heart, the fear comes: that Linda won't have a chance to finish the second puzzle.

She *will*, thinks Anvi. Positivity is key.

She notices that the blood from Linda's feet has been washed away. Arthur hasn't brought in anyone other than the police; he must have cleaned it himself. It breaks her heart to imagine him watching Madeline's grave, alone, as he scrubs the floor clean of his living daughter's blood.

Anvi turns to tell him he should have asked her for help—and she sees Linda's VR headset and gloves sitting on the kitchen counter. A dim red light by the earpiece indicates sleep mode. Instinctively, she picks up the headset and goes to put it in its charging station. And then she stops, staring at that little red light.

Arthur's pulling something out of a bag on the couch. He comes to stand beside her. "I found those on the floor," he says.

The headset feels suddenly heavier in Anvi's hands. Linda left her system running. There could be a clue here: a chat record with a gaming friend who could be sheltering her; a record of locations she's researched; a skills program that provides some vital clue.

But putting on Linda's headset and diving into whatever world she last escaped to feels like a new level of intrusion. Yes, Anvi has her *Butterflies* alert, but anything caught by that is from the public sphere. This is a closed system. Whatever's here belongs to Linda alone.

Looking could help.

It could reveal a horrible secret.

It could do nothing at all.

But it could help. In the end, that's all that matters. Anvi tells herself this is why she taps the wake button and slips the headset onto her forehead. As she grabs the gloves and pulls them on, she thinks it's probably even true.

She settles the headset over her eyes. Fury and Honor's familiar *You're Dead* screen flares before her. Anvi loads the last autosave and soon finds herself standing beside a dirt road, a puppy yapping at her heels. *Pickles,* the game tells her. He shouldn't be out here; dogs are easily killed in this game until they're grown. A strange, dark quirk in a mostly light game.

She checks for in-game messages. Nothing. Linda hasn't gone multiplayer.

She goes into settings to turn off the autosave feature so nothing she does affects Linda's game, then she checks the map. Linda's character—Briggs, the same name she used at Anvi's—is outside Rothram City with a side quest active. Anvi zooms out, and far to the east she sees it: *Home*. A fast-travel tag you can assign to a single lo-cation of your choosing.

This time the decision's easy. As the *Home* location loads, she feels a presence beside her, then a light tap on her shoulder. She shifts the headset to free her ear.

"Anything?" asks Arthur.

"Just a game," says Anvi. Then her borrowed eyes blink open to find a beautiful yellow house. Nothing about it is familiar—and yet, strangely, something about it is. Anvi checks Briggs's skill stats; Linda managed to become an adept at carpentry in only a few days. Anvi moves closer, studying the front steps, the door, trying to understand. It's all meticulously, gorgeously constructed. There's even a section that can only be described as a garage, though it's wide open, without any door Anvi can see.

It hits her: This is Linda's house. An empathetic pang swells in her chest. The time that must have gone into this. The *love*.

She pauses the game and peels off the headset. Arthur's sitting on the small couch, holding a blue-and-green rope chew toy. "You should see this," she says.

Rather than try to explain the headset and gloves to him, Anvi fetches her monitor and keyboard from her apartment and connects it to Linda's system. When it's all set, she unpauses the game.

"That's our house," says Arthur, surprised.

"She built it." Anvi navigates Briggs around the house. They see the shed and what looks like an empty chicken coop, though it's big-ger than any chicken coop Anvi's ever seen. They find a dock Linda's built along the shore of a neighboring lake.

After Arthur and Anvi reported Linda as missing, the police asked if there was anywhere she might go. Arthur gave them the co-ordinates of a neighborhood park, and out of a desperate need to contribute, Anvi mentioned the grocery store—but they both knew there was only one real answer. The Cedar Lake property was the first place the police checked. There was no sign of Linda, but as Anvi navigates Briggs around the lake, she thinks of the dense forest, the charred, run-down house with its pit of a basement. If Linda was there and didn't want to be found, it'd be easy for her to hide.

"I don't understand how she can miss it so much," says Arthur. "It's not like she had a happy childhood."

"Maybe not," says Anvi, "but it's still home." She pauses and leans back. She's seen everything she needs to see. "If she's anywhere by choice, it's there."

Arthur nods and rubs at his face. The dog toy is still in his hand. "You're right," he says. "I'll go. I'll look for myself."

That's what she was hoping he'd say. "I'm going with you," says Anvi. She sees the objection forming on Arthur's lips. "I was just there. I'll notice if something's changed."

Arthur's hesitating, looking for a way to say no. She's noticed this similarity between him and Linda—father and daughter both have trouble accepting help, much less asking for it. But they're dissimilar in how they handle their aversion: Linda shies away; Arthur takes control.

"Arthur." She softens her voice. "Please."

Her turning it into a request allows him to say yes; he nods as though he's the one helping her. "Okay, but stay away from the stairs. I don't want you getting hurt again."

Part of her is annoyed. Part of her is suddenly, fiercely upset that her own father is no longer around to issue unnecessary warnings. She swallows her emotion and asks, "When do we leave?"

"Tomorrow. I have a meeting with Detective Lopez this afternoon."

They first met with Detective Lopez the morning after Linda disappeared. She listened earnestly and promised nothing. The IP address of the post revealing Linda's address traced back to Eastern Europe, which was unhelpful and likely a mask. Lopez also told them the rantings of Internet trolls aren't considered credible threats unless they're specific—otherwise, every bored idiot in America would be behind bars.

After tracing the post turned out to be a bust, Anvi took it upon herself to track down the worst of SocialHub's offenders when it came to Clone Girl: a cretin named Gregory T. He seemed to pop up in every discussion circle even remotely related to Linda, usually spewing vulgarities that never quite tipped over into the realm of "specific threat." His location was easy to confirm: a small town outside Montgomery, Alabama. He'd posted from there the day Linda's address was revealed and again the morning after. With a little digging, Anvi learned he was a cashier at a Safeway and had been arrested for a DUI two years earlier. He was forty-three and living in his childhood home, and nothing about his Internet presence suggested he was capable of masking his IP address.

She needed to dig deeper. So she sidestepped SocialHub's identity confirmation—easily accomplished as long as you don't draw conduct complaints—and created a virtual alter ego: Henry Anderson. As far as the Internet knows, self-employed Seattle native Henry Anderson is every bit as real as Anvi Hendrickson. He already has over three hundred contacts. They're mostly bots, but all Anvi needed was the illusion of authenticity as she crept into the sleazier corners of the Internet, looking for clues and instigating just a little. That's what she was doing this morning before Arthur rang her doorbell—scratching the itch of productivity. So far it's accomplished nothing except to make her feel gross and misanthropic.

An in-person search would get her out of her apartment, where anytime she's not staring at a screen, all she can think is: *I should have kept her here.*

"I'll be here whenever you're ready to go," she tells Arthur.

He smiles. The expression brings a dash of youth to his drawn face, and he reminds her a little of her father in his final hours—how hard he worked to mask his exhaustion and pain. His focus on looking forward, getting better.

"In the meantime," he says, "I'm going to bring out the big guns."

"What's that mean?"

"Cash reward. Someone has to have seen her. Someone has to know something. We've been keeping this quiet, but I think it's time to get loud."

Cash reward. It suddenly becomes harder to imagine her friend hiding in the trees.

With a fervency others might call prayer, Anvi hopes that's where Linda is: hiding.

20.

Linda takes a deep breath and knocks on the door. "I'll do it," she calls. "I'll help."

It takes a few minutes, but Percy opens the door. He's wearing an old gray sweater, and his hair is sticking up at odd angles. He hasn't shaved since bringing her here, and the sprinkling of white in his scraggly facial hair is becoming more pronounced. Linda waits while he considers her. "You'll do it?" he asks. She nods. He watches her a moment more, as though he might be able to calculate her sincerity by looking hard enough. "Give me a minute," says Percy. He shuts her back in. Linda hears the stairs squeak, then silence. Another series of squeaks, and he's back. He nods for her to follow. This is the first time she's been allowed farther than the bathroom in days.

Lorelei is standing at the base of the stairs. Her hair is up in a loose bun, but she's dressed in the same robe as before.

"I'll transfer the money," Linda tells her. It's so much easier to say yes. "You're right, it belongs to you."

"Good," says Lorelei. Linda wonders what happened to her white sweater. In every childhood memory she has of her mother, she's wearing that sweater. Without it, Lorelei seems almost skinless. "Arthur can take you to the bank." *Arthur*. It throws Linda, and she sees Percy flinch. But he doesn't correct her, and Linda wonders if Lorelei makes the slip often.

Lorelei hands Linda a plastic bag from a cupboard. "Go shower. I don't want people distracted by how dirty you are."

Linda's hand sneaks up to the base of her neck, her fingers brushing the greasy edge of her hairline. Lorelei speaks as though Linda decided to lock herself up. As though Linda should be able to control her body's automatic excretions. As though she is any dirtier than Lorelei herself. Percy escorts her to the bathroom.

"I need longer than three minutes," she tells him.

"Take your time."

As she closes the bathroom door, she hears Percy's voice from the main room: "I can't take her now, it's . . ." She presses her ear to the door, but the rest of the exchange is indecipherable.

Linda opens the bag Lorelei gave her. There's a towel and some rolled-up clothing inside, all with price tags. She puts the bag down and shifts the green shower curtain aside, exposing mildewed tile. Pipes groan as she turns on the hot water, and she waits until the temperature warms before undressing, wary of the unlockable door. She tosses her dirty clothing against the base of the door, then steps into the shower. The steam, the pulse of warm pressure against her scalp and shoulders. For years, showers have been a chore, but this—she can't remember a shower ever feeling so good. Looking up to douse her hair, she sees a tiny spider in the corner of the ceiling. It doesn't move as she lathers. Linda wonders if it's dead or perhaps just a husk and is tempted to touch it, but this is one answer she doesn't need to know. The scent of the shampoo hits her nose, fresh and welcome—though nothing like the "summer rain" the bottle advertises. She uses the shampoo for her body too, not wanting to touch the hair-brindled bar of soap sitting in its own scum on the tub's edge.

She stands under the shower long after she's done washing, not wanting to return to the cold. Not wanting to face Lorelei's demands or Percy's looming silence. She wishes she was back in her apartment, about to head out on an excursion. She'd text Anvi; ask her if she wanted to share dinner or perhaps network their VR systems to try one of the cooperative puzzle games she's read about. Or they could explore Rothram together in Fury and Honor. She could show Anvi the home she's building there.

That feels so long ago: sitting on the replica of her dock, killing the deer.

The hot water fades to cold. Finally, Linda cranks the faucet shut. *Click.*

Linda stalls with her hand on the faucet. The sound came from the other side of the shower curtain. Goosebumps pimple her skin as she stands dead still, listening. Nothing. She peeks around the curtain.

The room is empty.

She begins to relax, thinking she made it up or that the sound was a quirk of the old house, something to do with the pipes. Then she notices her pile of dirty clothing on the floor—there's a clean-edged gap of several inches between it and the door.

Maddy was my one true love.

She died because of me.

Hurriedly, Linda towels off and dresses in the clothing from the bag: black leggings and a green sweatshirt. Everything but the socks, which she doesn't want to get wet. In her haste, she puts on the sweatshirt backward; the hood dangles down her chest. She squirms the shirt the right way around. Clothed, she stares at the door. She doesn't want to go into the hallway, doesn't want to look at Percy or be looked at by him. But she can't stay in here forever. She picks up her dirty clothes and opens the door, then walks quickly back into her room.

Linda sits and puts on the socks, tearing the pair apart so that the little tab of plastic between them flies off into the air. The price sticker reads WALGREENS. She knows that doesn't mean they are from the Cedar Lake store she and Anvi visited—but she can't help but think it's likely.

Percy hasn't come back. Linda steps into the hall. She sees him standing in the kitchen. There's a kettle on the stove that's beginning to whistle. When he sees her, Percy turns off the kettle.

"It's too late," he says.

Linda's heart thuds with sharp worry, and she notices the armchair has been moved directly in front of the front door. A blockade.

Percy pulls two mugs out of a cabinet. Linda tenses, ready to run or fight. "The bank will be closed by the time we get there," says Percy. "We'll go in the morning."

Relief floods through Linda. Percy motions for her to sit on the couch, and she does. Her gaze ricochets between Percy and the stairs. She's surprised Lorelei isn't here and annoyed at herself for that surprise.

Percy walks over, holding the mugs. He hands one to Linda. Hot chocolate. She breathes in its rich scent and tucks its warmth to her chest like a battery. But she doesn't drink it, and she keeps her eyes on Percy as he sits in the armchair and takes a sip. She thinks of him opening the bathroom door, watching the thin shower curtain. "Do you think she'd look like me?" she asks.

Startled, he briefly makes eye contact.

"If Madeline hadn't died," insists Linda. "Do you think she would have grown up to look like me?" He must think about it; he already said Linda looks more like her in person.

Percy lowers his mug. "Your eyes are wrong," he says. "She had the most beautiful eyes. And the nose, obviously. But it's impossible not to see similarities." There's a long pause. "I'm not stupid, I know Maddy's gone. But Lorelei needs this."

Like she needed Linda and Emmer? But Linda doesn't push; she doesn't want Percy to think she's having second thoughts. She rests her mug on her lap. The leggings she's wearing feel strange; she's used to baggy fabric. She wonders why Percy chose this clothing—if this is how Madeline dressed.

It almost feels more like she's mid-quest in Fury and Honor than sitting in a real room in the real world. Lorelei is the boss, Percy her minion. Linda needs to steal their secrets, defeat them, and escape.

It helps, thinking like this.

"What was Madeline like?" she asks.

Percy's eyes spark. This is the key to him, thinks Linda. This is what he wants to talk about.

"She was an angel," he starts, but then there's a loud *thunk* from above. His eyes shoot toward the stairs and he stands. "Go back to your room," he tells Linda. "Now."

Linda does, expecting Percy to lock her inside—but instead he goes straight upstairs. "Lorelei," he calls. "Are you okay?"

Linda stands in the doorway, unguarded for the first time. She decides to risk it: not an escape—Percy would hear her move the chair—but a different transgression. Percy's room is just down the hall. She creeps toward his door and tries the handle. It opens, creaking slightly. Linda holds her breath but doesn't hear any change in the murmuring above.

Whatever she expected, it wasn't this. The room is crammed with memorabilia, the walls lined with faded and curled posters, mostly of bands with their names in sharp, angry fonts but also a few of large-chested women in bathing suits. There is a bookshelf in one corner, three small trophies and a handful of picture frames mixed among the books. Next to the twin-sized bed is a small desk. The base of its lamp is shaped like a football. It's as though she's stepped through time to Percy's youth. Only the shine of fingerprints atop dusty matte surfaces tells the truth of the room's age.

A glimpse of red atop the desk: the notebook she saw him holding days ago. She glances back into the hallway, listening. Percy is still upstairs.

She grabs the notebook. Flipping it open, she finds page upon page of printed-out emails.

She thumbs back to the beginning:

From: Percival Hunter   1:46 A.M. 6/29/2002
To: Maddy Niequist
RE: hi

Maddy,

I can't stop thinking about you. Little Madeline Niequist all grown up. I hope you didn't feel pressured about the beer. I was just kidding around. I respect that you said no and I def don't want your dad to set the cops on me!

P.

From: Maddy Niequist   10:21 A.M. 6/30/2002
To: Percival Hunter
RE: RE: hi

Percy,

How did you get this email address?! j/k No worries about the beer. I'm a big girl. My parents are dragging me to the BBQ at the firehouse this weekend. Are you gonna be there?

Maddy

From: Percival Hunter   7:05 P.M. 6/30/2002
To: Maddy Niequist
RE: RE: RE: hi

Not only will I be there I'll be grilling. Rite of passage for new volunteers. I hope you like your burgers raw on the inside and crispy on the outside cause that's the only way I know how to do them.

P.

From: Maddy Niequist   8:11 P.M. 6/30/2002
To: Percival Hunter
RE: RE: RE: RE: hi

Aw shucks. I only eat mine raw on the outside and crispy on the inside.
Too bad!

From: Percival Hunter   2:04 A.M. 7/1/2002
To: Maddy Niequist
RE: RE: RE: RE: RE: hi

For you, anything.

There are dozens of pages of these messages, each taped carefully into place. Linda has no idea when Percy might return—or what he might do if he catches her reading this. She thumbs forward, scanning increasingly flirtatious and intimate messages.

I'm pretty sure my mom cares about those foxes more than she does about me, writes Madeline in one. *Sometimes I want to take an ax to that stupid hutch and kill them all.*

I'll do it for you if you want, replies Percy. *Make it look like an accident.*

She flips forward again, heart pounding, until a date catches her eye: August. The month Madeline died. This email chain starts just a week before her death.

From: Maddy Niequist   9:21 A.M. 8/10/2002
To: Percival Hunter
RE: See you tonite!

Perc,

I think I got ten minutes of sleep last night. Part of me kept expecting my mom to come barging into my room, like some latent maternal instinct might kick in and she'd be able to tell. As if. She's so fucking blind. They both are. We could probably walk into the fundraiser holding hands and my dad would just be like "Eeeer . . . microchips! Blah blah processing power blah blah derp!" God, I can't wait until we don't have to hide. There should be an application or something where I could be like "just b/c I'm young doesn't mean I'm stupid." And you'll be certified soon and SAVING LIVES!!! That should mean something.

Anyway, I can't stop thinking about you. See you tonite!!!!!

XOX

Maddy

From: Percival Hunter   10:12 A.M. 8/10/2002
To: Maddy Niequist
RE: RE: See you tonite!

You are an angel. I still don't know what your doing with an oaf like me. Holding you in my arms last night was a dream come true. I don't know how I'm going to keep my hands off you tonite.

Luv,

P.

    Linda turns the page—it's blank. She flips wildly, but the rest of the yellowed pages are blank. She is about to go back to the beginning and read everything she skipped, when she realizes the house is silent. Percy might be downstairs already, he might be—there's no time to wonder. She places the notebook on the desk and goes to the door, peeking her head around the frame. She doesn't see Percy—then the stairs creak. She steps into the hall, closes the door quietly behind her, and hurries back into her room, where she sits as softly as she can on the bed. Percival Hunter. His full name feels vaguely familiar, though she still can't place it. Her heart thrums with transgression— and with discovery. It's as though she's found pieces of a puzzle, pieces that make it clear the puzzle is much larger than she ever suspected.

From: Lorelei Niequist   Draft Saved 8:16 P.M. 11/12/2004

To: Arthur Niequist

RE:

I feel faint all the time. Tight chested. Off. I don't remember it being like this. Advanced maternal age. Internet says I'm lucky I got pregnant at all.

That's me all right. So. Fucking. Lucky.

21.

nvi's stomach knots as she watches the video on Arthur's Sheath. They're sitting together in Linda's apartment. As soon as the reward was announced last night, tips started flooding in. Almost none are credible—there's no way Linda's stripping in Las Vegas or selling organic seedlings in a farmers market in New Orleans—but one man sent a video: Linda barefoot, her face racked with pain, turning a corner a few blocks away. It's a short clip, her appearance an unintentional cameo in the tourist's video review of a coffee shop across the street. Linda looks absolutely heartbroken. She looks like someone who's been rendered incapable of making rational decisions.

For the first time, Anvi fears something worse than her running away or even being kidnapped may have happened.

"I didn't mean to upset her," whispers Arthur, stricken. "I came over to apologize and it all just went to hell."

"I know." Anvi thinks of Linda's quiet stillness, the way her eyes often do all her talking, and she guesses that stoicism is the side of Linda that Arthur knows best too.

Arthur lowers his Sheath and begins fiddling with an old, dirty gaming-console controller they found on Linda's kitchen counter.

I could have stopped her, thinks Anvi. She imagines Linda's body washing up in the sound.

No. Linda wasn't suicidal—was she? Would Anvi know? Beside her, Arthur presses buttons in a repetitive pattern.

Anvi thinks of the house Linda re-created virtually, a loving homage to what Anvi's only ever thought of as an ugly past. She wants to ask Linda all about it—not the neglect, but the beauty Anvi never even considered must have existed too.

"Do you still want to go?" she asks Arthur.

"Yeah, let's." He puts down the controller and stands, looking around the room as though there might be some clue they missed.

"Do you mind if Nibs comes along?" asks Anvi. "Linda likes him."

"Sure," says Arthur. "He probably has a better chance of finding her anyway."

They collect Nibbler from Anvi's apartment, then head down to Arthur's rental car.

Instead of driving toward the freeway, Arthur takes them down the street where the video showed Linda walking. Anvi scans the storefronts, wondering if any of their security cameras will show anything helpful. That's what Detective Lopez is up to today: collecting footage. She might even be in one of those stores now. It's a comfort, a chance: facial-recognition software.

As they creep through a construction zone, Anvi watches Arthur's eyes dart for clues.

"We'll find her," she says.

He nods and turns toward an on-ramp. As they merge onto I-5, Anvi syncs her Sheath to the stereo and, in an attempt to lighten the mood, asks, "Podcast or music?"

"Anything but *TASTMEs,*" replies Arthur. The car is a simpler model than the one Linda rented, a small electric Toyota—nonautonomous. Anvi wonders if he always drives himself or if it's a control thing to combat his feelings of helplessness regarding Linda. Nibbler pants in the back seat as Anvi scrolls through her podcasts. She settles for a show where triplets discuss their favorite childhood movies while railing against the short attention spans of "today's youths."

"We used to do this drive almost every weekend," says Arthur as they creep south in a sea of taillights. "You used the brakes a hell of a lot less back then."

The podcast's intro music blares; Anvi turns it down. "Do you ever miss living out here?" she asks.

"I miss things about it, like the trees. The East Coast grows them stumpy. But leaving was the right call."

Anvi thinks of her need to get away from Ithaca after everything with Tasha went down. She too fled to the opposite coast—after a much smaller loss. They drive, the podcast droning on. Anvi plays a silent game in which she tries to make sense of license plates. PLY2274, she sees. That's one strong paper towel.

Arthur chuckles, and for a second Anvi is confused—she made the joke in her head, and it wasn't a very good one—but the podcast hosts are laughing too. She's lost track of what movie the triplets are talking about.

After a while, she says, "I don't think I've ever said I'm sorry about Madeline. I can't imagine how difficult that must have been."

"It's an indescribable pain," says Arthur, a blunt statement of fact. "Have you lost anyone close to you?"

"My father, last year."

"I'm sorry to hear that. Can I ask what happened?"

"Cardiac arrest." Her father had a heart attack on a Tuesday evening, falling unconscious halfway between the master bath and his bed. Anvi's mother initiated CPR and he burst back to life, only to have his heart stop once and for all on Thursday morning. Anvi made it home just in time to say goodbye, though of course neither of them said any such thing. They said he was going to be fine and spoke of what they would do together once he was out of the hospital. Holding his hand, trying not to look at the bruise on his temple where his head had smacked the floor, listening to him talk about his childhood, her childhood, how he hoped her younger brother would find his path soon, Anvi refused to acknowledge aloud the possibility of his dying. But years earlier, during the pandemic, fear for her parents' lives had settled in her chest like a solid, suffocating object, easing only after the vaccine was developed—and seeing her father in that hospital bed had brought back all her long-simmering terror. She was out of the room when his heart gave out, but she saw him after: a simulacrum emptied of her father. It was horrific, really, and she doesn't want to talk about it.

"What was Madeline like?" she asks.

"She was our everything," says Arthur. "Such a sweet, smart girl."

As awful as Anvi's father's death was, at least he was old. At least he'd lived a full life. At least Anvi had always vaguely assumed she would outlive him. At least he didn't die like Tasha's father: blue-lipped in a hospital hallway, deprived not only of oxygen but of touch. Of family.

"When I think about who Maddy could have become," says Arthur, "the kind of impact she could have had on the world . . ." Something in his voice makes Anvi think he envisions her traveling the world with the magic wand of her amazingness, stopping disease and war and individual psychopaths. The quippy, reactive part of her wants to ask if he thinks Madeline could have stopped the bombing in Munich last year or the two school shootings just this month.

She understands the instinct, though. She doesn't think her father could have changed the world if he clung to life for a few more years—he'd had an entire life in which to meet his potential—but now that he's gone, it's easy to forget his flares of temper or how after a glass of wine too many one Thanksgiving, he told Tasha he hoped Anvi would bring home a man next year.

"She would have loved Nibbler," says Arthur. "She always wanted a dog."

Anvi's thoughts shift, and she thinks of the orange-furred character Linda created in Fury and Honor. "Her mother raised foxes, right?" That had always struck her as a fascinating hobby.

"Yeah. Mads would help with them whenever we were at Cedar Lake."

"What about when you were in the city? I'm assuming you didn't bring them with you."

"No, we had a local boy help us out. Sad story, that one. He lost both of his parents in a car crash when he was a toddler and lived with his aunt and uncle. His uncle was a drunk, his aunt this meek little thing—good heart but no spine. Anyway, we got to know them a bit through the community center; we'd take Mads over for activities when she was little. He was a few years older than her, and we hired him to check on the house while we were away. Water the plants, feed the foxes, stuff like that." Arthur switches lanes. Their exit is only a few miles ahead. "I hope he got out of that town," he says. "Percy was a good kid."

Linda wakes to arguing: Lorelei's voice loud, her words lost as Linda rocks into awareness, then Percy's sharp but soft reply. She hurries to the door to listen. The word *wait* from Percy. A shouted *no* from Lorelei. A crashing sound that makes Linda flinch—glass breaking. Percy, louder: "Stop, you'll hurt yourself." Creaking wood as Lorelei retreats upstairs. Linda listens a little longer, then sits on the bed, extracting the blue marble from a fold in the blanket. Light is creeping in from the window; she doesn't know how she slept so late. She was expecting Percy to wake her and take her to the bank, and she tossed and turned late into the night, thinking about what she would do once they got there.

When the bedroom door opens, Percy looks exhausted. "We can't go," he says.

"Why?"

Instead of answering, he gestures toward the bathroom and leaves. Linda guesses her three minutes start now.

She pees, rinses her face and mouth, then—an itch of a thought—instead of hurrying out of the bathroom, she waits. Counting seconds in her head, she reaches five minutes, and still Percy hasn't come. She stops counting but keeps waiting. Another few minutes pass. Last night she prepared for bed as quickly as she could, not wanting Percy to open the door on her, but now she suspects that wasn't necessary.

Is this modicum of freedom the result of her cooperation—or because Percy feels guilty about watching her shower? She thinks of emails taped into an old notebook and tries to imagine the boy Percy would have been back then, what about him could have appealed to Madeline. It's impossible. Almost as difficult is imagining what he could have seen in Madeline: Linda always pictured her as a little girl, too young for romance, and it's strange having to adjust her perception. Madeline was just shy of fifteen when she died. Linda thinks of all that had happened in her own life by the time she was that age. Emmer's disappearance. Leaving the property. Dr. Tambor's death.

She leaves the bathroom, then, after a brief hesitation, turns toward the main room. Percy's standing in the mouth of the kitchen. "Coffee?" he asks.

Linda shakes her head, bewildered. It's like he wants her to feel like a guest. "Why can't we go to the bank?" she asks. It's almost a relief to see that the armchair is still blocking the front door. Percy isn't entirely pretending she's here of her own free will.

"We just can't," he says. "Not yet." He takes a sip of his coffee. Linda sees a shiny patch on the tile floor by his feet. He wiped up something there—whatever Lorelei broke. "It's just as well," he adds.

"I'd say there's at least a sixty percent chance you're lying about wanting to help."

He thinks there's a chance she's sincere. That's a start. "I just want to go home," she says truthfully. "And it's her money."

"Sure," says Percy. "Have a seat."

Linda sits on the couch. Minutes pass as she tries to decide what to say next.

Then Percy asks, "Has it been hard?"

Standing at the counter with his coffee, he looks so harmless. Linda doesn't understand him, this man who claims to have both loved Madeline and been responsible for her death. This man who attacked her in an alleyway, crammed her into the back seat of his car, and shuttled her here—but who now can't meet her eye.

She hates that she sees herself in his slumped posture, his averted eyes.

"Yes," she says.

Percy leans against the kitchen counter, still not looking at her. "When I found out you existed, I . . . Seeing you in the window, it was like Maddy was staring at me."

"Why were you there?"

"I went to the gate to lay some flowers, like every year," says Percy. "Lorelei spotted me a few years earlier and we talked through the bars. It became a ritual. But this time she invited me in. We talked about Maddy and . . . I was trying to convince her to let me help her with the place. It was a wreck, nothing like it used to be. Then you popped up in the window. Lorelei started yelling and I was just— I didn't know what was happening. You ran off into the woods and I started after, but Lorelei stopped me."

Be scarce. How many times did Linda sit in her tree while Percy and Lorelei talked through the gate—her missing Emmer while they mourned a different sister she didn't know existed.

"And then you both left," she says.

"She got some stuff from the basement, and I brought her here." He sighs and rubs at his face. "I was going to go back, but Lorelei was so upset. I was trying to convince her to let me take her to the hospital. By the time she calmed down, my phone was ringing, and a buddy from town was talking about how a kid just walked out of the woods onto Main Street and fuck all if she didn't bear a striking resemblance to Maddy Niequist." He opens a cupboard and takes out a box of the same brand of cereal Linda buys. This throws her as much as his newfound loquaciousness. Of all the cereals out there, she and Percy eat the same unsweetened O's.

"You know," he says, "if it'd been any other night, they might not have recognized you. Fucking morbid town, her death was the biggest thing to ever happen to them. It's like they celebrated it, gathering at the bar each year to tell ghost stories." He closes the cupboard, hard, then holds up the cereal, offering Linda some. She shakes her head. Percy makes himself a bowl.

"Why are you telling me this?" she asks.

He shrugs. "It's going to be at least a few weeks before I can take you out," he says. "Might as well get comfortable." Weeks. What could have possibly happened to delay their plan by weeks? Percy catches her looking at the stairs and says, "Not *that* comfortable. Upstairs is off-limits. Upstairs and my room."

Linda's breath catches at the mention of his room—but Percy just keeps eating his cereal. If he knows she was in his room, he's hiding it well. He puts his empty bowl in the sink, then pulls his tablet out of a drawer and sits in the armchair. "If you want a book or something, help yourself," he says, and he points to a bookshelf by the woodstove. Not knowing what else to do, Linda goes over. The shelf is stacked with ratty paperbacks. She pulls one out and pretends to read the back cover while she thinks. She can't be here for *weeks*. She was planning to end this today.

She pulls out another few books—the cover of one looks like a scene from Fury and Honor: goblins rushing from a cave, a warrior with a shining sword. The spine is heavily creased and faded. She takes the book and sits on the couch.

"That's a good one," says Percy. "One of my favorites when I was a kid." Like they're just two people sitting in a room. His nonchalance makes Linda nervous. *You kidnapped me,* she wants to shout. Instead, she opens the book and begins to read, shooting intermittent glances at Percy, trying to determine what it might be safe to ask him about. She has time, she thinks. Despite the tension, it's oddly comfortable to just sit here, her attention split but some of it on a book. The story opens with an orphan boy helping a girl and refusing reward. A wizard soon tells him he's been chosen by the gods to save the world. It's a simple book, but appealing.

After a while Percy rises to make sandwiches, taking his tablet with him. He gives Linda a sandwich, then says, "Don't move," and takes another upstairs. Percy's voice mumbles. Linda doesn't hear a reply, and a few seconds later he's back.

She was waiting for Lorelei to come down to eat, but apparently that's not going to happen. After Percy settles back into his chair, there's the sound of running water above. Linda takes a bite of her sandwich. It's thick with mayonnaise and heavily processed meat, and it settles in her stomach like a clump of raw dough. If Lorelei has her own bathroom, then she has no reason to come downstairs. Waiting for her is useless. This changes things, and Linda's not sure what to do.

Percy rises to fill the woodstove. "I have to get ready for work," he tells Linda. He nods toward the bedroom. "In you go."

Linda takes the book and sandwich with her. Percy locks her inside.

She hears the sound of the shower. Footsteps. Various patterns of shuffling and silence. It feels like forever before there's the scrape of the armchair being moved, the slam of the door. Finally the gas engine sputters to life, disappears down the driveway, and Percy's gone.

It's just Linda here, and somewhere above her: Lorelei.

Linda forces herself to read another couple of chapters of the book, just in case Percy turns around. The orphan boy learns to fight and falls in love.

Linda's so distracted, she forgets the love interest's name within seconds of reading it.

If she's going to do this, now's the time.

She rises from the bed. "Lorelei," she calls. She bangs on the door three times, then calls again. She waits, bangs. Minutes pass. She clears her throat. She needs volume; she can do this. "Lorelei!" She slams her fist against the wood. It hurts her throat to shout so loudly. "Lorelei, I remember the password!"

It feels like it takes hours, but Lorelei finally opens the door. There's a foggy look to her eyes, and she stares at Linda as though she doesn't know who she is. It throws Linda—did she wake her?—but she forges ahead. "I can log in to my bank account," she says.

Blankness, like Lorelei doesn't understand. She squints at Linda, strangely distant.

"I can give you the money," insists Linda. And then, as eager to please as she can make it sound, "I just need to use Percy's tablet."

Lorelei cocks her head; her squint blossoms into wide eyes. "Emmer?" she says. The name, that look, the softness of Lorelei's voice—it sucks Linda into a black hole. Before she can extract herself, Lorelei is blinking and rubbing at her face. "No, no, no," whispers Lorelei.

She slams the door in Linda's face.

From: Lorelei Niequist   Draft Saved 3:05 A.M. 11/22/2004
To: Arthur Niequist
RE:

Its not her I can feel it this thing in me its not her it can't be what am I doing. I closed my eyes and I saw it it's a monster not her. I came this close to walking to town and saying get it out but if they

I don't know what to do. I cant what if its not her what if I'm

22.

Linda stares at the grain of the door where Lorelei used to be.

Your mother wasn't well. How many times did Dr. Tambor tell her that? Linda thought she understood—but nothing compared to seeing this. It was like a switch clicked Lorelei into different emotional states. That flicker of loving softness when she thought Linda was Emmer.

It's the first time she's heard Lorelei say Emmer's name since she was a little girl. The loss there—any lingering shred of hope Linda had that her twin might still be alive melts away. Lorelei wouldn't use that tone for someone who just walked away.

What happened in the basement that day?

Sunlight creeps through the crack in the window. Linda watches it shift and dim as she rolls the marble through her hands. After maybe an hour, the door opens again, startling Linda. She was so lost in thought she didn't hear Percy return.

But it's not Percy, it's Lorelei—and this time it's a Lorelei that Linda recognizes. Sharp. Cool, with an edge of annoyance.

And she's holding Percy's tablet.

"Do it," says Lorelei, as though there was nothing unusual about their last encounter. She hands Linda the tablet. Holding it is like having the world open up before her. Lorelei has no idea what she's just given her.

Linda opens the default browser—it looks like the one on her tablet, not the one Percy had her use before. A good sign, she thinks. Lorelei hovers beside her as she types her bank's name into the search bar. As she taps through, a notification pops up on the bottom of the screen: *Where is Clone Girl? Cash Reward Offered for Information.* Linda's heart thumps; she minimizes the alert. She holds her breath, expecting an outburst from Lorelei, but she doesn't seem to have noticed.

People are looking for her. *Arthur* is looking for her. Because who else could—would—offer a cash reward on her behalf? This must be why Percy wouldn't take her to the bank this morning; people are looking. She wonders how much the reward is for. It must be less than Lorelei needs, or else Percy would just find a way to take that—wouldn't he?

"Hurry up," says Lorelei.

Linda scans the page, taps the log-in. "Before I do this—"

"No conditions," says Lorelei. She takes a slip of paper out of her robe's pocket. The account number Linda's supposed to transfer the money to. "Do it."

Tremors sneak through Linda. This shouldn't be so hard to say. "I need you to tell me what happened to my sister."

Lorelei looks at her with heavy disdain. "You know exactly what happened."

Laying Emmer's body into a grave suddenly feels like too tender an act for the woman beside her. All the softness from earlier is gone, and Linda can now easily visualize Lorelei stuffing Emmer into the hole in the basement. She thinks of her twin's body waterlogged and rotting, decaying into mush. She can barely breathe; suspicion is suddenly fact: Lorelei killed Emmer.

Lorelei reaches for the tablet. "You're bullshitting, aren't you?" she says.

"No, I—"

"Then do it. Now."

Linda is still reeling. She can't think straight. She continues with her plan. *Linda_Russell,* she types. And for the password: *percival-hunter.*

She doesn't know how it works, if incorrect passwords are recorded. But she has to try.

This username and password combination doesn't match our records.

"What happened?" asks Lorelei.

"Typo," says Linda. She sits on the bed. "I'll try again."

Username: *Linda_Russell.* Password: *cedarlake.*

This username and password combination doesn't match our records.

As quick as she can, again.

Username: *Linda_Russell.* Password: *loreleiishere.*

Due to too many log-in attempts, your account is temporarily locked. Please contact customer support.

There, thinks Linda. They have to record that. Arthur will notice that. And even if they can't see the passwords, hopefully this browser can be tracked.

"Why did you stop?" asks Lorelei. "Try again."

Lorelei can't read the small text, Linda realizes. That's why she didn't notice the news alert.

"I must be wrong," says Linda. "It's not working."

"Useless," says Lorelei.

A car door slams outside.

Could they have tracked her so quickly?

No. It's Percy's voice that rings out as the front door opens. "Lorelei? What is it?"

"I should have known you'd fail," says Lorelei. "Now I paged him for nothing."

"Lorelei?" calls Percy again. Lorelei turns toward the voice, and as Percy's footsteps clomp upstairs, Linda sneaks the tablet under the blanket.

Lorelei gives Linda a sharp look, then follows Percy.

She doesn't take the tablet—and she leaves the door open.

Linda stares, astounded. She should be celebrating, but instead she feels a weird nub of disappointment: Lorelei shouldn't be so easy to fool.

She pulls out the tablet and searches for *Percival Hunter Cedar Lake.*

Madeline Niequist was found, severely injured in an apparent fall, by eighteen-year-old Cedar Lake local and EMT-trainee Percival Hunter.

Of course: Percy was the volunteer who found Madeline. He was one of the two men who were with her when she died.

She died because of me.

Does he feel guilty because he didn't know how to save her? Is that the basis of his loyalty to Lorelei? She scrolls and finds a picture of eighteen-year-old Percy at some community barbecue. Maybe the same one from his emails with Madeline. He's a skinny teenager holding a spatula.

Percy's voice, loud from upstairs: "You did what?" And then the thudding of his rushing downstairs. Toward Linda.

Linda slams the door, braces herself against it, then taps Percy's email app. She was stupid not to run when she had the chance, but if she can get a message out—the app opens, and her plan slips away.

Percy slams into the door. The tablet flies across the floor as Linda stumbles, but even as Percy rushes inside, Linda can't take her eyes off the screen.

Sitting just a few messages from the top of Percy's inbox is a message from Anvi Hendrickson.

*   *   *

"Percy?" asks Anvi. Her heart thuds, hard. "As in Percival Hunter?"

"Yeah," says Arthur, looking over. "You know him?"

"He's the one who found Madeline."

"Him and Paul, yes."

"I . . ." *Fuck,* thinks Anvi. "I did a little research after I met Linda, and I came across his name. And I emailed him."

"What?" asks Arthur. The car swerves slightly as he twitches to look at her. "Why?"

"I don't know. I'd just met Linda and it was exciting. She's . . . she's *Clone Girl.*" Anvi flinches even as she says it, and she sees Arthur stiffen. "You know what I mean. I was curious."

"That doesn't explain contacting Percy."

She isn't sure she can explain that impulse without explaining her whole secret filing system. The night Linda searched for her on So-cialHub and Anvi figured out who she was, she stayed up until nearly 3 A.M. researching the Niequist family's history. Huddling in the light of her computer—this endeavor was too extensive for her Sheath—she stumbled across a grainy video of an interview with one Percival Hunter, a lanky white kid in a baseball cap. The clip was from the morning after Madeline died. The reporter had ambushed the young man outside the police station, and though Percival had been polite, he was clearly exhausted and devastated. Anvi became entranced by the thought of an eighteen-year-old kid being the one to find Madeline. She couldn't find any follow-up reporting, any ex-amination of the effects of that awful discovery on the boy's life. And so she decided to search for him herself, curious to learn what kind of man such a boy might become.

There was nothing useful online; none of the Percival Hunters on SocialHub were even from Washington State. So, assuming he was still alive and living in the same general area, Anvi generated a list of possible email addresses, using combinations of his first and last names, his initials, and his birth year. Twenty-four combinations to start, each of which she then attached to the current-day most popular email server, three of the most popular email servers from the year Madeline died, and the biggest Internet provider in Cedar Lake. One hundred twenty possible addresses. She sent an email to each, hoping.

Fifty-one bounced back, seventeen garnered replies along the lines of *Sorry, wrong person,* one earned her a vague and poorly written death threat, and the rest brought no response at all. Then a few days later, as she was contemplating sending a second batch of emails, she received a reply from a Yahoo address: *I have no current connection to the Niequist family, and my life since that day is my own concern.*

She followed up, of course. Percival's denial was too strong to resist. Their brief back-and-forth was mostly useless; she learned Percival worked as a part-time delivery man for AmazonFresh but little else. Still, she feels guilty about it—this evidence that her interest in Linda isn't strictly friendly. That she's interested in her as an idea as well as an individual. But she hasn't told anyone she knows Linda—not even her mother, who she's been lying to all week. The same lie she told her group leader, that she's sick with the flu.

I'm not exploiting her, she wants to tell Arthur. *I'm just curious.* A certain amount of curiosity is justified, she thinks. All things considered. But she's wary of sounding defensive, and she thinks she has an angle he can relate to.

"I like to collect data," she tells him. "It's like an itch. When I found out a teenager was the one who found Madeline, I just . . . I needed to know more." Arthur knows she's about to start at SocialHub; they had a conversation about her hope to build a better reliability algorithm the other day. She told him about Scrub too; he laughed and confessed that he was glad he got out of the software game before social media took over the world.

Arthur switches lanes to pass a sluggish pickup. As he merges back, he asks, "Did he have anything interesting to say?"

The tension in Anvi's neck dissipates. "Not really," she says.

"That kid spent as much time at that house as I did."

"It must have been hard on him."

They drive in silence for a few moments, then Arthur continues with a guilty tinge to his voice. "I didn't think much about Percy after everything happened. What it must have been like for him. Maybe I should reach out."

"I have his email if you'd like it."

"Sure. Thanks."

Miles drift beneath them, the voices from the stereo like white noise, punctuated by the occasional snore from Nibbler in the back. Arthur's acceptance of her emailing Percy feels like tacit approval of her curiosity. Eventually, Anvi asks, "What was your wife like?"

His answer comes easily, like he doesn't mind being asked. "Coddled, but a sweetheart. I tried to do right by her."

The answer throws her. "I'm sure you did your best."

"It wasn't enough, apparently."

"You can't blame yourself for what Lorelei did—"

"Oh!" says Arthur. "You meant Lor. No, I'm sorry, I was talking about Claire. My current wife."

Embarrassment flushes through Anvi. This is different from talking about an ex who's been missing for years and presumed dead. More intimate. *Coddled,* she thinks. An odd thing to say about a grown woman.

"Sorry," says Arthur again. "She—Claire—asked for a divorce not long ago. I'm still adjusting."

"I'm sorry," says Anvi. She's surprised she hasn't seen any headlines about this. The papers must not be filed yet. "Are she and Linda close?"

"No. Claire tried, but . . ."

Anvi wonders whose fault lies at the heart of that *but.* Did Claire not try hard enough, or did Linda not try at all? She thinks of the way

Linda sat so stiffly on her couch, like she was scared to breathe lest that be an imposition on Anvi.

"Anyway," says Arthur, his voice suddenly chipper as he changes subject. "Lorelei. She was something else. What do you want to know?"

"Did you ever suspect she could do something like . . . Linda?"

"No. Though perhaps I should have. Her mother had an undiagnosed bipolar disorder, we think. And her brother—officially his death was an accident, but I know Lor always feared intent."

"But Lorelei wasn't ever diagnosed with anything, was she?" asks Anvi.

"No, but I wonder if Madeline's death triggered something. You know how it is: All these studies show how you can carry the genes and be completely fine as long as they're dormant. But if chance or your environment makes them switch on, you're in trouble. The heritability of mental illness wasn't as well understood back then as it is now, and the stigma was still strong. Mostly, we ignored that possibility. And things between us went bad so quickly afterward that I just . . . honestly, I gave up. I asked her to get help, but Lor refused, and I was dealing with my own grief." He pauses and drums his fingers along the steering wheel. "It's amazing, really, how quickly love can flip to . . . not hate but something like it."

Anvi thinks of Tasha, of the complicated washes of emotions she feels toward her ex. And they were together for less than two years.

The podcast ends. She taps at her Sheath to select something different before autoplay kicks in—and is flung forward against her seatbelt as Arthur slams on the brakes. Anvi's face snaps up; on the road ahead—too close—is a huge brown mammal—deer, elk, moose? And then the animal flashes out of view as they careen off the road and Anvi's head smacks the side window.

23.

Percy swipes the tablet off the floor and turns to Linda. "You remembered the password, huh?"

She scrambles to her feet, dazed. *Anvi.* Anger and sadness hang thick in her throat.

"I was wrong," she whispers.

"Like hell you were." Percy's tapping at the tablet. "Which browser did you use?"

Linda's thoughts stretch, desperate to find some benign explanation for why Anvi would be exchanging emails with her kidnapper. But the only answer she can find is that Anvi is part of this.

"Which browser?" demands Percy. He's staring at her with a firmness she hasn't seen from him in days.

"You're the one who found Madeline," says Linda, deflecting. His attention, her own thoughts. Anvi—*why?*

"Finally connected the dots?" says Percy. "Good for you." He pats at his pockets. "Goddammit," he whispers again. "Don't move." He storms past Linda, slamming the door. "Lorelei! Where's the key?"

The key. If he doesn't have it—Linda tries the knob. It turns.

Percy's footsteps rush upstairs. Linda doesn't have much time. She has to get out of here. Now that Percy knows she isn't really cooperating, she doesn't know what he'll do.

You can do this, she tells herself. *You* have *to do this.* Anvi doesn't matter. Her betrayal doesn't matter.

She leaves the room.

Percy's car keys and pocketknife are on the kitchen counter. Linda snags the knife and turns to the front door. It's closed, but Percy hasn't put the chair back yet.

Lorelei's voice comes from above, raised: "She's a mouse, Percy. What's she going to do?"

Indignation flares through Linda; she snaps the knife blade open, grips the handle tight.

She opens the front door. *Silent as a mouse,* she thinks as she slips into the chilly dusk.

Outside. She's *outside.* Evergreen air flows across her face, glorious and energizing. For a fraction of a breath that's all she knows. Then her attention snaps back to her situation.

Move.

Within a few steps, her socks are soaked.

"Hey!" Percy's voice, sharp and loud. Linda flicks her head around and sees him darting out the front door. Lorelei is standing in one of the upstairs windows, staring down at her with a frown.

Linda abandons any attempt at stealth and sprints down the driveway, slipping across sleek gravel and little pits of mud. Her wet socks drag and slap around her toes.

Behind her, a car door slams.

She doesn't hear the engine start, but maybe her breath is too loud, her pulse too urgent in her temples. Maybe he is about to run her down. She should have taken the keys. Why didn't she take the keys? *Stupid.*

She rounds a curve and glances back—no car, no Percy, not yet. There's no sign of a road ahead; the driveway here is long and straight.

She darts into the woods, slapping her way through wet cedar and young Douglas fir. The pocketknife is still in her hand. If he doesn't see her, maybe he'll think she made it past the driveway's next bend.

"Linda!" Percy's voice isn't far. This is the first time she's heard either him or Lorelei use her name. She keeps running. Her left foot lands on something sharp. There's a deep pain as she feels her skin slicing open, and she stumbles. A rock, a root, a glass bottle thrown into the woods—she doesn't know. She fights her body's protective urge to limp.

"There's no one for miles," Percy yells. "Nowhere for you to go."

A lie, it has to be. They're in Cedar Lake, or near. If she runs far enough, long enough, she will come across a road or a house. A person. She will shout, *I'm Clone Girl,* and they'll give her shelter, if only for the SocialHub post that will inevitably follow.

"Linda!"

The light is fading, the forest growing dim. She's crashing through the trees; he must be following the sound. She can barely breathe.

A dense thicket of brush erupts ahead of her. Her left foot yelps with every step, and she's lost her right sock. She ducks behind the thicket.

She can't hear Percy. Maybe she's lost him. Maybe now that she's silent—

"This is pointless!"

Slowly, she turns her head. Percy emerges as a shadow between two trees, walking calmly. He's maybe fifty feet away.

Linda clutches the pocketknife as Percy advances. Her cut foot pulses with pain, and she fears Percy must be able to hear the shallow huffs that aren't bringing her enough oxygen. He's drawing closer in the falling light; she watches him through the thorny brush, able to make out the shape of him but not details.

He's stopped calling out. Linda doesn't know if this is good or bad. Maybe he thinks she's too far away to hear him. She hopes so. She hopes he keeps walking and never turns around. Instead, he stops and picks up something from the ground. Her sock. Linda's chest is tight with need: The need to gulp down air; the need to spring from her hiding place and run. The need to make Percy leave her alone, whatever it takes.

Percy rubs at his face. He's too far away for Linda to ambush him, too close for her to run. Suddenly he punches a tree and yells, "God-dammit!" The shout fades, and he stands there shaking out his hand. Then, so softly Linda can barely hear, he says, "Haven't I done enough? When will it be *enough*?"

Light-headedness settles over Linda. This is not the body language of someone who will calmly march her back to the house. Percy starts walking again, and Linda closes her eyes, just for a few seconds, and takes a deep, quiet breath to settle herself. She wishes she could start this day over and try again.

She wishes she could stand up, splay her hands, and bring down Percy with a lightning spell.

Something snaps, near. Linda's eyes pop open and she goes as still as stone.

Percy is standing on the other side of the bramble. She can hear his labored breath. He walks around until he's standing directly in front of her, facing away.

She imagines jamming the pocketknife's short blade into his throat and twisting it in. She wonders if she could do it, what it would feel like.

Go, she begs silently.

He turns around.

Their eyes meet. Linda watches surprise blossom across his face. Then she's on her feet, shoving past him. He grabs at her sleeve, but she pulls free, and she's running full tilt. She doesn't care that her foot hurts. She doesn't care that she doesn't know where she's going. The knife is still in her hand.

A thunderous roar, like a firework going off just behind her. Linda stumbles but keeps going, darting through the trees. Her ears ring.

The gun from when Percy first took her.

He just *shot* at her.

He's not trying to recapture her—he's trying to *kill* her.

She finds a burst of speed—and then there's a wall before her. Out of nowhere: sheet metal, towering above. Linda nearly smacks directly into it. She looks side to side, quick. There's a tree to the left with branches hanging over the wall. She darts that way. She can't hear Percy over her own ruckus. She can't think. She's overwhelmed by the need to get away.

She leaps to grab one of the cedar's lower branches, then scrabbles her feet up the trunk and heaves herself into its limbs. Her arms are screaming; it feels as though her shoulders might pop out of their joints. She tears her way higher. She's above the wall now; the branch in her hands extends past it. If she can inch over, she'll be able to drop down.

"Linda!" Percy's voice cuts through the twilight. "Stop!"

She can feel him raising the gun. She thinks of Dr. Tambor, of that school in Arizona. Of all those who have faced a lifted barrel with no means to escape.

She jumps.

Nibbler tumbles, slamming against the back of Anvi's seat. His yelp pierces her despite the screeching brakes and her own scream. The car's headlights spin through the twilight; she can't see, she's waiting for impact. Then they stop. Anvi's seatbelt is tight to her chest. Her temple throbs from where it smacked the side window.

Slowly, she realizes the airbags didn't deploy. They didn't hit anything.

"Are you okay?" asks Arthur.

Anvi cranes her sore neck toward him. He's flushed, sweating, and his hands are suctioned to the wheel. "Yeah," she says. "You?"

Arthur nods.

A whimper from the back seat. Terror latches onto Anvi. She un-buckles and topples out of her door onto the road's shoulder, then scrambles to open the back. Nibbler is a lump on the floor. She reaches out, her heart breaking—but Nibbler's head lifts, and he licks her hand.

"It's okay," she tells him, summoning a soft, happy voice. "You're okay." She hopes it's true. Nibbler crawls out of car, his tail tucked, and rubs his skull hard against Anvi's stomach. She wraps her arms around him and sniffles as her fear loosens. "Maybe we should get you one of those stupid-looking seatbelts, after all."

When she lifts her head, Anvi sees Arthur standing at the hood of the car, talking into his earcuff. His legs intersect one headlight, send-ing long shadows across the road. Two other vehicles have pulled over, and Arthur waves the Good Samaritans ahead. "We're fine, thank you." She blinks her attention back to Nibbler and runs her hands down his body to make sure he's not hurt. He whimpers and pulls away when she touches his left hip. There's no blood, no obvious wound. She hopes it's just a bruise.

The burned smell of overused brakes is heavy in Anvi's nose. She wants to talk to Arthur, but she also doesn't want to leave Nibbler—especially this close to the road. So she waits. A woman calls over to her, asking if she's okay. Anvi gives her a thumbs-up, then gently leads Nibbler to the grass and sits, her hand tucked around his collar. Nibbler noses her chest again, then sits tightly against her, facing the opposite direction.

"Don't worry," she whispers to him. "I've got your back too."

It's getting darker and there's a wet chill in the wind. When Arthur walks over, Anvi feels a nip of guilt; he's moving like an old man who's just had a near-miss car accident. She should be helping him.

"Are you okay to keep going?" asks Arthur.

"We don't need to wait for the police or anything?"

Arthur shrugs. "The car's fine, and we didn't hit anything."

"Then who were you talking to?"

"My doctor's office." At Anvi's confused look, he explains, "My Sheath monitors my heart rate. I had a scare a few months back, so they check in when there are abnormalities."

She thinks of her father and what his scare so quickly foretold. "Are you okay?" she asks.

"Yeah, it's just a precaution." He pauses. "One sec." He answers his Sheath. "I'm fine, Victoria. A deer just jumped out in front of us while I was driving. . . . No, and I already talked with Dr. Hammond. I . . . Wait, what?" His eyes widen. "Yes, let Detective Lopez know," he says. "Thank you. . . . No, never mind that. Good work." The call ends and he turns to Anvi.

"What happened?" she asks.

"We got an alert about log-in attempts to Linda's bank account," says Arthur.

"IP address?"

"I pre-authorized the bank to release it. All the police have to do is track it."

"That's great," says Anvi. "That should take like three seconds." She thinks of how awful Linda looked in the video they watched before leaving, but if Linda's trying to access her bank account, that at least means she's alive.

Assuming Linda's the one trying to access it.

"In the meantime," says Arthur, "I think we should stick with our original plan."

Anvi can hear the hope in his voice. She climbs to her feet, keeping a hand on Nibbler's collar. "Let's go."

From: Lorelei Niequist   Draft Saved 1:03 A.M. 1/1/2005
To: Arthur Niequist
RE:

I miss who we were together. I miss wanting to dive into your arms and tell you about my day. Sitting with you and wondering what our child might be like. I miss the night we decided we wanted to find out. I even miss all the hardship that followed. The tests and procedures and all that pain, because it brought us her.

Sure, I'll say it. I miss you.

At least if this pregnancy kills me, I won't be alone anymore.

24.

inda's foot catches the top of the wall—there's wire, and it bites deep—and instead of landing and rolling, she hits the ground with a wrenching crunch on her left shoulder. Pain comes, sharp and huge. She rocks onto her stomach. She can taste the forest floor. She scrambles to her knees, then pushes herself to her feet with her right arm, gritting her teeth so hard her jaw aches. She's lucky she didn't land on her head. She spits out the muck in her mouth, and there's a coppery tinge of blood too. Then she runs—a shuffling, pained gait—keeping her left arm tight to her side.

She doesn't know what happened to the pocketknife. She must have dropped it when she jumped into the tree. A wild hope: Maybe Percy will trip and impale himself.

The ground here slopes uphill. Linda's breath tears through her as she pushes into the woods, stumbling through ferns and weeds.

Suddenly her tree is there, towering above her in the twilight. Linda reels and tries to blink away what must be an illusion: the big-leaf maple she loved as a girl. But she knows the pattern of its bare limbs better than she knows her own body, and it's the same, all the same, just smudged thicker by time.

She stares at the tree, still thinking that she must be wrong. But the colossus swelling from the ground before her is unmistakable.

All these days, she's been next door to her old home.

All these years, Lorelei has been hiding in the adjacent property.

All those years, Percy was just beyond the wall.

She stops at her tree and leans against it. Shadowy branches stretch above her, inviting.

Her left shoulder screams when she lifts her arm; Linda bites back a sob and tastes more blood. She can't get the arm above shoulder height. The pain fades when she leaves it down. She lifts her other arm and digs her fingers into the bark.

The ridges in the trunk are still there, barely. It takes imagination to see how this used to be more than one tree. That, or memory.

Her other sock has sloughed off, who knows when. Linda presses her toes into the ridges and uses her right arm to pull herself into the tree. She climbs with heaving breaths, the bark sharp against her toes.

She makes it to her branch and presses herself into the nook where she used to be scarce. Her shoulder throbs. There are pains in her knees too, and her feet feel destroyed. She wonders how badly she's bleeding, but she doesn't care quite enough to check.

It's raining. It's perhaps been raining for a while, and she's only noticing now because she's not moving, or because she's in the limbs of a winter-bare maple instead of under heavy bows of cedar and fir. It's a mist-like rain, chilly little pinpricks that feel like they're suspended in the air.

This is a terrible place to hide. She's totally exposed, to Percy and the elements. She should run to the house, lower herself into the basement. He'll never find her there. If he tries, she can leap out at him from the bathroom or from behind the desk, tackle him to the cement floor. Smack his head against it until he goes limp. Shove his body into the well to rot beside Emmer's.

His body would never fit. And Emmer's remains deserve better than that.

She could leave him under the hole in the stairs. Maybe it would look like he fell.

But her tree feels safe. Safer than the basement. Safer than anywhere she's been since the day she last sat in this very same nook.

Curled and shivering, her ears pricked for any sound of Percy, there's a part of Linda that's okay with the idea of dying here—not at Percy's hands, but by simply fading into the cold and her exhaustion. At least she'd be outside, sitting in her favorite tree. That's how animals do it, remove themselves from the pack for a quiet end. Dying is easy in Fury and Honor. Maybe it wouldn't be much worse for real. Maybe this isn't real. Maybe she would wake up at her last save point, just after tumbling over the wall. Maybe that's already happened, and she doesn't remember because she's been reloaded. Maybe she's done this dozens of times. Maybe Percy's the playable character and his decisions are all that matter. Or maybe Lorelei is, and the being controlling her is lost in the crafting element of this too-deep world. Wouldn't that be funny, if Linda's perception of existence existed only to support one woman's poor impulse control?

Even funnier: It does. Game or not, simulation or not, that's why she exists—Lorelei's single-mindedness. And it couldn't have all been madness—she bribed a technician, impregnated herself. Set up monthly deliveries of supplies, found black-market vaccinations. There was intent, forethought. She *planned* for Linda and Emmer, rewarded them for their similarities to Madeline, punished them for their differences—and in the end discarded each when they were found wanting.

If this were a game and Linda the player, maybe she wouldn't reload at all. Maybe she would just quit.

A creeping sense of shame: Dr. Tambor would be concerned by these thoughts.

But Dr. Tambor abandoned her, just like Lorelei did.

No. Even as the sad, bitter girl within Linda thinks it, she finds herself correcting the thought. Dr. Tambor didn't choose to die. Dr. Tambor didn't want to die. Linda wonders if it was even a conscious decision, leaping to take those bullets. Maybe it was the same instinct that led her to become a doctor. Maybe her instinct was always to help. To shelter.

Linda wonders if she regretted it after the bullets hit her.

She hopes she at least regretted not having time to say goodbye.

There were so many people at the funeral. Linda remembers sitting in a hard pew beside Arthur. A woman sobbed behind them, and sniffling was everywhere. People stood and told stories about a woman named Gina, whom Linda didn't know. A sweet child who blossomed in college. A daughter who brunched with her aging parents every Sunday. A mother with two grown children. Foster parent to a dozen cats in six years. All these aspects of Dr. Tambor's life of which Linda had been totally ignorant.

The love in that room suffocated her, convinced her that she couldn't possibly have been anything more than just another patient to Dr. Tambor. To Gina. That's the part that hurts the most, all these years later: the thought that Dr. Tambor probably didn't spare a single thought for her at the end.

Footsteps slide through the underbrush, soft but unmistakable, and Linda's attention slinks reluctantly to the present. It's dark enough that she can barely see her own hands. If she doesn't move, Percy might not see her. She stops rubbing her arms, but she can't stop shivering.

Percy's silhouette skates through the trees. He's coming from the pond. He must have entered the property at the same place as he did when Linda was here with Anvi.

Anvi. Have she and Percy been working together this whole time? If only Linda had time to read the email.

She presses her body tight to the tree, keeping her legs long and flat along her branch, letting her feet drop to the sides so the silhouette of her toes doesn't give her away. She thinks of the hidey-hole where she kept her first-aid book. It should be by her right hand, but she doesn't feel it. Misremembered or engulfed by time.

Percy passes under her.

She was stupid to think her friendship with Anvi might be true. She feels empty. Empty and stupid and so fucking sick of being used.

Percy takes another step.

She should wait him out. But every part of her hurts, and she's tired of waiting. Of hiding, of running. She thinks of another world, one where she feels free.

Percy's trying to *kill* her.

Linda flings herself from the tree.

She grabs Percy as she drops, smashing into the ground atop him. Her chin bashes into his shoulder; a gush of blood in her mouth as she bites the inside of her lip.

An explosion. Linda's head rings; she doesn't think she's been shot. Percy's rolling to his feet. Linda grabs his knees, but her left arm is nearly useless, and Percy pulls free.

Scrabbling forward, Linda's hand lands on something hard, rectangular—inorganic.

Her palm finds a handle, her finger a trigger.

Percy is a shadow rising to its knees. "All you had to do was give her the money," he says. She can see him patting the ground, looking for the gun that is in her hand. "You owed her that much."

Anger flares again through Linda. What could she possibly owe Lorelei?

She raises the gun. Percy must notice the change in her body language. He freezes. He's a man-shaped mass blending into the maple's trunk. She can't see his face, his eyes. She wonders what level enemy he'd be if this were a game, how many experience points she'd gain from killing him. What kind of loot.

She knows he's not. She knows he's flesh and blood and bone, like her.

There's an unexpected ridge under Linda's finger, like a slice of the trigger's middle is extending outward. She wants to press it, to see how easily it moves.

"Why are you helping her?" she asks. Percy shifts slightly but doesn't answer. Linda thrusts the gun toward him. "Why?" she demands. "You know she can't take care of a baby."

"That's not important," says Percy.

"Yes, it is. Look at her. She—"

"There's not going to be a baby."

That stops her. She blinks a few times and feels a return to herself. She's calm, almost. "What?" she asks.

"It's a scam. Or, I don't know, maybe he'll try, but the likelihood of it working before the money runs out is tiny. The doctor said so himself."

She's talking to a shadow. "But what if it does?"

"Then I'm the one who's going to fly to São Paulo to get her."

It takes Linda a second, but then she understands: He wouldn't come back. He'd leave Lorelei here, alone, waiting. Forever. She can't decide how this makes her feel, if his plan is villainous or brave.

"What did you mean when you said you were responsible for Madeline's death?" she asks.

The patter of rain. The soft howl of wind through branches. Then finally, "I couldn't save her."

The pain there. She believes him.

"Did Lorelei tell you what she did to Emmer?"

"Emmer?"

"My twin."

Another pause. He doesn't want to upset her, thinks Linda. He's trying to find a way to soften the truth of Emmer's death. "Tell me," she urges, her voice tight.

His shadowy form shifts slightly, closer to the tree. But her eyes have adjusted and she can see him, the moonlit glint of his wary eyes.

"As far as I know, it was only you."

Liar. Her finger twitches atop the trigger; the tab at its center depresses slightly, easily. She can feel herself shaking with nerves and cold. She wants to ask about Anvi, but a dark part of her knows that hearing Percy confirm Anvi's complicity might make her pull the trigger. "Why did Lorelei leave?" He told her the how already, but not the why.

"I convinced her to. She broke down and started crying about how she didn't know what to do. How she'd gotten herself stuck in this trap—"

"*She* was stuck in a trap?"

"You don't understand what it was like for her, watching this little doppelgänger of Maddy haunt her house."

Heat rushes to her cheeks. She wasn't a doppelgänger or a ghost. She was only ever a little girl who didn't understand why her mother couldn't love her.

"You left me there," she says. "Alone." A flash of memory: Walking into the house. Expecting punishment. Finding emptiness. The basement door, open. Looking down into the dark from the top of the steps. But that last part didn't happen, did it? Maybe her mind is playing a trick on her, creating memory from suggestion.

"She said you were used to taking care of yourself," says Percy.

Did she go down into the basement? Would she have? No, a few days after the fire, that was the first time she'd ever set foot down there. She would have remembered otherwise. Still, an image lingers: the stairs, unbroken. The shine of the concrete floor reflecting in an overhead light.

"I was going to go back for you," says Percy. "I thought that once I got her out, I could calm her down and go back—"

Linda knows this part already. She interrupts: "All these years, she's been with you."

She can just make out his nod.

"The police never checked?"

"They searched the woods, but they never had a reason to come inside."

Linda envisions it: Lorelei curled up somewhere on the second floor—or maybe even in the room where they've been keeping Linda—while uniformed men and women combed the forest, searching for her.

"Twelve years." It's all she can say.

"Linda," says Percy. He reaches out with one hand in a calming gesture. She can see it in the easy slope of his shoulders: his dismissal of her.

To him, she'll never be more than a lesser version of Madeline.

"I read your notebook," she says.

His posture goes rigid. She thinks it's with anger, but she wants more than that. She wants to affect him in some permanent way. She wants to be more than a dead girl's ghost.

"Does Lorelei know about the emails?"

"Shut up," says Percy. The hot tremor in his voice surprises her. There's something here she doesn't understand. Something important. She thinks about the printed-out emails. Madeline lamented the difference in their ages. Percy talked about holding Madeline in his arms.

She remembers a story that flared across SocialHub last year: A fifteen-year-old boy had bragged about having intercourse with his twenty-year-old ex-babysitter. There was a flurry of outrage, an arrest. The age of consent in Washington State is sixteen.

"You had sex with Madeline," she says. "Right before she died. You had sex with her and then—"

Percy lunges at her. Startled, Linda steps back and pulls the trigger. A thoughtless, easy pull—instinct—and she feels a jolt through her palm like she's caught something heavy as the gunshot echoes through the woods. Linda's ears ring and Percy lurches backward. For a second, she thinks he's pretending—and then he moans and falls to his knees. A few more slow, cold seconds pass. Percy slumps to the ground, becoming a lump in the dark.

Linda stares for the length of one long, shuddering breath.

And then she runs.

Without thought, without intent: *away*.

The landscape funnels her downhill, and soon the fire-eaten house looms ahead, broken in the wet moonlight. Linda stumbles to a stop. The gun is still in her hand, warm and heavy.

She didn't mean to shoot him.

He's the one who attacked *her*, who abducted *her*.

The world is better without Percy in it—or at least not worse. Big picture, he's inconsequential. Big picture, everyone is, she thinks—except for Madeline, whose death caused such a domino effect of misery. Hysteria is creeping through her; dark laughter skitters up her throat—of course Madeline still matters. More than Linda, more than Percy.

He attacked me, she tells herself. He pulled the trigger first. He tried to shoot her first. He was going to *kill* her.

She tries to shake her doubt from her mind, but she doesn't tell herself she had no choice—because she didn't make a choice. All she did was flinch. Her palm aches from recoil and gripping the gun so hard.

She's so cold she's becoming numb. She's stumbling. Her shoulder is a dull ache. Her ears are still ringing.

Soon she's standing before the back deck of her childhood home. The place where it all began. The place where it all ended. She feels sobs swelling within her, and she chokes them back down.

Lorelei, she thinks. This is Lorelei's fault, all of it, and she's just sitting in that house, blind to all the pain she's caused. Blind to the horror of her actions.

Linda wants to fall to the ground, to melt into the cold dead grass and be *done*. Instead, she shambles away from the house toward the pond and Percy's access point.

Toward Lorelei.

Annoyed, *Graham watched as the fox hissed and paced around the kitchen. They could do better than this, he thought. They needed to do better than this.*
He tapped his thumb and forefinger together.

GLITCH HUNTER—Beta Test
    Save
    Load
    Options
    Quit

"It's not a cat," he said, as he peeled off his headset and blinked his vision to the popcorn machine sitting just beyond the taped edge of the play-testing area.

"The software doesn't have fox," said Sergei behind him. "Would you rather it barked?"

Graham extracted himself from the CircleTread and turned to his partner's workstation. "Just google it," he said. "And use something close." He and Sergei had been roommates their freshman year at UW, and they'd grown weary and bearded together in the decade since. Sergei was used to Graham's brusqueness, just as Graham was used to Sergei's froggish stares.

"I still think we should scrap the mission," said Sergei. "We don't need it for the release."

"We've been over this."

"Just because you're obsessed with Clone Girl doesn't make her a current event."

They'd had this argument so many times it was practically a bit. Even so, Graham prickled. Fascination and obsession weren't the same. "She's better than current, she's everlasting," he said. He didn't bring up how he hadn't argued about Sergei designing a mission around the fictionalization of a talentless prima donna he loved to loathe. Sergei just needed reassurance and a moment to vent. Graham walked over and gave his friend's shoulder a squeeze. "I've got to take a piss. Need anything?"

"A Coke," said Sergei. "And a Hot Pocket."

Graham cuffed him lightly on the back of the head, and Sergei's tired grimace upended itself.

Graham pushed out into the hallway, tossing a wave toward the accountant across the hall, who always kept his door open. In the men's room, he checked the stalls, then flicked off the lights and fanned the fingers of one hand over his eyebrows, pressing hard. He could feel a cluster headache coming on.

They were so close.

It was a gamble. Anything outside a franchise always is, but an indie game that wasn't crowdsourced was practically unheard of these days. He and Sergei both had day jobs at Microsoft—though Graham thought it was unlikely either of them would survive the next round of layoffs—and they'd been pouring every spare cent and hour into this secret passion project for years. They'd spent over a hundred grand on outsourcing code alone. Silence was risky, but they had a plan. They were going to scream onto the scene.

Once they got this mission right.

25.

Anvi steps out of the car. Cold rain needles her cheeks. "Stay here, Nibs," she says as she closes the door. Nibbler presses his nose to the window, which they've left open a crack.

Arthur locks the car, and Anvi pulls up her sleeve to activate the flashlight on her Sheath. She can see the rain now, like a series of thin rents through the air. She wishes she'd worn a warmer coat; she keeps thinking that her years in Ithaca have given her an immunity to winter, forgetting that rain can be worse than snow. Snow-cold nips at you, but rain-cold seeps through your skin to the bone.

The driveway is a quagmire; their footsteps squelch through the mud as they walk side by side. Anvi's light slices through the dark before them.

Their near accident. The intensity of the last week. Walking through the dark together. She dares to ask, "Why isn't Linda's last name Niequist?"

"She didn't want it," says Arthur.

The mud sucks at Anvi's foot; she jiggles her boot free. "Really?"

"Her therapist helped her pick, not me, but Niequist was the first name on the list. She didn't choose it." He laughs a sad little laugh. "I've never felt so rejected in my life—and I'm about to be divorced for the second time."

They reach the gate. A padlock shines against the rusty bars. Arthur must have had the property secured since Anvi and Linda were here. He taps his Sheath to the lock, then pushes the gate open.

"You don't know why she picked Russell?" asks Anvi.

"I never asked. I was trying to support her decision." He wobbles, then steadies, looking down. "Dammit." His shoe is stuck in a particularly deep patch of mud, his socked foot dangling above it.

"I got it," says Anvi. She crouches to retrieve the shoe, then hands it back to him.

"Thanks." He slides it back on, then searches for a drier patch of land.

The house is a dim outline ahead. Now that they're here, Anvi has a hard time imagining they might find Linda. The cold, the wet, the rubble—it's unlivable.

And yet Linda lived here for twelve years, neglected by a mentally ill woman who never should have been left alone. Anvi wonders if Lorelei could even be held responsible for her actions—legally or morally—if she was still around. Where does one draw the line of responsibility when mental illness is involved? When exactly does normal human variation dip across a line into diagnosable disorder? And if Lorelei isn't responsible for what happened within these walls, who is?

Arthur could have stopped her. The lab tech who gave her the embryos could have called the authorities, or at least said no. People at Lorelei's now-defunct foundation must have recognized she needed help; any one of them could have stopped her—could have *helped* her.

But how far back do you go? Do you blame the volunteers who didn't find Madeline in time? Do you blame Madeline herself—for storming off, for falling, for pulling the shard of wood out of her chest? There's no need to even stop at Madeline. You could go back forever, finding fault. Anvi shifts her thoughts toward more worthwhile territory: finding a way to make things better moving forward.

To do that, they need to find Linda.

Anvi glances over at Arthur, picking his way through the mud. Linda's lucky, so many have said. Lucky that he stepped up. Lucky that he is who he is. Just imagine if she'd gone from that awful childhood into the real world without the cushion of wealth.

Coddled, Arthur called his current wife.

"Does Linda have any sort of education?" asks Anvi. She angles her light along the ruts and ridges of the driveway's curve.

"A GED. I made it a prerequisite for moving back out here."

"Have you ever thought about having her get a job? Or go to college?"

"I haven't been able to get her to show interest in anything," says Arthur. "I'm pretty sure if I didn't mandate excursions, she'd just sit in that apartment 24/7." Anvi hears frustration in his voice. "I know what you're thinking," he says. "I'm doing my best. It was going okay until her therapist died. Everything since then has been . . . hard."

"What happened to her therapist?"

"She was at Target and some asshole stormed in with a rifle," says Arthur. "He was hunting his girlfriend, but he got eighteen other people instead."

Fuck, thinks Anvi. There was a study not long ago that showed the average American was only two degrees removed from knowing someone who was injured in, killed in, or witness to a mass shooting. Anvi is now average. "Was that the one in Connecticut?" she asks.

"Yeah."

She remembers that shooting. It was memorable for the sick jokes that followed. *Target.* She kicks a fallen branch out of her way, then it hits her: "She wasn't the psychologist who saved the man and his baby, was she?"

"She was."

The woman was everywhere for days—friends, family, and former patients all coming forward to tout her virtues and call for gun-control reform. But the shooter had stolen the gun from a cousin, and the political consensus seemed to be that stricter background checks couldn't have stopped that. Or maybe that part was another shooting; Anvi isn't sure. She cringes as she remembers a meme. The psychologist was a large woman, and it was about how overweight people could be heroes too. Trolls usurped it, of course, and turned it into something ugly.

"How old was Linda when it happened?" she asks.

"Fourteen. We couldn't get her to see anyone else afterward. We couldn't get her to talk about it at all." Arthur sighs. "It was awful. When I told her, she attacked me."

"What?" Anvi pivots toward him, and he flinches away from the light of her Sheath. "Sorry," she says. "But . . . *what?*"

"It's the only way I can think to put it," says Arthur. "She was tiny, so I was able to restrain her pretty quickly, but she smashed a mirror with her elbow and cut herself pretty badly." Anvi's light is aimed at his thickly mudded shoes. Leather. Expensive. She tries to imagine a teenaged Linda flipping out and slicing her arm open on a shattered mirror. She thinks of Linda's bloody feet and how Arthur's shoes used to be flesh. "Claire and I took her in for stitches," Arthur continues. "When we got back, we were too exhausted to clean up the blood. The next morning our cleaning lady came in and started screaming. She thought we'd all been murdered."

The house rises up before them, a sodden, abandoned mass of shadows.

"The crazy thing," says Arthur, "is I probably felt more comfortable with Linda then than I did at any point in the previous year and a half. It was the first time she acted anything like Maddy."

Anvi shines her Sheath along the landing; the front door is

boarded up again. Presumably whomever Arthur had install the lock on the gate took care of this too. "Did Maddy attack you often?"

Arthur chuckles. "No, but she sometimes gave me this look like she wanted to. Normal teenage stuff, I suppose, though—"

Crack.

The sharp sound echoes from the woods, like a firework exploding just out of sight.

Arthur's hand shoots out, grabbing Anvi by the forearm.

They stand in silence for a long moment. It could have been a snapping branch, Anvi tells herself. It could have been a bear or an elk or any number of natural things. It could be Linda trying to scare them off.

Then Arthur says in a soft voice, "Go back to the car."

"That was a gunshot." She meant it as a question, but from his demeanor, she knows. A spasm of superstition runs through her: Is this because they were just talking about a shooting? Of course not, but some strange instinct thinks it must be—that part of being human that seeks cause and effect everywhere, that discards randomness to see a man's face on the moon or the Virgin Mary in a potato chip.

"It's probably a hunter," says Arthur. "They used to trespass along the outskirts of our property all the time. But you should go back to the car, just in case."

"And what are you going to do?"

"I'm going to look for Linda."

"Alone. In the dark. With trespassing hunters skulking around?"

"Anvi, please," he says. She shakes her head and he adds, "What if the noise scared Nibbler?"

She almost laughs. "That's low, Arthur."

Crack.

This time Anvi doesn't hear it as anything but a gunshot. Her pulse thrums: *runrun-runrun.*

"Turn off the light," says Arthur.

Anvi does, knowing that Arthur can't possibly believe the shots are from hunters. If he did, it would make sense to be as bright and loud as possible.

They stand together in the dark, silently waiting for their eyes to adjust. Anvi thinks of the drugstore where she and Linda stopped: The unfriendly air that was almost certainly because she's brown. How such an atmosphere can still exist so close to a city as proudly progressive as Seattle. How badly she doesn't want to run into an armed local in these woods.

Runrun-runrun.

She shouldn't talk. She should just wait. But nervous energy is coursing through her, and Anvi finds she can't stay still and quiet both. "When was the last time you were here?" she whispers.

Arthur glances at her, then whispers back, "When I flew out to get Maddy." The briefest pause, then, flustered, "*Linda*. When I flew out to get Linda." Anvi's heart aches for Arthur and Linda both.

"It must be—"

"*Shh.*"

Anvi clamps her mouth shut, listening hard. All she can hear is the wind and the rain. Her eyes have adjusted enough that she can distinguish individual trees, and she can see the worry in Arthur's posture. But there could be a person standing a hundred feet away, and she wouldn't notice. They could be surrounded, and she wouldn't notice.

Rustling in the distance. A branch snapping.

Anvi edges closer to Arthur. *It's just an animal,* she tells herself. Then she remembers they're looking for a person. She should *want* the sounds to be a person—to be Linda. But the gunshots are still echoing through her mind and she desperately wants whatever's making the sounds to go away.

And then the rustling's gone. She feels Arthur relax beside her.

"I thought I heard someone," he says. "But it might have been my imagination."

Anvi almost tells him it wasn't, but she's suddenly no longer certain what she heard. "It's so hard to be sure in the rain," she says.

"Is there any way I can convince you to go back to the car?"

She wishes she was back with Nibbler, doors locked, scratching the hard nub of his brow—but she can't leave Arthur here alone.

"No," she says. "Let's check out the back."

From: Lorelei Niequist   Draft Saved 12:37 A.M. 2/9/2005

To: Arthur Niequist

RE:

It's starting. I'm trying to think of my foxes, how easy they always made it look. Maybe I should go to the hutch instead of the bathroom. Joke. I've already prepped the tub.

I feel so calm. How am I so calm? I've made it this far alone. I can make it a little further.

I wish you were here.

26.

A silhouette moves in the depths of the second floor of Percy's house. Below, Linda's feet are dragging, her heart racing. Parts of her so slow, others so fast, the disparity might tear her apart. She puts her hands on her knees and ducks her head, hoping to steady the aching throb of her head. Her eyes lock onto the gun hanging over her thigh. The gun with which she just shot a man. The shock of red welling between his fingers, oozing over his hands. The way he fell to his knees. The way he looked at her.

She didn't see all of these things. It was too dark for red, and Percy's eyes were only holes in the night.

Linda pushes open the front door. Entering the small house of her own volition changes it; it's no longer a prison but a path. The stairs to Lorelei beckon. There should be swelling music and flickering candlelight as Linda climbs, not just this creaking wood and a bare bulb. She crests to find a short hallway with two doors. The nearer is open: a bathroom. She sees a towel on the floor, a pump bottle of soap by the sink. The second door is closed. Linda turns the knob to reveal a cluttered den. The walls are covered in paper: graphs and charts and lists. There's a small dresser, a twin-sized bed, and in the corner a large desk.

Lorelei sits at the desk, hunched over papers with her back to Linda. There's a bulky old monitor in front of her, switched off. Headphones cup her ears. She doesn't turn around. Linda takes another step inside, and Lorelei still doesn't notice. Linda doesn't understand how Lorelei could have gone through all the trouble of having her kidnapped and then not care when she escaped. Maybe she's forgotten. She wonders if she knew Percy was planning to kill her or if she was just expecting him to drag her back.

Part of her wants to raise the gun still clenched in her hand toward that bundle of gray hair, if only to make Lorelei finally, truly pay attention to her—not because of her dead sisters but because of who she is and what she might do.

Keeping Lorelei in her peripheral vision, she steps toward the far wall. It's covered in a patchwork of papers, some sheets white and crisp, others creased and aged. The whole thing is dotted with different-colored sticky notes. A timeline, Linda realizes. She strains to read it, not wanting to turn her back on Lorelei. There don't appear to be actual dates, but at the far left of the timeline she catches the word *Birth*.

She's looking at a chart of childhood milestones and events—first solid food, first word, first steps.

Christmas. Her eyes snap to the word about a third of the way along the x-axis. She blinks and steps closer.

A hash along the axis reads: *Four years, three months. Snowy Christmas.*

Below that:

Script: There was a snowstorm the night before. A real storm. We got several inches of snow, maybe half a foot. Christmas morning you walked into the living room and there it was: a bright-green sled. A round one, like a disc. It was new and beautiful and wrapped in a red bow I'd made out of my scarf. You were so excited when you saw it. You tore off the scarf and ran for the door. It was all I could do to get you to put on your coat before you were outside, trudging up the back hill. You stood at the top for a moment, red-cheeked and glowing, and then you were off! You cascaded down the hill, laughing, and spilled off the sled at the bottom, toppling through the snow. I was at the bottom, waiting, my arms extended, and then I ran to you and wrapped the red scarf around you, brushing the snow from your hair with its ends. You were so happy, so beautiful. And then I held your hand and helped you up the hill so you could go again. It was a beautiful day. A happy day. One of our best.

Focal points: Green sled. Red scarf. Me waiting at the bottom, arms wide. Happiness.

A handwritten sticky note beside the printed text reads: *Reintroduce Art figure, subbing in P?*

Linda can't parse the addendum; her mind is spinning too fast. She reads the description again—and again. Images pop in her head as she reads. The sled, the scarf, Lorelei waiting for her, a sense of laughter and joy. Her eyes slide to the top of the huge swath of paper. All-cap lettering announces: *M.R. TIMELINE.*

She scans the rest of the chart, panic building in her chest. *Lake*—it snags her eye.

Four years, eleven months: Rattlesnake Lake

Script: You bounced up and down in the back seat of the car the whole way, and when we got there you hopped out and ran toward the lake in your bathing suit, which was blue with little frills around the arms and legs. As you ran, the grass gave way to rocks and pebbles and then to an expanse of crackled, drying-out mud that looked like kitchen tiles. The lake surprised you, it was so small! And there were giant tree stumps popping out of the water and the mud. You came to a halt in the squishy mud, staring at the lake. You'd expected it to be bigger. You'd come to swim. "There's not enough water to swim, Mommy," you said. I told you, "Then climb," and urged you forward. It took you a moment, but then you ran ahead, squishing through the mud, to one of the tree stumps, and you scrambled up like a bug. Up there you started laughing. "Mommy, I'm the Queen of the Lake," you yelled. And you were. You were the Queen of the Lake that day. You had the time of your life.

    Focal points: Blue bathing suit. Grass to rocks to mud. Small lake. Giant tree stumps. "Not enough water to swim." "Then climb." Queen of the Lake.

Linda's mind is overloaded. *Scripts.* Scripts are meant to be read, performed. Why is Lorelei writing scripts about Linda's experiences?

For a few breaths she simply doesn't understand. Then the implication of the timeline and its instructive tone shatters her.

These weren't Linda's experiences; they were Madeline's.

The sound of a clearing throat tugs Linda's numbed gaze toward the desk, where Lorelei is standing, staring at her. "Where's Percy?" asks Lorelei in a perfunctory, almost annoyed way.

I shot him.

He's under my tree, bleeding from a hole in his gut.

By now he's probably dead.

He deserves it.

So do you.

Linda can't say any of these things. The timeline is pulling at her, absorbing her.

Her trip to the lake was her talisman: her proof that Lorelei had loved her once. Rattlesnake Lake. She didn't even know the name until now; she'd assumed her memory was of this town's titular lake.

Maybe there's another explanation, she thinks. If Lorelei at least reenacted it, then maybe it's not all false. Maybe—

It's an almost physical jolt: Enough with the *maybes*. Enough with trying to find a silver lining; enough with assuming anything but the worst. Of Lorelei. Of anyone.

"Did you ever take me to a lake?" she asks. *Enough.* She knows, but she needs to hear it.

Lorelei's brow furrows. It's enough of an answer. Too much of an answer.

"I remember going," says Linda. "I can see it." The crackling mud, the monstrous stumps. Lies, all of it. Worse than lies: someone else's truth. "And Christmas," she says. "The sled." *Her* sled, wrapped in a red bow. Already the image is turning to poison.

Lorelei's confusion blossoms into a smile. "You remember?" she asks. She's staring at Linda, so hopeful, so happy. Linda's silence, Linda's misery—it just makes her smile grow. "This is great," says Lorelei. "With you I barely had a plan, and I stopped when you were so young. I never thought—This is *great.*"

False memories. Linda read a book about them once, how children were convinced by overeager psychotherapists that they'd been sexually abused by their fathers or involved in satanic rituals. Hundreds of pages she read, fascinated and disturbed, and it never once occurred to her that something like that could have happened to her. But it seems so obvious now. Of course Lorelei never would have taken her anywhere, given her a true gift.

She clenches the gun so tight her hand throbs.

I'm not excusing your mother's actions, Dr. Tambor once said. *But it might be helpful for you to understand that she wasn't well.*

A nicer way of saying *sick.*

Lorelei has faded back into the kind-eyed stranger who first walked down the stairs over a week ago. "It's not your fault," she says to Linda. She seems so rational, so sure, that part of Linda aches to hear more. "The genes were wrong," says Lorelei. "Even with the memories, you never could have been her."

Linda turns away from Lorelei. She can't bear to look at her as she asks, "So why didn't you just kill me like you did Emmer?" She examines the sheets of paper covering the wall, tacked and taped along the timeline. *M.R.,* she sees.

"What?" asks Lorelei.

Once she keys into the shorthand, Linda sees the initials everywhere: *M.R. M.R. M.R.*

Madeline Rose.

Most Revered Madeline Rose.

Mother's Real Madeline Rose.

Maybe Replaceable Madeline Rose.

More Recent—

A schism of knowledge cuts through Linda. This realization, it's worse, so much worse. She's wrong. She *has* to be wrong. She needs to be wrong.

Emmer.

She always assumed favoritism, that Emmer earned her name as a reward for passing Lorelei's cryptic tests. Or that Linda had her own name once upon a time but forgot it after Lorelei stopped speaking to her. Though why would she forget her own name if she remembered her sister's? She never thought of that before.

"Emmer," she says, turning back toward Lorelei and searching for some sign of recognition. "My twin," she pushes, desperate. "She was your favorite. She was the one you loved. Until she—"

Disappeared.

"I don't know what you're talking about," says Lorelei.

She's lying, or in denial. *She's* the one whose memory can't be trusted. *She's* the one who *wasn't well. She's* the one who's been hiding in this hovel for twelve years, plotting, obsessing, allowing the world to believe she's dead.

She's the one who told Linda the memories of a dead girl until repetition made them hook into her mind as her own.

Emmer disappearing down the basement steps, her hand tucked into Lorelei's. Linda remembers it as clearly as she remembers Chrono the fox, or the cawing crows who came to visit. As clearly as she remembers her tree nest or the picture book tucked into her garage hidey-hole.

As clearly as she remembers a green sled at Christmas and running toward a too-shallow lake.

As far as I know, it was only you.

Her stomach is a knot of pain, her entire body quaking. "I remember her," she whispers. They played in the hutch together. They ran through the woods together. They confronted the monster in the shed together.

"Emmer," says Lorelei. It's not quite a question. Lorelei is looking at her like she's a puzzle barely worth the effort of solving. Then she says it again, more slowly and with a slight tweak to her pronunciation: "Em . . . ar." Her eyes alight. "Fascinating."

Linda feels like she's going to vomit or perhaps implode.

"You pitted us against each other," she pleads. "You *loved* her."

"You really think there was someone else there with you, don't you?" says Lorelei. "This is—" She turns her back to Linda and hunches over her desk, where she starts jotting a note.

"The kitchen table," says Linda. There are *two* sets of fingerprints on the underside of the kitchen table. This isn't just memory but verifiable fact. The table's in her apartment: *proof.*

Lorelei ignores her.

"The table," yells Linda.

Lorelei spins around. "What?"

"The kitchen table has two sets of fingerprints on it," says Linda. *"Two."* She sees Lorelei's back stiffen, and relief flares through her. She's caught Lorelei in a lie. Her memories *are* true; some of them, at least.

"Her constellations," says Lorelei. "You desecrated them."

Lorelei's voice, echoing through the years: *Emmer wouldn't have.*

Lorelei turns back around. "When I found you under there that day, I could have strangled you."

Emmer's cheek, covered in ink. Linda feeling the blame in her mother's eyes, heavy and aimed entirely at her. Emmer innocent, as always. Perfect Emmer, who could do no wrong. The image flickers and for a breath Linda is alone under the table, tapping her fingers along the trail of the one who came before. Then Emmer's back, smiling, insistent.

Linda doesn't remember ever touching her twin sister. In every memory she has of her, there's space between them, even if it's just a hairbreadth. Emmer never took her hand. They played Hide-and-Find but never Tag.

She turns back to the paper-covered walls. One sheet is a list labeled *Favorites*. Several of the items leap out at Linda as rewards she remembers Emmer being given: *strawberry milk; stuffed puppy; ABC book*. She took the book after Emmer disappeared; its moldy remains are back in her apartment now.

Beside the list is a faded photo of a naked infant sitting in a sudsy bucket. Next to that: a pinned piece of yellowing paper containing a green-colored circle. Shaky lettering underneath: *M-A-D-D-Y*.

"I remember getting a sled for Christmas and I remember climbing the trees at the lake," says Linda. Her head aches; her blood is pounding through her too fast. "I remember having a sister and you taking her away."

"Madeline Rose had an imaginary friend too," says Lorelei. "Squeaky. No, Squeakers. A big purple mouse."

But Emmer wasn't a purple mouse. Emmer was her only friend. Her sister. Her *twin*. A better version of herself.

Emmer's not in Linda's Christmas memory. She's not in her memory of the lake. In any of the rare memories Linda has of being rewarded, Emmer's never there to see it.

Emmer's gone.

M.R.'s gone. She can hear the difference now. Could this be a trick of memory too? But after the kitchen table, Lorelei started to ignore her. After that day, Lorelei gave up on her system of rewards and punishments. That was the day everything changed.

You desecrated them.

"Emmer never existed," whispers Linda. As she says it, she knows it's true.

Lorelei is back to taking notes at her desk. This life-shattering conversation for Linda is to her an inspiration. Linda runs her fingers along the timeline. There are memories here she doesn't hold—*First Time Feeding the Foxes; Planting Day Lilies*—and she wonders if that's because they didn't take or if Lorelei has expanded her arsenal for this second try.

Clipper was your favorite. You liked to touch his floppy ear.

You were wearing a purple dress and a yellow hat, and you kept calling yourself a sunflower.

There isn't a single negative memory among them. Madeline's life reads like a series of happy dreams.

"Percy's dead," says Linda. "And he was never going to let you have the baby."

Lorelei pivots toward her. Linda watches her face closely, and this time she sees what she's searching for as Lorelei's features sag. Then Lorelei's eyes fall to Linda's hand.

"You have a gun," she says.

"It's his."

Lorelei looks back and forth between the gun and Linda's face. "Percy went out," she says. "He'll be right back."

"No, he won't."

Percy falling to his knees. The catch of his labored breathing in the dark.

He deserved it.

Even so.

Confusion flickers across Lorelei's face, like when she was standing at the bedroom door earlier, when she mistook Linda for

Emmer—for Madeline Rose. *Not well*. Still, an ugly part of Linda wants to hurt Lorelei even more—to make her feel a fraction of the turmoil she feels. "He had sexual intercourse with Madeline," she says. "And she thought you loved your foxes more than you loved her. You should read these emails, Lorelei. They're all printed out downstairs. See what your daughter really thought of you."

"I don't . . ." Lorelei is shaking her head. "No," she says. Her voice sounds so old and pained, a crackle of remorse runs through Linda. But stronger than the remorse is the anger. A lifetime of anger.

"Percy's family," says Lorelei.

"He was a liar," says Linda. "And now he's dead."

Lorelei's robe brushes Linda's arm as she pushes past her into the hall. Linda watches the bathroom door slam, closing Lorelei inside. As silence settles, Linda feels sickened by her own cruelty.

But everything she said was true.

She glances down; her foot that hit the barbed wire is horribly torn, trailing blood. She's soaked and shaking, and she can't lift her left arm. She should leave, walk to the road, find the police. Lorelei won't be able to do anything without Linda's money, Percy's help.

Her gaze brushes the timeline again, and a memory comes at her strong; more a sense of grief than actual words or images:

Mommy, where's Emmer?
She's gone.
Where, Mommy?
Don't call me that.
Mommy, why?
My name is Lorelei. Call me Lorelei.
Mommy?

She remembers how she hugged Lorelei's legs—*Mommy, I love you*—trying, maybe, to make up for Emmer's being gone, trying to be enough. She remembers Lorelei shoving her off—Linda's fist catching her sweater, Lorelei tearing away—and disappearing into the basement for what felt like days. Linda crying and clawing at the locked door: *I'm sorry, I won't say it again, I'm sorry, please come back.* And when her mother did finally reappear, Linda was dry-throated, sore, shaking with fatigue and fear. *Lor-lei,* she croaked, and while Lorelei didn't acknowledge her, she didn't leave either.

Linda tries to envision the sequence as it must have actually happened—Emmer an invisible construct, Lorelei thinking she was asking where Madeline was. She squeezes her eyes shut for an instant, sees that oft-remembered image of her twin walking down the stairs, hand in hand with Lorelei. She tries to erase Emmer from the memory and fails. But when Lorelei emerged from the basement without Emmer that day: That was when she became Lorelei. That was not only the day Linda lost her sister, it was also the day she lost her mother, a mother who had never loved her for *her* but who had at least sometimes loved her for who she might become.

Linda wanders over to Lorelei's desk. The top note, freshly scrawled, reads, *No third-person references! YOU only!* She sees a Post-it with her address written on it. There's a book titled *Epigenetics and Environmental Triggers.* There's also a bulletin board above the desk, filled with more notes and a handful of pictures of Madeline— pictures Linda hasn't seen before. There's one of her around the age when she died. She's rolling her eyes but half-smiling, her thumbs hooked into the straps of a backpack, greenery behind her. Her perfect button nose with its splash of freckles. Linda's hand rises to her own nose and she feels its subtle hook. Arthur's nose, or similar enough. Madeline had Lorelei's. But babies' noses all look the same; Lorelei wouldn't have known about this defect at first. Another unconscious failure Linda could neither control nor avoid.

In her mind, Emmer has Madeline's nose.

Emmer standing across the pond. She'll never know why it was that day and not another she created a sister. If Emmer was born from a single precipitating event or an accrual of small pressures.

An aftershock of her new understanding: She was only ever following her own footprints while playing Hide-and-Find. This one hits her hard, and she tears the picture of Madeline off the wall, jarring a necklace that's dangling next to it. The necklace is an ugly thing: a nylon strap with a small plastic watermelon slice hanging from its end. It's pinned below another picture of Madeline, this one of her as a toddler, her face smeared with chocolate. Linda takes the necklace and slips it into the pocket of her soaked sweatshirt along with both pictures. She doesn't care if the damp damages the items, she just wants to take them away from Lorelei.

She can feel her knees wanting to give. She crosses the room and lowers herself to the twin bed; she goes to rub her forehead, but her shoulder shrieks and she has to drop her arm back to her lap. Tears press against her eyelids. If she could redo her life, what would she do differently? *Everything* feels like too easy an answer, but it also feels true.

A sob catches her ear. Lorelei, crying? Linda takes to her pained feet, curious to witness such a thing. Clutching the gun, she makes her way into the hall. Silence. Maybe she was mistaken. She stops outside the bathroom door and turns her ear to it. Nothing, not even running water.

Then: A sniffle. A nose being blown.

Linda's breath catches. She doesn't know what to do. She slips her free hand into the pocket of her sweatshirt and rubs the watermelon necklace between her fingers. She suddenly feels guilty about taking it and the photographs, and this guilt reignites her anger. A couple of tears change nothing, she tells herself. Lorelei never cried over *her*.

The bathroom door swings open. Lorelei's eyes are red and puffy, and her face flashes through confusion and fear. Pity swells in Linda. She shouldn't be able to feel so many contradictory emotions at the same time: anger and pity, guilt and tenderness, all these layers of pain.

"Lorelei," she starts, but she doesn't know what to say next—and she doesn't have time to decide, because the name is like a trigger: Lorelei's eyes flash with sharp, feral anger.

"Get out," Lorelei snarls, and she shoves Linda toward the stairs. Linda grabs for the handrail, but it's on her left side and her abused shoulder fails with a roar of agony. She topples, pain exploding in places old and new, and her head smacks the wall or a stair, hard, and she slides to a crumpled stop on the floor below. Everything is spinning. Everything hurts, great stabs of pain in her shoulder, her breast, her ankle, her head. Screams are building in her chest, imploding on themselves, rending her innards. There is blood in her mouth. She tries to spit it out, but the best she can do is allow it to dribble over her chin. She manages to roll off her ruined shoulder, and she blinks, trying to banish the dizzying spin of her head. Slowly the world comes into soft focus, and she sees the railing she could not grasp. She sees the glowing woodstove on the far side of the room. She sees Lorelei standing on the stairs above her.

She sees the gun she doesn't remember dropping, now in Lorelei's hand.

From: Lorelei Niequist   Draft Saved 10:09 A.M. 2/9/2005
To: Arthur Niequist
RE:

She's here! Her perfect little nose, I can't stop kissing it. It hurt so much I didn't think I was going to make it and you weren't here. I imagined you were but you weren't but that's okay, she's here. She's sleeping now and it's all I can do not to wake her and kiss her again. You should have heard it when she cried. Strong lungs and the way she raises and squirms her face when she's lying on my chest and how she kicks her little legs to springboard up me it's all the same.

She's here, Art. She's back. Our little MR is back.

From: Lorelei Niequist   Draft Saved 4:53 P.M. 2/16/2005
To: Arthur Niequist
RE:

She wont stop crying I don't remember her crying this much and my ankles are so swollen I can barely walk. It hurts so much my whole body shakes and I can't rest because all she does is cry. Sometimes I think she's telling me

From: Lorelei Niequist   Draft Saved 10:17 A.M. 3/28/2005
To: Arthur Niequist
RE:

Quitter. You fucking quitter, leaving me to do this alone. YOU MOTHER-FUCKING PIECE OF SHIT QUITTER.

27.

nvi follows Arthur through heaps of weeds and dead, wet grass to the back of the house. The rain has softened, and its patter against the foliage masks their steps. It feels like months since she watched Linda walk this same path. Sometimes it's hard to believe that day actually happened. She remembers the rush as she fell, scrabbling. The surprising strength in Linda as she yanked her up.

"She was like a different person here," whispers Anvi.

"What do you mean?" asks Arthur. "How she helped with your leg?"

"Not just that. It was the only time I've seen her comfortable. Confident. Even the way she walked was . . . more present, I guess." It was like she got a glimpse of the kind of woman Linda could be. But that's not something she can say to her father.

The dark lump of the back deck rises before them. Anvi runs her gaze along the tree line. The rustling sounds earlier would have come from around here.

"Maybe I made a mistake," says Arthur. "Maybe she wasn't meant for the city. But I thought it would be good for her to be around people, and Maddy—I know, I *know* this shouldn't have factored in, but Maddy was such an outgoing girl. The last couple of years, she got so mad when we dragged her out here for the summer. I thought Linda might be like that a little, once she settled in."

Anvi touches his arm softly. "That's the stupidest thing I've ever heard," she says. "Have you *met* Linda?"

An eruption of laughter. "You're right," he chuckles. "I should have set her up with the little cottage in the woods that she wanted. I—"

A hoarse cry reaches them on the wind, wordless and thick with agony.

Anvi turns toward the sound and sees a shambling, indistinct figure. A moment of terror as her heart whispers: *Runrun-runrun.*

The shadow stumbles. Another groan, and this time the word *help.*

"Call 911," Arthur tells her, and he hurries forward. In his posture, Anvi sees Linda striking out to find water with which to clean a wound.

"Crap," whispers Anvi. She follows, cramming in her earbud as she hits the emergency button on her Sheath.

A dispatcher answers and asks the location of the emergency. Her soft, measured voice is discordant with the situation. Rather than calming Anvi, it pushes her further toward panic.

"Cedar Lake," says Anvi. The hazy figure gains definition: a slumped-over white man. Arthur kneels at his side. Anvi's mind is spinning as she tries to remember the address. "Mill Lane, something Mill Lane."

"We need the actual address," says the dispatcher. "If you can."

She knows this—she *knows* this. But her fear is refusing to settle, to accept that the threat before her is actually someone who needs help. *Fuck it,* she almost says. "It's the Clone Girl house."

"Oh," says the dispatcher.

Arthur helps the man to a more upright position. The stranger's chest is bare—a pale patch in the night. That seems ludicrous, until Anvi notices the large wad of cloth he's pressing to his stomach.

The man looks up at them. "Mr. Niequist?" he asks, his voice faint and shaking.

Arthur freezes. After a few seconds he says, incredulous, "Percy?"

Anvi is so startled that she forgets the phone call. Could this really be Percival Hunter, sitting before them shirtless in the rain? The dispatcher calls for her attention. "There's an injured man here," says Anvi. Not just any man, Percival Hunter. How? Why? "I don't know what happened. There were gunshots earlier."

Percival's voice is a pained whisper Anvi can barely hear. "Mr. Niequist, I'm so sorry," he says.

Arthur shrugs off his jacket and puts it around the younger man. "What happened, son?"

Anvi's mind is whirring, trying to come up with a scenario—any scenario—in which the sight before her makes sense. Coincidence is immediately discarded; her thoughts seek cause, effect, and she can't think with a voice in her ear.

"We're behind the house," she tells the dispatcher. "I think he's hurt pretty badly. Please hurry."

"Help is on the way. Has the man been shot?"

"I'm not sure. I think so."

Percival is saying something to Arthur. Anvi can't hear over the dispatcher's asking, "Is he armed?"

"I don't know." She scans the ground. "It's dark. I have to go. I have to help." She has to see—to hear. "We're behind the house," she says again. "Hurry." She hangs up and taps the flashlight app on her Sheath.

Arthur flinches away from the sudden light, but Percival sits there dumbly. There's blood everywhere: smeared up his chest, covering his hands, leaking into his lap from the shirt wadded against his stomach. Dribbling from the corner of his mouth over his chin.

He shouldn't be alive, bleeding like this.

He won't be for long.

She aims the light toward the ground, then tamps down her fear and tries to solve the problem before them. "Where's Linda?" she asks.

Arthur looks at her as though he didn't realize Linda's disappearance must be connected to this. Or maybe he just didn't want to be so forward. But the blood—they don't have much time.

Percival's gaze is unfocused. He ignores Anvi, blinking slowly in Arthur's direction.

"Hang in there," Arthur tells him. "Help will be here soon." His hand is on Percival's and glistens with the younger man's blood.

"It was my fault," says Percival. The words are a husky gasp.

"I'm sure that's not true," says Arthur.

Percival closes his eyes. "I killed her."

Anvi's breath catches. *Linda.*

"What are you talking about?" asks Arthur.

Percival's muddy focus wavers off toward the house. Anvi wants to shake him, kick him, anything to make him talk.

"Percy, son, you need to tell us what happened."

Percival closes his eyes, his breath rasping, and leans his head back. "It was still in her chest," he says. "I'm the one who pulled it out."

Arthur jerks away. His posture stiffens. Then his voice grows cold as he says, "You lying son of a bitch."

"What's going on?" asks Anvi, newly panicked. "What happened to Linda?"

"He's not talking about Linda," says Arthur. "He's talking about Maddy."

Anvi looks back and forth between the two men, confused.

And then understanding clicks.

Madeline Niequist's injury was a stroke of terrible, terrible luck. Part of her fall was sheer, and she had to have struck the broken tree limb at precisely the wrong angle for it to have pierced between her ribs. But the worst bit of luck was that she'd removed it. This was the teachable moment over which so much coverage lingered: Her lung wouldn't have collapsed until she yanked out the obstruction. If she'd made it to the hospital with the wood shard still intact, she might be alive today: a grown woman with a scar and a story to tell.

But if Percival was the one who pulled out the obstruction.

He was training to be an EMT, Anvi remembers. He'd just graduated from high school and was training to be an EMT. He should have known better. *Anvi* knows better. But is the reason she knows because she's read so much about Madeline? She's not sure when she learned you should never remove an impaled object away from medical care.

"I panicked," whispers Percival. "I'm so sorry."

Arthur rocks into an inelegant seated position. His hair is slicked to his forehead and his shirt is soaked, sticking to his slight potbelly. He looks old and soft and broken.

Percival's chin is lifted to the wind, his eyes pinched shut. "I replay it every night in my head, Mr. Niequist. She's sitting there, crying, with a spear through her chest, and she looks at me like I can save her. And I just—I forgot everything. All I could think was it didn't *belong* there. But as soon as I—" He bites his lip and shakes his head.

"Why didn't you tell us?"

"I tell you every night." His eyes flicker open, dazed and distant. "This is just the first time you've been here to hear it."

Arthur looks like he wants to lunge forward and grab Percival by the throat.

"Arthur," Anvi says softly, kneeling beside him.

Arthur wipes at his eyes and nods. "I forgive you," he tells Percival. From his tone, Anvi doubts it's true, but Percival hears what he needs to hear, and he smiles a bloody smile. Anvi remembers seeing a similar smile on her father's face—during a promise to take it easy. Her father's smile said he would finally listen and take care of himself. This smile announces the end of a different kind of fight. This is a smile that doesn't see a future. The blood, the mud, this bottomed-out smile—everything about this man's death is so much less clean than her father's.

Anvi hadn't thought of her father's death as clean until now.

She watches Percival's chest, waiting for it to go still. But Percival jerks and coughs, then he meets Arthur's eyes with something close to clarity. "Lorelei," he says.

"I'm sure she would forgive you too, son," says Arthur. He's regained control of his voice and sounds almost sincere.

"No, she won't," says Percival. "All these years will mean nothing if she knows." Panic is rushing into his voice. "Don't tell her, please."

"I won't," says Arthur. He takes Percival's hand again and squeezes.

He's humoring him, but Percival's panic strikes Anvi as too urgent, too lucid. This is more than deathbed absolution. "Where's Lorelei?" she asks.

Percival hesitates, and then a measure of tension melts from his face as he says, "Upstairs. Waiting."

Arthur glances toward the ruined house behind them.

"He can't mean here," says Anvi. "The upstairs is destroyed."

A beat of silence, then Arthur presses Percy, "Are you talking about your aunt and uncle's house?"

"*My* house," Percy says. "I earned it."

"Is Linda there too?" asks Anvi.

Percival gives a short, ugly laugh, and a bubble of bloody saliva bursts on his lip. "Probably," he says. He took her, thinks Anvi, and she feels herself harden. This is the asshole who took Linda.

Arthur leans back and starts fumbling at his Sheath. "We have to call Detective Lopez," he says. "If Lorelei and Linda are both there—"

"Go," says Anvi.

Arthur looks at her, startled.

"Lopez is following the log-in. Call the police on the way, but you know where the house is. Go."

"But Percy—"

"Arthur." Anvi squeezes his hand. "I've got this. Your daughter needs you."

He holds her eye and her hand for a long second. Then he nods and his hand slips from hers. He takes off running. Anvi watches him disappear into the dark, then turns back to Percival.

"Who are you?" he asks. His curiosity is gentle and distant. Waning.

"Anvi Hendrickson." She settles onto the wet ground. "We've met on email."

Percival makes a sound somewhere between a cough and a laugh. "I thought it was pronounced like *Ann*."

"You're not the first," she says. "And you kidnapped Linda."

He looks away, but he doesn't deny it.

"Is she okay?"

"I don't know. She shot me and ran."

A tremor of surprise; it hadn't occurred to Anvi that Linda could have caused his injury. Though perhaps it should have. The death of someone Linda trusted made her attack Arthur, and who knows what she's been through this last week. The thought of Linda being pushed so far makes Anvi wants to dig every bit of information from Percival. But he's slumped and pallid, not shivering despite his bare chest. Arthur's coat is hanging from his shoulders, but there's no way that's keeping him warm. Despite her anger, Anvi shrugs off her own jacket and lays it atop Arthur's.

"Why did you take her?" she asks.

Instead of answering, he says, "How did you know Lorelei was with me?"

He must be in shock. Anvi wonders how much longer it will be before an ambulance arrives. "I didn't know until you told us just now," she says. "No one did."

"But you threatened me."

"No, I—" She tries to remember what she wrote that could have seemed threatening when read through the lens of a guilty conscience. She has no idea. She taps her Sheath to open her email.

Percival coughs again, and this time Anvi feels it as a slap.

He may be a kidnapping asshole, but he's dying—and she's checking her email. She puts down her arm. This isn't about her.

Unless—

"Is that why you kidnapped Linda?" she asks. *Because of my curiosity. My stupid, unnecessary prying.* She remembers asking if he'd had any contact with the Niequists in recent years. If Lorelei was hiding in his home, could that have been enough to push him to abduction? The oddest comparison leaps to mind: biologists studying primates and only realizing decades later that their presence caused the animals to change their natural behavior.

Percy dips his chin to his chest. "No," he says. "Not really. But the timing was—we had everything we needed except for her. And then I looked up and there she was. Just *standing* there. I almost didn't tell her. I almost didn't follow, but it was like fate. And even then I thought —She told me to drive her out, so I did, but—" A distraught sigh slips from his throat. "Why would she go out alone after that? Why would—" He blinks suddenly toward Anvi. "You're the brown girl from the car," he says.

Anvi can't quite follow his logic. She blinks away the rain. Please, she thinks, whatever her own role in this mess might have been, please let Linda be okay.

"I was supposed to be a hero," whispers Percy after a while. He's still staring at the ground. "I was going to be the man she thought I could be."

Anvi wonders if she should have recorded this conversation. But the confession has passed, and whatever wrongs this man has committed, she feels an obligation to be present for him as he fades. They can worry about evidence, about justice, if he survives. It feels like a big if. He's vampire pale, his eyes unfocused. She should probably take his hand, but it's covered in blood, and she knows too much about pathogens to touch a stranger's blood without protection.

"Tell me about Maddy," she says instead.

Percival smiles, bright and bloody. "She was an angel," he says. "My angel."

From: Lorelei Niequist   Draft Saved 12:20 A.M. 8/15/2005
To: Arthur Niequist
RE:

Do you remember how we used to say it didn't even sound human when she laughed? How we joked someone must have slipped us a robot child? I reminded her about the lake today, and she giggled that gorgeous baby giggle. She's still so young, but I think she remembers.

From: Lorelei Niequist   Draft Saved 2:07 P.M. 3/22/2006
To: Arthur Niequist
RE:

Her eyes are getting darker. And the nose, I swear it's sharpening. And she pulled your mother's lamp down by the cord and tried to eat the broken glass. Why would MR do that? I'm scared something's wrong but still I tell her. I tell her about sledding and climbing the trees at the lake and how she helped me with the foxes. I tell her who she is and what she will do and I think she understands but then she does something like this and I just

From: Lorelei Niequist   Draft Saved 11:19 P.M. 5/1/2006
To: Arthur Niequist
RE:

She pointed at your chair today and said Dada.

It's so hard and I'm barely sleeping and sometimes I doubt. Then something like this happens.

From: Lorelei Niequist   Draft Saved 9:52 P.M. 6/7/2006

To: Arthur Niequist

RE:

Every night we lie together on the floor, and I tell her. Remember, I tell her. Anytime I pause, she'll roll her little head toward mine and say, "More 'member. More 'member." So I tell her again, and I ask, "Do you remember the green sled?" or about planting the sunflowers or that day at Rattlesnake Lake. And she says yes. And she laughs and she paws at my mouth to feel all my teeth. "Big flowers," she'll say. Or "MR climb." And then, always, "More 'member." Until she falls asleep, over and over again, "More 'member."

It's beautiful, Arthur. She's beautiful.

I should tell you, I know I should. It's been long enough. But you said goodbye, and I'm not sure I can ever forgive you for that.

28.

Lorelei stands above Linda. Her mouth hangs open. She looks confused. She almost looks sorry. Then she clamps her lips into a tight grimace and steps over Linda to the couch. She picks up something and tosses it toward Linda. Percy's tablet. It smacks Linda in the chest, setting off a hellish spike of pain.

"Give me my money back," says Lorelei.

Linda's head is ringing and she can't catch her breath. There's something wrong with her chest. The only breaths she can take are quick, shallow rasps. She stares at the ceiling. The kitchen light flickers, sending a burst of fluttering shadows across the room. She squeezes her eyes shut. Panic thrums through her, and nausea rises in her belly. She sucks in another breath, but her lungs refuse to fully expand.

The thought slams into her: *I'm going to die.* A threat more imminent than Percy skulking through the woods—her life leaking from her as she lies broken at the base of the stairs.

She feels a fresh burst of fear: She doesn't want to die. Not like this and not at all. But she can't breathe, and she can't live without breathing, and—

A swelling revelation: Linda slaps at her chest, feeling for the shard of the stairwell that must have impaled her. Lorelei's voice is running in the background, issuing demands like static. Linda wants to tell her: Can't you see? I am your daughter, after all. But her blind patting reveals nothing jutting from her chest. She presses down, expecting her fingers to slide straight through into her lungs, but all she feels is the solid barrier of her rib cage under her shirt—and more pain. A spot that's tender but unyielding.

A muddle of relief and disappointment confuses her further. She's not pierced. She's not Madeline. She's not dying. She's failed again. She still can't get a full breath. She might still be dying. She's wrung out with fear and panic. She's a puddle at the base of the stairs awaiting further punishment. She's—

A wet something slaps Linda's face, sudden and shocking. She chokes on a stunted gasp and her eyes pop open. A shriek suffocates in her chest—above her is an open maw, sharp teeth. Her panic spikes—and then the beast licks her face.

It's a dog.

A shaggy black dog has materialized from the ether.

Its tongue smears across her eye, and Linda catches a glimpse of the dog's collar. A patch of white fur.

It's Nibbler.

She's so shocked she forgets her pain. She stares at Nibbler's muzzle. Her head is swimming, but she focuses on the white splotch under his chin. Maybe she's imagining this. Maybe this is her subconscious idea of safety: dog slobber and hot, fishy breath. So much of what she knows about her life was never real—why should her death be?

But Nibbler's arrival has stripped the edge from her panic, and Linda realizes she can breathe again. Her breaths are still shallow but slower, and she can feel a heady calm pouring through her.

She can breathe.

Why is Nibbler here—how?

The kitchen light flickers again. Or maybe it's Linda's vision. She rolls her head toward Lorelei.

Lorelei is standing unnaturally still. The gun hangs at her side as she gapes toward the front door.

Nibbler whines and presses against Linda, licking her face again. He must be tasting blood, she thinks. She pushes his face away, not wanting to turn him into a man-eater.

That's when she sees the old man in the doorway. He's ragged and filthy, his shirt soaked and stained red. There's blood on his hands and smeared across his thighs. For a second Linda thinks it must be her blood, but that can't be right. Her head is pounding and it's hard to make sense of what's happening, who the newcomer might be.

He's wearing a tie.

A paisley tie she's seen before.

Beneath streaks of dirt, Arthur's face shifts into focus.

As Linda struggles to convince herself it's actually Arthur, his gaze flashes back and forth between her and Lorelei. His eyes settle on Lorelei, and only then does Linda fully believe it's her father standing there.

"Hi, Lor," he says.

"Art." Lorelei's voice is full of wonder. "You're back."

"I'm back." He steps inside.

Lorelei rushes to meet him. "This changes everything," she says. Her voice is awed and hopeful and so painful to Linda's ear. She presses her hands to Arthur's chest. The gun is forgotten in her grasp, its muzzle pointed at his chin.

Arthur jerks away. "Careful, Lor."

"We don't need Percy now that you're back," gushes Lorelei. "We don't even need *her.*" She waves the gun to indicate Linda, and Linda feels a flush of concern: If Lorelei pulls the trigger now, she might hit Nibbler. She digs her fingers tight into his fur, knowing she can't protect him but trying to anyway.

"You can pay him," says Lorelei to Arthur. "I've taken care of everything else. All you need to do is pay him."

Linda wonders if Lorelei will feel anything when she shoots Linda, if she felt anything when she killed Emmer.

That's not right. There is no Emmer. There never was.

But Nibbler is warm beside Linda. He exists, and he shouldn't be here. And yet he *is* here, so where is Anvi?

A tickle of a thought: an email Linda didn't read.

But thinking hurts. Everything hurts. That's all Linda can feel: hurt. She remembers a yellow reptile girl stabbing her in the stomach. That didn't hurt.

"Why don't you put the gun down and we'll talk?" says Arthur.

Lorelei glances at the gun, then lowers it toward the floor. "You're not listening," she says.

"Yes, I am," says Arthur. "Who do you need to pay?"

"The doctor. He's agreed to do it. He has a surrogate lined up in São Paulo. We just have to pay him and send him the DNA and then we'll have her *back,* Art. We'll finally have her back."

Linda stares at the two of them standing together, and it strikes her that these two people are her *parents*. In a world where Linda was born instead of Madeline, they would have raised her together. In a world where Linda was born instead of Madeline, they might still be together. Maybe the three of them would be sitting down to dinner right now. No—Linda would be older, almost Percy's age, an age where he ended but that is still in her future, maybe. Percy would have known her instead of Madeline. Would he have loved her? Could she have loved him?

"Okay," says Arthur to Lorelei. "We'll see about paying him." He puts one of his hands gently around the gun. "But first you have to let go of this."

Lorelei shakes her head and pulls away. "You're not listening. You never listen."

Linda thinks of the video of Arthur and Lorelei after Madeline's death, holding hands at a podium: a single unit. She wonders if anyone ever suspected they could shatter into this.

"Let go of the gun, Lor, and we'll get you some help."

Yes, Lorelei needs help. Lying broken on the floor, Linda sees it so clearly now, how badly this woman needs help. Help that Linda could never give but that she wouldn't deny either.

"Let go," says Arthur. "Please."

Linda thinks of how Percy allowed the guilt he felt over his failure to save Madeline dictate the rest of his life, and now here's Lorelei, still plotting the impossible return of a daughter decades dead.

"We can have her back, Art," says Lorelei. "Come, I'll show you." She tugs him toward the stairs. "Once you see, you'll understand. We can have our little girl back."

Arthur shoots a worried glance toward Linda. She stares back, impassive. He would have to step over her to go upstairs.

"It won't be like last time," Lorelei tells Arthur. "I have her DNA. She'll be perfect. Come upstairs, look at my plan. We can do this."

Nibbler whines and presses his snout to Linda's side. She thinks suddenly of Chrono and wonders if he was real. She doesn't remember seeing his name on Lorelei's timeline. Foxes were mentioned and there was a name, but it wasn't Chrono's. Maybe he was truly hers.

Arthur allows Lorelei to lead him a few steps toward the stairs. "How do you have her DNA?" he asks.

Lorelei pauses. Now that her anger has sapped away, Linda feels her pity deepen. It's heartbreaking, really, that Lorelei has allowed her grief to turn her into this.

"How, Lorelei?" insists Arthur.

Lorelei's face has hardened again. She's trying to come up with another explanation, another plan. "That doesn't matter," she says.

It hits Linda that she's no better than Lorelei: All these years beyond the wall and she's refused to live. She's been clutching at the past, just like Lorelei, clinging to a history that she's not even remembering accurately.

Let go, she thinks.

There's an opening in Linda's chest: an awe-filled understanding like when she first saw that photograph of earth. She's part of a system, a cycle she can never hope to control. The best she can do is accept her place in it.

Let go. Of the anger, the fear. The regrets and resentment.

But who is she if not a failed Madeline? A lesser Emmer?

Perhaps Lorelei never had a choice. Perhaps every decision she's made since Madeline died has been determined by malfunctioning brain chemicals, and the rational woman she used to be is lost entirely in their swell. Perhaps the same is true of every bad decision anyone's ever made: They're just glitches. Linda doesn't know. But she knows she feels like she has a choice.

She can choose to do what Lorelei never could. She can let go of the past. Maybe then she can find out who she really is.

"You're serious, aren't you?" says Arthur. Linda turns her eyes back to him, his muddied, bloodied clothes. She realizes she doesn't understand him in the slightest.

"Of course I'm serious," says Lorelei.

"So you've got her DNA and you're going to what—*clone* her?"

"He says he can do it. It might take a few tries, he might need more money, but—"

"A few tries?" hisses Arthur. "You'd be reducing our daughter to an illegal experiment, Lorelei, and each failed round—that's a genetic duplicate of our daughter *dead.*" Lorelei recoils as though struck. "How would you feel about that, Lorelei? How would you feel about broken copies of Madeline rotting away in test tubes and jars?"

Linda is fascinated. He keeps repeating Lorelei's name, just like he does with her.

"Arthur," says Lorelei. She's backing up, confused. "You don't understand."

Disgust and fury flare through Arthur's voice. "You dug up our daughter's grave."

"Arthur."

"You cut off our daughter's fingers and put her back in the ground."

"It wasn't like that. Percy did that part. I—"

"That poor kid," says Arthur. "Did you make him set fire to the house too?"

Lorelei freezes, then cocks her head at him. Her bun has loosened, and gray hair flits around her shoulders. "What are you talking about?"

"Our house. It burned down. It's all over the news. Hell, it's next door. Did you not know?"

"No, I—" Fresh confusion flares across Lorelei's face. Linda's pity deepens. She never thought to mention the fire to Lorelei. She just assumed she knew. She wonders what it means that Percy never told her. "We can rebuild," says Lorelei.

"We're not rebuilding anything," Arthur tells her. "We're not paying any doctor. And we're sure as fuck not sending Maddy's fingers to Brazil."

"But, Arthur," says Lorelei. "It's for M.R." The phrase impales Linda—she still hears her twin's name—and she grips Nibbler tighter.

"Madeline is gone, Lorelei," says Arthur. "You're not doing any of this for her."

Lorelei wails softly. An inhuman sound.

But, no, her mouth isn't moving. It's a siren. A distant siren Linda can hear only because of the harsh silence that's settled between Lorelei and Arthur. The only other sound is the *swish-pat* of Nibbler's tail hitting Linda's leg.

Lorelei lifts the gun and points it at Arthur's chest. Her hands are shaking. The kitchen light flickers again.

The sound of the siren changes pitch, a brief lengthening, then deepening as it passes. Wherever it's going, it's not here.

"Lorelei," says Arthur. "You're not well." His voice has turned toward a patronizing tone Linda knows well. "Put the gun down, and we'll get you help." Linda wonders suddenly if the tone isn't patronization but the one he uses when he cares. The thought is as shocking, as impossible, as anything else that has happened today.

Lorelei shakes her head. "I can't," she says.

Arthur takes a gentle step forward. "I'm so sorry," he says. "I should have come sooner. I didn't realize how bad it was."

"I'm so close." Lorelei's voice breaks.

"Lor, it's never—"

"Police! Lower the weapon!" The voice startles everyone, and Linda's eyes shoot back to the door. A uniformed woman stands there, a gun in her hands too. For the briefest moment Linda thinks it's Anvi, but a quick series of blinks reveals a stranger.

"It's okay, Detective Lopez," says Arthur.

The woman looks at Linda but keeps her gun trained on Lorelei. "Are you Linda Russell?" she asks.

It strikes Linda as absurd that the essence of her being can be summed up by two words she chose randomly from a list. *Lin-da. Russ-ell.* No, that's not her.

She rolls her eyes back toward Lorelei and is startled to find her mother staring at her—not just appraising or dismissing her but actually looking at her. Linda sees all her own suffering reflected back at her, magnified. There's something new in Lorelei's eyes too: a sharpness, an understanding.

It's a look that makes Linda think maybe it's not too late after all.

Let go, she thinks and tries to say.

Lorelei breaks eye contact and looks to the gun in her hand. The police officer starts talking, soft reassuring words that wash over Linda, meaningless, as Lorelei raises the weapon to her own head. Arthur's voice is there too, pained. Linda hears the word *don't.*

Lorelei's lips part in a soft exhale as she pulls the trigger.

Her head rocks back and a flash of red splashes the wall, then her slim body is falling. It's nothing like when Percy fell. Lorelei falls like an empty sack, and by the time she hits the floor, she's no longer human.

Linda stares at the heap of flesh and fabric that used to be her mother, trapped by the seeping red, by the flaccid robe, by the bottoms of Lorelei's feet—her filthy socks. Desperate but unable to look away, she locks onto that detail—the browned heels, the hole showing a pink pad of flesh below Lorelei's big toe. A few awful beats of her heart pass as she stares. Her ears ring from the gunshot, from all that her body has endured, from all that has changed.

Then her view is broken by Arthur rushing toward her, calling her name.

Third time's the charm, *thought Graham as he entered the kitchen and initiated the scan.*

CODE ERROR DETECTED

A hellish scream shot out—shrill and throaty and short. Graham pivoted toward the doorway to find the fox glowering at him.

His heart pounded as he unsheathed his reprogramming device.

The fox pounced. The device fell to the floor—that was beyond Graham's control, a programmed inevitability. The fox screamed again, its jaws opening wide to reveal blackness and a ridge of needle-sharp teeth. And then it began to pace. Silently.

Graham needed a weapon. Inside a cupboard, he found a stack of rusty pots and pans. He threw one at the animal. It sidestepped the assault, then leapt at him. Graham grabbed another pan and smashed the fox across the face. The fox flew across the kitchen, smacking into the wall.

Graham picked up the reprogramming device, keeping his eye on the fox, which limped to its feet. The fox stared at him for a moment. Graham made a shooing motion and brandished another pan. The fox bared its teeth, then crept out the door.

Graham took another look around, admiring the shadows, the desolation. And then he initiated the reprogramming sequence. The house began to shake. Graham's instincts wailed, Get out of here, *but the sequence was only 40 percent complete. A piece of the ceiling crashed down to his right—80 percent.*

REPROGRAMMING COMPLETE

Graham rushed out through the back door. Away from the house, he turned to watch. As the roof crumbled over the kitchen, he thought of how Sergei had argued that this mission was too boring, too easy, without a person to change. But Graham didn't care; it was beautiful, and it meant something. He liked to think she might see this someday. That the connection he felt between them could finally flow both ways.

With a sound like thunder, the house became a pile of rubble.

Graham ripped off his goggles, ducked out of the CircleTread, and rushed over to crush Sergei in a hug. "That was perfect," he said. "What did you use for the fox?"

"I condensed a banshee wail. It's actually pretty accurate."

Graham laughed. "You genius bastard. It's perfect. It's all perfect. Well, not perfect, but anything left is minor league. We're ready. It's time to post."

"You don't think we should wait?"

Graham ruffled his friend's hair. "Sweet, cautious Serge. No. We've still got time. Two weeks from the first post to build buzz, then *bam.* We release. That's plenty of time for polish."

"You're right," said Sergei, and then he too was smiling, his ever-present worry momentarily contained. He craned his neck and stretched his long arms to the ceiling. His coder's fingers twitched. "Post it!" he declared.

Graham rushed to his terminal, logged in to his secondary account, opened their buzz file, and copied the text of the first document there. Seconds later it was done: *The world needs to know what is happening within spitting distance of downtown Bellevue. I was part of a group of software engineers focused on creating ancestor simulations making use of immersive VR technology. After more than a decade of work, our efforts paid off in a way we never anticipated: We created a world indistinguishable from our own . . .*

"And we're off," he said.

Sergei was standing over his shoulder. "Holy shit," he said. Only seconds had passed, and there was already a comment. That comment read *Bullshit,* but that was fine—it *was* bullshit. All attention was good attention.

They dove back into work, riding the high of being but a hairbreadth from the finish line.

The next evening, bleary and ecstatic, Graham posted their second teaser, promising proof of the simulation hypothesis. The first post's engagement rate was astronomical—this was going better than they ever could have hoped.

Graham rubbed his eyes, then shoved his hand into the popcorn machine, extracting a salty handful. He hadn't eaten anything except popcorn and Hot Pockets in two days.

"Let's get out of here," said Sergei behind him. Sergei—who Graham usually had to peel out of his chair. "Let's celebrate."

"*Yes,*" said Graham. "I have the perfect idea."

A few hours later, the tires of their car crunched into a long-abandoned driveway. Headlights revealed reaching brambles, hanging branches. Deep divots lined with weeds. The car was barely big enough for the two of them, a lightweight electric nothing meant for city streets. Graham shifted into park.

"What if someone notices the car?" asked Sergei.

"It's like two A.M.," said Graham. "Besides, they won't be able to see it perched in their hick pickups."

"Graham . . ."

Graham looked over with a playful smirk. "You want to camouflage it with branches?"

"Just pull in a little farther."

Graham revved the car ahead a few feet, then Sergei opened his door and unfolded into the night.

Graham followed, snagging their bag of supplies from the back. "Relax," he said, rounding the car to pat Sergei's shoulder. "This is a *celebration*. Loosey-goosey, man. Loosey-goosey." It was an old joke, and it made Sergei smile. He shook out his arms and neck.

Graham extracted a flashlight from his bag, flicked it on, and led the way down the driveway. A slight curve, the squish of cold mud beneath their feet, pockets of old snow here and there. Graham was shivering; it was colder here than in Bellevue. He lifted his flashlight; a closed gate sliced the beam into segments. Graham couldn't help imagining her here, sequestered. He slipped his bag over his shoulder and handed the flashlight to Sergei, then scaled the gate more awkwardly than he would have liked. Sergei handed the flashlight back to him through the bars, then followed, his lanky form landing in a soft, elegant crouch.

They approached the house, more gray than yellow and overrun by brambles and weeds.

"Spooky," said Sergei. "Maybe we should have set the mission at night."

"No, dusk is thematic." Graham cut through the overgrowth to the back of the house. He tried the door, and it swung open with a creak. Sergei had jimmied the lock last time, when they brought their 3-D mapping supplies, and it seemed no one had been here since. Graham lingered before stepping inside. Her hand had touched this latch; her feet had crossed this deck. He wondered if she'd been back since she was a child. If she would ever come back.

They cut through the dusty kitchen—their old footprints shone in the flashlight's beam—and into the living room. Graham pulled a bottle of cheap champagne and a short stack of red cups from his bag. Sergei took the cups, and Graham untwisted the bottle's wire.

"To Glitch Hunter," he said. The liquid didn't spray, which was fine—more to drink.

"To the smoothing of final bugs and a successful launch," said Sergei.

To Clone Girl, thought Graham.

They tapped their cups and drank.

Half an hour later, they were laughing, sprawled across the filthy floor. The champagne bottle was empty and they were sharing a joint, a six-pack of beer between them.

"How many comments now?" asked Sergei.

Graham rolled down his sleeve to access his Sheath. "Four hundred twelve."

"Not bad." Sergei took a slow, dreamy inhale of the joint.

"Not bad? It's fucking awesome." With each of those comments, his posts were being pushed into more and more feeds. They'd achieved the marketing dream: They were trending.

Graham sat up to sip his beer. Alcohol and euphoria coursed through him, but his elation was dampened by the chill seeping through his backside.

His eyes locked onto the dusty fireplace.

He imagined her as a girl, sitting before a fire.

He wondered if she'd ever roasted marshmallows. If she knew what marshmallows were.

Graham nudged Sergei with his foot. "It's fucking freezing in here," he said. He envisioned a soft warm glow, and he wondered if she'd liked to imagine faces in the flames. "Pass me your lighter."

From: Lorelei Niequist   Draft Saved 3:13 P.M. 4/17/2010
To: Arthur Niequist
RE:

For years I've been determined to see what wasn't there and this morning she broke a pen and she ran her hands all over the table. I found her there covering up MR's fingerprints and at first it was like a memory and I just watched her play but then I saw it. Her fingerprints are wrong. And it made me see the nose, the eyes, and how she always points at the dog when I ask for the bear and it made me think of all the things she's done that MR wouldn't and it's not her. I've begged her to remember and she can't it was never her and I don't know what to do it's too late and I feel

I'm trapped down here and I hear her banging on the door and she's up there crying. She thinks I'm her mother but I could only ever have one daughter and that thing up there it isn't her.

I don't know how I ever could have thought it was her.

29.

A flaming arrow hisses past Linda to pierce the ghoul's chest. The monster howls, its green-gray face twisting with pain and fury, then Linda-as-Briggs casts *Enhance* and he ignites. The ghoul is reduced to ash. There's no blood. No charred corpse. Linda has her gore setting at its lowest level.

Anvi-as-Leela sprints past Linda—Linda spent all her coin on a tiny, acid-spitting dragon that flies around her head, dissolving enemy projectiles; Anvi spent hers on boots with a 3X speed modifier. Reaching their wagon, Anvi hops inside.

Linda approaches the ash pile and collects the few coins spread around it. It's been months since Anvi and Linda witnessed real death. Linda still has nightmares about it, and she knows from their conversations that Anvi sometimes does too.

"Do you have time to collect the bounty, or do you need to go?" asks Anvi. Her character is a tiny dark elf with a purple ponytail; she's hunched over her storage chest, immobile to Linda's eyes as she manages her inventory.

Linda taps her fingers to check the time—11:13 A.M. "I should go," she says. She enters the wagon, triggering an autosave. In the corner, Pickles rises from the floor, fully grown, and wags his tail.

"Good luck," says Anvi. "Let me know how it goes?"

"Thanks, I will."

Linda calls up the main menu and quits, then peels off her headset. A view of the woods immediately greets her: lush greenery swaying in the breeze beyond the bay window. The mix of cedar boughs and maple leaves is accented by a single blooming lilac bush. Arthur looked at her askance when she said she wanted to set up her VR system here, but she loves emerging to the trees: a reminder that reality can be beautiful. The window seat is lined with pillows; sitting there with the window open is even better than sitting in a tree. Softer, and scented with lilac. And mosquitoes can't breach the screens.

She turns away from the windows and docks her headset.

It's a small house, smaller than Arthur wanted to get her. Downstairs is just this main room, the kitchen, a bathroom, and a mudroom. Upstairs is two bedrooms and a larger bath. Linda still sleeps in her nest chair, which she's placed by the window in the smaller room—it has a better view. Anvi's slept in the larger bedroom a few times, when she came for weekend visits, and Linda secretly thinks of it as her friend's room. She's thinking of hanging a poster from Anvi's favorite show on the wall.

She's been in this house almost two months. It's starting to feel like home—more like home than her old apartment ever did. Her gut still pulls toward the Cedar Lake property at the word *home,* but the pull is getting weaker, and she's leaning toward selling the property. Or maybe she'll donate it to a nature-conservation organization. She's pretty sure she never wants to go back. She's pretty sure she'd be okay with the house being razed to the ground. It's been weeks since she visited the version she built in-game, but she'll always have that.

"I'm so sorry," Anvi said to her in the hospital. Over and over she said it, apologizing for contacting Percy, offering condolences over

Lorelei and what Linda had been through. She let Linda read the emails she exchanged with Percy. They were innocuous, Anvi scratching some curious itch Linda doesn't entirely understand but which she's accepted as part of Anvi's engineering self.

"I forgive you," Linda told her. She'd never said those words before.

The car is supposed to arrive at eleven-thirty. Linda slips on her sandals, wincing against the lingering pain in her shoulder. She declined surgery for the separation. Her hospital stay had been awful enough; she couldn't imagine going back, staying longer. Letting them knock her unconscious with drugs and dig into her body. But her shoulder should feel better by now. Soon she'll have to decide if she'd rather live with the pain or undergo the surgery. She hasn't told Arthur how much it still hurts. It's been getting easier to talk to him since Cedar Lake, but she knows what he will advise and it's still hard to tell him no. She wants to make this decision on her own.

Linda grabs the first-aid book she's been reading from a table by the door and slips it into a bag with her water bottle. She doubts she'll want to read, but just in case. She walks outside, tapping her Sheath to engage the security system—a concession to Arthur, though it makes her feel safer too.

He was with her every day at the hospital. He brought her flowers and told her stories—about Madeline and Lorelei, and about his childhood spent running through the woods. In some small ways, Arthur as a boy sounded not too different from Linda as a girl. Though he had a warm home to return to. Dinner on the table, a pair of parents who loved him.

Sometimes he held her hand as he talked. One day, he even showed up without a tie.

I forgive you, Linda thought.

A concussion. A sprained ankle and knee. A bruised rib. A broken pinky finger she never even felt. Countless contusions and lacerations, the worst on her feet. They'd kept her at the hospital for four days. Linda suspected it would have been less if she wasn't who she was. If there hadn't been such a media frenzy. She was lucky, really, that she wasn't hurt worse. That she wasn't shot in the stomach. Or the head.

She blinks against the thought and sees a flash of blood splatter. Lorelei collapsing. Anxiety thrums through her. She looks at the trees across the yard. Breathes in the heady lilac. She remembers leaving Percy's house only in flashes. A brown-eyed paramedic leaning over her face, telling her she was there to help, asking Linda her name and if she knew where she was. A mesmerizingly calm presence, and Linda had a surprising thought: *You—I want to be you.*

The house has a small front porch. A bench that swings. She sits, rocking gently on her toes and watching a spiderweb that wasn't there yesterday. It's seventy degrees already; this spring wants to be summer.

Soon she won't have to wait when she wants to go somewhere. She starts driving lessons next week. She's terrified, but living out here— it's only twenty miles from the city, but it feels much farther—she needs to be able to get around on her own. All she has to do is get her license, and then she can buy a self-driving car. A hoop she doesn't understand but she'll jump through.

Soon she hears tires crunching up the gravel driveway, and the car pulls around the bend. Linda recognizes Cora's brown skin and white hair behind the wheel. Linda's had her as a driver before: a quiet black woman who retired from Google last year. "I have bad knees and the grandbabies are yet to come, so this keeps me busy," she explained when Linda gathered the courage to ask.

She's been practicing being friendly, initiating conversations. It's easier now that she's alone for long-enough stretches to build up a natural curiosity about the next person she sees.

"Did you hear about those boys from Bellevue?" asks Cora as Linda settles into the back seat.

Graham Williamson and Sergei Burkov. They came forward while

Linda was in the hospital and confessed to starting the fire at her house. Rather, Burkov confessed. Williamson went on the run and was arrested in Oregon a few days later. It still makes Linda's head swim: Not only were they responsible for the fire, they were G.H.

Glitch Hunter: a VR game in which the world is a simulation and the player is an enforcer from the base reality, charged with eliminating "glitches." Her home was a mission. They trespassed to map the house, then set it ablaze—accidentally, they claim. In the video Linda saw of Burkov, he looked like a hunted man: greasy-haired, with huge bags under his eyes. Guilt had clearly been eating at him. Williamson just looked angry.

"What did they do now?" asks Linda.

It still sends anger flaring through her: All that drama, all that worry, and the G.H. simulation-hypothesis posts were just a publicity stunt for a game. They had more posts planned, leading to some grand reveal. But their plans were thwarted by fire—and panic. Linda remembers wishing it were true, that nothing she knew was real— that *she* wasn't real. The thought had even provided an odd sense of comfort. Now she just feels embarrassed.

Cora twists around to look at Linda. "They declared bankruptcy to get off the hook for the civil suit."

"Huh." Linda isn't sure what to make of this news or how it affects the criminal case. She's been letting Arthur deal with the lawyers. She doesn't want anything to do with the two men. If the case ends up in court, she won't go to the trial.

Somehow it makes everything worse that Glitch Hunter isn't even a good game, not according to the handful of reviews Linda read in the hospital, flicking the tab closed on her Sheath whenever someone walked into the room. The game was available only briefly— Williamson released it against Burkov's wishes the same day Burkov confessed to the fire—and the reception was primarily one of scorn.

"Don't want to talk about it?" asks Cora.

"Not particularly."

Cora gives her a little smile, then turns back to the wheel and puts the car in reverse. Soon they're heading down the driveway to the main road.

There was an upside to Burkov and Williamson's actions: People rallied behind Linda. The public seemed to have reached a consensus that the men stepped over the line in using her life in their game. Linda suspects the reaction would have been different if their choices didn't also lead to her house being set ablaze. To Percy stumbling across Linda at her old home, to his following and ultimately abducting her. To Lorelei and Percy both dying.

During her recovery, she watched a live feed of a group of people outside the hospital. GET WELL, LINDA read one of their signs.

Not Clone Girl. *Linda*.

Something she hasn't told even Anvi: She downloaded the game. She hasn't played it. She doesn't know if she ever will, but it's on her system, waiting for her to make her choice.

She gazes out the window as the car winds down a long, wooded road to the highway. Turning right would take them toward the ever-expanding tech hub that rubs against Seattle's eastern edge. Cora turns left.

After about ten minutes, they traverse the main street of a run-down town. The gun shop catches Linda's eye, as it always does. She's faced no penalty for ending Percy's life. According to the law, it was self-defense and she did nothing wrong. She's not sure she agrees. "He lunged toward me and it just . . . happened," she remembers saying. But it wouldn't have happened if her finger wasn't already on the trigger.

They cross a river. Linda watches families splashing below the bridge, and there is a flotilla of yellow inner tubes. "Still a little cold for that, if you ask me," says Cora, and Linda murmurs agreement, though she's not sure she means it. They pass a fruit stall on the side of the road and snake their way up a heavily wooded hill. Next come the tourist stops: an overflowing parking lot for a waterfall overlook having to do with some old TV show; a small, cramped town with a train museum.

Soon they're inching along with a stream of cars into a packed gravel parking area. The line stops while a car ahead tries to navigate a tight spot.

"Why don't you get out here," says Cora. "I'll come back when you're ready to go."

A dart of fear runs through Linda; she'll be stuck.

No—having to wait isn't the same as being stuck. And she wanted to come here. She promised herself she would come here.

"How long do you think you'll be?" asks Cora.

"I'm not sure." For all Cora knows, Linda is just here to enjoy a day in the sun. "The latest I can stay is about three." Three hours feels impossibly long, but it's good to have an outer limit.

"Okay, great," says Cora. "I'm going to head back to those outlets we passed. Text me if you want to go earlier; otherwise, I'll meet you here at three."

"Thank you, Cora." As Linda opens the door, she synchronizes her breath with the breeze and imagines the air carrying her feet out to the gravel. Standing, she stares down for a moment. There's a lighter patch of healed skin where she cut herself on the barbed wire. The cuts were among the least of her injuries, but they've been slow to fade.

Laughter ahead. Linda shuts the car door. There are vehicles everywhere. Pockets of people are gathered around the cars, collecting items or packing them away.

She didn't intend to come on a crowded weekend afternoon—but she set a deadline and then procrastinated. In the end, her choice was to come today or break the promise she made to herself, and she fears if she breaks this promise she'll break another. She fears she'll skip tonight: the first session of an EMT training course she signed up for. It's just a two-hour orientation, but a commitment nonetheless. And a declaration of intent: If I start this, I will finish it. Her hand slips to the book in her bag. It's not the textbook for the class—she gets that tonight—but she's been reading it every night, dreaming of a day when she might be in a position to alleviate pain.

Eleven weeks. Three days a week. It simultaneously sounds like forever and like no time at all.

She *will* finish this course.

Anvi's the only person who knows about the class—she helped Linda navigate the sign-up requirements. How strange and right it felt to type her new name into the online form: *Linda R. Niequist.* All because Anvi took Arthur by the shoulders, pointed him toward Linda's hospital bed, and said, "Talk."

She sets herself a new deadline: three weeks. She'll tell Arthur about the class by then. Once she finds her feet.

Cora's sedan inches away, and a dark-haired family hustles past Linda. The father is carrying a cooler, the mother holds a young boy, and two girls balance an inflatable raft over their heads. Linda listens to their excited chatter without understanding a word—she's pretty sure they're speaking Spanish—then she follows them. Gravel crunches beneath her feet. The first sign she sees points toward a trail: RATTLESNAKE LEDGE.

She's not looking for a ledge.

The inflatable raft bobs to the left, taking a different path. Linda follows. The raft is bobbing ahead faster now, and the glisten of water flares through the trees.

There's not enough water to swim.

She still remembers it so clearly. The cracked drying mud. The tree stumps. Lorelei's hand on her back.

But this is the first time she's been here.

She remembers, Lorelei wrote in an unsent email she'd saved for years on a USB drive shaped like a watermelon slice. Anvi recognized the device and helped Linda access the messages. The emails are like diary entries: Lorelei explaining herself to Arthur, Lorelei railing against Arthur for being absent, Lorelei bouncing between joy and despair. Linda has most of the messages memorized, and sometimes she lies awake at night, reciting them to herself—trying to understand. Trying to forgive.

She's found she can forgive Anvi for snooping and Arthur for struggling, but she can't forgive Lorelei. Maybe this will change someday, but for now she's working on forgiving herself instead. For now she's focusing on letting go. On moving on. On making and keeping promises.

Linda steps off the paved path into the grass. The inflatable raft has disappeared into the distance. Ahead is a set of fenced-off garbage bins and a series of porta-potties. One's door is open but has the lock engaged. It bangs softly in the wind.

She walks forward, and then there it is: a deep, glistening, and expansive blue framed by a dipping mountain ridge. Children and dogs splash at the water's edge. A baby that Linda can't see cries. The scene is as bright and crisp as an oversaturated landscape in Fury and Honor.

Rattlesnake Lake.

She's read about how this land used to be a town and how that town was overcome by flooding. How the water rises and recedes with the seasons and rainfall, at times exposing the many great tree stumps that used to pepper the town, at times burying them in its depths.

It must have been a dry season when Madeline came. But this is a spring day after a long, wet winter, and the lake is massive. From where she stands, Linda can see only a single stump breaking the mirror-like surface, and it's topped with a smattering of fresh green growth where other plants have taken root. A child is pointing at it and laughing, joyous. It's impossible to tell from here, but Linda imagines the child is a little girl. The child scrambles toward the green-laden stump, and Linda takes a deep breath. She smells the woods but also the smoke of a charcoal grill and an undertone of waste coming from the bins and the porta-potties. It's imperfect, complicated—real.

A gentle smile unfurls across her face. *I'm Queen of the Lake,* she thinks.

It's nothing like she remembers.

Acknowledgments

First off, a mighty and somewhat bewildered thank you to all the people who worked through a pandemic to make this book happen—especially those of you who had children underfoot the whole time.

Thank you to Kara Cesare for not only our pandemic phone calls, but her years-long excitement for this story, her incredible insights regarding structure and tension, and for allowing me to take the time I needed to get this book right. Thank you to Jesse Shuman for his sharp eye, quick replies, and a kickass title. Thank you to Jennifer Hershey, Anne Speyer, and Sarah Peed for their thoughtful and extraordinarily helpful observations. Thank you to Kelly Chian and my copy editor, who had many great catches. Thank you to the designers responsible for the look of this book, inside and out. Thank you to Scott Biel for a gorgeous cover. Thank you to Kara Welsh, Kim Hovey, Kathleen Quinlan, Melissa Sanford, and everyone else who is helping present this book to the world.

Thank you to Lucy Carson and the rest of the team at The Friedrich Agency. Any author would be lucky to work with such a group, and I feel fortunate beyond words to have a champion as dedicated, passionate, and savvy as Lucy behind my writing.

Thank you to Alex and Libby, whose enthusiasm for this story helped me push through a difficult first draft, and whose insights and honesty helped me make that draft stronger.

Thank you to Andrew for his steadfast nature and for making sure I had the time and space to write after our son was born. Thank you to Simon for (eventually) learning how awesome sleep is so I could use that time well. Thank you to Codex—and Banks—for the doggy inspiration.

Thank you to my son's childcare providers. Who knows how much longer it would have taken me to finish this book if I didn't have a safe, loving place to deposit my toddler for a few mornings a week.

Thank you to my ninth-floor suities for their continued support and friendship—and the occasional Hindi phrase. Thank you to my family for meaning it when they say "I can't wait to read it."

Thank you to my climbing partner, Kirsten, for letting me blather about the ups and downs of the publishing process during our sessions, and for pushing me to try routes I would otherwise assume are beyond my abilities.

Thank you to the many authors and publishing professionals I've met in the last few years who have made me feel like a member of a community. Thank you to the booksellers, librarians, and teachers who have been excited by my writing and shared that excitement with others.

Thank you to the Catto Shaw Foundation for a gorgeous getaway where I not only put the finishing touches on the last book, but figured out much of the backstory for this one—and found Linda's pond.

Thank you to Mark Tavani for helping me get this beast off the ground years ago, and for his continued belief in my work.

Thank you to David Weed for answering my many questions about house fires. (It goes without saying that any inaccuracies in the novel are my fault, not his.)

Thank you to Liam Downey and Greg Gaskin for a truly illuminating and inspiring ten days; dipping my toe into the world of wilderness medicine proved key to my figuring out this story. (Again, any inaccuracies are on me.)

Thank you to Daron Schreier for "stuff."

Finally, to my readers: Whether you've been waiting five years for this novel or this is your first introduction to my work, thank you. There is a part of me that still can't quite believe anyone other than me would be interested the worlds and characters I work so hard to create and explore. But I'm so glad you are.

ABOUT THE AUTHOR

Born and raised in the mountains of upstate New York, ALEXANDRA OLIVA is the author of *The Last One*. She has a BA in history from Yale University and an MFA in creative writing from The New School. She lives in the Pacific Northwest with her husband, dog, and young son.

alexandraoliva.com
Facebook.com/olivaauthor
Twitter: @ali_oliva
Instagram: @ali.oliva

ABOUT THE TYPE

This book was set in Minion, a 1990 Adobe Originals typeface by Robert Slimbach. Minion is inspired by classical, old-style typefaces of the late Renaissance, a period of elegant and beautiful type designs. Created primarily for text setting, Minion combines the aesthetic and functional qualities that make text type highly readable with the versatility of digital technology.